Chapter 1

'Is that for real?' Eli leaned over the rail and pointed at a small cruiser that was sailing parallel with the ferry. Trance music blared out from the cabin and, in the darkness, Eli could see the wash as the driver ramped up the speed and the small boat skittered and scudded over the waves.

'Isn't this a shipping lane? Stupid kids, that's a great way of getting killed. They think they're immortal, nothing bad is ever going to happen to them,' Eli said as the boat veered sharply away and bounced over the wake.

Twenty-five-year-old Segev, head watcher and also lead in charge of tech at the Mossad's London Station, ignored the comment. Eli knew he would. It was one of the perks of being head of station, Eli could muse unchallenged.

'Paper Doll is on board,' Segev said. 'His car parked forward, his wife and kids at a table in the lounge on deck three. He's on the way up here. Lev is in position.'

'Thanks.' Eli felt behind his ear for the listening device and he pressed the button to open the comms channel and at the same time watched the screen on his phone engage.

There he was. Lev, planted at a table on the outside deck. Alone in the dark, as the ferry juddered through the choppy Solent.

'You there, Lev? Ready to rock and roll?' Eli said.

'All set.' The voice in Eli's ear sounded about as ready to rock and roll as a coma patient but Lev was Paper Doll's *katsa*, his case officer, and as such, it was his job to meet the agent and do the debrief.

It was bad enough that Eli was on the ferry on a Friday night, there to observe the debrief in real time, worse that this contact location was both expensive and inconvenient; they'd had to allocate two motorbikes and one car to tail Paper Doll on the journey between London and Portsmouth, all to make sure the agent was clean. For one meeting. If Lev hadn't been such a lazy bastard, he would have found a way of insisting that the meeting was somewhere more convenient and at a better time.

Eli glanced around the deck and saw the watchers. They were eating sandwiches and drinking coffee. No doubt these over-priced props would end up on their *heshbon* too.

'Eyes on Paper Doll,' Eli heard in his ear. 'He has his son with him.'

'His son?' Eli said. This was exactly what they needed, a curious nine-year-old telling anyone who might listen that Daddy talked to a strange man on the ferry as the family went for their weekend away on the Isle of Wight.

'Abort?' Segev said.

'No. Give him a few minutes. Paper Doll might take the kid inside after he's thrown up over the side of the ferry.'

As he watched Paper Doll walk back and forth along the deck, hand in hand with the child, something nagged at Eli. Maybe the situation was more complicated than a lazy agent meeting a lazy case officer. The agent had missed the last two of his meetings with Lev. While that wasn't unusual for Paper

Praise for Merle Nygate

'Intriguing and atmospheric. Merle Nygate is a writer to watch'
**Charles Cumming, *Sunday Times* Bestselling author of
Box 88 on *The Righteous Spy***

'There is no black and white just varying shades of grey,
this is the twilight zone all good spy novels should reflect.
Gripping and well written, fans of a serious spy fiction
will love this'
Paul Burke, Editor of Crime Time FM on *The Righteous Spy*

'For all her deft delineation of character, of spies as people
not superheroes, Nygate is not afraid to get her hands
bloody, and this is shaping up to be a series with heft'
James Owen, *The Times* on *Honour Among Spies*

'Merle Nygate writes intelligent and genuinely
thrilling spy novels'
Jake Kerridge, *The Telegraph* on *Honour Among Spies*

'Absolutely gripping and so well written. A strong plot
which sustained itself right through to the final page
and a great cast of characters'
**Alex Gerlis, best-selling spy fiction author on
*Honour Among Spies***

'Modern day espionage served with a side of geopolitics and
lashings of tension, suspense, believable characters and dialogue.
Nygate writes realistic yet thrilling espionage suspense'
Shane Whaley, Editor of *Spybrary* on *The Protocols of Spying*

Also by Merle Nygate

Honour Among Spies
The Righteous Spy

THE
PROTOCOLS
OF
SPYING

THE
PROTOCOLS
OF
SPYING

MERLE NYGATE

NO EXIT PRESS

First published in the UK in 2025 by No Exit Press,
an imprint of Bedford Square Publishers Ltd,
London, UK

noexit.co.uk
@noexitpress

ISBN
978-1-915798-48-0 (Paperback)
978-1-915798-49-7 (eBook)

2 4 6 8 10 9 7 5 3 1

Typeset by Palimpsest Book Production Ltd, Falkirk, Stirlingshire
Printed in Great Britain by CPI Group (UK) Ltd, Croydon CR0 4YY

The manufacturer's authorised representative in the EU for
product safety is Easy Access System Europe,
Mustamäe tee 50, 10621 Tallinn, Estonia
gpsr.requests@easproject.com

PART ONE

Anger

Then my anger shall be kindled against them in that day, and I will forsake them, and I will hide my face from them, and they shall be devoured, and many evils and troubles shall befall them.

Deuteronomy 31:17

How much more grievous are the consequences of anger than the causes of it.

Marcus Aurelius, Emperor Rome, 121–180

Doll, who was systemically disorganised, maybe there really was an issue. When the agent had surfaced to pick up his retainer, Paper Doll told Lev that the reason he'd missed the meetings was because his wife was becoming suspicious about the extra money. Money he'd been spending on her and the kids. He said that he'd even caught her going through his workbag, which was never a good sign. This meant Eli was there, on a Friday night in early October, to observe the meeting. To see if he, the head of the Mossad's London Station, with his superlative spy-running skills, could identify what the issue was, and whether indeed the agent was lying and perhaps trying to get out of the relationship with Lev because he'd had enough. If so, he wouldn't be the first agent to claim, whether it was genuine or not, that a partner was suspicious. It was such a constant that the Office had developed a number of slang expressions for it. *Lichporkaki*, angry shit-dropping bird was just one of them. The unsolvable problem was that when you sleep with someone for years, when you eat with them, talk to them, experience both joy and pain with them, they know when you're lying.

Eli shrugged off the thought about his betrayal of his own wife and looked out into the darkness as the ferry chugged along. That was past. They were on a relatively even trajectory now and he wanted to keep it that way. Eli concentrated on the small screen in his hand, where he could see Lev, still sitting at the table at the other end of the ferry, on the outside deck. The only other people in the space were a couple of men, drinking beer from bottles and surreptitiously vaping – and Paper Doll. He was holding his son's hand and the boy seemed to be excited as the lights of Fishbourne got closer, a black mass speckled with light.

But, as yet, there was no contact between agent and case officer.

Maybe the wife had put the fear of God into Paper Doll and she'd got the kid to keep an eye on him. Not impossible. A popular tactic in authoritarian regimes, and Qatar was hardly California. Eli's finger hovered over the call channel at the base of his screen. Abort or no?

He was there to observe the meeting and protocol dictated that, if conditions were suboptimal, then a contact should be aborted. But that would mean the entire effort to come down here would have been wasted and made worse because Eli should have been hosting a *Simchat Torah* party at the apartment and he was missing it. But for all Eli's complaining, there remained the unshakable sense that this meeting was important, and Eli needed to give it every possible chance to succeed.

Paper Doll was a Human Resources manager at the Qatari Embassy. Lev, who Eli considered to be the laziest and most inept case officer he had ever had the misfortune to meet, let alone have on his team, had been running Paper Doll for three years, so far without mishap, beyond the agent's apparent inability to meet for regular debriefs.

A face-to-face debrief was always the first-choice contact, an opportunity to check in with the agent, but failing that, the compromise with Paper Doll was USB chips with the contents of his computer and a document summarising changes in personnel and noteworthy events within the Qatari Embassy. Besides the contact issue, it was the type of account that ran on tram rails, so it was suitable for a deadweight like Lev, whose only claim to fame was his ability to pass himself off as a Syrian to a Syrian. So authentic was Lev's grasp of the language and the nuances of the culture, and the Byzantine internal politics of the Assad regime, that Lev had held on to his job through multiple HR assessments. Perhaps it was Lev's background in *Shabak*, the internal intelligence service, an organisation renowned for its slow thinking and slow action, that made him so thorough. Perhaps he had sucked in his Syrian alter ego with his mother's milk, a Syrian Jew from Qamishli. Whatever it was, in that one area Lev shone like the bright light of the lighthouse on the headland up ahead, and he even showed glimpses of not just enthusiasm, but actual intellect, as he kept up to date with the shifting sands in the one-party state. What's more, nobody had ever challenged Lev's cover story. Nobody could. When he was working, he was transformed. He became that creature: a Syrian businessman, an Alawite loyalist, who was distantly connected to the Assad family, with broad interests in industry, technology, consumer electronics, minerals, textiles, medical equipment and construction. Wanting to know what the mood was in Qatar in terms of their economic plans.

However, although economic intelligence about Qatar gave the analysts back home product to feed the insatiable appetite of their algorithms, what was more enticing for the Mossad was the geographical location of Paper Doll's office within the Qatari Embassy. Human Resources at the Qatari Embassy was situated on the second floor, right at the back of the property in South Audley Street. The office itself, which comprised two rooms and overlooked a brick wall, was conveniently right across the passage from the suite that the UK political wing of Hamas had been occupying for the last twenty years. They even shared the same coffee station, which was supplied daily with an assortment of the choicest delicacies from nearby Selfridges food hall.

That's why Eli was on a ferry crossing the Solent towards Fishbourne. That's why Paper Doll was so important.

Glancing down at his phone, Eli saw the bodycam images, and Paper Doll take his child by the hand and coax him towards the sliding doors into the lounge. He disappeared into the light, leaving Lev at his table, alone, on deck. If the agent came out again, there just might be a chance for contact, but the likelihood was fading the closer they got to shore.

What was going on? There could only be two possibilities: the agent either had something significant to say to Lev and he was nervous, or he was giving them the runaround. Given his profile, Eli didn't think the man was bold enough to play them. He was also strongly motivated by money and, as noticed by his wife, had developed expensive tastes for everything from the finest caviar and £500 bottles of whisky to Savile Row suits. All of Eli's instincts and his experience told him that Paper Doll wasn't going to turn off the money tap without a good reason.

Behind Eli, a PA system sprang to life. 'We will shortly be arriving at Fishbourne. Would passengers return to their cars on the car decks, making sure they have left none of their belongings behind. Thank you for—'

'He's back,' Eli heard in his ear. 'He's back. No kid.'

He must have been waiting for the bustle of travellers preparing to get off the ferry.

Gripping his phone, Eli watched as Paper Doll approached Lev. The agent wasted no time and Eli saw an outstretched hand slip something into Lev's pocket. Then the agent leaned down over Lev, who was still sitting, and muttered something. His voice was soft, urgent. Eli could only make out one word.

He said it twice, '*i'tidaa*'. Immediately, Paper Doll swivelled around and marched back towards the door into the lounge. And that was it. Lev was left sitting at the table like an unloved date on a night out. They were going home with one word, and what looked like a USB chip slipped into Lev's pocket.

If they'd brought the Techtruck with them, they might have washed and debugged the chip before examining its contents, but the truck with several million dollars of high-end toys was in the lock-up in Ladbroke Grove. Eli had decided it was only to be used when absolutely necessary, because it ruffled too many British feathers. That was a mistake. It would now take them another four hours to get the ferry back to Portsmouth and drive into London.

Theoretically, this might have waited until the next day, but the word '*i'tidaa*', combined with the tension in the man's body and the way that he'd possibly used his child to shield further interrogation by Lev, bothered Eli. Why would the agent make such a drama out of this meeting? Was it really just a case of his wife getting suspicious and wanting to meet out of London or was there something else?

Eli strode into the lounge and joined Segev on the steps with the rest of the crowd, heading towards the car decks.

'We're not going straight home, Segev,' Eli said. 'We get the next ferry back to Portsmouth as planned but then we go straight to the embassy and decrypt the chip. And Lev is coming with us.'

Lev was nearby.

'What did Paper Doll say?' Eli said.

'Just the one word. *I'tidaa, attack.*'

Chapter 2

Later the same night, Petra sat in front of her laptop, at the kitchen island. The night was still, with only the hum of the fridge and some light snoring that drifted down from upstairs to disturb her. There was order at her perch on the bar stool: the laptop at right angles to the notepad and pen, the pendulum lighting that directed pools of task illumination onto the granite worktop. Everything was within reach, everything well organised, no surprises.

Since Petra hadn't been able to sleep and had lain awake in the dark for over an hour, listening to the rhythm of Matt's breathing, she'd figured that she might as well get up and do some work. Now was as good a time as any to get her report done. The dark silence of the pre-dawn hours might aid concentration.

Petra was trying to write up a report on behalf of a consortium client, who wanted to invest in a subsidiary company within the National Grid. It was part of what she did for Corudon, the intelligence and security company. The report was based in part on her interview with the Internal Communications Director. Under the pretext of an article for *Finance Times*, a cover magazine owned by Corudon, Petra had said she wanted to write a piece about new initiatives in developing corporate culture. It was boring business bollocks and of course, the comms manager agreed to the interview. *Finance Times* was considered to be a prestigious magazine distributed throughout the City and it also had an international online presence. But Petra had had a second agenda.

Over a fancy lunch that included a bottle of rosé plus two extra glasses, Petra had not only gleaned everything she needed for the article, but she'd extracted the information she really wanted – the background of the target company that was in the iron sights of the client. And Petra had opened a rich vein; it seemed that the company was covering up a small matter of embezzlement by the Finance Director. The middle-aged accountant had developed a taste for hookers and cocaine. Of course, these things happen and listed companies were bound to cover up the truth, but it was exactly the type of information that a potential buyer wanted. Not only would it help with negotiations but it meant that due diligence would be escalated so there'd be no further nasty surprises if the deal went ahead.

As the kettle reached peak and switched itself off, Petra slid off the high stool and refreshed the teabag in her cup. She checked her phone to see if her feeds had anything interesting or distracting. They didn't; it was back to the boring report. She carried the cup back to her laptop and tried to settle down. From upstairs there was a snort from her bedroom, followed by an audible sigh; no doubt Matt had just turned over in his sleep.

Despite her good intentions, things weren't great between them; they'd got worse after she was approached by MI5 and they'd told her to ask Matt to assure her that they were the good guys.

Once she'd got over the initial shock of the MI5 approach, Petra had taken herself off grid for three months to a cottage on the Welsh coast. The place was a former fisherman's cottage owned by Bob, a man who had his own secrets but who believed he owed her. He didn't owe her. All she'd ever done was what any first-aid responder would do, because she happened to be there and knew what to do. But it was useful. Bob had connections and, most importantly, Bob never asked questions.

For three months that's where she'd sat, in the inaccessible stone cottage, often wondering what she was doing in such a dump, as she looked out over the sea and planned her next moves. High on that list was not getting involved with intelligence agencies of any flavour or description. That meant attending the meeting with MI5 and closing the door.

When Petra had fronted up to the address in Page Street, near Millbank, she was surprised. The offices were above a coffee shop and the exterior was unprepossessing. However, once inside it was different, with a mixture of institutional shabbiness and high-tech shine. She was left in a room on her own for five minutes and then joined by the two people who'd made contact with her. Two people who'd said they worked for the government. Forgettable Bill, who'd worn a beanie and probably liked hiking, and petite Southeast Asian Sonja, who was charming and over-enthusiastic – she made Petra think of Tigger.

The room they showed her into was a neutral space. It might have been a low-rent law firm with its big table, utilitarian chairs, wall screen, and the homely touch in the corner of an unemptied bin that contained the remains of someone's breakfast sandwich.

Once the meeting got going, Bill and Sonja, as they continued to call themselves, sat on one side of the table and Petra on the other. Coffee was offered and declined and then they got down to business.

'You were interviewed by our colleagues after the suicide bomb attack at RAF Fairborough. Two of the victims were in the EFL class you were teaching in Oxfordshire.' Bill consulted an A4 yellow pad, no doubt government-issue.

'That's correct.'

'We happen to know that another government was involved at some level with the incident.'

Petra said nothing as she assessed the situation. How much did they know? Then she smiled and said, 'I did go through all this at the time with some of your colleagues. There must be a report somewhere. Matt, that's my boyfriend, well, he was away, I was fed up with my job and I thought I'd try something new for the summer. The outcome was tragic.'

It was Sonja's turn. She emoted, 'It must have been truly awful for you.'

'It was.'

Bill continued, 'Then, just last year, a young man who was an intern at Corudon, where you work, was killed by far-right extremists when he infiltrated their group.'

'There are six to twelve interns at Corudon each and every year – I don't remember the names of most of them. In this case I do, it was Tom, but I really don't know what he did after he left, because he didn't get a job offer at Corudon.'

That lie was harder, because she did know, but Petra kept her face still and relaxed.

'Are you a talent spotter for the Mossad?' Sonja said.

'I'm not entirely sure what a talent spotter is, but I can guess,'

Petra said. 'Are you suggesting that Tom was recruited by the Mossad? If you are, that's quite a wild idea.'

There was no answer to the question. Bill consulted his notebook for the next question.

'An American who was on our watch list was murdered in Tom's flat,' Bill said. 'Were you aware of that?'

Petra's heart rate increased.

'No,' Petra said. 'No, I wasn't.'

'Are you sure?'

'Yes.'

'Why did you call us?' Sonja said.

'Because you asked me to. I want to know about this watch list you said I was on, and I also want to know what Matt, my boyfriend, has to do with me being here. And I want to hear it from you, before I hear it from him. Call it... call it curiosity.'

That's when the mood shifted and they made Petra the job offer. It seemed they wanted to partner Matt with someone who could give him cover in a specific operation and he'd put her name forward.

'You're kidding,' Petra said. 'Matt works for Corudon, like me. He doesn't work for you.'

'Sometimes we outsource specific projects to experts and this is one of those times,' Bill said.

'Why didn't he just ask me?' Petra said, now certain that she wasn't about to be arrested. 'I'm Corudon's high-end divorce investigator and I also cover their finance journalism. I've got no idea what Matt gets up to when he goes off on his jaunts, because we never talk about it.'

'The reason we asked you in was because you have to have

a certain amount of clearance before he could ask you,' Sonja said.

'Okay, so what's the gig?' Petra said.

It didn't take long for Petra to politely decline the notion of attending a series of cocktail parties at London embassies on Matt's arm so he could covertly assess the security arrangements. If there was one thing that Petra wasn't prepared to do, it was to be diversionary eye candy, and she couldn't imagine why Matt would ever think that she would. It showed just how little he understood her.

Of course, the real problem wasn't Matt; it was her. He seemed to think that, if he took a London-based job for MI5, they could live and work together. Do the couple thing. And here she was now, trying to make it work, despite the problem that he had no idea who she really was. That it was more than a coincidence that she'd taught a suicide bomber English. And that the American who'd died in Tom's flat was by her hand during a Mossad operation.

But she was done with all that. No Mossad and no MI5 camouflage jobs. She'd closed the door behind that part of her life. From now on it was just Corudon and its Risk and Financial Advisory Solutions.

Petra took a sip of tea and studied the paragraph on the screen in front of her. It was clunky and needed cutting. As a displacement activity, she picked up her phone again and checked out her newsfeeds.

'What…?' There was a notification of an attack. On her phone there were live images of a woman on a motorbike, a woman who was being kidnapped by Hamas terrorists. Was this real?

Chapter 3

Eli didn't go home at all that night. It was now 5 a.m. in London on October 7. The contents of the USB chip, and that single word, whispered in Lev's ear on board a Solent ferry, had been confirmed with blood-soaked authenticity. There was no need for an analyst to assess the grade of the product and write a report to be circulated within the organisation. The veracity of Paper Doll's product was being played out in real time on the monitors in the unit's meeting room at the embassy in Kensington.

Thirty people were crammed into the room, all the overnight staff, the security jocks and those who had been pulled from their beds by emergency calls. They'd crossed London in the darkness of a Saturday morning to sit in the meeting room and watch the screens.

'This can't be happening.' The ambassador sat at the beech table next to Eli; she was in a tracksuit that looked as if it had been grabbed from a pile of washing. Her face was white, and Eli noticed her manicured hands clench and unclench. As image after image streamed onto the screens, the ambassador seemed to be moments away from wailing. There was no sound on the feed, the only noise was from the people in the room – a sob, or a groan of anguish, as they watched, transfixed.

'Where's the army?' the ambassador said. 'Why aren't they there?'

Eli knew. Even though the incursion and massacre were ongoing, he'd already had first look at the signals. Before attacking, Hamas had systematically knocked out the sensors and the cameras on the border. End result, there were no eyes, no electronic intelligence, so they were all in the dark, apart from the social-media footage taken by exhultant attackers and the desperate WhatsApp messages from people trapped in safe rooms, on kibbutzim and in shelters, begging to be rescued. Messages that trashed the feeble hope that what they were seeing in the London meeting room was fake. It wasn't.

Nothing on this scale had ever happened before and the implications and outcome were beyond Eli's imaginings – but what he did know, what he was certain of, was that they had to keep clear heads for whatever lay ahead.

It was now obvious why Paper Doll had avoided a face-to-face briefing with Lev. Even though the Hamas military wing had kept the preparation for the operation under wraps, they were obliged to tell the political wing before the event itself. That meant an increase in signal traffic between military and political offices. Paper Doll either knew what was afoot or he suspected. And he was well aware that in any face-to-face debrief he'd have been asked what was going on with Hamas. Paper Doll might not have known the details, but the bastard definitely had known that there was something major afoot.

Eli glanced across the room at big Lev, who was propped up against the wall. He was looking down at his hands, and not at the screens. Slow though he was, he'd have drawn the same conclusions as Eli. They'd been bested by a mid-ranking HR gonk.

At Lev's side was Nathan, the man who by rights should have been the Paper Doll contact. The wiry-haired man, eyes closed, swayed back and forth, muttering. The man was *davening*, praying. Like that was going to help now.

Eli turned away and saw two other members of his unit on the other side of the room, by the door, Michael, the comms guy and Segev, chief watcher. Segev has his arm around Michael's shoulder, squeezing it tight.

Just then Urit, the unit analyst, was at Eli's side. She nudged his elbow.

'Station heads' meeting with Yuval in ten minutes.'

'Thanks.' Eli stood up. He'd seen enough.

'It's station heads' and analysts',' Urit said.

'Okay, we'd better get up to my office.' Eli bent over the ambassador. 'I've got to go. I have a meeting with Yuval.' With a hand Eli indicated the crowd in the room. 'They're expecting you to say something.'

'What?' she looked bewildered. 'I… I don't know what to say.' Her voice cracked.

'Make it up,' Eli said. 'You're the ambassador.'

As soon as the news had broken, everyone in the room had started to call relatives, friends, people they knew who lived on the kibbutzim, people who had children at the music festival, where a bunch of stoned, hung-over kids had been easy pickings for trained attackers. People with kids doing their service on the borders. Kids. For a surreal second Eli thought about the kids on the boat who had criss-crossed the shipping lane in the Solent, and the trance music that had blared out. That's all they were, just kids, being murdered by other kids. At that moment, Eli nearly lost his composure, but he clenched his muscles and got himself back under control.

'Just make it up,' Eli repeated. 'Say something about serving the country and that's why we're all here. Say it's our job not to let people down at this terrible time and how we have to be strong and support each other.'

The ambassador grasped his hand and used it to haul herself up.

'Thank you. I'll do that.'

Eli strode out of the room, keen to get to his office and away from the miasma of terror in the meeting room. He made his way to the men's room on the third floor. He had just enough time to piss and wash his face, in an effort to try to cool down his brain.

Even though he knew that it was true that people were being brutally murdered as he stood there, he recognised a sense of unreality. It was exactly the same sensation he'd had when he was a student, and he watched the TV screen in the cafe on the campus. 9/11. A plane flying into the Twin Towers. It couldn't be real, but it was.

As Eli let the cold water run over his hands, he looked in the mirror, shaven-headed and hollow-eyed. He was strong, muscled, he'd lost weight under Rafi's tutelage and felt better for it. It would be good to get Yuval's take on the situation; Washington's head of station was unorthodox, but he was a steady hand on the Mossad tiller and that's what they damn well needed.

The door of the men's room swung open and Rafi stood in the door frame.

'I went to your office,' Rafi said.

'I had to have a piss, man,' Eli said. 'I'm only human.'

This drew no response from Rafi. No put-down. Under normal circumstances there would have been, but this was far from normal.

'I've got to go home,' Rafi said. 'I want you to sign me off now and I can get out on a cargo transport in a few hours.'

Eli looked at the taller man, still handsome despite the savage beating he'd got only months ago. Since then, the broken nose had been reconstructed, the ribs mended and the tough fitness regime had left no visible trace of either the injuries or the surgery.

'It's my kibbutz,' Rafi said. 'They're my people. I have to be there, Eli, I've got to help. Have you seen what they're doing to them?'

Eli approached him, he opened his arms and pulled Rafi in close. He squeezed him tight, tried to give him a chance to regroup, then he held Rafi at arm's length. '*Achi*, bro, you can't go. Think. Think for a minute. So I agree, I say yes, you find a transport, the airport, the five-hour flight, you tool up and drive down there. You're talking ten hours minimum.'

Rafi pulled himself away and stalked to the end of the men's room. He had his back to Eli and his head was down. Rafi's voice was muffled as he struggled to get the words out. 'I can bury them, can't I?'

That was too much for Eli who covered his eyes with his hand. He swallowed. 'I'll talk to Yuval, he'll know what to do.'

Four minutes later, Eli sat at his desk with Urit on a chair by his side. She had her laptop open and her entire attention was on the screen. That suited Eli, who didn't want to have to reassure Urit that they were all going to get through this just fine.

Bang on time, Yuval hove into view on the big screen on the wall. Usually in meetings, whether face-to-face or on screen like today, the station heads indulged in chit-chat before it began. Talked holidays or kids, books or exhibitions, but today, no one was talking.

Yuval launched in, but even he looked rattled. 'This is what we've got so far,' he said. The screen split vertically and a map was superimposed over half of it. 'There are incursions at all the points ringed in red. They've knocked out the army bases, overrun two kibbutzim, and we're still trying to get in.'

There was an audible groan from Boaz, the young German head of station. Yuval looked annoyed.

He went on, 'They've taken a lot of hostages and killed a lot of kids. It's still going on. So…' Yuval paused, 'the situation is like this.

As Yuval used the well worn phrase Eli felt some sense of order restored to his life. The world was not going to end. At least, not just yet.

The general meeting lasted ten minutes, and all the station heads were tasked with setting up immediate emergency security protocols within their embassies. That meant making sure that the security teams were tooled up and the armoury had been checked over more than the current protocol of every two weeks.

Then the analysts were asked to identify all intelligence leads in the territories and Gaza and grade them. This type of focus was usually carried out by *Shabak*, the internal intelligence service but for now, anything that was germane to the attack would be fed into a central data bank and Unit 8200, army intelligence.

Yuval dismissed the analysts and eyeballed the other station heads. His large head filled the computer screen, and it would have been less intimidating if he'd sat back, but that was Yuval, he was sending a message. Take control. Eli glanced at his colleagues on the screen, Boaz with his furrowed brow, Csilla for once not the perfectly groomed middle-aged blonde but with her hair dragged back and no make-up, and Carmel with her cropped grey hair, lean and wiry and scared. Her son was in one of the border outposts that had been attacked and she had yet to hear whether he was safe. The only person who seemed unperturbed was Harel, head of France and Belgium. No doubt having his head up the arse of the Minister for Homeland Affairs gave Harel superpowers in terms of sangfroid. Today, Harel had eschewed his Italian suits and was wearing an open-necked polo shirt with an outsized designer logo over the pocket. The grey hair was groomed, and he'd retired the Tag Heuer watch and chosen a Rolex. Thank God he was across the channel and Eli rarely had to work with him.

'So, people, I've been in a meeting with the boss, *Memune*, and this is how we see it,' Yuval said. 'No surprises, we will be going into Gaza within the next few weeks. It will be dirty and there will be casualties. Our job is to think about what happens afterwards and try to prepare the ground for the regime that will be in place after Hamas has been destroyed or, if not destroyed, decapitated. Understood?'

There were some nods around the table. It wasn't an invitation to interrupt.

'The expectation is that there will be a hostage deal and we will send a lot of their people home. That's what's happened in the past and that's what will happen this time.'

'And then they murder us,' Csilla said. Eli could see that the comment had just slipped out; they weren't supposed to comment politically, their job was just to follow the demands of the government. Yuval went on, 'In your boxes you will find a list of the people we expect to be negotiated for. Among them is Dawood Al-Arikhi, a very important man, code name Butterfly. He's been our guest at the Ketziot prison for twenty years. As you may know, he was an acolyte of dear old Yasser Arafat and acted as his aide during the Oslo Accords. He's secular, that's important.'

'Why?' Harel was flicking a fancy pen between index and middle fingers. It was irritating.

'Good question,' Yuval said. 'Because the way forward is secular. Dawood Al-Arikhi is the best hope of replacing Abbas. Our projections are that he's likely to emerge as leader of the Palestinian Authority and thus our best hope of peace. Your job is to recruit someone who will be capable of working within the new administration as a *lochesh*. Okay? We need a whisperer. Not some low-life who sells product for cash and burns out after five minutes, but someone who is capable of becoming a minister or a diplomat and can impact policy.'

'I disagree, Yuval,' Harel said. 'Who knows what's going to happen down the line? We need to be dealing with the immediate problem and that's gathering intelligence to support the war. Maintaining legacy arms supplies with our partners. Because if this gets as bad as it's likely to, Europe and the US will be screaming about civilian casualties, then it will be arms sanctions and then what?' Harel said. 'We need spare parts; we need the bunker buster bombs we've paid for.'

'If it's over quickly, we're in, we're out, then it won't be a problem,' Boaz said. 'And that's when we need to be prepared for regime change in Gaza.'

'And if it goes on for months? Then what?' Harel used his pen to stab the air and emphasise the point. 'You're not listening to me, Yuval. We need ordnance, we need bunker buster bombs and we need spare parts now. You know that as well as I do.'

There was silence in the virtual meeting room and Eli could almost hear Yuval thinking it through. Finally, he spoke.

'I am listening, Harel. Let's not kid ourselves, we have hard times ahead. Bad mistakes have been made, the army has been run down and we've relied too much on SIGINT. It's a massive intelligence failure and not just for *Aman*, for all of us. We underestimated Hamas. But there's no point killing ourselves or each other, not now. You're right Harel, we need to think about today and at the same time, we also need to plan for the day after.'

'Assuming there is a day after,' Csilla said quietly.

Yuval frowned and only by the smallest shake of his head acknowledged that he'd heard her.

'Eli, I want you to source, recruit and train the perfect *lochesh* agent. Get it done. And, Harel, come back to me with a proposal for getting what we need to fight this war.'

Chapter 4

The train pulled into Finchley Road tube station and Eli woke up with a jerk.

He looked around the carriage, aware of the discreet and not so discreet glances from other passengers, who assumed that an unshaven man asleep on the Jubilee line at 4 p.m. on a Saturday afternoon had to be a drunk. Not someone who'd been up since before dawn the previous morning, October 6 – the day before.

After a deep breath, Eli hauled himself upright and made his way towards the doors, where he could prop himself up. Was he hallucinating? He felt as if was hallucinating as he tried to keep his eyes open. He needed to get off at the next stop, walk to the apartment block, shower away the day and then sleep. Blessed sleep. There was nothing more that he could do, not today.

Once outside the station, Eli trudged towards the apartment, step by step, negotiating the space with passers-by who were out on a sunny Saturday afternoon, young and old, on dates, enjoying their time. A cyclist ahead of him swerved onto the pavement by a letter box and skidded to a halt. That's when Eli had to stop. The images he'd seen on the screen that morning crashed in on him. With an effort Eli pushed them away and focused on his breath and the steps he was taking to get ever closer to the apartment, to home. To safety. But that was the problem, there was no safety. Not any more. Not for any Jew, anywhere.

Earlier on in that interminable day, Yossi, the deputy ambassador, had crashed in on Eli's meeting with Urit for what, at the time, seemed like no particular reason. The visit was camouflaged as thanks for supporting the ambassador and the encouragement Eli had given her to make the rallying speech to the shell-shocked staff. Yet, after the thank-you, Yossi didn't go. He wanted to talk, to share his feelings, and at first Eli couldn't work out why Yossi, who always seemed to hate him with an unremitting passion, had chosen Eli to unburden himself to.

Usually, Yossi looked like an accountant with his boring suits and white shirts. Today was no different – he was as buttoned up as ever on the surface but all you had to do was tap and he cracked open like a soft-boiled egg.

'Here we go again,' Yossi said.

'What?' Eli said.

'Same old, same old,' Yossi paced up and down Eli's office. 'Rape the women, kill the men, smash the babies' heads against the walls, it was a fucking pogrom, Eli. It's what happens to Jews. It's the exact same story that my great-grandfather told my mum when she was a kid. Every year at Easter the mob came into the village, raped the women, killed the men and smashed the babies' heads against the wall.'

In response, Urit's shoulders hunched tighter over her laptop, which was starting to look more like a safety blanket than an extension of her brain.

'Yossi, it's bad, I'm not denying that,' Eli said, hoping to get him out of his office and also wondering why he'd been chosen for this outburst. He didn't have long to wait.

'I really dislike you, Eli.' The deputy ambassador stabbed his finger in Eli's direction. 'I dislike every single thing about you. Your arrogance, your intellectual snobbery, your fancy education, your languages, your background and more than anything, this work you're supposed to do.' He sneered over the word 'work' before he went on. 'This so-important work you do, that was supposed to protect us and, once again, it didn't. Did it? You people got it wrong, so fucking wrong that we'll never get over it.'

Eli got up from behind his desk and assumed his most sympathetic expression. If he couldn't guide Yossi towards the door, he'd either have to hit him and bundle him out or call security, but those guys were tied up with the emergency protocols. Eli reached out and put a hand on Yossi's shoulder; when the man turned his agonised face towards him, Eli smelt whiskey. Okay. Now he understood.

'Mistakes have been made,' Eli said as he guided Yossi in the direction of the door. 'And people will be accountable, but short-term, Yossi, and medium-term, we need to sort out this mess. And that's what Urit and I are trying to do.'

'Oh yes, there'll be inquiries and sackings and the blame game, which has already started but the point is, Eli. Why? Why us? Why can't we ever be safe?'

By now Eli had opened the door and nudged Yossi into the hallway. 'Because we're the chosen people?' Eli said before he shut the door and punched in the code to slam the bolts. Eli's office was a safe room, at a switch a metal shutter would come down, to protect against bomb blasts.

'Sorry about that, Urit,' Eli said. 'Are you okay with the door bolted just in case Yossi wants to come back and continue his enlivening conversation?'

She nodded.

'Right, where were we? You now have a list of every contact we've made during the last twenty years and their connections to the prisoners who are likely to be exchanged. That's clans, families within the clans, shared geographical locations. How long is the list? I don't want to know. Is there anybody we've worked on who has the right profile to be a *lochesh*?'

She tapped away as she spoke; it was almost a nervous tic. Or maybe she was typing fast so that he wouldn't see her chewed nails and how she'd ripped the cuticles. Urit usually dressed herself like a crazed fashion influencer but today she wore jeans and a tee shirt and no make-up. That made her seem younger and more vulnerable. Maybe that's why she usually chose to paint her face like a clown, to try to protect herself. Or maybe he was just dog-tired and getting fanciful.

'So go on, who have you got for us to play with?' Eli said.

'There are three, maybe even four, but there's one standout possibility with an eighty-five per cent chance of success.'

'Eighty-five per cent? I like it,' Eli said. 'Hit me.'

'He's at the younger end of the optimum age profile at 24, but he comes from the Al-Arikhi tribe, which is the same one as Butterfly; his branch was displaced in 1948 from Ramallah. They are actually third or fourth cousins. The subject has an uncle in Kentucky who sponsored him to go to university in Kansas, where he's been studying engineering.'

'I presume that the fifteen per cent is the geographical issue,' Eli said. 'Sounds perfect apart—'

'Actually, the geographical issue is eight per cent.'

'Sorry, Urit. Okay, don't give me the statistics, just the facts.'

'Those are the facts.'

'Never mind, just go on,' Eli said. 'How does the fifteen per cent break down?'

'Geographical location, age and a brief contact initiative achieved nothing. The subject didn't want to engage with our people.'

'Maybe our people didn't want to schlep to Kansas if there were easier targets closer to the coast.'

'Possible, based on the data from the US in its entirety.' Urit tapped away again.

Eli sat on the corner of his desk and closed his aching eyes for a second. This was promising but he was too tired to think any more. He badly needed to sleep. He needed to go home.

'Send me the file on the guy.' Eli stood up and started to shrug himself into his jacket. 'I'll read it overnight and we'll take it from there. Thank you. Good work. Also, and this is important, Urit, it's been a bad day for everyone. If you feel anxious, it's no surprise and if you think you may need some help sleeping, Menachem has some anti-anxiety medication. He's going to be in his office until midnight. Okay? I'll leave it up to you.'

'Thank you. I'm good, so far everyone is okay,' she closed her laptop. 'There – I've just sent the file to you.'

By the door Eli keyed in the door code and the bolts drew back. In an attempt to lighten the mood, he made a play of gingerly pulling at the door and peering outside to see if Yossi was outside, then he held it wide open for Urit.

'By the way,' Eli said, 'what's the target's name?'

'Wasim Al-Arikhi. He knows you as Abu Marwan, hence the high chance of a positive recruitment. His sister was Sweetbait.'

'Sweetbait? Oh no, not him, did it really have to be him?'

Eli stepped inside the flat in West Hampstead, closed the door behind him and spent a moment leaning against the door. He'd got back. Only a few more actions before he could stretch out on the bed and slip into unconsciousness. What a joy that would be.

'Hey, you're back.' Gal appeared from the kitchen into the long hallway and strode towards him, her arms open.

'Barely.' Eli let himself be hugged. They stood for several seconds, locked in each other's arms, saying nothing. Gal pulled away first.

'Are you all right, babe?'

Eli said nothing. Just shook his head. 'Let's not talk about it. I can't, Gal. I really can't. Have you spoken to Doron?'

'Yeah, he's okay, but Eli... we have to talk about it.'

'Not tonight. Let me have a shower and a sleep, we can talk tomorrow and the next day and the next day. Nothing is going to change. I don't want to talk now.' Eli opened his eyes and noticed that Gal was wearing what he always called her flying outfit; the navy velour tracksuit she used when she travelled, because it had zipped pockets for documents and she was able to sleep in it. It was one of things he admired about her – her planning and organisation.

'Why are you wearing that?' Eli said. 'Are you going somewhere?'

He didn't expect the answer he got.

'Yes, I'm going back tonight,' Gal looked at her watch. 'I've got to leave in about two hours.'

'What?'

'Come and sit down in the kitchen. I'm nearly packed. I'll make you some tea, then you can shower and sleep.'

Eli felt himself being led into the kitchen and seated at the kitchen table almost as if he was a decrepit relative. Meanwhile, Gal busied herself with kettle and cup and, minutes later, she was sitting opposite him and there was black tea in front of him.

'I tried to phone you,' Gal said. 'But all I got was someone who said you were in meetings and she'd pass the message on. I'm just so pleased you got here before I left. Why is nothing working, Eli? It feels like the whole country is falling apart.'

'It is. And so am I. Why are you going? What have I done now?'

Gal laughed. For the first time in thirty-six hours, Eli felt a lightening in his spirits.

'Nothing. Nothing at all. I got a call from Oded at the institute this morning. They're screaming for people with paediatric PTSD skills and, as you know, the quicker victims get treatment after an event, the greater their chances of recovery. They're bringing the kids in directly from the battle zones and they've got no one to treat them.'

'But it's not over, it's a shitstorm. There are people who were trapped for six hours in safe rooms who were picked off by Hamas, and soldiers who didn't go in because the comms had been blown out. I've been getting through the day, Gal, pretending it's okay but it isn't. Rafi tried to go back because his kibbutz was a target but Yuval said no. All we're doing is planning operations when the whole thing is going to shit around our ears and now you're leaving me.'

'Hey, hey,' Gal reached across the table and took his hand. 'Eli, you're tired. Physically and emotionally exhausted. Also traumatised, as we all are. You're the most grounded and balanced man I've ever known, either in or out of my practice. You'll be okay, Eli. You're a strong man and we all need to do what we can in the best way that we can.'

Eli said nothing. He just looked at her for a long moment. 'You're right, I'm tired. Too tired to think. Have a good flight.'

Chapter 5

Two days later Eli was in the reception area of what was known in the intelligence community as the wedding cake, the MI6 building in Vauxhall. He'd been scanned, searched and badged up, and was now waiting to be escorted to one of the diplomatic meeting rooms on the sixth floor. No matter how many times Eli had been to the stone building, it still fascinated him. From the outside it looked less of a wedding cake and more like a futuristic fortress with towers louring over Vauxhall, but inside, in the reception area, it was all light. On one stone wall there was a massive carved wreath with a crown and ER inset into the wall. Artfully lit, the shadow enhanced the beauty of the sculpture. To its right there was a spiral staircase that led to the gallery and some of the administrative offices, and, of course, on the wall on the ground floor there was a portrait of the King. But what fascinated Eli and where he loved to linger was in front of two crystalline sculptures. A portion at the centre of each had been polished so it was possible to look through it while the remainder of the block was rough and opaque. It was a perfect metaphor for the artistry of intelligence work and Eli knew just how much Gal would have admired it if she'd ever been able to see it.

Eli had had a busy couple of days since his wife had flown home, so busy that he hadn't processed that she'd gone. That was good. No time to think about anything except moving ahead. He had back-to-back meetings with his unit, with the embassy security jocks and with the nervy diplomats, half of whom were stoned on the meds that Menachem, the embassy doctor, was dishing out like a corner dealer to anyone who wanted them. Whatever. Eli was in no position to suggest how anybody else should cope with the situation, not when it was still a fucking mess and there were hourly updates on just how bad the attacks had been.

So now here he was, at the feet of the old mandate coloni- alists, about to beg for a favour. A favour for which there would be the inevitable quid pro quo at some point, because there were no free rides in intelligence and that's the way it worked.

The reception area at MI6 was architect-grey-and-white, with an atrium that showed glimpses of blue sky inside the anodyne interior. If it wasn't for the armed police detail inside the build- ing, it might have been any corporate headquarters. Only the burly presence of the boys in blue indicated otherwise.

After two days' research, there was now no question that Wasim Al-Arikhi was head and shoulders above the other likely targets as having the best potential to become a *lochesh*, an agent who could rise so high that he could shape policy. He had education, he had connection and the only thing he didn't have was immediate geographic availability for recruitment. Before reaching that conclusion, Eli had spent a few hours considering the notion that he could ship out to Kansas with a capsule team and both develop and run the target from there, but the logis- tics plus the expense made that an unattractive idea. Better to get the target to the UK.

Urit, diamond that she was, had dug and discovered that the

target had completed his undergraduate degree at Kansas State University and then applied to do a masters at both Illinois and Imperial College, London. He'd been accepted by both, but he hadn't been awarded a bursary or a research job in either faculty to support his studies. For some reason yet to be understood, the target's funding from his uncle in Kentucky had been cut. A bursary from a newly established UK foundation that would pay for his studies and living expenses while at Imperial College would be irresistible, hence the favour begging. While the Mossad could set up a bursary from a dummy endowment charity, it would have to go through all the academic protocols. Ever since donations from the likes of Purdue Pharma and assorted Russian oligarchs, universities now liked to know where their money was coming from. Who could blame them? Only MI6 liaison would be able to speed up setting up a bursary for a particular applicant with a phone call and polite request from one old Westminster boy to another.

'Forgive me, Eli,' Milne was at Eli's elbow. 'Sorry to have kept you. My morning meeting overran and I'm not in a position to kick out the new Minister of Defence.'

Eli got to his feet and held out his hand. 'No problem. I'm grateful you found the time to see me so quickly. I only messaged you this morning.'

Milne gripped Eli's hand a second longer than necessary in a gesture of unspoken sympathy. 'I was expecting you to call. Follow me.'

They said nothing more until they were seated in the sixth-floor meeting room. The view of the city was spectacular, and London glittered in the autumn sun. At one end of the table there were some utilitarian china cups next to a thermos of coffee and a plate of assorted biscuits, supporting the notion that this was a government department and costs were considered.

'The coffee is just about drinkable,' Milne said. 'Next time we'll go to the Travellers or come for the Friday afternoon drinks and canapés.'

'I'm not here for the refreshments,' Eli smiled.

'I know that. I presume you've already seen Charlene.'

Charlene was the CIA liaison, and Eli had indeed already made a brief courtesy call to her on the way to Vauxhall. He'd already had the 'What the hell went wrong with your intelligence?' conversation with her and he wasn't keen to go through it again, but it was necessary.

'She was deeply sympathetic. She may be too young to remember 9/11, but it was the same damn thing and it left the same big scar, although ours is still gushing blood as we speak. You know as well as I do that the Americans had the intelligence in 2011, but it wasn't analysed and it didn't get passed up the chain. It's as simple as that. Intelligence is inexact. There are variables. We can run it through as many algorithms as we like but ultimately, it's up to the government to decide what they want to do with the product.'

'We've had our own cock-ups. WMD to name but one.' Milne sipped at the black coffee. 'That was expensive on so many levels, not least the human cost. Have you ever wondered what might have happened if we hadn't trundled into Iraq on the back of a report from a single unreliable agent?'

'Saddam might have survived. He would probably have had to expend his energies on subjugating the rebels to prop up the regime, rather like Assad. My guess is that he would have had to get closer to Russia.'

'Mmm.' Milne nodded as he considered the geopolitical equation, then said, 'Speaking of Russians, did you know Nicolai is back in London?'

'Nicolai? Not as Rezident, surely,' Eli said. 'He was recalled and replaced.'

'Yes, he was, after that unfortunate incident with the Ukrainian who was defenestrated out of a first-floor window. You may remember, Eli, the one who worked in a British drone facility and whose son your wife just happened to be treating for PTSD,' Milne said.

Eli had reached for one of the biscuits and was chewing on it. Even without looking up, Eli knew Milne's eyes were on him. Best to brazen it out.

'My wife is extremely grateful for the recommendation you gave us to that Dorset prep school. I understand that the child is flourishing in the environment and, not only that, but the Ukrainian's wife has moved to the area and is working in some up-market restaurant.'

Milne nodded and gave the smallest of smiles. 'Well, well… a happy outcome to a tragic incident.'

'Yes, yes, you could say that. But tell me about Nicolai, is this anything to do with Prigozhin? I never understood exactly why Nicolai was reaching out to you and Charlene when he did. At the time Putin looked weak in relation to Ukraine but now… well, now with no effective opposition to Putin with Navalny in prison and Prigozhin dead—'

'Another tragic incident,' Milne said. 'Whatever was Prigozhin thinking of? If anybody should have known that actions have consequences in Russian politics, he should have.'

'It's always been the Russian way, you know – ice picks,

polonium,' Eli said, having successfully steered the conversation away from the Ukrainian problem. It wouldn't do at all if the Ukrainian incident stymied his chance of getting some help from the British.

Meanwhile, Milne seemed keen to meander.

'It's not just the Russian way,' he almost drawled. 'It's one of your organisation's strengths, isn't it?'

'I can't deny it,' Eli said. 'Even though I've never been convinced of targeted killings' tactical benefits from a strategic point of view there have been advantages. You may recall, Oliver, we assisted with a targeted execution of members of the IRA at the request of your very own Margaret Thatcher.'

'Indeed,' Milne said. 'For which we were extremely grateful.'

'And it cemented the relationship and co-operation between our countries, did it not?'

Milne pushed his undrunk black coffee away from him. It was as clear a signal as any that Milne had stopped playing for the moment. The MI6 man smiled a warmer and more genuine smile. 'Come on, Eli. Why don't you just tell me what you want and I'll tell you if we can actually do it.'

Chapter 6

An hour later, Eli tapped his numeric code into the wall-mounted touch pad outside his office and waited for the light to turn green. It didn't. Fuck's sake, he needed to get into the room and prep for the meeting with Yuval. Just then the door swung open from the inside and Rafi beckoned him in.

'I thought I heard you scratching at the door like a little pussy cat,' Rafi said.

'Sure.'

Rafi stood over Eli. He was holding a tablet in one hand and tapped it as he spoke. 'You need to change your code, Eli. I can't report that all embassy security protocols have been updated if you're still using your son's birthday reversed with two numbers transposed.'

Eli walked past him into the elegant office with its panelled walls, and his precious library shelves stacked with books and magazines on international relations and political biographies. As he made his way to his desk, he ran his eyes over Rafi and assessed him, trying to gauge his number two. The bigger man looked clear-eyed and his customary lazy smile was pasted on his face. That was a relief. Rafi had obviously gotten over his meltdown and was everything you would expect from a former platoon leader in an elite combat unit. He knew what it was to take a hit. He knew what it was to regroup. Good. They were all bound to hold it together and hold each other together for as long as it took.

'I hope you didn't go through my drawers,' Eli said as he threw himself down into the leather chair behind his desk.

'Of course I did. What do you expect?'

'Nothing less, asshole. What have you got for me?'

Rafi glanced down at his tablet again but Eli sensed that it wasn't just to consult whatever was on the screen. Something had happened. The man was steadying himself. Eli barked at him, 'Get on with it. We've got Yuval and the rest of the European station heads in six minutes. What do I need to know?'

'Embassy internal security has all been checked. I've had meetings with British Special Branch. They've allocated us with two more teams externally, plus a ready response unit.'

'Good of them,' Eli said.

'They don't want a replay of the Iranian Embassy siege in 1979. The Brits have long memories.'

'So do we,' Eli said.

Rafi ignored the comment and rattled on. 'They've also got more street police in the area, as the expectation is that there will be demonstrations and marches. Unfortunately, we're conveniently close to Hyde Park and Speakers' Corner.'

'There's damn all we can do about that.' Eli glanced at his watch. 'What about the unit?'

'All fine. All on track,' Rafi said. 'Nathan has been out meeting the leaders of the local Jewish community and assuring them of our support. He went with two security jocks, which I think might have helped calm down the locals.'

'Good.' Eli glanced at his watch again and flicked on his laptop to give it a chance to go through its security somersaults before the meeting. 'Anything else?'

'We've got a preliminary list of the hostages and casualties,' Rafi said.

For a moment Eli's hand, which had been flicking across the keyboard, froze.

'And?'

'One of them is Alon's widow. Hamas knew where the ex-intelligence officers' houses were and they went for them.'

There was silence within the room. Eli felt Rafi's eyes on him. The last time Eli had seen Alon's wife was at Alon's funeral; an 80-year-old woman with diabetes burying her husband, she was bent but not yet broken. That was a few years ago, what sort of state was she going to be in now? Thank God Alon wasn't alive to witness this, to know that they'd been unable to keep his wife safe.

'Thanks for letting me know.' Eli tapped his desk with a finger. 'Someone is going to have to tell Trainer. Have you heard from her?'

'I've been trying to reach her for days on the work phone, ever since... ever since it happened. Calls, messages, nothing. Just to see how she was, but nothing. Maybe she's away.'

'Someone's got to tell her about Alon's wife and check up on her. Keep trying to reach her,' Eli said. 'Okay, you got any other delicious presents for me?'

Behind Eli, on the wall, the black screen for the conference call flickered into life to show thumbprints of half a dozen grim-faced people, all on mute, all waiting for the meeting to begin.

'One more thing,' Rafi said.

'Best till last?'

'When I was on the way up here, Nathan told me that Yuval is going to make a big announcement.'

'It's probably the hostage list,' Eli said.

'I don't think so, not the way he said it.'

'Rafi, why didn't you find out? You were there.'

They were interrupted by Yuval's voice calling them to attention. 'The situation is like this…' The dark-haired man with the small hands and the heavy fringe opened the meeting.

Eli swivelled round to face the camera and sat back in his chair. Today they were one station head short, Carmel, head of Spain and Portugal was absent and her deputy, Oren was standing in. Carmel's son had been in one of the army posts near the border and had been killed in the initial attack. She was now on indefinite leave. Eli doubted that she'd be back any time soon. Oren was smooth-skinned with an open face and he was bright. Eli had seen him working an agent and he had a frank and open style. He'd do. Boaz from Germany looked heavier than ever. No doubt it was his new young family and the feeds through the night, never an easy period. Csilla was back to her immaculate self with newly coiffured hair and a carefully painted face. Eli always thought she looked as if she ought to be working for Chanel and not the Mossad. He'd told her, and she'd said she'd have rather liked it. But she'd also told him, during a late-night stake-out in Paris, her secret, that the worst she felt the more carefully she dressed. How she liked the ritual of dressing and painting her face and how it gave her a sense of control. No doubt she was reaching out for that now.

Only Harel looked relaxed, even smug. Had he managed to recruit Sinwar's dear old mother in the last two weeks? That's what the level of smugness on his face suggested as he tugged at his cuffs to make sure the slim gold Omega picked up the light. How many damn watches did the man have?

The meeting started with the station heads feeding their embassy's current security status into the meeting. Eli shifted to one side as Rafi reeled off where they were at. Yuval nodded, and gave one-word acknowledgements. Only Boaz got picked up for his security status, which in Holland was as yet incomplete. Wisely, Boaz didn't attempt to sidestep the criticism.

Next was a roundup of operations and Eli was able to report with some satisfaction that the British had been more than accommodating and that Wasim, the target, now designated Silver Dove, would be relocating to Imperial College to start his MSc within the week.

Eli said, 'He has all the attributes required to become a *lochesh* and we've already had contact with him with some success. While no agent recruitment operation is guaranteed, this is as good a chance as any.'

'Good,' Yuval said. 'And further to our last meeting, Harel has come back to me with an operational plan that he assures me will secure the continued supply of spare parts for the army as well as the 2000-pound bunker busters. Would you like to outline it to your peers?'

It was clear to Eli that Harel's plan had been forced on him either by expediency or by *Memune*, the man in charge, himself. Either way, Yuval looked as if he'd trodden in some shit and the stench was close to his nostrils.

By contrast, Harel was unperturbed. 'With respect, Yuval, I'd prefer to wait until I have all my people in place. Is that okay with you?'

Eli waited for Yuval to say that it wasn't and to launch into Harel. He waited in vain.

'Need to know,' Harel said.

'Very well,' Yuval said. 'It's your operation and since it is our job to implement government policy and not to set it, then this is what we are tasked to do.'

Eli frowned and glanced over at Rafi, who was off camera and who shrugged back at him.

'I have several announcements before we wind up. As most of you know, Carmel's son was killed on October 7. She has elected to stand down and Oren will be replacing her in a permanent role. Most of you have worked with Oren in the past and I have every confidence in his ability to maintain our operations in Spain and Portugal. Some of you may be aware that one of our own, Alon, lived at Nir Zev. Alon died some years ago but I'm afraid that his wife is one of the hostages.'

There was a mutter from the screen, so obviously this piece of news wasn't common knowledge. That must be what Nathan was going on about. But Eli was wrong.

Yuval continued, 'Finally, I have to inform you that I am joining *Memune*, the boss, in the hostage negotiations. Until the situation is resolved, Harel will be taking over as head of Washington Station.'

What? Harel? No… that couldn't be right.

Eli looked at other heads of station. Their expressions confirmed what he'd just heard and couldn't believe to be true.

Chapter 7

Petra sat on the side of the bed by the open Shaker-style wardrobe. Despite the central heating being on downstairs, it was cold in the bedroom, and she could hear the wind rattling around the sash windows of the Victorian cottage. Soon it would be full-on winter and tonight's early chill was a hint of what was to come. Between the two wardrobes was a small fireplace, and once upon a time she and Matt had roasted chestnuts in the bedroom as if they were having a secret picnic. It seemed like a long time ago.

In her hand she held a book, and she stroked the cover as if it were animate. It was a journal and usually concealed in the wardrobe safe she'd built beneath a shelf. It was a neat safe and she'd been proud of her handiwork; it held all manner of useful and even sentimental items, like this journal. Every so often Petra took it out from its hiding place and examined it, as if, in the Arabic script that she was unable to read, she'd be able to find answers. It was absurd. She knew that. Ever since she'd got the book translated, she realised that she needn't have bothered. The woman who wrote in the pink-bound book was deluded. She'd believed that by killing herself she'd make a difference, but during these last two weeks, Petra had repeatedly returned to the journal and the translation and wondered what Sahar would make of what had happened on October 7 and what was going to happen now. Because Petra knew her, she knew the girl was gentle, shy, sometimes humorous and always generous, intelligent, hardworking, even perceptive – as she sat on the side of her bed, Petra could see her, the slight form, the wild wiry hair that the young woman bound back and the strands that escaped, the specs that shielded her dark eyes. Her one real beauty. What would Sahar have said? She was from Gaza, her family had been displaced in 1947 and she'd only ever known life on that narrow strip before she came to the UK and death. And what a life, to have grown up in privation, managed to find a career as a nurse, but then to be married off and, when she failed to produce a child, sent back to her own family, disgraced because of her barren womb. The only way for Sahar to win respect from a critical and disappointed parent was to become *shaheed*, a martyr.

What would Sahar have made of October 7?

Would she have she have danced in the streets, joyous that a blow had been struck against the Zionist monkeys who had ground their boots into her people ever since the *Nakba*, or would she have quailed at the thought of the terrible repercussions that would surely come, the pounding bombs, the mangled bodies that would be buried under rubble when the angry Jews sought revenge, or might she have had some compassion for the old and the young, snatched from homes and lives, the babies and the raped, the mutilated and murdered?

'Ready in five minutes,' Petra heard Matt calling up to her through the thin walls of her cottage.

'Just coming, I've found a bottle of red that will be perfect.' Deftly, Petra replaced the journal in the safe then nipped across the landing into the second bedroom that she used as an office and which also housed a wine rack. Then she was down the open stairs into the living area and kitchen, where Matt stood hunched over the hob, stirring a pot and frowning into it.

'Come here, I want you to taste it and tell me if it needs something else. Maybe a little more lemon, or maybe a little sugar to…'

'Search me. You know I can't cook,' Petra said. 'Your genius is wasted on me, but it is nonetheless genius.' She said it mechanically as she reached inside the drawer for the bottle opener, then slid out the cork before sploshing the wine into two glasses that were ready and waiting on the kitchen island.

'Hey, I thought that was a special bottle,' Matt said. 'To go with my osso bucco. Show some respect for the vintners, if not for me. What were you doing upstairs anyway?'

'Just tidying up. I've mislaid one of my pens so I was checking the pockets of my running hoodies.'

'Why would you put a pen in a running hoodie?' Matt said.

'No idea. I didn't find it anyway.' Petra took a gulp of the red. 'Nice wine. Hurry up. I'm starving.'

But Petra wasn't hungry. She played around with the lump of meat in its tomato sauce, all the while drinking the wine and watching Matt tuck into his plate with relish. Could she tell him, should she at least try to tell him?

'I don't like what's coming along the track in the Middle East,' Petra said. 'You know my father had a close friend who ended up in Israel. They were fostered together.'

'Total shitstorm.' Matt sounded unconcerned. 'Hard to see how the so-called start-up nation could have messed up so badly but it was ever thus. Too clever by halves, some of you Jews.'

'That's not funny, really. I'm uncomfortable with all this.'

'Sorry, but it'll give our arms guys a new beta theatre to trial kit when the Israelis go in. Never mind the income stream.'

'So long as someone's happy,' Petra said.

Just then a trill interrupted what Petra was about to say. It came from her white Bakelite phone, a retro gift to herself, that sat on a corner table in the sitting area, across from the TV. It was still attached to a land line and was hardly ever used but it was an extra layer of security.

'I'd better get that.' Petra jumped up and strode across the space towards the phone, expecting to find a canvasser or someone asking about a car accident that she hadn't had. Anything to get away from the table and Matt and the pointless conversation she shouldn't have started.

'Hello,' Petra said.

'I've been trying you on the work phone for days, messages, calls, ever since… Are you okay? I need to talk to you,' Rafi said.

'I'm sorry, I wasn't involved in a car accident recently and I certainly don't talk to people I don't know about my finances. But if I did, I would most certainly call you.'

'I get it,' Rafi said. 'You can't talk but are you able to call me back? Are you okay?'

'Yes and yes, I have adequate insurance and yes, that's both car and house contents.'

From the table Matt said, 'Just tell whoever it is to piss off.'

'Thank you for calling,' Petra said and put the phone down. She walked over to the table and held her hand to her head.

'Matt, I've got this crashing headache, that's why I'm not eating. Give me five minutes, I'm just going to go upstairs and get a paracetamol.'

'You never have headaches,' Matt said.

'Then it's probably a brain tumour.' Petra was already halfway up the stairs.

Back in her bedroom she reached into the wardrobe safe again and found the work phone. She hadn't used it for months, ever since she'd decided to have nothing more to do with the Office. It was predictably dead and she sat on the loo in the en suite with a lead and power pack, waking up the phone to see the messages that had stacked up. Petra didn't read them, she just messaged Rafi.

I'm okay, you okay?

She saw the wavy dots as he wrote a response. It seemed to be taking some time.

I need to see you, I'm in the car park at the end of your road. Can you get out?

Petra leaned against the back of the loo and thought for a moment. Only a moment. Then she changed into her running kit and clattered downstairs, where Matt was still at the table, still eating.

'I'm going to run this headache off,' Petra said. 'I'll be back in forty minutes, I might even have an appetite.'

Before Matt could say a word, Petra was outside her front door and gently jogging along the dark street away from her house and also away from the car park, where Rafi was waiting. She found a stretch of clear road, crossed it and then ran up the hill inside a private road. There she paused and looked down. She had a clear view. The street was quiet. The village was quiet. Matt hadn't attempted to follow her.

Once she'd got to the open car park, it wasn't difficult finding Rafi, there were only three other cars there and he'd tucked the black estate car in a corner. It was unlike Rafi to be so careless, but the car was backlit by a security light from the deserted scout hall at the edge of the car park and the clean car shone in the gloom like an oil slick. Petra continued to jog until she was right by the car, where she glanced once more behind her and slid into the passenger seat.

She was out of breath. Wordlessly, Rafi handed her a bottle of water.

'I hope it wasn't too hard for you to get away,' he said.

'To be honest, I needed some fresh air.' She gulped at the bottle and some of it spilt down the front of her tee shirt. 'And I needed to speak to you.'

'Why didn't you have your work phone charged up?' Rafi said. 'I've been trying you for days, ever since…'

'You know why, I promised myself that was all over – all of it.'

There was silence in the car.

'I wanted to at least try to give it a go with Matt and have a normal life,' Petra said.

'But you're not normal.' Rafi held out his hand for the water bottle and took a gulp from it.

'How is everything?'

'How do you think it is? That has to be the stupidest thing you've ever asked and you're not a stupid woman.'

'Okay, thank you for the compliment, but I don't know what to say, Rafi. I'm sick with it. I can't process what happened and I'm terrified about what's to come. I'm pleased my father's not alive – it would be his nightmare all over again.' Petra let out a ragged sigh. 'You?'

'Shit. All shit. My kibbutz was one of the ones attacked.'

'Oh, Rafi.' Petra reached out a hand to his forearm. He pushed it off without looking at her. He was staring straight ahead and his hands gripped the steering wheel.

He went on, 'I tried to go back immediately, while the attack was ongoing and I could have done something, but the Office convinced me that there was no point. I know that. It would have been too late.'

'I'm sorry, mate. I'm sorry I wasn't there for you and I'm sorry I didn't pick up your messages. It was cowardly, but it was easier for me not to, to stick my head in the sand and try not to think about it… How's Eli?'

'Saving the world, one operation at a time,' Rafi said with disinterest. 'You know what the hardest part is? I have to tell my girls, and Hannah, that it's all going to be all right. That they have no need to be scared, that they're safe and that I'll protect them. And I'm lying. I'm pretending all the time that it's all going to be okay. And in the Office we all have to keep up this pretence, that it's all okay, start new operations, plan for when the fighting stops, have meetings, recruit new agents, blah blah blah. But none of it's working, Petra. None of it. Because we can't tell our children that they're going to be safe.'

Petra reached out to Rafi's forearm and this time he didn't push her hand away but took it and squeezed it between his own. It was so tight it hurt but Petra didn't flinch. Rafi went on, 'Yeah, and I've got some bad news for you. That's why I'm here. Your father's buddy Alon.'

'He's dead, he died a few years ago,' Petra said. 'Lung cancer.'

'I know, but it's his widow, she's one of the hostages. Eli thought you'd want to know.'

'Oh, no, I didn't think she could have been one of them. She must be eighty if she's a day,' Petra said.

'Yeah, they knew where the ex-intelligence officers' houses were. Eli said she was eighty-five and diabetic. Big mouth, big heart. She was some sort of peacenik, apparently.'

'Was?'

'Who knows?' Rafi's hand slackened his iron grip on hers. 'I can't imagine it's going to be like the Dan Hotel in the tunnels.'

'What can I do, is there anything I can do?' Petra said. 'Is that why you're here?'

'No, no, Petra, for once, besides telling you about Alon's wife, I have zero agenda. You're out of this mess. We're starting something with the brother of that girl you worked, Sweetbait, but there's nothing for you to do there. Eli already has the connect with him. The brother thinks Eli is some sort of Hamas commander who was running suicide actions and persuaded him to go back to the US. We're in the process of getting him over here, but there's nothing for you to do.'

Petra sat for a moment thinking before she spoke. 'You know, I never told you at the time, but before she blew herself up, the girl gave me a journal that she wrote in. She wanted me to give it to her brother.'

'Why didn't you give it to us then?' Rafi sounded cold. 'What were you going to do, track the kid down and give it to him? Say you're sorry about his sister and you didn't mean her to get killed?'

'Something like that. It doesn't matter. Tom translated it.'

'Another innocent death. So what's in this thing? Anything that might be useful?' Rafi didn't sound overly interested.

'Not as far as I can see, just a lot of sad stuff about how she was doing the right thing and it would make a difference. Do you want it?'

Rafi flicked the ignition into life and the engine thrummed. 'Keep it for the moment, Petra. If we need it, I'll get in touch. I'm sorry to have barged in on your evening and I'm sorry to sound like a shmock.'

'I've got news for you Rafi, for once in your life, you don't sound like a shmock.'

Petra got out of the car and walked away. She barely checked herself between car park and home, so deep in thought was she. When she drew abreast of her cottage, she could see through the window, Matt was sitting on the vermilion sofa. The TV in the corner flickered with images of a rugby match. Petra hovered outside at the end of her path, ruminating before she took out her key and prepared to open the front door.

She was inside.

'Good run?' Matt said. 'How's your headache?'

Petra came into the sitting area and sat down on a low chair so she was at eye level with Matt.

'There's no easy way of doing this but I want to be clear with you – we're done.'

'What? Why? Why now?'

'I got some bad news today, Matt, and it struck me, once again, that you don't know me, you never have, and you never will. While most of that is my fault, the fundamental problem is that I don't want what you want.'

'What do you want?'

There was a long silence in the room. Finally, Petra said, 'I don't want you.'

She saw his face crumple with hurt, then his expression shifted to resolve as he started to get up and reach towards her, arms outstretched as if he was about to try to hug her. Quickly, Petra stood up and stepped back. 'I'm not kidding, Matt. Let yourself out.'

Chapter 8

It was clear to Eli that, in his new role as acting head of Washington Station, Harel wasn't going to waste any time. Two weeks after Yuval had made the shock announcement, before Eli had the chance to process the seismic shift in the chain of command, Harel was doing a tour of European stations. It was Eli's turn today and Harel was in his office, striding around the space like a nouveau-riche buyer sizing up a property, deciding which walls he was going to knock down.

He was in Eli's face, kitted out in an Yves St Laurent suit, fingering Eli's books. To see Harel idly turn the pages of a book that Alon had given him was distasteful, not just because Harel was an oaf, who concealed his ignorance behind a cloud of cologne. It was because he was a bully, with one skill, internal politics, and at that he was world-class.

'Nice office,' Harel said as he abandoned the leather-bound book and strutted towards the window, to gaze at a view currently obscured by a shedding tree. 'Nice office,' Harel repeated, 'but a little too classical for my taste.'

'What, you mean not enough style magazines?' Eli said, before he could stop himself.

Harel smiled and turned away from the window to face Eli, hunched behind his desk. 'As you know, I prefer something a little more current, Roche Bobois or something similar that's not necessarily High-Street. Because, Eli, being current is important, indeed being current is crucial for survival, because as times change, well, we all need to keep up with new ideas, and if we don't…'

'I'm aware of that,' Eli said. 'If you're here to go over our internal embassy security before you go to Washington, Rafi will be here in twenty and will be happy to brief you. Or maybe you'd like to sit in on the morning meeting, give the unit a pep talk. I'm sure they'd all appreciate that.'

The chances of Harel demeaning himself by going through the nuts and bolts of internal embassy security were as likely as his expenses being accurate. Eli guessed this surprise visit was more likely to be about lunching with the ambassador and her deputy in the private dining room before catching the afternoon flight to Washington, although Harel might, time permitting, get himself down to Bond Street to gauge the street atmosphere in London.

'That won't be necessary,' Harel said. 'I'm here to brief Nathan for a specific operation that will have a London angle to it.'

'Nathan? What do you want with Nathan?'

As far as Eli was concerned, Nathan was dead wood that he'd inherited when he took over as head of London Station. Eli knew that Nathan spied on him and that he was Harel's creature but, as a devout Jew and former head of *Tsafririm*, the unit charged with protecting Jews in the diaspora, he had certain uses in his ability to liaise with the orthodox elements of the British community. But working an operation, a specific operation, loaded with the expectation that Harel wanted – no, needed – a career-defining success to secure him in a permanent place as head of Washington Station? Never. Choosing Nathan would be career insanity for anything that involved logistics and precision and, whatever Harel might be, he wasn't insane. Opportunistic for sure, but not insane.

'Sure,' Eli said. 'No problem. I can shift Nathan's ongoing operations to other members of the unit. Do you want to take him back with you to Washington?'

'No, he'll be based here, reporting directly to me.'

'That's a little unusual, isn't it?' Eli said.

'Protocol. I don't mind telling you, Eli, that it's a sensitive operation that's come down direct from the Prime Minister's office. It's strictly need-to-know.'

'Understood,' Eli said for form's sake, although his mind was turning over all the possibilities that the Prime Minister would entrust a sensitive operation to Harel and his creature. Presumably, this operation was bypassing the Minister of Defence, who so far hadn't lost his scruples in the ride up the greasy pole to power.

'I want one of your safe houses for a contact meeting, but I won't need watchers or a tech team, as I've got them coming in from home.'

'Fine.' Eli pulled his laptop towards him, as much for something to do as to see what the status was on their individual safe houses. 'Any particular location or other requirement?'

Just then there was a knock on the door and the armed security jock who was now placed outside his office during office hours stuck his head around the door.

'Rafi's here, are you still in conference?'

'No, come on in, he can chat to Harel if that's okay with you?' Eli glanced up at Harel, who pasted on his customary smirk.

'Always happy to see our very own movie star,' Harel said, a comment clearly meant to belittle Eli's deputy, and a proxy put-down to Eli. Ever the professional, Rafi was unperturbed.

'Good to see you, man.' In one swift move Rafi held Harel's arm and clapped him on the back, a move that only emphasised how much taller Rafi was than Harel but also how much fitter he looked in his leather jacket and white tee shirt.

'Sorry to interrupt, Harel. Congrats on Washington, but I've got something for Eli that could have a major impact on our operation. Eli, I've just seen Trainer and I picked up both—'

Eli held up his hand, 'Rafi, stop. Don't bother Harel with this. He's only here for a short while and our priority is to facilitate his requirements while he's in London.'

Just for a moment, Rafi looked taken aback but then he nodded. Eli looked up from his laptop and smiled at Harel. 'Would Mayfair work for you? We've got a small apartment near Shepherd's Market we rarely use, as it's not wired and it's too close to the old MI5 building. Five still use it for their internal communication training programmes. Would that do for you? Or would you like something in Westbourne Grove? Or Ladbroke Grove?'

'Mayfair would be perfect, particularly if it's near Berkeley Square and the Connaught. Most convenient.'

'Good, let me know if you need anything else.' Eli stood up from his desk and walked Harel to the door.

'I will. You can be sure of it.'

A moment later the door was shut behind Harel and Rafi was helping himself to juice from the fridge in the unit under the bookcase.

'What was all that about?' Rafi said.

'You're spilling that green shit on the rug.'

'I'm not.' Rafi licked the side of the bottle where it was dripping down. 'Happy now? So go on, why's Harel here, why are you letting him treat you like yesterday's cold pasta, and why didn't you want me to tell you what I've got from Trainer in front of him? He'll see it in signals when it goes back home for analysis.'

'He won't.'

'What?'

'Sweetbait's journal is not going back to HQ.'

Rafi threw himself down into one of the two armchairs by the side of the window, an action which nearly spilt his drink, which Rafi managed to save with a flick of his wrist.

'I'm sure there's a very good reason why we're going to keep what could be a significant piece of intelligence about Hamas to ourselves at a time like this.'

'There is a very good reason,' Eli said. 'Harel will use the fact that Trainer has been holding onto it for years as ammunition. Therefore, you and I will examine it carefully, and if there is something pertinent, then yes, of course, we'll get it back to HQ. If there isn't, then we bury it.'

'Bury it? Are you crazy, Eli? What about protocol, what about rule of law, ethics and any of that other shit you used to teach at the Country Club? Wasn't that your thing, Eli, ethics in intelligence gathering?'

'I'm surprised to hear you were listening during that module.'

'I wasn't. I just know you made a big deal about it,' Rafi stood up and paced. He went on, 'What's going on with you, bro? When did you change from being buttoned up, by the book, follow the rules, don't improvise, into this. Man, if ever there was a time when we need to follow protocol, shouldn't it be now?'

'No, and you know why. Because everything has changed, all the rules. You want to know why Harel is here? Let me tell you. He's got some secret operation that he's overseeing, direct from the Prime Minister's office in London, which is why he wants a safe house, and he's seconded Nathan to his team.'

'Nathan?'

'Yes, Nathan.'

'It can't be that important if Nathan is involved,' Rafi said.

'I agree. My guess is that it's probably something dirty to do with shifting assets for the Prime Minister and his cronies from the US to the UK in preparation for the election that's going to come after this mess is over. But what if it isn't, Rafi? Harel can't be trusted, neither can the Prime Minister's office, and my point is that we can't give Harel ammunition to sideline us, not when he can do a lot of damage. It's up to us to make sure that doesn't happen.'

'Even if it means breaking rules that at the very least could lead to an inquiry and at worst could see us in jail.'

'Us?'

'I'm not going to let you fuck this up on your own,' Rafi said.

'Thanks. I appreciate that,' Eli said. 'Now, how good is your written Arabic?'

'Not as good as yours but I can certainly do my own translation, if that's what you're asking,' Rafi said.

'Good, we'll have mine and yours and we'll also have the translation from Tom's chip. With three versions we should be able to identify if there's something in the content that's pertinent. And if it is, then we'll find a way of getting that intel to HQ. Agreed?'

Rafi nodded but he didn't look happy.

Eli ignored the hangdog expression on his deputy's face. 'Rafi, they don't have to know where it's come from, they just need the intel. Just do it, Rafi. Stop overthinking. Remember the crap you like to quote that your old grandmother said. '*Quien mucho pensa, no se la fada Yersalaim.*'

'Your accent is shit.'

Eli ignored the jibe, though he was pleased to get it. It meant that, despite the long face, Rafi was on board. 'We haven't got time to mess with this, *achi*. Silver Dove will be here in three days and I'd like to make the contact the moment he arrives at Heathrow.'

Chapter 9

Eli knew that there were those in the Office who accused him of hubris but, when it came to recruitment and subsequent spy running, he didn't feel the need to feign modesty. He was good at what he did and his ability to tease out that first dribble of intelligence from an agent that led to a stream and sometimes a torrent was never questioned. No doubt that was why Harel disliked him.

In Eli's opinion, the craft of spy running wasn't only about planning, although that was certainly a significant part of his methodology; it was military science, specifically being able to understand the difference between strategy and tactics.

What Harel, and his cadre within the government, failed to understand, was that without an endgame plan for Gaza and the wider region, in other words, without a clear strategy, there would only be noise before the eventual defeat, as Sun Tze had put it so succinctly. But since the morons in the government probably thought that Sun Tze was a breakfast cereal, Eli was intellectually isolated. Yuval understood, Yuval who was a student of military history certainly understood, but he wasn't around.

It was now a month after the October 7 attacks and ground troops were in the north of Gaza. The situation grew uglier as each day passed, with the displaced population evacuated south.

Fortunate Palestinians with dual nationality were able to get out and cross the border at Rafah into Egypt, while the rest were stranded in conditions that generated harrowing footage for an increasingly hostile international community.

And still there was no strategy for the day after. This made his operation to recruit a *lochesh* superspy all the more important.

The path from intelligence work into the government itself was well trodden and it was a route that Eli held tucked at the back of his mind. After all, how much dirtier would it be to seek election than to manipulate an agent? In both cases, it was to make a positive difference. Eli was mulling over this idea as he stood in Terminal 3 under the arrivals board, waiting for American Airlines, Flight Number 734 to clear through the baggage hall. The plane itself had been delayed because of stacking over Heathrow, so Eli had sat down at Costa Coffee and enjoyed that extra half-hour thinking about how he might one day have a political career.

It would be a long way from this.

Eli looked down and fingered the fabric of his *thob*; the floor-length garment was perfect. Imported from a shop in Rafah, it had been aged by stains and detergents and now gave the impression of a garment that was neat, but well-worn, owned by someone who didn't care for such fripperies.

The outfit was the result of an afternoon session at the facility in Great Pulteney Street. There, with the assistance of Kia Kholman, Eli was kitted out. He'd even done a twirl in front of the full-length mirror, to the amusement of a couple of watchers who were sitting in a corner on two beaten-up sofas, playing backgammon. With his grey eyes, shaved head and unshaven beard Eli looked convincing. He could have passed on any street corner in Gaza City. Eli was ready and waiting for Wasim.

Across the concourse, by the arrivals barrier, Segev was posing as a driver to pick up passengers. The young man with the bored expression held up a tablet with the name of a fictional passenger. The tablet had a secondary function; it wasn't just a prop – Segev was filming the arrivals as they came through the doors.

Dotted around the airport, three other members of the unit were in position: one in the arrivals concourse, one in baggage handling and one outside. Each of them had seen a recent image of Silver Dove and they had confirmation that he had boarded his connecting flight at Charlotte for the flight to Heathrow. If they couldn't pick him up and make a contact, then they really all should pack up and go home.

At least, that was Eli's estimation. No doubt Harel would have insisted on double the amount of manpower and found some way of making a contact that involved a limousine and, if at all possible, a private jet, but even if he had been so profligate, resources were tight with the ongoing war. With relish Eli recalled how Harel had been duped out of seventy per cent of his budget by a canny Egyptian who'd supplied him with open-source intelligence culled from the internet with a smattering of colourful fiction. One more cock-up like that and Harel must surely be out and the chances were his oh-so-secret operation just might be the one.

Eli saw Segev touch his right ear – the signal to turn on his comms. Eli responded by pressing the app on his phone. By necessity comms were cut to the minimum amount of airtime necessary. This was because Heathrow was one of the most monitored locations in the UK and Eli didn't want their data finding its way to GCHQ via a conscientious security wonk before they'd had a chance to do what they were there to do. As Eli had said in the briefing meeting, the contact protocol wasn't totally vinyl tradecraft but it was certainly heading in that direction.

It seemed that Silver Dove had cleared passport control and was now in the luggage hall, that meant he'd be out any minute and Eli needed to be in position. Ready to collide into him, feign surprise and joy at meeting him again. Rejoicing in the coincidence, he would offer the young man a lift to London and, before Silver Dove could think twice, he'd be guided towards the waiting car.

Timing would be everything.

'Silver Dove is by the belt,' Eli heard in his ear. 'He's just helped an old woman get her case off the luggage belt and onto a trolley.'

'A gentleman, is he?' Eli muttered.

'It's a massive suitcase. He's helping her with a second one, she's thanking him, they're talking. He's got her case onto her trolley. It looks like she's now waiting for him. Probably the trolley is too heavy for her to push.'

'Why doesn't she get a porter?' Eli hissed.

Eli was tapping his fingers against the phone. How many times did people strike up conversations with strangers in baggage halls? It just didn't happen.

Segev's voice maintained its usual neutrality. 'He's got his case, which is on the trolley, and they're heading towards customs. He's pushing the trolley and they're talking. They've stopped. He's looking after the trolley; she's walking away, I think she's heading towards the toilets.'

Now would have been good for that chance meeting if he'd been in the luggage hall, but he wasn't. Eli was outside, unable to do anything except listen to this description of the events that seemed to be spiralling out of his direct control.

'She's out,' Eli heard in his ear. 'They're heading towards the green channel.'

There was silence. Eli focused on the door that opened and shut as travellers from all across the world filtered into the hall and the outside world.

At last. There was Silver Dove wheeling the old lady's trolley. The kid could have been taken for the woman's son, so careful was he with the way he was guiding both her and the trolley through the doors. Seeing him in real time jolted Eli; in the three years since Eli had last seen him, he'd changed. Then he'd been a teenager, foul-smelling, sobbing, curled in a foetal ball under the bedcovers in a run-down apartment, bereft after the violent death of his elder sister. Yes, he'd changed. He was still slight but he was taller, more athletic, while the wiry hair he shared with his sister was now covered by a baseball cap. It was certainly Silver Dove, in jeans and high-top trainers. The young man had the same unmistakable gait, Eli had noted before – a way of bouncing on the balls of his feet. But the specs were different. They were round and oversized. Modern, stylish.

Now outside, the old woman, who, in Eli's view, shouldn't have been travelling without assistance, tottered across the concourse towards a young couple and a toddler. There were cries of welcome and the toddler slipped under the barrier and nearly knocked over her grandmother, while Silver Dove held onto the trolley, waiting for the family to notice him. Once they did, there was hand-shaking and obvious thanks and then, to

Eli's chagrin, Silver Dove was wafted with the family through the airport and towards the car park.

'Contact aborted,' Eli said. 'Return to base.'

'Whoever said no good deed goes unpunished was a shmock.'

It was two weeks later and winter was closing in. In London it was dark at 4 p.m. and in Israel there was a one-week truce, where hostages were exchanged for prisoners. Eli and Rafi were in the meeting room, watching the newsfeed of the exchange. Lists had been circulated before the exchange and Alon's wife wasn't among them.

Besides the newsfeed, the wall was a kaleidoscope of screens that showed maps, nearby streets, stills of Silver Dove, as well as interiors and exteriors of both Imperial College and Silver Dove's apartment in Eastbourne Terrace.

Eli massaged his eyebrows, trying to squeeze the tension away, trying not to think about Alon's wife. 'There's got to be an easier way of doing this. And fast. We do not have time for some long-drawn-out recruitment.'

'You know, I always thought the FBI's method of two people approaching someone in the street had its advantages,' Rafi said. 'Direct and to the point, no messing about with cover stories and shows.'

'That would only work if we posed as Americans and that option's off limits unless we really want to destroy the relationship. They won't forgive us. It's also clumsy and it's about as insecure as you can get.'

'Dove has an Uber account,' Rafi said. 'Say we hack into his account, you pick him up as if you're his Uber driver and then you make the pitch.'

'Possible.' In his mind, he pictured Silver Dove amid a composite of some of the agents he'd recruited over the years and the moment, that sweetest of all moments, when they agreed to work.

Eli shook his head. 'No, it won't work. I need eye contact to make the pitch and I can't do that if I'm driving. It might work on a three-hour journey but not between South Kensington and Bloomsbury.'

Rafi got up from the armchair by the window and paced, before taking up his favourite position on a corner of the desk by Eli's side, both men staring in silence at the wall of screens. There had to be a neat way of doing this. Eli was thinking hard, wishing that they had Yuval in the meeting with them but, since he was now tied up with the hostage negotiations, they were on their own. What would Yuval say? Probably something about keeping it simple.

That's why Eli found himself three days later sitting in the dark on a rainy night waiting to hear the key turn in the lock of Silver Dove's flat. This was about as simple as it could get. Just a couple of watchers monitoring Dove's journey from his afternoon tutorial to the apartment via a supermarket, where he picked up a ready meal and some toiletries. Dove was on his own and he stayed on his own. In his earpiece, Eli heard his progress towards the flat.

Getting inside the flat had been simplicity itself, since it was their flat, or at least they held the short-term lease on it and it had seemed only sensible to use it as part of the research bursary for Dove. It was one bedroom in a secure block, and they'd used it as a safe house in the past. It had been the home of another agent, Tom. Since Tom's occupancy, the flat had been redecorated and the furniture shifted around. Only the wall TV screen was still in place, and a gimcrack cabinet beneath it. As well as changes to the placement of the furniture, the previous wooden floor was now carpeted; it needed to be, since it had been irreparably damaged.

As Eli sat back in the dark on the hard chair, he remembered the last time he'd been in that flat, when he'd struggled to push open the door to this room because a hulk of a man had collapsed against it and was bleeding to death on that hard wooden floor. Despite the murk, with only the light from the street outside creating shadows, Eli could visualise the exact spot. Almost see the shape of the man and the image of Petra, as she'd stood, still holding the knife.

Just then the earpiece burst into life and Eli heard, 'Dove now inside the courtyard, approaching the building. He is alone.' Eli sat up and focused. It was showtime.

Chapter 10

Eli crossed his hands across his padded belly and pasted onto his face an expression of beatific solidity. He'd been practising both the expression and his pitch for days and he was now word-perfect. He'd also identified the likely emotional arc of the target; there would be the initial shock of the unexpected visitor, the fear of a physical attack, the moment of recognition, then interest, curiosity and, finally, the establishment of trust. Eli needed to get to trust as fast as possible while still maintaining his authority throughout the process. It was a big ask but no more complicated than many of the complex agent contacts he'd worked. Silver Dove's sister was a case in point.

When running Silver Dove's sister, Eli had spent months in this guise as Abu Marwan. He'd nurtured the agent, flattered her and acted as her guide and commander in her quest to become *shahida*, a martyr. And she was convinced. She thought he was wise, perhaps like the father who'd disappeared from her life. Eli knew the girl had been convinced. He'd read what she'd said in the journal that Petra had kept to herself. Sahar had written that she wanted to make Abu Marwan proud of her. For a moment Eli could see the young woman, the big doelike eyes and a hopeful expression, and her kindness for anyone she met, unless they were the Zionist monkeys.

Eli thought about the journal and recalled much of its content. It was mostly mawkish, all he and Eli had gained from it was a reference to an Uncle Fahed, who'd helped with Wasim's university fees and American visa and he was already on a watch list. The rest was a saga of sadness. The young woman wrote about how she looked after her brother as a child. Eli remembered the words, 'Mawmia was ill after you were born. It was winter, wet and cold. The house was draughty, even though we stuck newspaper in the window cracks and covered the cold floor tiles with sacking.'

What a way to live... and die. How cold would it be there now in the tunnels underground? In tents above the ground? On the road moving from place to place. Sirens, explosions, terrified screams of pain, silent screams of misery. What suffering must be going on.

The door to the room opened and the overhead lights came on and Eli blinked as his vision adjusted.

'*Marhaban Al'afw*, Wasim,' Eli said, using a warm tone and his perfect Arabic, with a hint of the Djebdahi accent he'd worked on. Deliberately, Eli didn't stand. He needed to establish his seniority. 'Please forgive the intrusion into the privacy and sanctity of your home, but I did not want to speak to you in a public place, for what I have to say is for you and you alone.'

'Who the hell are you?' the young man said in English with an American accent. For a bad moment, Eli wondered whether this aggressive man, who was certainly the one at the airport, was the same young man that he'd cajoled years earlier into going back to the US and safety. Up close, and from his seated position, Dove seemed taller and he had more of a beard, but it was definitely him. Wasim was blinking hard behind the designer specs.

Eli went on, 'Maybe I have grown older and more frail since we last met, maybe harder for you to recognise, while you, a young lion, have grown in both stature and power. I salute you, Wasim. I stand before you and I honour you with all my heart, I, Abu Marwan al Djebdahi, was the commander of your blessed sister's *istishhada*. Sahar was a credit to the Al-Arikhi clan.'

At the mention of Sahar, the colour drained from the young man's face almost as if there was an invisible tap under his chin but, in no more than a second, he'd recovered, and Eli saw his mouth tighten.

'What do you want, old man?'

'To talk. Just to talk. It is good that you remember me. I remember you well. As Ali Ibn Abi Talib said, "Everything expected is happening, so expect what you wish." And it is happening, Wasim. It is happening.'

Wasim said nothing. He was still holding onto the rucksack that no doubt contained his laptop. He walked into the kitchen area and with deliberation placed his rucksack on the kitchen worktop. With his back to Eli, he opened the fridge door, grabbed a beer and flicked open the top. Then he turned, looked at Eli, tilted his head and drank deeply. Dove wiped the back of his hand against his mouth. Once more, Eli had the sense that he was talking to someone he'd never met before.

Silver Dove said in English, 'I don't know what you're talking about, old man, but, whatever it is, I don't want any of it.'

'You are Wasim Al-Arikhi, born in Rafah, studied at University of Kansas, now studying for an MSc in Biomathematics at Imperial College.' Eli was striving to regain control of the contact, despite the sensation of sweat running down his armpits. 'The time has come for you to return the gift of your education. To do something for your people and for your heritage.'

'Is this anything to do with my uncle, old man?'

'No,' Eli said. 'This is to do with you and your future. And your obligations.'

'Obligations?'

'If you remember me, then you may remember that it was our actions that stopped you getting arrested when you came to the UK, looking for your sister. If we hadn't warned you, you would have been arrested and, as such, unable to go back to the US to complete your first degree. I am sorry to be blunt, Wasim, but you have an obligation to us.'

'And just who is this "us" that I'm supposed to be obliged to? Hamas, Fatah, Muslim Brotherhood, Al Shabaab, al-Qaeda. Or maybe you're something new.'

'That will come later.' Eli raised a hand, open-palmed. It was designed to be a gesture of harmony. And for a moment Eli had the sense that he'd corrected the tilt and could steer the meeting into less choppy waters. 'For now,' Eli said, 'we just talk. How are you enjoying your studies? I hear this university is very fine.'

Wasim ignored the question and drained the rest of his beer in one long gulp. Eli saw his Adam's apple shift up in his throat. Once again, the young man wiped his hand across his mouth, then stared at Eli through his specs.

Eli continued, 'Now that we have met again, we want to know what we can do for you. Later, there will be time to talk about the future.'

Wasim scoffed and smashed the beer bottle against the side of the sink, he held up the green shard and came towards Eli. 'What you can do for me? You've done enough for me and my family and my poor sister. She'd have been alive now if you hadn't got your claws into her and made her think that she was actually going to make a difference.'

The young man was using the broken bottle, like a green finger, to emphasise his words. 'You used her. You and people like you have done nothing for the real people of Palestine except use the weak to get what you want. And you know what that is? Power. It's not what's good for us. Never has been. You get the hell out of my apartment before I call the English police and tell them you threatened me. And if you ever so much as come within a metre of me, I will kill you and take the consequences.'

While the speech was going on, Eli stood up from the chair and moved behind it. He was confident that he could overpower the younger man but didn't want to reach that point. More than anything, he had to establish some authority.

Eli spoke to him as if he was his own son. 'For many people your sister was a beacon of hope and, if you choose to turn your back on me, then you are turning your back on Sahar and everything she believed in.'

At this, Wasim lunged at Eli who picked up the chair and smashed it across the younger man's arm. He yelped and the bottle shard fell to the ground. Losing no time, Eli grabbed the arm, spun Wasim around and hoicked it up into a savage half-nelson. Using his other arm, Eli slammed it against the young man's throat and yanked it back.

'Nicely, now,' Eli said softly, 'or I break your arm and strangle you. London is a violent city. This wouldn't be the first robbery that had gone wrong.'

Eli felt the gasp and a nod, so released the pressure on the young man's throat, still keeping his arm locked in the painful grip. Then he pushed the young man away from him and strode to the front door of the apartment. Outside, he clattered down the stairs and out into the street, hopeful that the boy wouldn't follow him. That would only compound his failure.

PART TWO

Wounded

A wounded deer leaps the highest.
> Emily Dickinson, USA, 1830–1886

When you go to war as a boy, you have a great illusion of immortality. Then, when you are badly wounded the first time, you lose that illusion, and you know it can happen to you.

> Ernest Hemingway, USA 1899–1961

Chapter 11

The afternoon meeting after Eli's botched contact with Silver Dove ranked in his mind as a low point, but nonetheless not an irredeemable failure. That's how Eli fought to look at it. He'd managed to catch up with Gal in the morning for a brief WhatsApp conversation while she drove to one of the newly-set-up therapy centres for the victims of October 7. She was full of the statistics, the resources and long-term damage resulting from PTSD and also the new initiatives and the new research that was coming out of it. Despite her visible focus on the job at hand, she did give him some comfort when he told her that he'd had an operational fuck-up the night before, and he was grateful for her advice.

Hours later, when the video meeting went live and Eli saw Harel's face, Eli held onto Gal's words as if he was on a life-raft paddling away from the sinking ship of his career.

Although he hadn't told her the details about the contact with Silver Dove, he'd told her enough for her to realise how serious this was for Eli.

'From what you're saying, Eli, this rival of yours is now your boss because he's got the Washington job for the duration. He obviously has an agenda; that's to get you out of the way. He'll try to goad you into defending your decisions in whatever you did last night, get you to make excuses, justify your actions and then he'll shoot them down one by one. Okay? Your best course will be to take responsibility and then offer an alternative solution, a better one.'

'But I don't yet have one,' Eli said. 'I've got some ideas and I've read—'

'Say you'll get back to him,' Gal interrupted. 'The worst he can do is scream at you for not having an immediate alternative and that will serve the purpose of taking the heat off whatever went wrong last night.'

'Okay,' Eli said. 'And—'

'Eli, I'm here now.' The sound of the car engine had stopped. 'I've got to go inside. Good luck.'

'And you,' Eli said, but she'd rung off before he'd had a chance to say anything else.

So now he sat waiting again, drinking coffee and waiting for the video meeting to start. Last night it had been waiting for Silver Dove to call him an old man and threaten him with a broken bottle. Now he was waiting for Harel to taunt him about his professional ineptitude. But he'd handle it.

The other station heads were now on screen but on mute. Eli thought he could discern a sympathetic smile from Boaz and a nod from Nurit who was now acting head of station in Paris and Belgium. But all of them would by now have read the overnight signals and know that Eli was going to be hung out to dry. Some were sympathetic, some dispassionate and others were no doubt relishing a little institutional bloodletting.

Despite the anticipation, protocol was maintained and Harel went around the different regional stations and asked for updates on significant operations. To Eli's chagrin, he was well prepared and asked pertinent questions; this thoroughness was a worry to Eli. No doubt Harel was enjoying the Washington chair and was planning to wedge his slick ass into the seat and oust Yuval. His meeting style was different to that of Yuval, who was master of the military approach. Harel was snake-like – he asked questions in a pleasant, even a relaxed, manner and then pounced on any inconsistencies or errors.

Predictably, Harel was saving Eli's humiliation until last, like it was the brandy and cigars after one of his overpriced dinners with an agent. Before they reached that point, Boaz was in the crosshairs of Harel's disdain.

'The operation with *Aman* is going well,' Boaz said. 'We've found a guy in a bonded warehouse in Budapest, where the pagers will be stored before they're shipped.'

'Ah, yes.' Harel consulted his laptop. 'I read your report. The guy wants an obscene amount of money.'

'It is a lot,' Boaz said. 'But *Aman* are coming up with a third of the budget. I think it will be worth it.'

'You do, do you? It seems like a fanciful waste of time and money, when there are other priorities,' Harel said. 'Explain to us again why you need a river ship cruising down the Danube, as opposed to a warehouse in a secluded location?'

'Because every day there are 151 river cruises leaving from Budapest, as well as day cruises and cargo boats. It is far easier to blend into a busy environment than put our people on a coach to a warehouse in the middle of nowhere, where locals and local police are going to be wondering what we're doing,' Boaz said. 'Harel, you know we have successful precedents for this type of show.'

'I suppose you're going to cite Operation Moses and the Red Sea resort. Wasn't your uncle involved in that?' Harel said.

'Yes, he was. And it was successful,' Boaz said. 'Eight thousand Ethiopian Jews rescued.'

There was silence for several moments while Harel pulled at his lower lip. Finally, he said. 'Well, if *Aman* are so confident that this is all actually going to work, get them to come in with half.'

'I'll do my best,' Boaz said.

Given how much money Harel had previously wasted on his own fanciful operations, this seemed a little too much, but Eli was in no position to make that point. Not when Harel had just unmuted him on the video call.

'And now to Eli,' Harel said with exaggerated weariness. 'Would you care to update us all on operation Silver Dove?'

'The target rejected me unequivocally.' Eli put down his coffee cup. 'I approached him in the guise of a known mentor and someone that he'd previously taken orders from. I didn't take into account that he's changed, and I take full responsibility for the outcome of the contact, which, as I'm sure you all know, was a complete failure. For that I'm sorry.'

After abasing himself with such success, Eli had the satisfaction of seeing Harel's smooth brow above the aviator tinted specs, crease into a frown. *Kol Hakavod*, Gal. She had that bastard's number.

'And what are your plans for proceeding?' Harel said. 'How is this attempt at establishing your super-agent going to go when you have so thoroughly ruined the contact, not to mention pulling in the favour with the British government? A favour that we will certainly have to repay.'

Before Eli had the chance to respond, another thumbprint image sprang onto the screen. It stopped him in his tracks. Nathan? What was he doing in a meeting of heads of station? He wasn't even a deputy.

'Ah, Nathan,' Harel smiled. 'Perfectly on time. Eli, it occurred to me that, given your failure last night, you might benefit from some additional help with this operation of yours. Nathan, who we all know to be a diligent member of your unit, has shown great initiative and, by analysing data from Silver Dove's file, he has come up with a plan.'

It took every gram of Eli's self-control to keep his face bland. It was clear that Harel was trying to publicly humiliate him and was goading him with a plan from Nathan, a plan designed to show that he, the head of London Station was incompetent and should be replaced. Cunning bastard.

'By all means,' Eli said. 'What's your *tochnit peoolay*, Nathan? I can't wait to hear it.'

Nathan's reedy voice set Eli's teeth on edge but that was nothing compared to the plan.

'I got our guys to run Silver Dove's file through the system and there's a seventy per cent chance that he's homosexual and, if he is… then we can use that to convince him to work for us,' Nathan said.

'What?' Eli said. 'Are you suggesting that we dangle a couple of rent boys in front of Silver Dove and then photograph him and threaten to circulate the pictures on social media. Is that it? Really?'

Nathan nodded but he didn't look convinced. Eli bet that this was all Harel's idea and Nathan was merely his mouthpiece. The notion strengthened Eli's response.

'When did we ever do this type of thing? It's not our style. It's what the Soviets did.'

'With some considerable success,' Harel said.

'And some considerable failure. Blackmailing a target only ever works short-term. The relationship is tainted from the start and, if Nathan wants to take his ass back to the archives, he'll see that. If you use coercion, the agent resents the *katsa*, the quality of the product is always second-rate – always. And, in my opinion, it's a waste of time and money.'

'But he's gay,' Nathan said. 'Can't we use that?'

'Probably, but not to compromise him. If that truly is the case, then it's another reason for him not to want to go back to Gaza, because Hamas have a lousy record when it comes to LGBT communities. They kill them.'

'Which makes him vulnerable to blackmail,' Harel said. 'And unless Eli can come up with a better idea, I propose pursuing Nathan's plan. That is my decision.'

Rigid with anger, Eli managed to wait until the meeting was over and the screen was black before he threw his coffee cup at the wall. It shattered; the grounds left a stain against the paintwork and dripped down like a splatter of oxidised blood.

Chapter 12

'I'm not an option,' Petra said. 'Just remember that.'

'I know, I know, you keep telling me. It's just a mercy fuck, isn't that what you said? But I'm still appreciative.' Rafi twirled a lock of Petra's dark hair between his fingers. 'Despite that, being with you gives me comfort. I hope it's the same for you.'

'Sure. You want coffee?'

Petra disengaged Rafi's hand from her hair and pulled away to get out of bed and end the conversation. But Rafi reached for her hand and held it. 'Seriously, Petra, you are the only person I can talk to. I can't talk to Hannah. She just cries, talks about God, and that's if she isn't high on meds.'

'What about Eli?'

'He's obsessed with this new operation and he's fighting some internal politics.'

'Internal politics? Isn't there enough crap going on without that?'

'You don't know these people.'

'Sadly, I do. I met one of that sort when there was that inquiry last year about the Ukrainian contact cock-up.'

'Of course you did,' Rafi said. 'Didn't you tell one of the interrogators to fuck off? Eli really liked that.'

'It was actually fuck off and die,' Petra said.

85

Rafi let go of Petra's hand and fell back on the pillow, smiling. 'There are still plenty of contact cock-ups to go round. Eli just had a bad one.'

'You really are an awful gossip, Rafi. You shouldn't be telling me this stuff.'

'Who are you going to tell? MI5? They wouldn't care anyway.' Rafi went on, 'It was Sweetbait's brother.'

'Wasim? That's a shame. Wasn't there anything in the journal that was helpful?'

'No. Eli and I both retranslated and then checked it against Tom's translation, which was accurate. There was nothing useful in it.'

'Poor Tom,' Petra said. 'What a waste.'

There was silence in the bedroom for a few moments, a silence born of mutual understanding beyond sex and beyond any friendship or camaraderie the two might have had. It was a silence of respect for the casualties that sometimes seemed to be all around Petra, to crowd in on her. It was also the silence of guilt. During this recent resurrection of their sexual past, Rafi had talked about his early years in the army when he was 22, and how he'd led a platoon into a firefight and three of them had died. It struck Petra that Rafi, with his irritating machismo and unsophistication, understood something of how she felt and who she was. She lay back down on the bed and nestled into his arms.

'I presume Wasim told Eli to fuck off, or was it worse than that?'

'Worse. Eli's burnt and can't be used again. Wasim knows him as the guy who got him out of the UK and safely back to the US. That's what we were banking on, that he'd remember how Abu Marwan had got him out of trouble. But, with Wasim, there's also the connection with his sister's death. End result, Abu Marwan is the enemy.'

'That's too bad. You know I had a good relationship with him. He knows I tried to save his sister. It's a shame Eli told him I died in that bomb blast.'

Rafi stopped stroking Petra's shoulder.

'What?' Petra said.

'I'm not sure he did.'

'That's what Eli told me,' Petra said.

'No... no, I was there,' Rafi narrowed his eyes as if he were replaying the memory. 'He said you'd been badly injured, he might have said you weren't expected to live, but that's not dead, is it?'

Petra raised herself on one elbow. 'No... that's definitely not dead. What do you think, Rafi? Would Eli go for it?'

'He has big respect for your skills, I know that. He's also desperate to recruit Silver Dove.' Rafi kissed Petra's shoulder and got up and started to get dressed.

'Let's have that coffee now and talk about how it could work? I'm seeing Eli tonight. He's coming for *shabbat* dinner. I can check it out with him.'

'Sure.'

Petra slipped on a tracksuit and padded down the open-tread stairs to the kitchen, where she turned on the coffee machine, got the coffee cups out and put a notepad and pen on the table. The idea of recruiting and running Wasim was more than intriguing, it was case officer work, above her grade and never done by anyone other than Israeli nationals. But if anybody could do it...

Her thoughts were interrupted by the doorbell. She wasn't expecting anyone on a wintry Friday afternoon, as day slid into dusk. There were no expected deliveries. Rafi was halfway down the stairs and he raised an eyebrow. The doorbell rang again and Petra shrugged and went over to the camera. Before she could reach the door camera, there was a sharp ratatatat on the black knocker, accompanied by a voice, a plaintive voice that was talking to the doorbell.

'Oh Petra, I do hope you're there. I so desperately need your help.'

'Sandie,' Petra said to Rafi. 'You met her before. Probably a problem with the rabbits. Do you want to go upstairs while I get rid of her?'

'No, if it was Matt, I'd be climbing out the window, but Sandie. I know her. She likes me.'

'Don't give me a headache, Rafi.' Petra checked the camera, as was her ingrained habit, and confirmed it was Sandie before she opened the door. Petra's neighbour almost fell through the door.

'Oh, thank goodness,' Sandie said. Over her neat beige trousers and neat print blouse she was wearing a neat apron. No doubt she was cooking something and needed some vital ingredient, although Sandie must be pretty desperate to think that Petra might have it, unless it was something like eggs. Or milk.

'Come in, come in,' Petra said. 'You remember…' Petra couldn't remember what Rafi had called himself the last time they'd met, when once again Sandie had invited herself around for a moment and then stayed for the evening.

'Dan,' Rafi chimed in and held out his hand to shake Sandie's. She preened with delight. The woman was lonely and sad and

Petra considered being kind to her one of the few charitable acts she did that had any worth.

Petra gestured at the notepad and pen on the table. 'We're brainstorming some ideas for a new initiative and there's no better time to do that than a Friday afternoon.'

Too much explanation, but it was supposed to imply that Petra was busy. She softened it by saying, 'What are you doing later?'

'That's why I'm here,' Sandie relinquished Rafi's hand. 'Do you remember Cameron?'

'No.'

'Bob's grandson. The one who choked on a bit of carrot when he was feeding the rabbits. You saved his life, Petra.'

'I just happened to be there. Is there something wrong with him? Do you have time for coffee?' Petra looked at Rafi over the top of Sandie's head. He shrugged.

'No, I don't have time. You see, they're coming for high tea. Bob and Cameron. It's Cameron's birthday and he wanted to set-off some fireworks, but Bob hurt his back on the allotment and he doesn't want to disappoint Cameron. He's staying with him for the weekend. You know the parents have split up.'

'Oh dear,' Petra said. 'Isn't it a little late for fireworks? That was weeks ago.'

'I know, but it's his birthday and things are difficult at home. And what with Bob's back. I don't want Bob to make it any worse, bending down and whatnot, so I just wondered, dear, dear, Petra... I just wondered, would you help me set up the fireworks and then tell me what to do? I'm so sorry to interrupt you and I can see that you're busy but...'

If she let Sandie do it on her own, the chances of Petra's

own house burning down certainly increased, and she did owe Bob a favour. After all, he'd let her use his off grid fisherman's cottage in Wales, no questions asked.

'Sure, Sandie. Give me half an hour to wrap up the afternoon with… Dan. And I'll be over.'

'Thank you, thank you so much.'

After ushering Sandie out of the door, Petra turned to Rafi who was gulping down the coffee and already had his leather jacket on.

'*Ainbayot*,' Rafi said. 'I'm seeing Eli in a few hours. I'll see how the idea of you recruiting and running Silver Dove sits with him.'

'Okay, he'll either go for it or he won't.' Petra was in the kitchen, going through the drawers. She took out a lighter and pocketed it, then rooted through her work bag on the kitchen worktop. She took out her purse and a plastic gizmo the size of a credit card.

'This has got a torch, a magnifying glass and scissors, among other tools. Because I bet you any money you like, Sandie won't have any of those things to hand.'

'You just need a hat and scarf,' Rafi said. 'It's cold out there.'

'Got one of those.' Petra pulled on the quilted coat that was hanging up in her utility room and wrapped a grey and navy scarf that Sandie had knitted for her. It would make Sandie happy if she wore it.

'Nice.' Rafi felt the fabric. 'But wear something else. It's acrylic yarn and possibly untreated.'

'Oh, don't make a fuss.'

'I'm not joking,' Rafi said. 'Wool is the least flammable material. Here.'

He unwound the blue cashmere scarf that was round his neck and wrapped it around hers. It was soft and it smelt of him. 'Take mine, you can give it back to me when I see you.'

'Okay. Thanks.' It would be foolish to argue for the sake of it when, if there was one thing that Rafi knew about, it was explosives. 'You'd better leave first,' Petra said.

'Sure. But tell me…' Rafi hovered by the front door. 'What's high tea and why is it any different from normal tea?'

Petra stood on her toes and kissed Rafi on the cheek. 'It would take too long to explain and I have to blow up some fireworks.'

'Sounds like my kind of evening.'

Chapter 13

Eli hacked away at the dry chicken and chewed at it with a mouthful of overcooked carrots that hadn't been thoroughly drained from the water that had boiled away all flavour.

'This is lovely, Hannah. You've no idea how good it is to have a home-cooked meal.' He smiled at Rafi's wife, who had the youngest girl on her lap and was feeding her with minced gloop. Across the table, Rafi winked at him. He knew Eli was just being polite. Rafi was next to the oldest girl, Netta, a tow-haired charmer, who had just regaled them all with her day at school, the preparations for Hanukkah, the other children in her class and the security drills they were doing. She liked to talk.

It was Friday night at Rafi's apartment in Child's Hill. The room was homely, untidy, with a basket of children's toys that overflowed onto the wooden floor. On the dining table the candles were lit, the tablecloth was white and, before they'd eaten, Hannah had blessed the candles and Rafi had said *kiddush* over the wine and bread – that was the best part of the meal, as the challah bread was soft and sweet. No doubt Hannah had bought it in.

While Hannah busied herself in the galley kitchen of the mansion flat getting the fruit salad, Eli nodded at the *shabbat* candles and raised an eyebrow. 'I didn't realise this was your thing,' he said in English.

'It isn't. October 7,' Rafi responded. 'Ever since then. It seems to be a trend going on with the wives, becoming more devout.'

'No doubt led by Nathan's boring wife – Malka, isn't it?'

'How did you guess? I'm not crazy about it, but I've got to let Hannah do whatever works for her. Malka, is one of the ones saying that October 7 happened because people aren't observant.'

'I suppose that beats the explanation that the government fucked up,' Eli gulped back a large mouthful of wine.

'It's all coming from the blacks, they've really got themselves organised,' Rafi said, using the slang term for the ultra-religious groups who dressed in black and were propping up the government.

Rafi went on, 'As I hear it, they're recruiting like crazy. And they're having a field day explaining to people like Hannah that the kids who were snatched from the Nova festival wouldn't have been raped and murdered if they'd been back home praying. They wouldn't be starving to death in the tunnels while we bomb the hell out of the strip.' Rafi shook his head. 'At least your wife isn't buying into any of that shit. How's she getting on back home?'

'Busy as hell but she's certainly not wearing a *sheitel*.'

Rafi chuckled. 'Not your wife.'

Hannah came in with a bowl of fruit salad, followed by Netta, who was proudly carrying the dishes. Hannah was an attractive woman, lean and long, with blonde hair and manicured nails. A gym bunny that Eli had previously discounted as being on the light side of the IQ spectrum. Before she'd met Rafi, she'd been a model and had a few small parts in TV series. No question, they made a handsome couple, and those two girls were beauties. It wasn't hard to understand how threatened Hannah might feel at the notion that the *blondinis* would have had their skulls smashed against the walls if they'd been visiting Rafi's kibbutz when the attack happened.

'What have we got here?' Rafi switched back to Hebrew as he took the plates from Netta and helped Hannah dole out the fruit salad. 'Who wants the blueberries?'

Thirty minutes later, Rafi and Eli were outside the apartment block, walking in the direction of Eli's flat which was half a mile away.

'You don't have to walk me home.' Eli unfurled a small umbrella. 'I haven't drunk that much.'

In answer, Rafi took out his sound buffer and switched it on.

'This couldn't wait, *achi*,' he said. 'I've got an idea for Silver Dove. Actually, Petra and I came up with it this afternoon.'

Eli raised an eyebrow but didn't comment. 'Go on, what's the idea?'

'Silver Dove knows Petra and he trusts her. If he is gay, he'll have fewer macho hang-ups about being worked by a woman *katsa*; if anyone can recruit him… well, then it just might be her.'

'But she hasn't been trained and she's a British national. It's against protocol.'

'I know that,' Rafi said. 'And Harel and Nathan will try to block it on those grounds, but you have to agree, she's the best person for the job. And she could do it.'

They'd both stopped stock-still and stood in the street as cars splashed through the Friday night rain. Eli thought about Petra, how quick she was, how resourceful. How she'd got the better of them when they were working the girl. Even how she'd handled the interrogators when the operation went wrong. Petra was powerful, there was no denying it.

'You're right, she could do it,' Eli nodded. 'Yes, not only could she do it but it could work on lots of different levels. I like it, Rafi. I like it a lot.'

On Saturday Rafi and Eli spent most of the day prepping and on Sunday afternoon, by a secure video link, they pitched the plan to Harel. As predicted, he was both obstructive and negative, but Eli held a trump card, a lure that would seem so sweet that he knew Harel would find it irresistible. It was Harel's expectation that the operation to recruit Silver Dove would end in disaster, preferably of the diplomatic type that would end Eli's term as head of London Station, and with it, his career. There was no way that Harel would be able to resist the opportunity of allowing Eli to screw up. What's more, Harel had, as expected, played right into Eli's hands by insisting that Nathan would be a part of the operation.

After the call, Eli sank back into his chair with a satisfied air. This was the best he'd felt since October 7, before the world had crumbled around his ears. Rafi was on the other side of the office, examining a brown stain on the wall.

'What's this?' he said.

'I spilt my coffee,' Eli said. 'Wishing I was smashing Harel's skull. But that's now all resolved.'

'Okay, you don't have to tell me about your irrational outbursts where you trash your office, but I don't understand why you're okay with Nathan being on Silver Dove. You know he'll be a pain to work with and he'll report right back to Harel.'

'What sort of spy are you, Rafi?' Eli twirled around in his chair. 'Of course Nathan will report back to Harel. Meanwhile having Nathan on Silver Dove gives us our best chance to find out what Harel's special need-to-know operation is all about.'

'And fuck it up?' Rafi said.

'No, not if it's actually going to make a difference but, knowing Harel, it will be expensive and unproductive. Remember the private jet he hired to impress that agent who was inventing the product? Harel should have been fired and would have been if he hadn't gone to school with the Minister of National Security.'

'So now what?'

'We cram a three-year training course into three weeks and set up the slickest contact between Petra and Silver Dove in the whole history of the Office.'

Chapter 14

It was a week later, and it seemed as if it hadn't stopped raining. Outside Petra's cottage it hammered at the windows as if trying to shatter them. Inside Petra had the wood burner alight in the open-plan sitting room and the orange flames leapt up behind the door and echoed the vermilion sofa. From where she sat at the dining-room table it looked alluring. But Petra was barricaded by books and papers. Far better to have been on the sofa in front of the fire, while the stormy night raged.

'How much of this stuff do I really need to know?' Petra said. With her hand she indicated the books and papers that covered the table to the point that the oak was no longer visible. 'I'm supposed to be a Brit, Eli. I am a Brit, for goodness' sake. How much do most people know about the history of the Middle East, not to mention clans and militias? Shouldn't we be looking at the target's backstory and working up a contact initiative?'

'Not yet,' Eli said. 'You're not ready and I'm surprised at you, Petra. You know the importance of preparation.'

He was right. She knew it, but she was also tired and not used to absorbing so much information so quickly. This part of the preparation had begun to feel like being back at school and cramming for exams, an activity in which she'd never excelled.

'Do you want another coffee?' She stood up from the table. 'I'll make you another coffee while I run through what I've managed to retain. Or would you like to set me some essay questions?'

Eli grunted in response. He didn't seem to find the comment amusing. The hell with him.

While she filled up the coffee machine from the packet in the fridge, she said, 'There's something else. I get the political facts, the dates, the treaties, the wars, but what's the truth behind the facts?'

'Truth? I'd say, geography and economics,' Eli reached into the pocket of his leather jacket and tapped a note into his phone. 'I'll bring you a book next time. Now give me the key shifts in regional power.'

Petra still wasn't convinced that this deep dive was going to help with a recruitment. She'd always tried to present a disinterest in international affairs to targets, not to arouse suspicion, but it was clear that Eli believed Wasim was no ordinary agent. 'The entire region was under the control of the Ottoman Empire from early in the sixteenth century – about the time that our Henry VIII was trying to produce an heir. That went on to World War I, when they sided with Germany. Okay?'

'So far,' Eli said.

'Thank you,' Petra said with some sarcasm. She flicked the lever at the sink and filled up the water reservoir. 'What happened then? Oh yeah. Massive regional shake-up after World War I ends. Britain supports Arab revolts against the Ottomans and promises self-rule. And around the same time, they also promise the Jews a homeland in Palestine.'

'It could be argued that this is the historical root of all our problems.' Eli had followed Petra into the kitchen area with his cup and rinsed it out in the sink. He put it on the granite surface and leaned back, arms folded, ankles crossed over each other. It occurred to Petra that he looked comfortable there.

'Why were those promises made?' Petra said.

'Geography, economics, as I said. Natural resources, lobbying and, like a lot of political decisions, the long-term implications weren't thought through. The law of unintended consequences, if you like.'

'You mean a cock-up.'

'I wouldn't put it like that. You need to remember that Europe was collectively shattered by World War I. France was screaming for revenge on Germany. The Russian Revolution had just happened, the Tsar's family had been murdered and Britain was terrified of a home-grown revolution. With all that going on, the Middle East was a secondary concern.'

The coffee machine groaned out its first cup and Eli reached for it. 'Thank you, you make the best coffee.' His voice was warm. With his free hand he reached out and stroked her cheek, then he jolted his hand away and seemed to recall himself. He said, 'So now the region is controlled by the British and French via mandates, as agreed by the League of Nations, which was the forerunner to the UN and just as ineffective as the current iteration. East of the River Jordan is Transjordan, west is Palestine. Immigration of Jews into Palestine picks up and there are riots with the existing Arab population.'

Petra was still processing the sensation of Eli's hand on her cheek. Something had just happened, but she let it go. Petra filled her own cup and sipped it as she leaned against the kitchen cabinets.

Petra said, 'I get all this. I get that promises were made and local populations were fighting against each other. And I get that the Holocaust led to a huge increase in immigration.'

Eli took his cup back to the table and sat down. Petra followed. 'There are two key points in all of these mistakes and lost opportunities. First of all, by 1947 Britain had had enough. World War II, another big shake-up. Britain is bankrupt, they've lost the empire, the last thing they need is aggravation in the Middle East. The UN takes over and suggests two states, one Arab, one Jewish. Ben-Gurion says, "Thank you very much, we'll take it." But the Arabs didn't accept it because they thought they'd get the whole lot. And the rest is a horrible and bloody history of Israeli/Arab relations, with the odd moment when progress is made. But the point is, Petra, not that people are angry and scared and violent and stupid,' he waved his finger back and forth before he went on. 'No. The point is, the important point is that after every massive shake-up, things change. Regimes change, leaderships change. They don't go back to where they were and we're at that point now. That's why Silver Dove is so important.'

Later on, after Eli had gone, Petra lay on the sofa and read about the clans of Palestine while the news spatter filled the TV screen. While she'd struggled to get her head around the alliances and factions, who was Sunni, who was Shi'ite, she found a document about clans in Palestine. She was aware of the Ottoman Empire as a power broker for hundreds of years, she hadn't known about the clans. They'd survived. And there they still were, in Gaza, different clans who ran different parts of the place; one clan might own all the hardware stores, and another one controlled smuggling on the border. It seemed that loyalty to the clan was more important than to either Hamas or Fatah or any other political group.

Loyalty. What did that mean? That you picked a team and stuck with it whatever happened, whether it was football, a partner, a boss, a country, a family or a system. Or was it to a belief, the idea that what you were doing was worthwhile? It was a curious question for a spy to consider.

Petra paused from her reading to watch the ice cubes clink inside the glass of gin and tonic that she'd just made herself. A few juniper berries danced with the lime segment. The fire was warm and the drink was cold. Between the grim news coverage there were Christmas ads, for pies and turkeys and luxury gifts. These images seemed to segue into fights for food on aid trucks, anguished wails from mothers who'd lost children and the Hanukkah table set in a Tel Aviv square with empty seats for the hostages.

And what of Eli? Petra thought back to the moment when he touched her cheek. Yes, he liked her, yes, he was attracted to her. But he wasn't the kind of guy to act on it and for that Petra respected him. He was loyal. He'd moved on from the little moment as if nothing had happened and having completed the history lesson, he outlined the plan. She smiled as she recalled him pacing up and down in front of the dining-room table as if it was a military briefing. All that was missing was a whiteboard and a bigger audience.

'There will be a hostage deal,' he'd said. 'There always is. The hostages are used for negotiation. In this case they will be exchanged for the Palestinian prisoners that we're holding. Their list will include Dawood Al-Arikhi, who has been enjoying our hospitality for the last twenty years.'

'Why is he so important?' Petra had said.

'He's the natural successor to Mahmoud Abbas, the ageing president of Fatah, who currently controls the occupied territories of the West Bank.'

'Okay...' Petra was two steps ahead. 'We recruit Wasim, Wasim manages to get a job in the new administration, we get the intelligence. Is that it?'

'Broadly speaking,' Eli said. 'But it's more than intelligence we're interested in, which is why your reading is important.'

Eli leaned across the table to make his point. 'Al-Arikhi and Wasim are members of the same clan. They have traditionally controlled the pharmacies, previously fairly marginal compared to the clans that control construction or smuggling through the Philadelphi Corridor. However, since Covid and the PPP, as well as the vaccination programmes, they have increased in power. They are ideally placed to support the regeneration of the Palestinian community when the truce happens.'

'Truce?'

'Yes,' Eli said. He was tight-lipped and looked grim. 'It won't be comfortable or easy, but there will eventually be a truce. That is the only way forward. Al-Arikhi has many qualities to lead. Among them is that he's secular. In other words, he hasn't signed up to the pan-Islamic world plan that hopes to take us all back to the Dark Ages, along with the rest of the end-timers.'

'You mean the evangelists?'

'Yes, and our very own ultra-orthodox. Also, he's a pragmatist who will be able to work with the other clans, who are going to need to step up and help rebuild Gaza.'

'Do you really think that recruiting Wasim is so significant?'

'Yes, I do. We can help without him knowing that we're

helping. Wasim is studying biomathematics, that makes him ideally placed to be Minister of Health in any administration. We don't just want intelligence from him. We want him to be a *lochesh.*'

'What's that?' Petra said.

'The literal translation is whisperer. It's far more important than just providing intelligence. And far more dangerous. It's someone who is placed in such a senior position in a government that they can affect policy. They're rare.'

'I'll bet they are.'

'Rare, but not unknown. Remember Sadat from your little history lesson? We had a *lochesh* in the Egyptian President's inner circle that we called Angel. He was Nasser's son-in-law and, being so close, he was able to influence policy. That's what we want from Wasim – we want him to help make peace. And keep peace.'

Petra felt overwhelmed. This was a lot more than she'd expected to have to do, a lot more than the responsibility that she'd tried to avoid for most of her life.

'Eli, do you really think I'm the best person for this?'

'You're the only person.'

Chapter 15

Eli was thinking about Petra on his way to a meeting the next day. The storm had blown itself out and left trees with broken branches, shards of bark scattered on wet roads and grey sky overhead. Despite being 11 o'clock in the morning, it was so dark that it felt as if the clouds were weighed down and it was hard to believe that if you were to soar through them, there would be blue sky above.

The question Eli asked himself was whether he'd placed too heavy a burden on Petra. Was she really the only person? Quite possibly. If it didn't work and Wasim was unrecruitable, then the chances of finding someone with the same potential were remote. You didn't need an algorithm to work that out.

The 176 bus trundled along past Denmark Hill and, as Eli looked out of the steamed-up window, he saw a group of students with placards and the instantly recognisable red, green and black flag. The war was underway again and the calls for a ceasefire were loud and discordant. Every day there was another signal about the increase in anti-Semitic attacks in European cities, never mind the protests on the US campuses. Eli hunched inside his coat. The chill December air outside and the fug in the bus made him yearn to be out of the greyness and London and somewhere else. Somewhere peaceful, where he didn't have to think all the time. Even though it had only been a few weeks, he missed Gal, he missed her presence, which is no doubt why he'd had that uncomfortable moment with Petra in the kitchen. If ever there was an endorsement for the Office's insistence that staff had to have a partner to get an overseas posting, this was it. He was just missing Gal. He resolved to try to phone her later when he got back home. But before he could do that, he had the rest of the day ahead of him, and this meeting with Nicolai.

Eli got off the bus and hovered for a moment outside the gates of the park to make sure that the watchers were in place and were tailing him. If there was sensitivity about this type of meeting before October 7, now alerts were constantly firing off; security was escalated and the new protocols, while necessary, were beyond onerous. It was tiresome. Everything took longer, whether it was the cyber somersaults that his laptop went through before he could write a damn report to this: a liaison meeting with another intelligence service. Despite his irritation, Eli did it, because he was, after all, a professional and this is what professionals did. They did the job properly.

Ahead of Eli, a watcher in green tracksuit trousers paused to stretch out an apparent cramp in her calves. As she stretched out her leg behind her, she held two fingers unclenched in her fist. This was the okay sign for Eli to proceed. It was a neat manoeuvre. She'd been well trained.

Eli felt in his pocket for his earbuds and, once they were in position and he could hear the chatter of the watchers, he strode towards the cafe in the middle of the park, aware of the watchers' box around him, one in front, one on either side and one behind. All the while above Eli there was the buzz of a lone toy drone wheeling about, checking out the entrances and exits of the park. All was clear.

Already seated in the cafe was Eli's contact: Nicolai Petrovich, formerly the Russian Rezident, now seeming to have some type of roving brief, according to the document that Eli had read the day before. Officially, Nicolai was a commercial attaché, which was an interesting choice, given the prevailing UK sanctions. Nicolai was meeting Eli to talk about the hostages who had dual Russian/Israeli citizenship, either from having been born in Russia or from having parents who were born there. The expectation was that another exchange would take place soon and many countries were trying to lobby for their citizens. Naturally, the American dual nationals had the least chance of getting their people out of the tunnels, along with the Israelis.

If ever there was a man who fitted the expectation of what a spy should look like, it was Nicolai. Tall, fit, longer than average hair that flowed off his wide forehead, he had high cheekbones and dressed the part in a leather jacket, over a cashmere rollneck. His English was as good as Eli's, a result of his second degree at Johns Hopkins, where no doubt he mixed achieving a degree in international relations with developing his own international relations on behalf of the motherland. Behind the smooth exterior, the man was a total bastard.

Eli nodded to him as he went to the counter and queued with the mums and retirees to buy an americano. Then he carried it over to the table, as Nicolai rose.

'Good to see you,' Nicolai smiled and the two men shook hands. 'How are you?'

Before responding, Eli put the coffee cup down and took out his sound buffer. He placed it on the table and noted that Nicolai was using what looked to be the same model he'd had when they'd last met a year ago. No doubt the sound buffer worked and the software would have been updated, but it was an indication that tech advances were not happening across the board and the war effort against Ukraine was taking its toll.

'Good to see you too,' Eli finally said, as he smiled back. 'Pleased to see you back in the UK.'

Nicolai's eyes narrowed, it was almost imperceptible, but Eli caught the moment and mentally uploaded it. At the same time, he concentrated on keeping his face neutral, like a pond without a ripple. Eli could make a very good guess as to why Nicolai was hostile to him. No doubt about it, it was the matter of the defenestrated Ukrainian mechatronics engineer deftly laid at Russia's door and an incident that had precipitated Nicolai's expulsion as London Rezident.

So Nicolai knew. He might not have all the details, but he'd worked out that Eli had something to do with it. Well, the hell with him, Eli thought. If the situation was reversed, the Russian would have done exactly the same to him, but Eli knew better than to show anything on his face beyond the blandness of professional camaraderie.

Nicolai had also recovered his sangfroid.

'I'm very pleased to be back but not under these circumstances,' he said. 'How are you getting on with all this? I saw the metal shutters have gone up on all the windows at your embassy when I walked past earlier. Have you been directly affected?'

'Everybody has,' Eli said, giving Nicolai nothing to feed on.

'I'm sure you people will find your way through this, you usually do.'

Eli hid how irritated he felt by Nicolai's use of 'you people'. It was one of the things that had made him relish being instrumental in his expulsion.

'That's the plan,' Eli said. 'Do you have the list with you?'

'Of course.' Nicolai's hand went into his inner pocket and he came out with a memory chip. With one long finger, the Russian flicked it across the table towards Eli. 'Everything is on here, names, birth certificates if available, citizenship documentation and also dental records if necessary.'

'Thank you.' Eli reached for the chip.

'There's an additional document in there. We've prioritised preferences in the exchange. Although, of course, we're aware that this is open to some degree of flexibility.'

Eli slipped the chip into his pocket.

'Thank you,' Eli repeated. 'I presume you'll continue to be our point of contact.'

'Oh yes, I'll be in London certainly for a few months. Protocol and all that.'

'I hope you'll find enough to do. There's going to be some waiting, I believe.'

'I'm sure I'll find something to keep me busy,' Nicolai said. 'Now we have concluded our business, I shall leave first.'

Eli sat at the table and watched Nicolai disappear out of the door. For several moments, Eli thought about Nicolai's last comment about finding something to keep him busy and wondered whether there was something in it or whether it was just a standard Russian wind-up, spreading paranoia and fears of disruption. It was the type of thing they liked to do, like the arson attacks and the daubing of anti-Semitic slogans in Paris. It was like a child having a tantrum, throwing their food at the wall; the activities in isolation were inconsequential, but the accumulated effect spread anxiety in the Western body politic.

While Eli was musing, he felt his work phone vibrate and saw that it was Boaz. Or Joe, as the contact details on the secure line stated.

'Hey, what's up?' Eli said.

'Where are you? It's noisy.'

'I'm out having fun. You?'

'The same. Listen, you know that thing we were talking about at the last meeting?'

'Yeah,' Eli said. He must mean the joint *Amal* operation that Harel was already rubbishing.

'I need a very small amount of help from you,' Boaz said.

'How small? Man, we're round the clock here.'

'I know, I know, that's why I wanted to speak with you and not just send a message. I figured you'd find it harder to refuse me.'

Eli chuckled. '*Mumsa*, what do you want?'

'Forty-eight hours of your valuable time, and I also want Trainer.'

'Trainer?' Trainer was the code name for Petra. Eli said, 'How urgent is this? I've got something big cooking and I don't want to take her off it.'

'I get that. It won't be for at least a month. We're in development but I want everything lined up. Checked and double-checked. You know, the way the guy we're missing likes to do it. "The situation is like this."' Boaz mimicked Yuval and then laughed his big man's laugh.

'It's good to hear your voice, Joe,' Eli said. What Eli really meant was that it was good to hear Boaz's laugh. These days there didn't seem to be much to laugh about with the rolling news of casualties and refugees, failure of the hostage negotiations, and the triumvirate of self-interest at the top of government.

Eli said, 'I'm in. Send me the details and I'll factor it into the schedule.'

'You're my man,' Boaz said and clicked off.

Chapter 16

It was dark by the time Eli had criss-crossed London with his escort of watchers and opened the door to his office in the embassy. The room smelt stale from the closed windows and the unemptied bin. Eli threw himself into his leather chair, determined to spend as little time as possible writing up the report on his meeting with Nicolai. After that he'd grab some food in the 24-hour cafe on site and take himself off home to watch the football in bed with a large glass of good red wine. If that didn't expunge the day, he didn't know what would.

'What?' Eli said in answer to the knock on the door and its immediate opening.

Rafi strode in and loured over the desk. 'How did Middle East geopolitics 101 go with Petra?'

'Petra?' With a rush, Eli remembered the odd moment when he'd stroked her cheek. 'Yeah, fine,' he said. That was one conversation he wasn't going to have with Rafi. 'It was hours ago. I've just been all over London for a fifteen-minute meeting with that snake Nicolai. He's up to something and, whatever it is, it will be bad news.'

'Really?' Rafi said. He'd picked up the memory chip in his hand and was tossing it in the air and catching it in what Eli considered to be an irritating way.

'You know, *achi*, I'm coming round to your way of thinking.'

'What's that?'

'I used to think you obsessed too much about details and your instinct but I'm now starting to think there's something in it.'

'What makes you say that?' Eli said, pleased not to be talking about Petra.

'I had a meeting with Nathan today to talk about training up Petra to have the skills to recruit and run Silver Dove, since that was part of the deal with Harel. And although Nathan's not saying anything specific about his secret mission, which, incidentally, is called Phuket, I think it's big.'

'Maybe they're buying in from Thailand?' Eli said. 'We sell arms to them, as does the US. Maybe they're doing some sort of deal on the spare parts? Swapping them around?'

Rafi was still tossing the chip from one hand to the other. 'I don't think so. Call it instinct—'

'Can you just put that damn chip down,' Eli said. 'It's got to go in tonight's bag to be cleaned back home before we can see what's on it and I don't want to have to go back to the Russian and tell him that it's not reading because you've covered it with sweat.'

'Okay, okay.' With exaggerated care Rafi placed the memory chip on the desk. 'There. Happy now?'

Eli didn't respond and Rafi went on, 'Anyway, I'm trying to be more like you and I'm thinking about clues and nuance. I'm also prepared to bet you fifty shekels that Phuket isn't an arms deal and it's big.'

'Arms or no arms, I bet it's a bullshit operation,' Eli said. 'I'll take your bet.'

Eli had pulled his laptop towards him and keyed in his

password. He sat back and waited for the system to go through its somersaults so he could write the report and go home.

'What is it?' Eli said. 'Why are you still here?'

'I've got some good news.'

'The only good news would be you getting out of my office so that I can write this report and go home.'

'Okay,' Rafi said and headed towards the door. 'I'll let you get on with it because you need to finish it tonight. Then you can take tomorrow off and I'll cover for you.'

'What are you talking about?'

'Your son landed at Heathrow an hour ago. He just managed to get on a plane at JFK so he didn't have time to message. He's now on the way into Central London and is expecting to see his miserable father tonight.'

Eli did complete the contact report before he left the office but it was brief and to the point. As he read through it before signing off and uploading onto the Office site, he considered that it said everything that needed to be said; a model report, aided by the shot of energy from the knowledge that Doron was on the way to West Hampstead and would certainly be hungry. Eli dashed from the embassy to Panzer's, where he stocked up at the deli counter, bought some ready-prepared schnitzel and, to be on the safe side, bought a frozen meat meal that could be thrown in the oven. Since Gal had gone back to Israel, Eli had either snacked on whatever he could find at the flat, eaten at the embassy commissary or eaten out. The cupboards were bare.

Even though Eli had rushed, Doron had beaten him to it and, when Eli approached the mansion block of flats in West Hampstead, he saw a slight figure sitting on a low wall, a bag at his feet and his head hunched over the phone screen as he either scrolled or played a game. Burdened by his bags of food, Eli didn't increase his pace, but that wasn't the only reason. The sight of his son made him well up and he needed the extra steps before hugging the boy to compose himself. Why? Eli thought. Why was he so emotional? He was just tired, that was all. That was the answer and that would just have to do.

'*Munyamin motek*,' Eli said when he was close enough to see the dark hair that curled around his forehead.

Doron looked up and grinned. He hugged Eli and kissed his cheek. Then he grabbed the bags and made a show of seeing what was in them. 'Panzer's. You shouldn't be carrying these heavy bags, old man.'

'If you want anything to eat out of these bags, less of the "old man",' Eli said, as he remembered for a moment that 'old man' is what Silver Dove had called him. 'I can still wrestle you down.'

'Sure about that, *Abba*?'

'Get on with you. Let's get inside.'

Five minutes later they were in the apartment and Eli was able to look his son over. It had only been a few months since he'd gone back to the US for his second year of aeronautic engineering at Dayton, but it seemed longer. It was longer, it was another lifetime, the one they all had before October 7. Eli knew that this was no mid-term break; Doron had been called up and was returning to his unit. Of course, since he was at university in the US, the boy might have deferred but he'd told his parents that if his unit was going into Gaza, he wanted to go back with them. Eli figured that if he was old enough to vote, he was old enough to decide what he wanted to do.

In the kitchen of the large apartment, Doron sat at the wooden table and Eli bustled around, putting the food away, putting the kettle on and talking about nothing much. Only when there was a coffee and some smoked salmon in front of him did they talk about the news, which was all bad. One of the kids who'd been killed at the Nova festival was at the University of Beer Sheva and was a friend of a friend. His girlfriend had been raped before she was murdered.

'How do we make sense of this, *Abba*?'

'There is no sense to it, unless you accept that they wanted to hurt us in the most profound way possible and they succeeded. But your mother says it's how we deal with it that will show who we are.'

'What's that?' Doron said. 'If it doesn't kill you, it makes you strong?'

'Something like that,' Eli said and took a pull on the beer in front of him.

'That's what she used to say to me when she gave me medicine.'

'Well, it seems to have worked,' Eli said. 'Tell me, what time do you have to be at the airport tomorrow?'

'It's the 10 o'clock, the red-eye, but the upside is that we have the day.'

'Shall we talk to your mom and then go out for dinner? And then maybe tomorrow we can go for a *tiyul…*'

'How far are we from Cambridge?' Doron said.

'Cambridge? You're not thinking of switching courses? I thought you were enjoying Daytona. There's nowhere like it in the world.'

'I am, it's amazing, but if I'm here, there's an aviation museum near Cambridge; Duxford.'

Doron had the exact same look he wore on his face when he asked for a birthday treat as a kid. He was cute and he knew how to play it, like his mother.

'Okay,' Eli said, though he'd have rather gone to look at art or some historic buildings than wander round freezing hangars looking at engines, but it was Doron's outing.

'I need a shower before we go out,' Doron said.

Eli picked up the empty plate and carried it to the sink. '*Tov*, take your shower, I'll book a table at the Singapore Garden for, say, an hour? Is that okay? And I'll try to get your mother on the phone so she can see you got here.'

Doron disappeared and a few minutes later, Eli heard the water running. He had a good ten minutes to get through to Gal and make sure she was going to be around to pick Doron up when he arrived in Tel Aviv. Ever since October 7 they'd talked about Doron and whether he would insist on going back to his unit. They were in agreement; it wasn't just about doing the right thing for the country when the inevitable war started, but it would be a waste for Doron to lose a year's study if he went back to Israel and his unit. As much as Eli was thrilled to see his son, he'd have been happier if he was back in Daytona in the campus air tunnel, measuring drag velocity.

If anyone could persuade Doron to turn round and go back to the US and continue his studies, Gal could. After all, she was a psychologist as well his mother.

Eli propped his phone up against the kettle and keyed in Gal's number. It rang once and then connected. She was expecting Eli. He'd messaged her as soon as Rafi had told him that Doron was in London.

'You're working late,' Eli said when he saw the backdrop of

Gal's office, a whiteboard with a kaleidoscope of sticky-back notes all over it, while behind her the Tel Aviv University night sky twinkled. Eli also saw a glass of red wine on her desk. Typical Gal, Eli thought.

'Tell me about it,' Gal said. 'How is Doron? Is he there?'

'He's in the shower. We have a few minutes before he comes out.'

'Probably more than a few,' Gal said.

Eli smiled. 'We're going to Singapore Garden. He'll move his ass for the chicken satay. He's on the 10.30 flight tomorrow night out of Heathrow, so he'll be with you by four in the morning. There's no chance you can pick him up, is there?'

'Eli, I'd rather not, I've got so much work to do. The only time I can catch up on the reports is now. I'm drowning here. I'll have breakfast with him. Eli, tell me, is it definite, is he really going straight to his unit?'

'I don't know. He's being vague. He's making me go with him to some air museum in Cambridge tomorrow.'

'Lucky you,' Gal said.

Just then Eli heard the wail of sirens, the rising crescendo that demanded they run to the shelters. They had ninety seconds to get there.

'Gal! Gal!' Eli heard someone call his wife's name in the background, '*Motek*, let's get out of here.'

'Eli,' Gal said. 'I'll talk to him, I promise. We'll do this.'

'Who's that?' Eli said. 'Who's calling you *motek, motek*?'

'Nobody, Eli, I have to go, we have to get out of here. The university is a target.'

The screen went black.

117

Chapter 17

Petra squinted against the glare. It was a glittering winter's day, the type of day Petra loved, where the cold air sliced into lungs and made her eyes stream. The sun was low and shone hard as if, for the brief hours it hit the winter landscape, creating long shadows and sharp edges, it demanded to be seen and remembered.

Petra put her foot down on the accelerator and pushed into the outside lane of the A3, nosing up behind a black Focus that needed to get out of her way. After all her studies, she had begun to feel confident about her ability to recruit Wasim and run him and it was reflected in her driving. No one else would be able to talk to Wasim about his sister with the same level of confidence, nobody else would be able to build a level of trust that was based on truth. After all, she'd tried to save his sister's life.

More than anything, Petra was sorry not to have had the chance to see Eli since their last meeting. There was so much she wanted to talk to him about, but as Rafi had explained when he'd delivered to her a book called *Palestine: Islamic Art and the Archaeology of Palestine*, Eli was tied up with Office work, and family.

Rafi had his head down and was fiddling with his phone as they barrelled along the motorway. 'His son's in town,' Rafi said. 'Wife's back home in Israel and he's trying to save the world.'

'Aren't we all?' Petra said as she flicked the indicator and slammed her foot on the accelerator to steam past a lorry meandering in the centre lane. 'By the way, your scarf's in my work bag. Don't forget to take it back.'

'Ah… you're now wearing the flammable one.'

'I like it and we're not setting fire to anything today.'

'Not exactly.'

She and Rafi were side by side in the hired Toyota Camry, heading out of London towards Hampshire. It was a big solid sedan with good acceleration and, although Rafi had driven the silver car to the agreed rendezvous, Petra had insisted he move into the passenger seat because his lane discipline was negligible, to say the least.

'You drive like you're in a tank and you're planning to mow people down,' she explained. 'We have something called the Highway Code here.'

'You also have speed limits, don't you?' Rafi said. 'You are driving aggressively, as if you're angry about something. Are you?'

Petra ignored the comment. 'Just give me the directions and tell me about the day ahead.'

They were on their way to a private facility, where she was going to do some hands-on training in firearms. Using the cover of the film facilities company in Great Pulteney Street, they'd told the owners of the shooting gallery that they were prepping for a casting session with a major Hollywood talent, who was very specific about their requirements.

The chance of Petra needing to use a gun was remote; case officers were rarely, if ever, involved in direct combat. After all, they were in the business of gathering intelligence and analysing it, yet it was one of the protocols within Petra's training as a *katsa* that she was to be as prepared as she might have been if she'd made *aliyah* and either emigrated to Israel or been born there and, as such, she would have gone through the army and learnt how to handle firearms.

'We have two hours at the shooting range,' Rafi said. 'All we're going to do is look at half a dozen guns, see how one or two of them strip them down, show you how to clean them and put them back together and then you get to fire them.'

'I really can't see me using a gun to persuade Wasim that he'd like to become an agent, can you?'

'No, but it's protocol,' Rafi said. 'After that we have a session with someone you haven't yet met, who is going to talk to you about Ethics and the Law and why the work that you're doing is so important.'

'What's that, a pep talk?' Petra slowed down and shifted into the inside lane as the Hook exit came up.

'Far from it. His name is Nathan but he's going to call himself Motti. He's one of the people who are making our lives more difficult than they need to be.'

'Our lives?' Petra said.

'Eli's and mine and all the good people in the Office, the country and the world.'

'Okay…' Petra stopped at the roundabout at the top of the slip road and glanced over at Rafi. 'Is this a bit of Office politics?'

'It's more serious, as everything seems to be these days,' Rafi said. 'I don't know how much to tell you.'

'For God's sake, Rafi, you know it never works when you hold out on me,' Petra said. 'I always know when you're lying so you may as well tell me.'

'You're right.'

Petra wasn't remotely surprised by Rafi's account that there was an operation being planned by one of the right-wingers in the organisation and he and Eli were being kept in the dark.

'But they've got governmental authority for it, haven't they?' Petra said.

'Yes, from the top, but it doesn't mean that this secret operation is strategically sound. Or even likely to be properly executed. Eli wants me to find out what it is. Eli thinks it's going to be a bullshit operation and we don't have to worry about it. But I'm not so sure.'

'Do you want me to do something?' Petra said as she reversed into a bay in the car park of the facility and switched off the engine.

'I'm not sure what you can do.'

'Tell me about him.'

'He's religious, he thinks we're doing God's work, he thinks homosexuality is an aberration, he thinks that October 7 and the Holocaust happened because Jews weren't observant.'

'Well, sometimes one can't help but wonder why all this shit keeps happening,' Petra said.

'That's their argument. Women should dress modestly, their place is in the home bearing children and their work is to support the men in their lives. You know I could live with that idea, Petra.'

'Why don't you shut up,' Petra smiled.

They were at the door of the reception area. Petra adjusted the bag over her shoulder and assumed this morning's persona of a locations finder, there to check out the facility's suitability for a film shoot with the production's arms expert.

Chapter 18

After two hours at the shooting gallery, Petra concluded that, although she had an aptitude for small arms, she had little interest in using them. A mechanical frame of mind helped her absorb all the information about cleaning and checking the weapons laid out for her, and while she could appreciate the different angles, weights, materials and shapes that were explained, and even discovered that she was a good shot, the notion of fetishising guns left her cold. The warehouse location had a reception area, where a couple of women were trying to keep themselves warm and offered Petra and Rafi tea and coffee while they waited to be seen. There was a glass case with accessories, gun bags with holders for ammunition and cleaning kit in pouches. In another glass case there were gun jackets and belts and bags. And the walls were lined with gun safes of different sizes for storing guns.

Shooting was a rich person's hobby.

Despite her lack of interest, Petra noted how comfortable Rafi seemed among the weapons. He was even excited about the mechanisms and weighed the weapon in his hand with a gesture that was certainly practised. But he was also a patient trainer, and his best tip was how to control her breathing so that she might concentrate on the target and become one with the gun.

On the way back to London, Petra was thoughtful and ignored all of Rafi's attempts to chat. The weather had changed and the clouds had gathered and rolled up into towers; it began to rain; savage drops battered the windscreen and the radio gabbled upcoming election news. Petra pushed on through the traffic and road-surface water, thinking, not talking. She was thinking about the afternoon session with the Office guy who was going to talk to her about ethics.

Eventually they manoeuvred their way around Shepherd's Bush roundabout. Petra said, 'You know, if you're going to meet this Motti character first, you could drop me somewhere near the safe house and I'll join you there a bit later? There's no point me sitting around in the kitchen waiting for you to finish, is there?'

'No,' Rafi said. 'Just make sure you follow all the protocols before you get there. It's unlikely we're being tailed but it still doesn't mean we take chances.'

Rafi dropped Petra at Paddington Station. It was far enough away from the Westbourne Grove safe house and it was also the perfect spot to circulate and thoroughly check herself. Once she was certain that she was clean, Petra did the shopping she thought she would need for her afternoon session with Motti and even went so far as to return to Paddington Station, where she changed from sweatshirt and jeans into her new outfit in a public toilet.

Suitably garbed, Petra took a taxi back to Ledbury Road and took a turn around the streets, slowing down and then speeding up, doubling back and crossing the road to go down an alley behind the houses before climbing the stairs up to the front door of the safe house.

This particular safe house was a shabby building. Outside the lower-ground-floor flat an overflowing wheelie bin with a broken lid sat on cracked paving and a broken bike was propped, chained to the railings, as if anybody would want to steal it. It was a sad house. White paint peeled from crumbling stucco plasterwork and the grand old villa was being eaten by damp and subsidence. It was also prey to the thud and roar of the traffic from the A40 that fought with the trains rattling into Paddington Station.

By contrast the camera on the door was high-tech.

Rafi let her in and Petra climbed the stairs to the second-floor flat, where he was waiting on the landing, the door to the apartment open behind him. When she reached him, Petra had the satisfaction of seeing Rafi do a double-take at her new outfit. She was now wearing a long skirt, a blouse with a tie bow and a jacket, all of which she'd chosen to be shapeless. To be modest. Only her dark hair didn't quite fit the look but she'd tried to tie it back in a scrunchy.

'What's with the clothes?' Rafi said softly.

'I felt like a change,' Petra smiled. 'What do you think?'

In answer Rafi shook his head.

She stalked past him into the shabby sitting room, where she found a small man with grizzled grey hair and a beard. He was sitting on the sofa, hunched over a coffee table, looking at a laptop screen. At her entrance, Motti sprang up, came towards her, all twinkling blue eyes with a sweet smile on his face.

'Petra, I'm Motti, very happy, and very honoured to meet you,' he said. 'What would you like to drink? We have tea, we have coffee. Whatever you like, we have it.'

'May I have a glass of orange juice?' Petra kept her eyes down in what she hoped would be seen as a demeanour that was modest. 'That would be very kind of you. Thank you.'

'Good choice. I'll have the same. I'll be right back,' Motti disappeared into the kitchen.

'I won't stay,' Rafi said. 'Unless you want me to.'

'No, I'm good. You run along.'

By then Motti was back in the room, balancing a tray of glasses overfilled with orange juice, which he placed on the table with exaggerated care. Then he sat himself down, right opposite Petra, and fixed her with a gimlet stare, as if she was a specimen in a display case in a museum.

After gulping back his juice, Rafi sprang up and said he would leave Petra in what he said were Motti's capable hands. As soon as Rafi had closed the door, Motti sprang up and started gathering the empty orange glasses onto the tray.

'That Rafi, what a guy. Always running to his next meeting. How about some coffee now?'

'Let me make it?' Petra looked up. 'There's no reason for you to be making me coffee.'

'No, no, no, it's a well-known fact that I make the best coffee in the Office and,' he paused, twinkling his eyes, 'I also have a small treat.'

'Are you sure?' Petra said. She widened her eyes as if in anticipation.

'More than sure.'

Petra relaxed back on the mildewed sofa and waited for Motti to return. Ever since Rafi had told her that he and Eli wanted to find out about a right-wing operation that Motti was involved in, she'd been thinking; it would be a feather in her cap if she could find out what it was. It would demonstrate her agent-running skills. What's more, she'd enjoy gaming one of the people she disliked.

Motti came back with two coffees steaming in their glass cups and an empty white plate. Once again, he laid the tray down on the scratched table and then in a swift movement, he dived into the 'bag for life' that he'd left at his feet. Out came a cardboard box that he opened with the same reverence he'd used for placing the tray and showed it to Petra so that she might peer in.

It was a box of biscuits.

'Is that...? Petra said.

'Rugelach.'

'Oh, my goodness, I haven't had one of those for so many years. My Papa used to buy them as a treat at Rosh Hashana. May I...?'

'Of course. We are blessed to enjoy varieties of nourishment.'

The biscuits were good. Petra didn't have to fake pleasure as she nibbled at a miniature stuffed pastry and was urged by Motti to eat on. The fact that she'd never seen a biscuit like it in her life was irrelevant. It was working, even though in reality, her father favoured Mars bars and hid them at the back of the fridge.

Motti turned to work and asked Petra how she felt about what she was doing and the plan to manipulate Silver Dove. It was a bald question, a trick question, she thought. He'd no doubt read her file and was looking for ways to trip her up.

'You know, Motti, I've been looking forward to this meeting more than any other aspect of the preparation,' Petra said. 'I'll tell you why. I think law and ethics is the most important part of what Jews do and how we live. I've even been reading about *Halakha*.'

'*Halakha*?,' Motti said. 'You surprise me, young lady. Do you know what the word means?'

'The law?' Petra said.

He'd asked her the question as if she was a seven-year-old child who needed to recount her daily lessons. She let him explain. He did.

'Its literal meaning is "the way to behave" from "*halakh*", which means "to walk or to go". In other words, it's the way to behave through our lives. But tell me, Petra, why are you reading about *Halakha*?'

Petra sighed before she spoke. 'In truth, I'd rather not talk about it until I know you better.' She dropped her gaze and looked down at the hands folded in her lap. 'I hope that doesn't offend you.'

For some moments there was silence in the room, only the tumult of the outside world, the trains, the planes, the police sirens and the traffic beyond the walls of the faded flat, speckled with black mould in the corners.

'I'm not offended,' Motti said. 'When it is time, we will speak but only if you want to. For now, I can explain to you some of the basic precepts of the organisation and how it relates to the law, both *Halakha*, civil and also international law.'

Petra looked up, anguish on her face. She blurted out, 'The truth is I've been reading about *Halakha* law, trying to find answers. Ever since October 7, I've been sad and desperately confused. Why did it happen? Why does it always happen? What did we ever do that's so bad that people want to keep killing us?'

'Big questions, Petra. If you're reading about *Halakha*, then you know how important it is that we fight to keep Israel safe, which is what we're trying to do.'

'I do, and that does make me feel less confused. I feel like I'm doing something and whatever I may be, I am a Jew.'

Motti leaned back into his armchair and nodded as if he was satisfied in some way. 'You know, there are many people now feeling the way you do. Confused. Lost. Searching. Some say we underestimated our enemies and we took our battles against Muslim countries too casually. But perhaps the bigger battle we fight is against ourselves.'

Petra nodded. 'That's true, aren't we all our own worst enemies? But my question is, what about the other enemies? Will people ever stop trying to kill Jews?'

'Such a question, Petra – how can I answer you?' Motti shook his head. 'Only maybe from another's wisdom. Not mine. You know there are 613 *mitzvot*, or commandments, in the *Halakha*. Six hundred and thirteen ways to behave so that we can live in peace. But, for the moment, many of these commandments can't be carried out. Some say it's as many as forty per cent.'

'Why? I don't understand.'

Motti sighed. 'The belief among many people is that when Jews return to Israel and the Temple in Jerusalem is rebuilt – then it will be possible to carry out all the commandments. And then there will be peace.'

'I see… I think,' Petra said. 'But if we have enemies, and we certainly do, what about our friends? However many people hate Jews, we do have friends. There are countries that try to help us, aren't there, like America?'

'Yes, there are, but we also have to help them. Or help the

people in those countries to have power so that they can continue to help us.'

'What do you mean?' Petra stood up and walked around the room as if the pacing might help her to think through these new ideas. 'Motti, please, explain to me what you mean. Is this something we can actually do to change the future, to stop this terrible cycle of hatred and destruction against our people?'

'Petra... I'm going to tell you something. I'm telling you so that you know that we are working for the future good... to make sure that we have what we need to fight our enemies. Okay?'

'Will it change the future? Will it keep us safe?'

'Yes, that's why I'm telling you. It's secret – you mustn't tell Rafi, even if he asks you what we talked about.'

'You can trust me, Motti,' Petra said.

'So there is a particular operation that I am involved in. We are going to do a *mitzvah* – a favour, if you like – for someone who is connected to the American candidate who would be best for Israel's future.'

'You mean Trump, of course. But what favour can we possibly do? It's not as if we can interfere with an election, after 2016 and the Russians, there's all sorts of checks and double checks.'

There was silence in the room. Petra could tell from the man's expression that he was bursting to tell her about this plan. It was almost leaking out of him but not quite. Finally, he said, 'There's a quote from the Babylonian Talmud,' Motti said. '"If someone comes to kill you, rise up and kill him first." That's all I can say, except that it will make a difference, I promise you.'

'Motti, I don't understand exactly what you mean, but this is the best I've felt since October 7. We have to win this war, don't we? Whatever the cost.'

'Yes, we do. That's why the work we are doing is so important.'

'I will pray for that every day and every night.'

Chapter 19

To Eli's chagrin, Yuval didn't want to know.

As soon as Rafi had relayed the report from Petra, he'd booked the meeting with what he still considered to be his boss, even though Yuval was at Rome Airport, waiting for a connecting flight to Cairo. The conference call lasted less than ninety seconds and, beyond Yuval saying in reference to Harel, 'Nothing that man would do surprises me', he made it clear to Eli that he was on his own and as head of London Station it was up to him to sort it out any way he could.

'You can't come running to me, Eli. There's too much going on. We are fighting with the Prime Minister's office over these negotiations and every day that passes more people are dying.'

'They're planning a targeted killing to curry favour with Driver,' Eli said, using the code word for the 45th president. 'Isn't that enough of a priority?'

'Not now. Not without more evidence. If this has been authorised by the Prime Minister's office and they've got a signed red page, then there's really nothing we can do. I have to go.'

The screen went black.

Eli leaned back in his chair and massaged his temples. When he stopped, he looked over at Rafi, who was sitting on the armchair by the window with his laptop open.

'Ideas?' Eli said.

'You heard the guy.' Rafi was massaging his beard with the heel of his hand. 'If they've got a red page, then that's it.'

'No, it damn well isn't,' Eli said. 'At the very least, if they've got a *Kidon* unit in London, we need to know what and where it is. If anything, in the interests of security and if it does go wrong, who's going to get sent back home on the shame plane. It'll be us, that's for sure.'

'We can hardly kidnap Nathan and beat the name of the target out of him, can we?'

'Appealing though that idea is, no,' Eli said. 'According to Nathan, Harel will be here in two days to progress the operation. Nathan had the audacity to tell me to talk to him.'

'He must be pretty confident that he's on the winning side, despite being so stupid as to tell Petra, just because she pretended to have found God.'

'Yes, I wonder how he's going to explain that lapse of operational security.' Eli took a deep breath; there were upsides to the situation. '*Plusim*, it demonstrates just how skilled Petra is. Harel's not going to be able to argue with that. I just need to work out a way of getting all the facts about this operation.'

'What are you doing now? Do you want to come to our place for dinner?'

'No, thanks. I'm going to work out a plan.'

That evening it came to Eli, if not in a blinding flash, certainly in a neat equation of simplicity and logic. Having eschewed the offer to go back to Rafi's place for another badly cooked meal, Eli sat at his kitchen table with a glass of Pinot Noir and a half-decent Fettucine Alfredo he'd made for himself. In the middle of the table his laptop lay open and, while he forked in the cream and cheese sauce, he reread Petra's report about the meeting with Nathan. And there it was, encapsulated in one word: law. Eli could hardly wait to finish what he was eating before he pulled the laptop towards him and dived into the documents he'd signed when he took over as head of London Station. He found the job description. It was unequivocal. By law he had to be apprised of all operations in his geographical area. It had been set up so that that there was some control over the cowboys that somehow wormed their way into the organisation. Even if there was a red page, the head of station still had to be kept informed of the details.

Eli sipped at the wine and sighed with deep satisfaction. Let Harel try to talk his way out of that.

Of course he did.

The following morning Eli met Harel in the unit meeting room on the third floor. It was a deliberate choice. For one thing, with its monitors and mostly monochrome interior, the space was more formal than his office and Eli wanted to try to exert some authority over Harel as head of London Station. There was also a more personal objection; Eli didn't want Harel touching his books and leaving behind his contrail of duty-free cologne.

Across the rosewood table, Harel's body language was a sonnet of arrogance; he leaned back in the chair, one leg crossed over the knee of the other, with his hands folded behind his head.

'I don't have a lot of time, Eli,' Harel said, 'but I understand from Nathan here that you want some details about Operation Phuket.'

'You can start with showing me the red-page authorisation for the operation,' Eli said.

'If you insist. Nathan, forward to Eli.'

Nathan was at Harel's elbow, for all the world like a courtier at the emperor's court. He had his own laptop in front of him and, within seconds, the document was in Eli's box.

'Happy now?' Harel said as he straightened and prepared to leave.

'Just wait,' Eli said. 'Exactly who is this guy, this target? Is he some sort of terrorist?'

'Depends on your point of view,' Harel said. 'An incoming administration might consider him to be a communist. Anyway, you don't need to know all the details. You've seen the red-page authorisation.'

'And that's exactly where you're wrong.' Eli pressed the send button on his own laptop. 'If I may refer you to the document that's now in your box, you will see, part three, clause seven, second paragraph. I highlighted it, Harel, so it'll be easier for you to read.'

Harel wasn't reading, he was just glaring at Eli from behind his aviator tinted glasses. By contrast, Nathan was reading. He was scrolling down the pages and his mouth moved as he read the words. He might almost have been *davening*, appealing to the Almighty, but for sure, this wasn't a prayer that would be answered.

Eli went on, 'You will see that since this operation is taking place in the region of my station, you are obligated by law, not just to show me the red page as proof that it has been appropriately authorised, but also to give me all the operational information that I request. Thank you, Harel. I am waiting.'

Harel shook his head, the smile still on his face, the smile that Eli wanted to punch to the back of the man's throat. 'I really don't have time for this.' Harel glanced down at his Omega watch as if to confirm what he'd said. 'No, I absolutely, do not have time for this. I'm meeting the American liaison for this operation in forty minutes.'

'Who is this American liaison? Where are you meeting him? What protocols are in place for the security of this meeting?'

'Eli,' Harel said. 'Can you please do your pathetic jobsworth crap some other time? And not when I'm on my way to a meeting with someone so important to our future.'

'Who is this American liaison? I demand to know.'

'Okay, if it makes you happy and stops you having a heart attack, his name is Grant D Miller. He is close to Driver, the man we hope will be the next leader of the free world; he currently lives in Thailand, for lots of reasons, so London is a convenient place for us to meet. He's impressive. If I didn't think you would be an embarrassment, I'd take you with me to the meeting.'

'I've never heard of him,' Eli said.

'Is that my fault? Get your people on to him and you'll see exactly how influential Miller is. He's advised us that it would be beneficial for our future arms supply if there is a termination operation against a specific individual.'

'You mean Driver told Miller in a "Who will rid me of this troublesome priest?" kind of way?' Eli said. 'That didn't work out well, did it?'

'I have absolutely no idea what you're talking about.'

'Becket. Look it up,' Eli said. 'Let me be clear then, make it easier for you to understand. Are you telling me that Driver phoned Bibi and asked him to authorise a termination operation?'

'No, I'm not. Driver's much too shrewd to do that. He learnt from the fall-out from his various phone calls that got leaked and ended up in the courts. That's why he's using Miller as an intermediary. We have masses of corroborating evidence that this is what Driver wants and what we get in return.'

'If we target a specific individual? What specific individual?' Eli said.

Harel sighed as if impatient to be dealing with Eli. 'His full name is James Michael Loxlee but he's known as Jimbob, he is both a law professor and a podcaster, he's an ex-US marine and was a deputy communications director in the Trump administration.'

'So what? How did this guy get to the top of the enemy list?'

'He wrote a book about the legitimacy of the 2016 election, another book about the Trump administration and payouts; he claims to have evidence about Putin and Trump's financial dealings. He's also closely connected to the Thomas Jefferson Project.'

'I still don't get it even if I have heard of the Thomas Jefferson Project. You'd be hard pressed to find anyone in the Trump administration who didn't write a tell-all book. It's a whole industry. Why this guy?'

'He's a comedian, really funny. You should see what he does with the Trump dance. He has twelve million subscribers, and he tells people how the system works and who to vote for.'

Eli had got up from his desk and was standing in the middle of the office. He felt, rather than saw, Rafi at his elbow and sensed that Rafi was going to stop him if he launched himself at Harel. 'Are you telling me that we are going to target someone that isn't a terrorist but who just happens to disagree with a possible incoming American administration and may have some dirt on it? Harel, we can't do that. You must know we can't.'

'Do I have to remind you that the Mossad implements government policy. It does not set it. Government policy is to secure the flow of arms from the US – regardless of who wins the upcoming election.'

Before Eli had the chance to say anything else, Harel had left the room with Nathan trotting behind him, his laptop still open as he sought to catch up.

'Get Urit up here,' Eli said to Rafi. 'Get Urit and also Segev, I want to see them within the next ten minutes. I want to know who this Grant D Miller is.

Chapter 20

The library at Imperial College was anodyne, an expanse of long white tables, where students could park themselves and create barriers with laptops and sealed water bottles. Here and there an attempt had been made to soften the clinical lines with banks of ferns and orange space separators but, as Petra sat at her own territory of desk-space with her laptop and water bottle, she reckoned you couldn't mistake a university library for anything else. There was a buzz of concentration that was almost electric.

After some discussion with Rafi, she was kitted out in a knee-length tartan skirt, a white shirt and a cable-knit cardigan. Tan knee boots completed the outfit. She was supposed to look British establishment but, in this sub-royal-family get-up, she felt fake. As if she was dressed up in her mother's clothes and was pretending to be a grown-up. It wasn't that it was a skirt – she'd worn one of those before in different operations – it was the county look.

Better get over it, Petra thought, and focused her attention on her surroundings.

Around her, students hunched over screens and there was hardly any conversation between them. Perhaps she was being fanciful but they were like brain islands on a sea of knowledge with the information waves lapping in as the tides changed. Yes,

Petra concluded, looking at the screen in front of her where she had a prop document, she *was* being fanciful, but then she had been in that library for four days – at different spots in the library, admittedly – but the boredom of waiting was getting to her. Her only breaks had been when she either went to get a sandwich or went to the loo.

During those four days she'd caught glimpses of Wasim and she'd even felt his eyes on her when she'd been eating a bowl of soup in the cafe. She'd glanced at him, and then went back to her meal, eyes down on the minestrone and sourdough roll, not looking up again. No more eye contact, despite the sensation that her pulse had quickened because he'd noticed her. Why? Because Petra was unequivocal about how the operation, her operation, would proceed. Wasim had to approach her, it would not be the other way round.

Experience was guiding her.

Years ago, when she was working with Alon, Petra had made contact with a junior diplomat at the Pakistani Embassy. It was in the cafe at the YMCA in Tottenham Court Road where the guy swam five times a week. The problem was that he didn't always go to the cafe and, worse, he swam at different times of day depending on his schedule. Petra had sat in that cafe for ten days without a sighting; consequently, when he did show up, she'd rushed it. It was embarrassing to remember. She'd approached the diplomat and asked a question about the swimming facilities. It was the type of question that ought to have been answered by the people at the front desk and Petra had known it. It also sounded like a feeble pick-up line, which, in the larger sense, was what it was.

The result was that the contact was aborted and Alon had

given her a bollocking for being lazy. 'You wasted the contact, you were impatient and too obvious. By approaching the target, you made the contact memorable and that's the last thing in the world you should have done. It was clumsy. What made you do it, Petra?'

For Petra to have said that she was bored going to the cafe day after day and that there were other things she wanted to be doing wasn't the right answer, even though it was true. But as she sat in front of her library desk in the Imperial College Library, trying to understand articles in the journals that were supposed to be associated with her PhD thesis statement, Petra smiled a little to herself as she thought of Alon. In a funny way, this contact was for him. No matter how bored she was, how long it took, she was going to make damn sure that this contact was perfect.

Petra had also given the same attention to detail to her cover story. It had taken her a few days to consider the options and to come up with a proposal for Eli. Despite the handicap that she was operating under her own name because Wasim knew her as Petra, once Eli had agreed, the Office enhanced her online profile. If anybody googled her now, besides her journalism for *Finance Times*, she now had an MA in Education, a profile on LinkedIn and endorsements from people with whom she'd worked at various NGOs who were science educationalists. As such, her proposed PhD in the cross-disciplines of literacy in science in developing countries gave her the reason to be spending hours in Imperial College waiting for Wasim to be curious enough or brave enough to approach her.

She looked at her watch. The library was closing soon, so it wasn't going to be today. Petra began to dismantle her citadel.

Another day had come and gone in the fruitless task of turning the glimpses of Wasim into a contact. Too bad.

As Petra put on her coat and wrapped the scarf around her neck, she thought how much he'd changed since she'd met him. When he'd come to the UK from America to try to save his sister, he'd been barely more than an indulged teenager. Petra had seen how indulged he was in the pages of Sahar's journal; there she'd described that, if thwarted, the child Wasim would kick the furniture until he hurt himself. In the years since, he'd soared into manhood. Although slim, he was above average height and carried himself with an air of assurance and self-possession that had been absent during his younger days.

Petra made her way out of the library, thinking about the evening ahead. These last four nights, after she'd completed what she started to think of as her shift in the library, Petra often read Sahar's journal. What would Sahar have thought of the young man? Petra asked herself. She knew the answer. She'd have been so proud of her Wasim *nadir*, her favoured little brother, who'd wriggled in her arms like a puppy when they went on family outings to the sea.

Still thinking about Sahar, her dead voice whispering in her ear, Petra pressed the button to summon the lift. She was tired. It would have been nice to go home and share her day with someone who would understand. For a moment she thought about messaging Rafi. He'd certainly share her day but he was a long way from understanding her feelings about Sahar.

Eli?

The lift arrived with a judder, the doors opened and Petra stepped in. There was a middle-aged woman already in there. She looked like Petra felt, tired and gearing herself up for the commute home. The lift doors started to close. They were nearly shut when Petra looked up at the sound of pounding feet. By instinct she reached for the button to hold the door. It slid open and Petra was face to face with Wasim.

'Thank you,' he said as he stepped into the lift. 'You're very kind.'

The lift doors closed.

He looked at Petra with intensity, scanning her features and frowning.

'Excuse me, ma'am,' Wasim said. 'Forgive me for asking, but you look like someone I used to know.'

'Me?' Petra glanced at the other woman in the lift as if the young man might be talking to her.

'Yes, ma'am. Your name wouldn't be Petra, by any chance?'

Chapter 21

Instead of finding her way to Waterloo and the train back to Surrey, Petra had a drink with Wasim in the h-bar in the Sherfield Building. Wasim led the way into the space, where there were long trestle tables with beech chairs. It was utilitarian but the overhead lights were dimmer than in the library and, as she followed Wasim past the till, she saw that he exchanged a cheery wave with the woman who was working there. He led her to a table in the corner with the easy familiarity of someone who was comfortable in his surroundings.

'Are you working here?' Petra said.

'Yeah, it's not just for the beer, let me assure you. I just find the library a bit bleak. Please sit, what would you like to drink? I've been seeing you around the campus and I kept thinking it was you, but I wasn't sure. And I didn't want to look weird. But now that you're here, at the very least, I must buy you a drink.'

'I don't know,' Petra said with genuine hesitation. 'Well, since we're here, maybe a gin and tonic, but then I really do have to go,' she added.

This was going too fast for her but, more seriously, Petra had lost the initiative. Wasim was driving the contact and it was important for her to reassert control even at this stage.

'A quick drink,' Petra said. 'My shout and then I really do have to dash.'

'Oh no, Rita won't take your money, you'll see…' Wasim was already at the bar and ordering. Petra had no choice but to pull out one of the chairs and make herself comfortable while she waited for Wasim to return to the table. Maybe he hadn't changed so much from the kid who liked to get his own way and would kick furniture to prove it.

But he was charming. The geekiness of his late teen years had almost disappeared and been replaced by a polite American style. He also reminded Petra of Sahar with the same mesmerising eyes behind his designer specs and the same wiry dark hair, but he was the plus version. She'd been gentle, he spilt over with energy. It was arresting.

The drinks were in front of them and Petra sipped at the gin as if she was relaxed, which she wasn't.

'What are you doing here?' Wasim said. 'I thought you were hurt.'

'I was, I still do hurt,' Petra said with a smile. 'And never travel with me through an airport security x-ray, otherwise we'd be there all day.'

Wasim had a quizzical look on his face. Petra went on like a woman who wouldn't tolerate sympathy, 'There's so much metal in my body that I set everything off. But I'm still here. I had a lot of operations and a lot of rehab, and bad scars and yes, it hurt like hell. But… well, here I am.'

'I'm sorry.'

'I'm also sorry. Very sorry Wasim,' Petra held his gaze. 'It shouldn't have happened. Your sister was a lovely young woman, who was in the wrong place at the wrong time.'

'You tried, I know that. Let's not talk about such sadness, not today. Tell me what you're working on.'

Petra met with Eli and Rafi later that evening. They both seemed distracted and were checking their phones in between eating the pizza that Rafi had brought to the safe house while drinking the unnecessarily classy bottle of red wine, which was Eli's contribution to the picnic. They were in the same safe house where she'd last met Nathan and, under overhead electric light, it looked even worse than it had looked in daylight. It also smelt worse but, beyond smearing her hands with antibac, Petra didn't consider this to be her problem.

'What are you doing?' Petra asked when Eli picked up his phone and checked his feed again. 'Checking the football?'

'Sorry, Petra, we've got something else going on and it's worrying me.'

'I hope it's nothing to do with that toad, Nathan. Has he forgiven me yet or is he raining down curses on the apostate Eve who tempted him with a possible conversion and then entrapped him?'

Rafi grinned while he wrestled with a messy slice of mozzarella-dripping pizza. 'You certainly did a number on him,' he said, chewing with his mouth full. He swallowed. 'And hats off, you did better than I did with him. A lot better. And now you're weaving your magic on Silver Dove. Tell us.'

Eli wiped his mouth with a paper napkin and pushed the greasy box away from him. 'Yeah. Let's take it from the top.'

Petra described the contact in all the necessary and indeed, unnecessary, detail. The woman in the lift, the shift to the h-bar the people she'd seen on the walk between library and h-bar, what

Wasim had been wearing, carrying, his general health, appearance and demeanour, what he'd drunk in the bar. Eli even asked about Wasim's hands and whether he had any notable marks, traits or tells. Did he seem nervous, relaxed, suspicious, angry, and Petra was aware that Eli was now giving her his full attention and was doing a deep dive into the nuance of the contact.

All the while, Rafi continued eating, now and then stopping and jotting something down with a Sharpie on his napkin, a letter in Hebrew, but not interrupting until Eli had finished and had turned to him, a questioning look on his face. It was clear to Petra that the two men, once adversaries from different sides of the track, who'd been only too keen to fuck each other up, were now a team. And she was a part of it, as integral as a door hinge. Being a part of it gave her an odd thrill.

'This is all very good. I don't think it could have gone any better, do you, Rafi?' Eli said.

'No, pitch-perfect. Just one thing,' Rafi said. 'Did he talk to you about his bursary package? Like the accommodation that came with it?'

Petra saw Eli look at Rafi and nod at him.

'Yeah, thanks for reminding me,' Eli said. 'That's important, you need to know about that, so we'll talk about it in a while, but first, I want to know what your thoughts are,' Eli said. 'So, how do you want to proceed, Petra? Do you have a plan?'

Petra had been waiting for this moment. Waiting for Eli to ask her. It was *Auftragstaktik*. Mission-type tactics. The question brought back memories of dear Alon, whose wife was probably dead or dying in a tunnel, and the theory had been repeated in some of the reading she'd done. Decentralised military doctrine that emphasised initiative and flexibility for subordinate commanders. People like her. A memo from Clausewitz across the ages, a methodology for maximum impact in an operation.

During all the hours that Petra had sat in the library at Imperial, after she'd memorised her so-called thesis statement and written down the bullet points of what she was supposed to know, she'd been developing her plan. And she was proud of it. It was the result of her years of experience as a *bat leviyah*, a junior case officer, and she knew that if it didn't work, there would be no second chance. Her position was unique and she meant to make the most of it.

'I've looked at lots of options and I keep coming back to the same one. I want to go for a frontal approach.' Petra looked at the two men, daring them to challenge her without hearing her rationale.

'There are several reasons. First, and most important, he already trusts me. He knows I fought to save his sister, and he believes that I was severely injured as a result of my attempt. I did try to save her.'

'We know,' Eli said.

'And I tried to save him. I'm going in there with a unique advantage. I don't have to build trust. I already have it. That's the first reason for a frontal approach.'

'I'm hearing you out, Petra, but it's also the riskiest approach and, as you know, he's already rejected Abu Marwan.'

'Because Abu Marwan is the enemy. I'm not,' Petra said. 'My second point is the journal; he may not want to talk about his sister just yet but, when I give him those pages that she wrote, and he reads them, he'll be in.'

'But he thinks she was misguided and entrapped by Hamas.'

'Yes, but it's a direct line to her. He will feel that she didn't die in vain.'

And so will I, Petra thought.

She could see Eli nodding as he considered and absorbed what she was saying. Both men were concentrating.

'Finally, the reason for a frontal approach is because it will be based on ideology, which is the best motivation of all, as we know. It's the one that works long-term. Silver Dove doesn't need money; once he achieves this degree, he will be highly employable, whether he chooses academia, government or work for a medical insurance company. A PhD in biomathematics is a ticket to a fat salary. The way I see it is that he needs a damn good reason for him to give all that up and go back to the moon wasteland of Gaza, where the climate is crap, it's over-crowded and polluted, and his life will be continually under threat. It's a lot to ask him to go back there when he could be building a life and career in some picket-fence community either in the US or here. Or anywhere else he fancies come to that.'

'And you really think sentiment is the key?' Rafi was leaning on the battered chair, swinging on the back legs.

'It's not just sentiment,' Petra said. 'Whatever that young man may say, I believe he's got his sister's genetic make-up. If I do this right, he'll do it because he believes that he's making a difference – which is, after all, what we're trying to do, aren't we?'

Behind her she could hear the whirr and hum of an arthritic fridge revving up its element to keep the milk cold. Outside there was traffic, in the flat upstairs a television was on at full volume and, from the same direction, she could hear the distant yowl of a baby crying. Petra focused on the two men and looked from one to the other.

'Well,' she said. 'What do you think?'

'Exactly what are you going to tell him in your pitch?' Eli said.

Petra whipped out a handwritten document from her work bag. It was grubby from being written and rewritten and then folded up, but everything was there, her whole plan. Eli reached towards it and opened it out. He gazed at it for a few moments, then muttered something incomprehensible and pulled a pair of reading specs from his pocket. Looking somewhat embarrassed, Eli put them on and read. Rafi grinned at her, enjoying the moment. The document contained her whole plan. At last Eli finished reading and passed it to Rafi.

'There's too much detail, but your plan is sound. From me, you have a green light.'

It was another five minutes before Rafi finished reading and he concurred with Eli. 'Impressive, Petra, but I didn't expect anything less from you. There's just one thing in your document and in your pitch to us, one thing that I... we... need to make clear to you.'

'What would that be?'

'You say here,' he pointed. 'You say here that we may be able to avoid the expense of using a safe house for your meetings and suggest that you could rendezvous at his apartment.'

'Yes, what of it? I'm more than happy to take and dress an apartment but if this is what's on offer...'

'That's not it, Petra,' Rafi said. 'You need to know that we put Silver Dove in Tom's old apartment. The one where you not only met Tom, but where that American...' He tailed off.

'Where I killed the American piece of shit?' Petra said.

Chapter 22

As Petra sat down at the beech table in Wasim's flat and looked around, she considered that it was a good thing she'd been prepared for the possibility of being in the location where she'd fought for her life. The place may have looked different but here was the same beech table, where Tom had sat with his books and computers. Now it was covered with a couple of place mats, some cutlery and two glasses, one of which was half full of red wine.

It had taken Petra three more weeks of intense development before she felt she was ready to make the pitch and this was the second time she'd had a meal at Wasim's flat. He considered himself to be something of a cook and in that he was right.

'Can I do anything to help?' Petra said.

'Nope. I've got everything under control.' He was standing over the hob, stirring a pot, and whatever it was smelt good.

Petra was nervous. But she recognised that it was performance nerves that went with the knowledge that she was as prepared as she could be and also that she was experiencing the sense of anticipation that would help her focus and get into her flow. Despite the subliminal discomfort of being in Tom's flat, a location she associated with tragedy, there was a tactical plus; the environment was controlled. If they'd been in a restaurant, there was the risk of a waiter interrupting them. If they'd been in the university, there might be a fellow student. Even if they were at a cultural event – say, the gallery that she'd visited with Wasim on a weekend – there was distraction. For the purposes of the work, the flat was a sealed unit. It was also wired.

On the way to the apartment, as she'd checked herself by going around the block and then reversing back on herself, Petra had even walked past the Techtruck. She recognised Segev in the front seat, since she'd been in that truck herself and she knew that Eli and Rafi would be in the back, on their swivel stools, crouched over the screens, listening to her in real time, just two streets away from where she was working. The awareness that she had a live audience gave her a fillip. She was about to show those two largely unreconstructed men just how it was done.

Petra looked at her coat, which was draped over one arm of the sofa, and then down at her work bag. It was by her feet and she repositioned it a few inches closer so that she had easier access. That was part of her plan.

'How did your meeting with your supervisor go?' Wasim said.

'Good enough. The thesis statement ticks all the boxes; however, I'm shelving it for the time being. Something more interesting has come up.'

'Oh yeah, what's that?'

'I'm not sure what you'll think,' Petra said. 'It's one of those odd moments of synchronicity that sometimes occur.'

'Ah, our friend Jung.' Wasim was heading towards the table with two steaming plates of food. 'Jamaican rice 'n' peas. Cultural appropriation meets collective unconsciousness in action.'

During the last two weeks Petra had got to know Wasim,

the adult. In many ways he was like his sister, open, on the geeky side of the spectrum, but also funny and smart. From the first he'd trusted her and talked about his educational choices, how he'd considered medicine and thought of specialising in psychiatry. As such he'd had therapy in the US when he realised that his sexuality wasn't 'strictly binary', as he put it. He'd told her how he'd explored relationships with both men and women and it didn't matter so long as you treated the other person with respect.

'He sounds like a fucking hippy,' Rafi had growled at the next planning meeting.

'Or maybe he's just being American,' Eli had said. 'What's wrong with that?'

'It's neither,' Petra had said. 'He's his own man, that's what. You know we like to put people into boxes and slots and say if this guy is a gambler or greedy or horny, or corrupt or angry, we can press his buttons and get what we want, but some people… some people defy categorisation. And that's Silver Dove.'

'Sounds like you're in love with him,' Rafi said in the same dark tone. 'Like you were with his sister.'

'No, I'm not, but I'll tell you one thing, Rafi. He's special, like her.'

What Petra couldn't decide was whether this awareness made it easier or harder for her. Here she was, the rehearsed sentence on her tongue, in the perfect environment, and she had the target across the table with a fork halfway to his mouth waiting for her to compliment him on his rice 'n' peas.

Petra said, 'Here's the thing, Wasim, and you'll get what I mean about synchronicity. I've been recruited by a think tank that wants to try to move things in the Middle East towards stability and democracy.'

'What? Who are they?'

'They're the real deal. They're talking to people on both sides, the Israelis and the Palestinians, both on the West Bank and Gaza, who want a future and not this endless bloodshed.'

'Are they British?'

'It's not Chatham House but they do have strong links with the UK. They're trying to identify people who can make a difference, who can step away from the religious extremists on all sides, not to mention the corruption.'

Wasim shook his head, as if disbelieving.

'That's what I thought, but you know what? It can be done if enough people buy into it. It can be done if there's a strategic plan, which is what they have. That's to get people who can change minds into positions of power in the region. It's not going to happen overnight. They reckon it'll take ten years to get enough people in place to effect the changes. To make that difference.'

Wasim's fork was frozen, halfway between plate and mouth and he was staring at Petra. He sounded wary.

'How did you get into this? Why you?'

Petra dived into the bag she'd placed by the base of her chair and took out Sahar's journal.

'Why me? That's an easy question. Your sister. When I met her, I was just teaching her in class. I had no idea what she was planning but, as soon as I did, I did everything I could think of to try to stop it. To stop her. And I failed. I didn't do enough, and I will have to live with that for the rest of my life. That's why me.'

Wasim was silent and Petra felt her voice cracking with emotion as she held out the journal, 'This is for you, Wasim. She gave it to me to give to you. You should also know, I had the journal translated. I wanted to know what she'd written. After it was translated, I was able to hear her voice in every line and it breaks my heart to think that a situation exists where a woman like Sahar thought the only way she could make a difference was to kill herself. Because what she did didn't change anything, did it?'

'No, it didn't. Not a damn thing.'

Wasim held out his hand for the journal and took it. In the dim light of the room Petra saw his eyes shine as he leafed through the pages and saw his sister's handwriting.

'If you want me to leave, I'll go,' Petra stood up, gathered her bag, slid her arms into the coat that she'd placed on the sofa and trod towards the door.

She heard Wasim get up from the table. 'Stay. Let's talk.'

Chapter 23

Eli strode into the reception area at the American Embassy's Nine Elms location and waited in a queue cluster by the white desk for someone to attend to him. The American Embassy was inconvenient to get to from Kensington, particularly when he had to adhere to necessary protocol to try to ensure he wasn't being tailed after he left Palace Gardens. It would have been preferable to have a video conference as part of the regular liaison between himself, Charlene Dineen and Oliver Milne but, when the senior partner wanted face-to-face, that's what they got.

From outside the monstrous building looked like a radiator, inside it was worse. Every time Eli had to go there, he marvelled at how, with all the resources in the world, all the power, all the wealth, they couldn't buy a little good taste. As he waited and looked around, Eli played the game that he often did, and that was to guess how high the ceiling was. He was reminded of the steps that Mussolini had built near the Garibaldi Monument. It was the same principle – small man, big steps. If ever there was an indication of an emperor complex, this must surely be it.

'Good morning, Eli. May I join you?'

It was Oliver Milne, the MI6 liaison. In his customary charcoal suit and highly polished shoes, even he was dwarfed by the ten-metre-high windows, windows that were studded with pillars designed to ward off a bomb attack. Well, there were reasons for the building's ugliness, Eli supposed. The US never knew when they might have to evacuate in a hurry.

'Good morning, Oliver. I'm pleased to bump into you before we go in.'

They shuffled closer to the front desk, where several harassed-looking men and women were checking identity and carding up the visitors.

'How's everything? Did your man arrive at Imperial *intactus*?' Oliver said.

'Very much so and we are most appreciative. In fact, I have something for you that's tangential to that particular gentleman.'

Milne's eyebrows above the tortoiseshell specs shot up. It was a gaze that questioned and was also sceptical.

'Is he getting into some bad company?' Milne said.

'No, but predictably we've been following the protests on the various British campuses for people of interest to us.'

'As are we, as I'm sure you're aware,' Milne said.

'Of course, and we're very grateful. However, we came across some information about a particular group who are active at Westminster University. Very active. With access to some of the equipment and facilities of the laboratories that are on site…'

'I see,' Milne said. They were at the desk now and Milne slammed his British Government identity card on the top and glared at an overweight woman who'd had too much lip filler. 'We're here to see Dr Dineen. Please facilitate our visitor cards with alacrity.'

The icy tone seemed to do the trick, because moments later they were badged up with an unctuous young marine at their elbow, who was preparing to escort them to the lifts and the upper floor.

'Ghastly place, monument to paranoia,' Milne muttered. 'Young man, would you be kind enough to collect my umbrella. I left it by the front desk. We'll wait here.'

'Yes, sir.' The marine scuttled off.

Milne turned to Eli. 'What were you saying about facilities and laboratories?'

'I have an address for you.' Eli reached into his pocket and took out the folded piece of paper he'd prepared. 'Could be nothing, could be something, but they're Westminster students and they have been… vocal.'

'Thank you, very kind. I'll get this acted upon.'

The marine reappeared. 'I'm sorry sir, but I haven't been able to locate your—'

Milne looked abashed and gave the marine the kind of smile that was warm and no doubt well practised. 'Stupid of me. I didn't bring it. Please, let us proceed to Dr Dineen.'

They were escorted by the marine to Charlene Dineen's office, a space that in style looked as if had been shoehorned into the building. It was near the top of the monolith, on a corner site with a magnificent view through floor to ceiling windows on two sides. It was overpowering, but Eli supposed that was the whole point. The CIA's head of London Station sat behind what looked like a redwood table that was so big it dwarfed the woman.

'Good to see you guys.' She uncurled from her chair as they came in and, with one hand, gestured them towards a seating area by a bookcase; a space that was backlit from the bookshelves and oozed golden light into the room's corner.

The seating area was two deep sofas and an Eames chair, stark lines and stylish, like the station head herself. In a corporate black trouser suit, Charlene looked like a lawyer. Charlene took her place in the Eames chair, while the men sank down into the heavily upholstered sofas. It amused Eli, because the Eames chair wasn't quite a throne, but there was certainly a sense of it.

Greetings were exchanged and the three spies settled down to the business of updating each other and exchanging information in the economic manner of professionals.

The American secretary of state, Anthony Blinken was on a European shuttle tour to establish who was going to weigh into the hostage negotiations, and a meeting was scheduled with the British Prime Minister. There was some housekeeping in connection with the diplomatic visit to ensure that security was paramount.

'I know it's not your fault, Eli,' Charlene drawled. 'But an election year is a real bad time for there to be a Middle Eastern conflict.'

'That was probably one of the reasons they did it,' Eli said. 'That and the thawing relations with Saudi. And, let's be blunt, our own domestic instability.'

'Well, we're inside the eye of the hurricane now,' Charlene said. 'No choice but to nail down those doors and sit it out with a quart of Jackie D.' She smiled sympathetically and Eli felt she was genuine.

Milne lifted the coffee cup of to his lips, sipped and, by the tiniest grimace, managed to indicate that it wasn't to his taste.

Eli took the initiative. 'While we're talking about your election, Charlene, have you come across Grant D Miller?'

'Who?' Milne said, now instantly alert. He had reason not to trust Eli during these trilateral meetings.

'My understanding is that he's connected to the Republican re-election campaign. A major donor, based in Thailand. He hasn't been domiciled in the US since Jeffrey Epstein's death—'

'One of those, is he?' Charlene said. She was tapping her nail against the stainless-steel strut of the Eames chair. It's what she did when she was thinking. 'Let me tell you something, Eli. I try very hard to stay away from shady politico donors. They're trouble. If you want to know who he is, well, that's gonna be one for the FBI, not me.'

'Forgive me for being blunt, Eli.' Milne placed the offending coffee cup on the glass side table.

'You're always forgiven, Oliver.'

The MI6 man's smile was thin. He continued, 'What's your interest in this character? In other words, is this something that His Majesty's Government should be concerned about?'

Eli was prepared. 'It's about money going to our settlers, as well as Trump's re-election campaign. *Shabak* want to know where the money is coming from. We want to make sure it's clean. If we find out it's dirty and that it's come through the UK, we'll tell you.'

'Thank you,' Milne said.

'And I also can't help you, Eli,' Charlene said. 'I've got so much crossing my desk right now that if some donor wants to kiss the Trump ring in the hope of a favour or perhaps a pardon, it's not on my priority list. There are just too many of them.'

Charlene looked a little worn down and Eli thought that the cheerleader mien was forced. Based on the Mossad's reports and contingency plans, there would be dramatic changes in the

CIA if there was a Republican government in January, so no wonder she was strained.

But Eli had got what he wanted, even if it was a negative. Charlene clearly didn't know Harel's influencer and Eli had gathered a little more intelligence, which is, after all, what he was trained to do.

'Have either of you come across Nicolai on the UK diplomatic circuit?' Milne asked. 'I thought he was in London and was going to be based here to try to facilitate an early hostage release for some of their dual nationalities. Our guys are saying that, in the build-up to the US election, the Russians are going feral. Low-level stuff mostly, arson attacks on Ukrainian arms supplies and disruption at a Swedish airport and, of course, cyber, but lots of it. Across all platforms. We don't want any of that here.'

'I don't know what he's doing but he's busy,' Eli said. 'I saw him recently at the Mexican Embassy national day.'

'And I saw him at an event at Somerset House,' Charlene said. 'I can't remember what it was but I do remember he was looking mighty pleased with himself, so I have no doubt he's into something that's not going to benefit any of us.'

'Any idea what it could be?' Eli said.

'Most of our energies are going into the outcome of the election and maintaining stability, whichever way it goes. Nicolai's people have their favourite, and they've got track record in election interference.'

'Do you think that's why he's looking smug?' Eli said. 'Or maybe he's just a smug bastard, who likes to wind us up and enjoys the idea that they worry us.'

PART THREE

Lies

This generation is seeing a boom in propaganda... technical progress has vastly increased the power of the propagandist. His campaign may be open or he may operate silently, like a thief in the night, moulding the pattern of a people's mind by subtle suggestion.

A J Mackenzie, 1937

History is a set of lies agreed upon.

Napoleon Bonaparte, France 1769–1821

Chapter 24

It was mid-January and cold in London. God knows what it was like in Israel and, by default, Gaza; the news had been unrelentingly bad for the past month. In mid-December Israeli forces had killed three Israeli hostages by mistake; the news made Petra wince. Meanwhile the trail of displaced people dragging their pathetic belongings continued across news outlets, coupled with escalating incidents of anti-Semitism. It had even come to her own Surrey village where a couple of sisters, daughters of a neighbour, had been abused for wearing Stars of David. According to Sandie, one of the young women was told by a stranger in a shopping centre that it was a pity her family hadn't all been burnt to death.

Petra's Christmas had been quiet and, besides having drinks with Sandie and Bob, who seemed to be edging towards a romantic attachment, she'd spent a good amount of time with Wasim. They spent sunny days walking in Hyde Park, wrapped up against the cold, they strolled around the Serpentine and talked. Much of the conversation was to build up the levels of trust and communication between them. The other part was talking about his future.

Silver Dove was an original thinker, a mix of liberal attitudes peppered with ideas that hadn't occurred to her. There was more than one occasion when, despite her crash course in geopolitics and continued reading, she felt out of her depth and recognised that Eli, in some other cover that wasn't Abu Marwan, would have connected better with the young man. Case in point was on a Saturday afternoon, when they got caught up in the tail end of a demonstration and had to manoeuvre through a crush of people with placards that said 'Fuck Israel' and 'Zionists aren't welcome here'.

'This is their Vietnam moment,' Wasim said, as he took her arm in a protective way. 'Most of them have no idea where Gaza is and the anti-Semitism has very little to do with how they're positioning themselves, it's just being part of a protest movement. You see, climate change is amorphous, there's no single specific, clearly identifiable enemy with climate change. Who do you target? The oil industry, aviation, fracking? And as for the attacks on paintings, that was one fucked-up idea. It only served to alienate the public. Or colonialism, it's too general, and it's grounded in history. The Romans were colonialists, Persians, Vikings, Venetians, take your pick, all colonialists, so to say that it's the UK or Europe or the US, it's too general. But Gaza is easy. Like Vietnam, good guys, weak but brave and bad guys, powerful and evil. And Jews.'

Later, over a hot chocolate in a noisy cafe on the Strand, Wasim described how he saw the current rise in anti-Semitism in Europe and how it was being appropriated by the far right to bludgeon the millions of Muslims in Europe.

'As I see it, that's the real risk and I don't think our zippy activists have considered how this may play out.' Wasim stirred the glass of hot chocolate to break up the cream. 'It's just fun and social to march and chant and conflate Jews with the actions of the Israeli government and churn up the old tropes without realising what they're actually doing.'

'Which is?'

'Feeding the far right with a narrative that will be acceptable to centrists. Okay, the far right have a head start with issues about immigration, but what better way for them to promote Islamophobia than by claiming that they are trying to protect Jews, who have been historically discriminated against? To say that they're coming to this position not from a platform of being racist and discriminatory but because they're protecting people.'

'That's a pretty depressing way of looking at it,' Petra said.

Wasim shrugged. 'Sorry, I just get really frustrated when I've gotta listen to some of the garbage that floats around the student body, most notably from the regional student union organiser. Man's a total dick.'

Unfortunately, it was this total dick that Wasim had to get onside. Petra had discussed it at length with both Eli and Rafi. Sam Scedding, or Samir, as he sometimes liked to be known, in his role as regional student union organiser, was connected to all the groups that would be needed to endorse Silver Dove as a person with a future career in Gaza politics.

Petra was less interested in Wasim's world view and more concerned about how this arrogant young man was going to get the endorsement he needed.

'You may not like Sam or even agree with what he's saying but you need to find a way to connect to him.'

Wasim leaned back in his chair and put his hands behind his head. 'The only thing I like about him is his girlfriend. She's much too good for him.'

'Do you think flirting or even screwing this woman is a good way for you to get Sam onside?'

Wasim put his head onto one side and smiled at Petra. It was a warm smile and one that would charm any young woman away from a worthy activist, as she imagined Sam to be. But Wasim's next comment brought Petra right back to the here and now.

'There is no think tank,' Wasim said.

'I'm sorry? I thought we were talking about Sam,' Petra said.

'You're a Jew, aren't you?'

'What makes you say that?'

'For one thing, you answered a question with a question,' Wasim smiled.

'That's hardly scientific,' Petra said.

Wasim changed his position and leaned across the table. He lowered his voice. 'I don't have a problem with it, neither do I have a problem with the notion that your think tank is the Mossad. That's because I know you, Petra, and I know that you tried hard to save my sister's life. I also know what she thought of you from her journal and, despite her religious beliefs, Sahar wasn't stupid when it came to people.'

Through the designer specs his eyes were magnified, and it gave his words a heightened intensity. The sense of just how pivotal her response was going to be to the future of the relationship and, by default, the operation was acute. It was like an out-of-the-box kitchen knife, dangerous but functional. It was either going to slash through the dross of maintaining the cover story or finish the operation in one move. Petra opened her mouth, ready to deny, deny, deny. She was sure that's what Rafi would have told her to do, but something held her back. This was about respect and about judgement. It was her call. If she was going to ask him to risk his life, she at least should show him some respect and tell him the truth.

'Yes, I am a Jew. And yes, this idea of you going back to try to make Gaza a better place is an initiative coming from the Israeli government, in other words, the Mossad.'

'Good. That makes life a lot easier, doesn't it?'

She paid for coffee and they left the cafe. Now warmed, they crossed the road into Green Park and walked among the bare trees, trees that had shed their leaves and had no secrets. Wasim was right. The rest of that afternoon's meeting was a lot easier. For one thing, Petra was able to set up the safety codes for when they spoke on the phone without dressing it up as some weirdness dreamt up by a paranoid think tank. Wasim got it immediately, even adding his own enhancements.

'Words associated with heat are a warning code. Words associated with cold are an all clear.'

'Exactly, simple to remember, hard to identify,' Petra said. She was already wondering how she was going to explain the change in Wasim's status to Rafi and Eli. The need for Wasim to understand safety codes was not going to convince them that it was necessary to break the agreed recruitment protocols. Would she have to tell them?

It was only later that evening when they were sitting on the sofa at Wasim's flat, watching a Christmas movie and eating popcorn, that she realised she would; the flat was wired.

'It's not just because of my sister. Though that's certainly a part of it. It's also about a friend I had in Kansas.'

'Go on,' Petra said, careful to give him space to explore the idea.

167

'It started when I came back… after Sahar. At first I didn't go in to classes at all. Just stayed in bed all day, watched the lectures on the feed. When I didn't turn up to anything my roommates set the counsellors on me, so I had to go to lectures. Day after day, I sat at the back of that lecture hall, didn't take anything in. Just looked at the clock, counted the minutes until I could get back into bed and sleep. Jonathan was in my biophysics group. He used to walk me back to the dorm, didn't speak, didn't nag. Sometimes handed me a takeout in a bag. Dear Jonathan. He brought me back. He said I was like a bird with a damaged wing.' Wasim smiled at the memory.

'He was right.'

Wasim sighed heavily. 'Jonathan was Jewish and his mom was okay with it when we got closer. She was a bit like you. His father was an asshole. I never worked out whether he hated me more because we were having a thing or because of my background, but Jonathan was everything anyone could want in a friend, a partner, a son. Big, big heart, and funny, so funny.'

'What happened?'

'It was the stupidest thing. He never cleaned his car windows before he started driving, there was heavy snow, it was early in the morning and he was late for class. He was driving too fast, hit some ice, smashed over the barrier, hit an oncoming truck.'

Petra took his hand and squeezed it. 'I'm sorry.'

Wasim stared ahead at the cavorting women in skimpy Santa costumes surrounding Bill Nighy on the TV. 'I blamed myself. You see, we'd made a bit of a night of it, the night before. I told him all about Sahar, and we talked about whether we had a future together. You know what he said?'

Petra shook her head.

'He said, "We have to live," and said that's what *l'chaim*, the toast was all about. To life. Not the death cult that killed Sahar. That's what I want to bring to my people. The mindset that life is precious.'

The fall-out from the change in Wasim's status wasn't as bad as Petra had anticipated. Much of that was due to the benefit of the wired environment of his flat. Eli and Rafi had heard exactly what was said and seen the images.

'It's clear that he trusts you,' Eli said. 'And it's clear that he's acting out of idealism that he can associate with a particularly positive experience. If we'd known this before, it would have made our lives easier and we could have got to him through the family, but Gaza was never a priority. Anyway, I'm happy with the development. Rafi?'

Rafi's expression said otherwise. 'I'm not convinced by him. Nor the *l'chaim* crap. It strikes me that's exactly the type of string we might tug if we wanted to shift an operation. But I still agree that we go ahead with the next stage; we just do it with clear fallback procedures.'

The university cafe at Westminster had long trestle tables that striated the floor space where pockets of students chowed down while they simultaneously flicked through their phones and talked at each other. To one side of the cafe, there were small tables for people who wanted to sit alone or share with just one other person. Petra had insisted on getting into the space a full hour before necessary so she might bag one of those side tables. That meant with her back against the wall she had the optimum 180-degree view of the space.

For the last week she'd been using the earpiece and, despite it looking like a commercial earbud, she was conscious of it. She was also uncomfortable with the chatter in her ear, much of it in Hebrew, in which she could understand only every few words. If she was going to make a habit of this, she would have to find a better way of staying in touch with the Techtruck that didn't give her a headache.

Her work phone was also connected to the Techtruck so, when she seemed to be talking on a call, she was waving the phone around so that Rafi and Segev had as clear a view as possible of the location.

'Just relax,' Rafi said. 'I'm sure your golden boy will do fine. This is his chance to impress.'

'I'm not worried about him. I can't work out how to lower the volume on this thing.'

'Is this a little more comfortable?' she heard Segev's voice. 'I've taken down the treble.'

'Yes… yes… thank you.'

'Okay,' Rafi said. 'We're all set. Our guy has just exited Baker Street Station, and he will be with you in just over seven minutes.'

'Got it.'

'Enjoy the show.'

Besides his position as regional student union organiser, Sam had further attributes that made him a desirable target for Silver Dove. He was already on an MI5 watch list, he had an established social-media profile in antifa and he even had connections to Hamas's political wing.

Yet his background was unexceptional. Originally from a small town in Devon, Sam's father was a Tory councillor, who owned a chandler's shop. His mother was a teacher and, according to the document Petra had read, Sam himself was a postgraduate media-studies student. After failing to get a job in the creative industries, he'd found his niche in the student union. Here he was able to use his skills writing copy and designing posters for the events that they ran. He also did the data gathering and ran the social accounts, which, in the three years that he'd been doing the job, had grown exponentially. While it was nothing like the sort of money he'd have earned if he'd got himself into an advertising agency, nonetheless he was able to sustain himself in the flat he rented in one of the blocks near Shepherd's Bush. There were other perks to the job, among them the supply of admiring undergraduate students.

As Petra studied him from her table on the other side of the cafe, she considered that he was exactly where he was supposed to be in life.

At that moment he was leaning against the makeshift stall, handing out flyers and information for the weekend rally to everyone who passed by. The stall itself was draped with the red, white, black and green of the Palestinian flag and a young woman with green hair and a Medusa cut was trilling on a recorder, while a fellow student banged on kettledrum and chanted, 'From the River to the Sea, Palestine will be Free.'

Behind them Sam smiled with the beatific indulgence of the senior student. Petra noted, from both the file she'd studied earlier and from observing him in the flesh, that he had a particularly interesting face. It was long, his brow was lined and he looked older than his documented 26. There was a worn-down look about him, as if he'd done some serious drugs and compromised his health before he got clean. He was pale and, from time to time, he held up the keffiyeh around his neck and coughed into it. That hadn't come up on the file but, as Eli said, they didn't know everything.

Regardless of Sam's status as a student union man and an activist, Petra was confident that Silver Dove had all the smarts needed to make this first contact. Petra was thinking about that when her earpiece buzzed into life.

'*Shin Daled* has just entered the building.'

Minutes later, Petra spotted Wasim as he walked into the cafe.

'Eyes on him,' she said and, at the sight of the agent, she almost shook her head in amusement. Almost, but not quite. For all the world he looked like someone strolling along the boardwalk at the beach, not making a contact with a prickly activist who might well be aggressive. In loose jeans and an overlarge sweatshirt, baseball cap and a bowling jacket, Wasim looked cool. No question about it.

'Stand by. He's at the desk,' Petra said.

Petra heard the channel switch as the young man bent over the stand and smiled at Sam.

'Hey,' Wasim said to Sam, 'I'll keep it brief. I'm a PhD at Imperial. Name's Wasim Al-Arikhi. I've seen you around and I've stayed away because…' Wasim pointed a finger. 'You're being followed.'

Sam frowned deeply, shook his head. 'I don't know who you are, and I don't know what you're talking about.'

Wasim shrugged, '*Salaam aleichem*, bro. I'm just telling you what I saw because I saw the same guys on me.'

Then Wasim picked up one of the flyers, ambled over to the coffee stand and ordered. While he was there, Petra saw him chat to the girl with the green hair in that charming way he had. Then he sauntered towards the exit.

'All okay,' Petra said. '*Shin Daled* leaving location. Target looks worried. I don't think it could have gone any better.'

'Let's see,' Petra heard Rafi say.

Chapter 25

Ever since Eli had met with Milne and Charlene, he'd been ruminating about Grant D Miller. It was like muscle sprain, always there. He'd spent hours both in his office and at home, at the kitchen table looking at footage on social media sites of the tall, urbane American with the slicked-back grey hair. He'd been filmed at Trump rallies, among a group in the White House and Mar-a-Lago when the former president was in power, giving a talk at an Ivy League university on the benefits of isolationism, and there were also posts about his association with Jeffrey Epstein that lent credence to the reasons why he had to meet Harel in London.

Eli delved further and found a print interview with the man for a local British newspaper, where he talked about his British ancestors, who'd been mill brokers in Nottingham but had fled to the US in the eighteenth century. There was even supposed to be a house associated with the man's family in some remote village in the area.

Despite all that colourful corroboration, something continued to nag at Eli and, as yet, he couldn't work out what it was.

Who was this Republican mover and shaker who'd got the ear of the former US president and was now the point of contact for this operation? How much influence did he really have over a quixotic leader? There were always satellites swirling around authoritarian powers who thought they were bigger than they really were. Look at Prigozhin, blown up mid-flight. Eli asked himself, was that it? The notion that Grant D Miller wasn't a power broker at all, and they were being led down a dark tunnel with a bomb at the end of it?

Eli neither trusted Harel nor rated him. But, worst of all, this targeted assassination was going to be carried out on his patch. If anything went wrong, anything at all, his head would be on the block.

'I need to do something,' Eli said to Rafi, who was lounging on the armchair in his office, laptop on his thighs, rereading Petra's report of the contact Silver Dove had made with Sam, now designated by the code name Treesmith.

'*Ma?*' Rafi said without looking up.

'I said I need to do something about this operation before it blows up in our faces as sure as water runs downhill. I want to do some due diligence to satisfy myself.'

At last Eli had Rafi's attention. 'Haven't you got enough to do? Can't we expect that this has already been done and when it comes to the negative treatment itself, even if it is in the UK, we can rely on *Kidon*. There are some great guys in the unit and their recent track record has been one hundred per cent.'

'You're only saying that because it used to be your unit.' Eli stood up from his desk and paced to the fridge, where he pulled out a beer and gestured with it towards Rafi. He nodded and Eli opened the bottle and handed it to him before he took his own.

It was 6 p.m. and they'd just had the unit's weekly forward-planning meeting, where they looked at the longer-term operations. Nothing much had changed. Adam was still jetting back and forth to Hungary working the pager operation. Nathan was busying himself with the Jewish community, trying to reassure them that Israel had their backs while ramping up security measures outside *shuls* and Jewish schools. Lev was doing the minimum possible as usual, and day by day they consumed every morsel of news coming from home. It was exhausting. Despite that, Eli's brain was still working and he was beginning to develop an idea.

'What are you doing now?' Eli said.

'Just rereading Petra's report before I go home. Then watching the football, Man City and Crystal Palace.'

'It'll be boring. Come on, let's get out of here. I'm inviting you.'

'Inviting me? Is this a date?' Rafi said.

'Fuck off. I've got an idea and I want your view.'

Rafi stood up, necked the rest of the beer and shrugged himself into his jacket.

On the way out of the embassy, they bumped into Yossi, the deputy ambassador, who was leaning over the desk where they collected their home cellphones. He looked worn out, dark shadows under his eyes and a face that was more pinched than Eli had ever remembered. They nodded at each other, Eli felt that they were both too exhausted to resume their customary state of open warfare.

Thirty minutes later, Eli and Rafi were sitting in an Italian restaurant in Notting Hill. It was a reclaimed pub and there was a bustle around them, people who just had normal problems, like work and money and love and kids. It was the perfect place to pitch his idea to Rafi.

Over a platter of prosciutto and olives, Eli jumped straight in.

'What do *you* think about this Grant D Miller?' Eli said.

'What's there to think about?' Rafi paused with a fork of prosciutto halfway between plate and mouth. 'I'm more worried about Silver Dove. The contact may have gone okay but I keep remembering a *Kidon* case. We studied it.'

'You? Study?'

'Yeah, me, study. I told Petra about it to warn her.' Rafi munched the ham.

'So what *Kidon* case was that?' Eli selected a piece of mortadella and arranged it on the sourdough.

'It was a monumental cock-up. One of the experts reckoned they could hypnotise a Palestinian prisoner to kill Yasser Arafat. The Office spent a fortune on training, even constructing room sets so the guy could slip into his assassin role when the time came. You know the story; the minute they released the Palestinian, instead of killing Arafat, he told him the whole story and we'd been conned.'

'What? And you think Silver Dove is conning us?' Eli said.

'Could be. How do we know we're not getting pulled into a really dirty trap?'

Eli thought for a moment, Rafi had summed up exactly what he was thinking about Grant D Miller. Were they getting pulled into a dirty trap?

'And you know what makes it worse, what's killing me?' Rafi tossed his wine back. 'I'm started to sound like you. Obsessing about nothing. But what if I'm right? Aren't we paid to make assumptions? Isn't that what Yuval says the whole time?'

Eli ignored the comment and went on, 'Let's look at the facts. Silver Dove rejected Abu Marwan in no uncertain terms. If he was playing with us, he wouldn't have rejected the initial contact. Okay? What's more, everything he's said has checked out, including him doing an acting course at the theatre in Jenin. We know he cut ties with the uncle who sponsored him to get to the US and we know he's bisexual. And we have now confirmed the story about the kid in his year at Kansas who died in a car crash. If ever there was a reason for someone to want to work towards a liberal and democratic system, he's that guy.'

'Petra thinks he's the Messiah.'

'Maybe he is. We could all do with the Messiah.' Eli looked at his deputy. 'Is this about Petra?'

Rafi said nothing, took another swig of wine and then glared at Eli. 'Maybe.'

'What? You think she's going to sleep with Silver Dove or something? Grow up, Rafi. First of all, she wouldn't, she's too professional. And second, it really isn't your business what she does, is it? Be reasonable, *achi*. The operation is running on tram wheels. Five raided Treesmith's flat two days ago. They found nothing but, since Silver Dove warned him, our guy has now got the student group leader's endorsement. That show was all we were trying to do and it worked, it was beautiful.'

'Yeah, I guess.'

'You know sometimes things actually do work out.'

A server cleared the platter and the two men fell silent. Despite having the sound buffers on the table and the volume level in the restaurant being high, it was protocol not to speak when someone was in proximity. They didn't even realise they were doing it. Around them tables of friends were laughing and talking, a hen party was underway two tables away and the bride-to-be was unwrapping small gifts to oohs and aahs. Some genuine, some exaggerated.

'I want to do something off grid,' Eli said. 'I want to check out this Grant D Miller, find out who he is and whether this really is coming down from Trump.'

'You're surely not asking me to help you do something that may not be authorised?'

Eli didn't have to answer Rafi's question because the server returned just then with bowls of pasta and salad.

'And I want Petra and Segev on the team. What I've got in mind is too big for just you and me,' Eli said. 'If I'm wrong, I'll take full responsibility and you will say that you thought it was authorised, is that understood? But if I'm right, well… let's see.'

'Why do you want Segev and Petra?' Rafi said.

Eli pushed the pasta in the bowl around before he spoke.

'What if Grant D Miller's cover story was just a construct?'

Eli watched Rafi as his deputy nodded a little, as if the action was helping him to absorb the idea.

'Who would do that?' Rafi said. 'I mean, this isn't simply posting some images on someone's Facebook page to make them look bad. It would be a massively complex operation. But who would actually do that?'

'We would, Harel would, if he thought there was something in it for him and his guys in the government.'

Rafi had his head down as he twirled spaghetti around and around his fork. Finally, the fork spinning stopped and he looked up. 'I don't know, Eli. That might be one step too far even for them. And there's another thing; operational. It would be really complicated because of date stamps. Our people would have had to check it out before the negative operation was authorised.'

'What if they didn't check it out thoroughly? Everybody is overworked, due diligence procedures are being skipped because of the war. That's why I want Segev on board. That's why I want to do it off grid. If we can't check it out internally, then we'll do it outside. And we'll do it right.' Eli pushed his uneaten pasta away from him. 'What do you think, *achi*? Do you think it's worth checking out?'

'I think you're an asshole, Eli, but you have a knack for smelling trouble. Count me in.'

Eli exhaled the breath he hadn't realised he'd been holding. '*Tov*, so here's how I'm thinking this is going to work: we're going to the place where Grant D Miller's family is supposed to have come from and we'll be out of contact with the Office for 72 hours. We don't use the Techtruck or the hire-car *sayan* or any of the internal systems and we say we're doing a security training exercise. We say we're testing it in the UK and plan to roll it out throughout the embassies and the local communities so we can establish new security protocols.'

'What about Harel?'

'He won't care. As soon as you say "basic security", he'll be bored.'

'Eli, I get that we can travel with cash, leave phones behind and disappear for a few days but we can't manage without access to our data if that's what you're thinking. Not when there's research to do.'

'Yes, we can. Petra can go into Corudon and use their data facilities and there's something else I want her to get from them.'

'Have you asked her?'

'Not yet,' Eli smiled. 'But I am the world's greatest spy runner, aren't I?'

'World's greatest asshole, if you ask me. What do you want me to do?'

'I want you to make contact with that old retired cop. You know, the one we used to find out about Red Cap's wife. He'll be able to get access to the police central computer so we can do some basic background checks.'

'Easy.'

Eli waved for the bill. 'No phones, only cash, vinyl tradecraft. Tomorrow I'm buying two new laptops that aren't connected to our network. And before I forget, make sure your plumbing kit is to hand. We're going to need it.'

'Plumbing kit? What are you thinking? It's one thing using old sources to gather operational information, quite another to do a break-in.'

Eli stood up as the server approached, 'When did you get so cautious? We do what we have to do. Bring the plumbing kit.'

Chapter 26

Petra rolled over in bed and enjoyed the quiet of the morning. Overnight it had poured and she'd been conscious of water cascading beyond her window. Being inside and warm, in her cocoon, with a sense that she was doing something useful with Silver Dove, something that only she could do, was pleasing. Sure, the future was dangerous for him but he was aware and committed.

Petra stretched diagonally before reaching for her phone and checking her newsfeed. Always a downer. She looked at the headlines and resolved not to read on. Just for today. Just for a few hours.

Eli had messaged her the night before asking to meet up for a coffee as early as she could make it. Petra's expectation was that it would be part debrief and part herogram – Silver Dove could not have gone any better, whatever Rafi suggested with his stories of operations that had gone wrong, where the Office had been duped by cunning Palestinians. Sometimes Rafi was about as subtle as a sledgehammer. Silver Dove was everything that Rafi wasn't – he was a thinker, not a glory boy. He had integrity and emotional awareness. In many ways he reminded her of Eli, other than that he was young and unscarred by the soul erosion of working for an intelligence organisation. An unwelcome thought came to her. Yes, Silver Dove reminded her of what Tom might have been if he hadn't been murdered.

Now out of bed, Petra padded to the bathroom and showered, still thinking about Tom. Well, what she was doing would be for him, it would be for Sahar, it would be for all the good people who had lost their lives trying to make lives better for other people.

Less than an hour later, Petra was sitting with Eli in a cavernous coffee shop on Esher High Street. It had taken her forty minutes to get there. She had driven around multiple one-way systems looking in her rearview mirror and then, after she'd parked, she'd walked up the road against the direction where she was supposed to go, crossed into a golf course, where her vistas were unimpeded and then circled in the direction of the high street. It was protocol. It was procedure. And now that she was on a roll, Petra was determined not to screw up.

Inside the cafe the ceiling was high and there were old tiles on the wall from its previous life as a dairy. The coffee was good, so was the cinnamon bun. But once again, Eli looked lousy, tired, worn out. She didn't know how old he was but he wasn't wearing it well.

'This is nice,' she said. 'You okay?'

'Yeah, lot going on.'

'I bet there is. You read my report, didn't you? Believe me, Eli, Silver Dove is one thing you don't have to worry about. Whatever Rafi may have said, I am confident that this agent can be trusted. Has Rafi said anything?'

'Yes, he has,' Eli said. 'But that's not why I'm here. Petra, there's something else where I really need your help.'

'Okay, go on, what is it?'

'How did you leave things with Matt?'

'Matt? What's he got to do with anything?'

'Do you know where he is? Is he still with Corudon or is he on a security operation somewhere?'

'Honestly, I don't know. The way I left it… it wasn't good. He was angry, I was angry, and I told Corudon that I wouldn't be available for a few months because I had something else going on. I'm freelance, I can do that.'

'What if I said that I'd like you to go into Corudon at the earliest opportunity and do some…' Eli paused, 'do some research for us?'

Petra was still for a few moments while she thought about what Eli had just said. 'I think I would probably say "No way and why can't you do your own research?"'

'A perfectly reasonable and rational response,' Eli said.

Around them there was a clatter of coffee-drinking mothers, pension-spending seniors, office geeks and gym bunnies, there to grab their caffeinated sweets and treats, unaware of the secret world buffering up against them. Why on earth did Eli want her to go into Corudon? Petra looked at him, in an attempt to gauge what was going on with him, how much of it was what she called, to his face, his spy-runner shit and how much was genuine.

Yes, she'd seen that look before. He wanted her for something and he was going to try to manipulate her.

Petra leaned back against her chair and smiled, 'Go on then, spit it out. I'm sure I'm going to love it.'

'Very well. There's an operation underway and, at best, I don't believe the appropriate due diligence has been carried out before it was greenlit. At worst—'

'Appropriate due diligence? What exactly do you mean and why are you dressing it up in Officespeak. Come on, Eli. I said "Spit it out", for God's sake.'

He opened and shut his mouth for a second, no doubt trying to work out what he was going to say. He also shifted around on the wooden chair and it wasn't to get more comfortable, at least not physically.

'Come on. What's the operation? Something dirty, I presume.'

'About as dirty it could get. Did Rafi ever talk to you about what he did when he was in *Kidon*?'

'Not really, but I get it.' Petra looked around, scanning the cafe afresh. Even with the sound buffers on the table and the hard surfaces all around them and the cacophony of other voices distorting sound in the cavernous space, she was wary.

In a low voice, she heard Eli describe the situation with what might be an American with fake cover. An American who was trying to initiate a targeted assassination that was supposed to benefit the continuance of arms supplies to Israel.

'Okay,' Petra said. 'You're suggesting it's the old quid pro quo?'

'That's only one of the problems,' Eli said. 'I don't know if what I'm thinking is true. And if it is, my other concern is that it could be us who've created the fake cover. I know that sounds—'

'Paranoid?'

'If you want to put it like that, but that's why our research and fact checking has to be done externally, hence Corudon.'

'You don't ask for much, do you?' Petra said. 'I presume there's something specific that you want me to try to find out.'

'Yes.'

He looked relieved. It was clear to Petra that this was hard for him and she almost reached out to pat his hand, but stopped herself. He went on, 'You told me that Corudon assisted one of the companies within the National Grid that had an issue with Ofgem and there was a payout.'

'I remember,' Petra said. 'It was one of the jobs I did, just a small part. I interviewed some of the senior managers for *Finance Times* to try to find out who was leaking stories to the media. I also did another National Grid job recently.'

'Even better. If we could get all the background tech on the grid itself, then it just might prove to be helpful.'

Petra leaned back in her chair and put her hands behind her head and looked at Eli across the table. It was clear that he was under stress. He was tired, most likely overtired. To Petra, Eli's idea of some sort of deep-fake cover, either by Israel or by some other actor, seemed unlikely. It wouldn't be the first time that Eli had got something wrong. They all made mistakes, herself included.

'Eli, I have to tell you, I'm not convinced. Yeah, I know we're paid to make assumptions. I had all that from Alon, as I'm sure you did. But this sounds… don't be offended, but it sounds like one of those conspiracies that float around on the internet.'

'You don't think I know that? I get it and I'm not happy about it. It's not my style. I'm just a regular guy trying to do a job, sitting in front of a friend asking for help.'

'Disingenuous, Eli,' Petra said. 'And unoriginal, being a pitiful homage to *Notting Hill*.'

Eli smiled. It made him look less weary.

Petra enjoyed seeing some of the stress drain away from him with the smile. She went on, 'Typical spy-runner shit, and just the type of thing you would do.'

'But will you do it?'

'If it makes you happy,' she said and only later on did she realise that she meant it.

'There's something else,' Eli said. 'Another job, in Europe, nothing to do with Silver Dove or this other business, but they've asked for you. And it's important.'

'When? Where?'

'Thursday, Budapest. Work Friday, come back Saturday.'

'Nice.'

'If you can get into Corudon before then, I'd really appreciate it.'

Chapter 27

It was a cold Thursday morning in early February and pouring with rain when Petra came out of Piccadilly Circus tube station and walked up Regent Street. Around her the shops advertised the tail end of the sales with '70% off' signs, slashes of red that brightened an otherwise grey day. London wasn't at its best, it looked run-down, waiting for spring, but to Petra it was the best day of the week. Petra was on her way to Corudon. Later on, she'd be at Heathrow, on the early-evening flight to Budapest. As she marched up Regent Street, she went at a clip; she had no time to waste.

Despite what she'd said to Eli, she did not expect that getting into Corudon would be a problem. At least, not a logistic one. Her pass was still current and Steve, the security guy at the front door, knew her; he even opened the door for her.

Petra marched up to the front desk and leaned over it with a smile.

'Hello, Jeannie,' Petra said to the rounded woman behind the desk. 'Is that some sort of new uniform?'

Jeannie was bursting out of a white shirt with 'C's' printed across it in orange. The other women behind the high desk were wearing similar tops.

'Yeah, what do you think?'

Jeannie wasn't just a receptionist, she'd been at Corudon for years and was more like a front of house, *maître d'* of the company.

'I like it, very taking.' Petra reached for the pen and prepared to scrawl a signature as Jeannie printed a day pass. 'Is Felix around? Or his assistant? I've been contacted by BBC Verification about a piece I wrote for *Finance Times* and there are some figures I need to check.' Petra grimaced an expression to suggest that it was all a big hassle and she'd rather be doing something else.

'Felix is off site today, a conference. His assistant is with him.'

Petra had known that. That's why it had to be Thursday. Today was the first day of the annual homeland security conference at Kenwood House in Hampstead and Felix wouldn't miss the event under any circumstances. What's more, he wouldn't be able to resist taking an assistant with him. How many times had Petra seen it, Felix in his tweed three-piece, ambling around the building, imagining he was a guru of the private security industry with his assistant and, if possible, an unlucky intern, in tow.

Boy, did he love those walk-and-talk rambles. All the while he'd spout his brand of corporate security bollocks delivered in an opinionated lowland Scots accent. For Felix, the annual conference was the most anticipated date in his calendar and then some, because it gave him the heady chance to mix with his old MI5 pals and pretend he was still relevant and hadn't had to leave under a cloud of what Petra suspected was incompetence. The conference was catnip to the creep.

'That's a real shame,' Petra frowned. 'I really need to get this wrapped up today. I'm away this evening until next week and it'll look bad if we don't respond promptly to verification requests. It looks like we're trying to hide the truth.'

'We don't want that, do we? How about I give you an access code for the archives,' Jeannie said. 'It's not as if it's any material you haven't previously been working on.'

'Really? Thanks, Jeannie. I owe you. If you need me, I'll either be on the fourth floor next to data depository or at the drinks station at the back. Are they still buying in those Italian almond biscuits with the chocolate chips?'

'I wouldn't know,' Jeannie said with a grin and handed Petra a scrap of paper with the scrawled code.

Petra winked at her.

It took Petra no more than fifteen minutes to download the data that Eli had asked for. There was barely enough time for her to drink her coffee and indeed she had it poured into a takeaway container. After she'd thanked Jeannie with one of the biscuits in a paper napkin, Petra was outside the building and walking along Savile Row towards Regent Street. It was still raining steadily and she hunched into her hooded Barbour, resolved to get out of town and get home. There was plenty of time for her to pack and she might even manage a workout before her flight.

'What are you doing here? Petra?'

Petra turned and found herself face to face with Matt. It was the first time she'd seen him since she'd told him to let himself out. As she stood on the street for a few moments, she was lost for words.

'Just some, er…' she picked up the thread and recovered. 'Some verification shit I had to do on an old story I wrote for *Finance Times*. You?'

'I've got to see Greg in an hour. Do you want a coffee? I want to talk to you.'

'I've got to be somewhere,' Petra said.

'That's not good enough,' Matt said. 'We have unfinished business. You slung me out, no explanation and just some half-baked statement that I didn't know you. I've sent you countless messages and nothing. I deserve more than that, Petra. I really do.' His face was contorted with anger and passers-by had noticed it.

'I'm sorry.' Petra didn't want to have a row in the street. 'Let's have a coffee, not at Corudon, somewhere else, and I'll try to explain why this isn't a good time for me.'

He seemed to be slightly mollified. Petra stalked in the direction of Beak Street and led Matt into a shiny little coffee shop that promised Arabica coffee and Buddha bowls of flavour. After ordering a decaf, she perched on one of the high metal chairs and prepared to be attacked for not wanting to have a relationship with him. Perhaps if he had his rant, he would feel honour had been done. But what he said surprised her, and Petra thought she was beyond surprising.

'I figured it out,' Matt said, stirring brown sugar into his espresso. 'This isn't about some deep-seated inability to commit. It's about being a Jew.'

'I beg your pardon?'

'And…' He was now pointing with his forefinger while still holding the spoon. 'You're not even a proper Jew, are you? You don't go to synagogue, you don't do anything Jewish. So that when this crap happens in Israel, you feel guilty for what you're not doing. And you would feel guilty if you forgot all about it and had a life with me.'

Never, in the entire time that she'd been seeing Matt or been in any other relationship, had Petra felt more alienated and also more stunned. And angry. It welled up inside her like a chemical reaction and she felt it in her chest, in her lungs, in her clenching and unclenching fists – Petra badly wanted to lash out. How dare he say she wasn't a proper Jew, what the hell did he know about that? What exactly did he think Jews were?

Petra swallowed hard. She *had* to contain her anger – there were bigger issues at stake. It took all her will to compose herself. She looked down and, when she looked up, she leaned forward, elbows on the table, and propped up her face. 'Matt, you're a nice man who deserves a nice woman. Jew or no Jew, I'm not that woman. I never was and I never considered us a long-term thing. I'm sorry if you thought that but you have to try to understand.'

'The only thing I understand is that you're a fucking bitch.'

'I'm sorry,' was all she could say. But she wasn't sorry at all.

Chapter 28

Before October 7, Eli had always enjoyed the side-trips to Europe. There was always an opportunity to find some time to wander around somewhere new and get a fresh perspective. But that was before. Now, as he made his way through the narrow streets of old Buda, taking a circuitous route to meet his contacts, all he could see were ghosts. Half a million Hungarian Jews had been murdered by the Nazis, some of them no doubt came from these same streets. Jews who considered themselves to be the crème de la crème, as Oded, a case officer and grandchild of Hungarian Holocaust victims liked to describe himself to Eli, thus distancing himself from the agricultural shtetls of Eastern Europe, where Eli's family had grubbed around, growing root vegetables for the pot in between pogroms. Oded was a pompous fool to say that the Hungarian Jews were the elite but, when Eli walked past the Dohány Street synagogue in the VII district, visible from afar with its twin minarets, he had to admit there was truth in the statement. It was a spectacular building, bang next door to the place where Theodor Herzl had been born, without whom maybe they wouldn't be in this damn mess. Or maybe they would.

What must it have been like for Holocaust survivors to come back and see their elegant homes and lives destroyed? To remember those Saturdays when the good and great of the Jewish community flocked to that beautiful building. Was it the same sense of anomie that he had in the moments before sleep took him? The sense that since October 7 everything had changed and he was in another reality? Is that how those long-dead people felt when their worlds started to crumble?

Get a grip.

Eli put the thoughts and the ghosts aside and continued to walk through Vorosmarty Square, with his briefcase of cash. He stopped outside a window selling an array of scarves. The stop was to give Boaz's watchers the chance to check him from all angles, as well as overhead. Boaz meant what he said when he'd talked about preparation. Having carried the cash through the diplomatic channel at Heathrow, all Eli had to do for the moment was look around him with the casual gaze of a tourist, admiring his surroundings. The scarf shop was splendid and Eli thought for a moment about Gal. That green one draped over a dress would suit her. She could wear it on the slinky dress she'd worn when they went to the opera in Covent Garden. What had they seen? *Carmen*, he thought. Yes, *Carmen*. It seemed such a long time ago, but it was only a year – but it was before. Before. Before. In the meantime, Eli hadn't spoken to Gal for days, at least not at length nor in any way that resembled a relaxed chat. He wanted to talk to her about anomie but Gal was always at work, around the clock, and, when Eli had managed to talk to her, the conversation had been fact-based, a check-in on family members and their status. Gal's sister's son was now on active service in a front-line brigade and, as a consequence, his mother was falling apart. Then, of course, there was Doron, back with his unit, only able to phone home when he was at base camp, because all soldiers' phones had been confiscated for fear of location tracking. *Carmen* and operas and scarves seemed like another life.

Just then Eli saw a man across the road with a beanie and a grey parka. He gave Eli an almost imperceptible nod. That was the all clear that he hadn't been followed, so Eli left the shop front and continued his progress towards the meeting point.

Ahead of Eli lay the hotel, the Novotel Budapest Centrum. It was a fine building and perfect for their requirements, with a mezzanine level suspended over the lobby that was used for conference break-out meetings, but seemed designed for surveillance. In the lobby itself there were side tables for two people, with a perfect view of the main staircase. Truly, it was made for spies.

Eli approached the main desk and launched into his flawless French, perfected after his spell at Ecole Jeannine Manuel. It had been his diplomat father's third posting in five years and the one that Eli remembered with the most horror. He'd arrived mid-term at the international school, small for his age and with neither fluent French nor English. On Sunday walks by the Seine with his parents and sister, they'd foraged through the second-hand books on trestle tables. That's where he'd found an old Agatha Christie book, *Le meurtre de Roger Ackroyd*. By the time the first term had ended, Eli had perfect French and a love of golden-age detective fiction, a guilty secret that he only owned up to, to Gal.

'Bonsoir, pouvez-vous me dire où se trouve la salle de réunion, car je suis attendu.' Eli was directed to an anodyne meeting room on the first floor with overhead lighting, a whiteboard at one end, white trestle tables and black leather chairs. It didn't just say 'work', it shouted the word. The dining room of the Art Deco hotel might be somewhere to linger when a deal was done but this meeting room was functional in the extreme.

Eli mentally prepared himself. He chose a seat at one end of the table; there he took out the laptop with its newly applied logo and opened up a spreadsheet. It looked genuine, and indeed, if anybody had bothered to examine it, they would have been convinced by the figures that supported his backstory. But it was all fake and part of the show. It didn't much matter whether or not the man he was about to meet believed it, it was necessary and, in an odd way, it was respectful. It showed that whoever they really were, and they certainly weren't owning to be Israelis, they treated their partners with respect and maintained the story.

After ten minutes the door to the room opened and Boaz came in with a slim, grey-haired man who looked as if life had permanently dissatisfied him. But despite the expression, he had the sharpest of eyes. They raked over Eli as if trying to scratch beneath the surface and discover who these alleged buyers were and why they wanted unrestricted access to his bonded ware-house for ten hours, no questions asked.

'I'm very pleased to meet you,' Eli said. 'Parlez-vous français?'

'I prefer to talk in English,' Laszlo Oszkar said.

'Very well, not my best language but I will try not to make too many mistakes,' Eli said in English with a pronounced French accent. He lifted the briefcase onto the table and pushed it towards Laszlo, who was still standing.

'You may count or you may take, but it is the figure that has been agreed in the denominations you stipulated. In exchange you have a document for me, plus pass and access codes and the assurance that we will have a full nine hours' unrestricted access to the site – including parking facilities. Is that clear?' Eli said.

Laszlo nodded. He opened the briefcase and Eli saw the light of greed in his eyes. Eli exchanged a glance with Boaz. He'd seen it too. It was a funny thing, some agents had to be convinced that they were working for a cause, whatever that might be. Others just wanted cash. Thank God for capitalism. Eli went on, 'After the nine hours and the conclusion of our access, I will meet you here with the same amount of money, plus a bonus if we're completely happy, to assure you of our good hopes for the next time.'

This bonus and the promise of further money-making opportunities was an innovation. It was Boaz's idea. Without saying as much, Eli was trying to suggest that whatever illegal activity was underway, whether it was drugs, stolen art or arms, there would be more briefcases from these well-mannered and respectful individuals. Over Laszlo's shoulder, Eli saw Boaz nod again. It was a nod of approval and Eli smiled to himself. It was a funny moment when someone one had mentored gave their approval. It felt as if a baton had been passed.

Laszlo Oszkar was also nodding, but more visibly. He almost doffed his non-existent hat, and it was clear from his body language that the arrangements were more than satisfactory.

'The day after tomorrow,' he said. 'At the same time.'

'Absolument. Exactly the same time. I thank you,' Eli said as he stood and shook Laszlo's hand, the signal that the meeting was over and the bond warehouseman could go.

Chapter 29

While Eli passed over the briefcase, Petra was in charge of 25 fake music students on a cultural excursion to Europe. Their starting point was Budapest, there, supposedly, to study the Austro-Hungarian Empire and its influence on Liszt, Strauss and the Romantic period. They were all between the ages of eighteen and twenty-one and were not music students but on active duty in the Israeli army, assigned to an arms and electronics unit. Petra's job was to get them and their instruments in place – without incident. If anyone in the group was challenged and asked to play the musical instruments they carried there would be a problem. There were twelve in the group who had competence with their instruments but, if they were to be professionally interrogated, not enough artistry to be convincing.

'What we need,' Eli had said, 'is for you to pick them up at the airport, take them for a tour around the city and get them to the quay. Once on board the boat, our people take over. Eight hours later the boat returns to the quay and you escort them to the train station and hand them over to the guide there.'

'Understood,' Petra had said but, when she saw the group, there was another problem. The group was too big, too noticeable. They came through the baggage hall into the arrivals hall in a noisy mass and gathered around Petra, who was holding up a Rendor Tours sign. They were attracting attention. Other tourists were looking at them. An elderly man and his wife were pointing at the instruments. Petra put her arm on a small blonde girl, who looked younger than 18.

'What's your name?'

'Tali.'

'We've got to get the group on the bus as quickly and as quietly as possible. Understood? Quietly.'

The girl was quick. She nodded. 'I get it.'

With Tali by her side, who glared and muttered in Hebrew, Petra checked the kids off with a clipboard and hustled them on to the bus. Once they were seated, Petra used a prepared script to describe the sights that they were passing; this was for the benefit of the driver. He at least didn't seem interested in the group.

The boat was moored on the Buda side of the river, a location chosen because it was a less popular location than the Pest side. It was near the Szilágyi Dezső Square and, when Petra herded the group off the coach towards the gangplank, she was relieved. Whatever was planned, this at least looked real. Convincing. Music wafted off the boat and lights lit up the main decks.

By the dock, boxes of supplies were stacked up in wire crates and only the presence of muscled porters wearing uniform hoodies with the Rendor Tours logo suggested that the boxes might contain not just the food and drinks needed for the mini-cruise, but goods of far greater value.

Once aboard, one of these fake porters directed the group towards a small lounge aft. There they sat in groups, in the armchairs or the sofas, near the baby grand piano, talking quietly among themselves, looking around at the unfamiliar surroundings. One of them, a kid with a shock of red hair, sidled up to the bar, leaned across it and tried to order himself a drink. The frown he got from the 'barman' quelled him.

Using another prepared script, Petra spoke. She welcomed the group on board and described the safety procedures on the boat and the evening's music programme. This was for the benefit of maintenance staff who had access before the boat left the quay. Even though it was unlikely that the men in blue overalls spoke English or if they did would be interested, Petra talked about Liszt and Strauss. During her spiel she saw Eli arrive and sit down by the window next to an overweight but attractive guy. A third man came up to them. He had a buzz cut and wore a short-sleeved white shirt with epaulettes, and a navy tie. He muttered a few words in the other men's ears; they nodded and he strode away. Minutes later the maintenance crew disappeared, the engines rumbled into action and the boat slipped its moorings.

This was the signal for the stony-faced barman to come into the middle of the lounge and address the group in Hebrew. He was army through to his bootstraps and Petra understood why he hadn't led the group through the airport. They would have been stopped in an instant. After a brief and precise speech, a screen connected to a laptop was brought out and a series of images was shown. To Petra it looked like small circuit boards sandwiched in a plastic casing with a lithium battery.

The next image was a pair of tweezers with a tiny tube.

The final image was in figures.

5000

8

25

'What's that all about?' Petra said to Eli who had just sidled up to her.

'There are 5000 units, 8 hours and 25 kids. That's without repacking into fresh blister packaging. But that's what those guys will be doing.' He gestured towards the guys in the hoodies who had acted as porters.

'What's this all for?' Petra said.

Eli gave Petra a long look. Then he said, 'If this works, you'll hear about it. If it doesn't, best you don't know.'

Just then, Eli's colleague made a short speech and then the kids got up and were led down the main stairs into the dining room where their workstations were already set up.

'So far, so good,' Eli said. 'Any problems?'

'They were too noisy. Too noticeable. People will remember the group, Eli.'

'That's not good. Despite our current relationship with the Hungarian government nobody wants to be embarrassed.'

'Maybe I'm over-reacting,' Petra said. 'Alon used to say, "The hat on the thief's head burns."'

' *Al rosh haganav bo-er hakovah*? Yeah. We only notice because we're the thieves. That's a way of ignoring risks.'

Eli gestured in the direction of the exit and the stairs down to the dining room. The boat's dining room was a long narrow space with tables on both sides of the area. But instead of tourists, there were two kids at each table. One snapped open the backs of the pagers and placed the components onto a rubber mat in the configuration that had been demonstrated in the lounge. Petra saw the second kid using tweezers to slip in one of the tubes from a tray in front of him or her. Then the first kid reassembled the pager and put it on another tray.

Each pager took less than a minute. The military type walked up and down between the tables, he watched, he adjusted trays for easier access and nodded at the guys who'd been on the deck in hoodies when a tray was near to completion. They came forward to shift it for packing. All the while Liszt's waltzes trilled in the background and seemed to be on a loop.

At the other end of the dining room there was an open buffet and a few eating tables for breaks.

Eli touched her elbow. 'Let's grab something to eat. I don't think we can contribute much except to get in the way.'

'Good idea,' Petra said.

Although she wasn't hungry, Petra helped herself to a sandwich and they found a sofa and a low table in a corner of the lounge, on the upper deck, away from the trestle tables, where the packing process was underway.

Petra looked out of the window, they seemed to be in the middle of the river, far away from either shore. 'We're quite far away from the shore. Is that part of the plan?'

'Well observed. Yes, it is part of the plan, in case we have to abort and evacuate,' Eli wiped his mouth and folded the cloth napkin. 'Now we need to talk about Corudon I read your report. You said you bumped into Matt and had a coffee with him. How is he?'

'Since you ask… not happy.'

'How's he ever gonna be happy without you in his life?' Eli said with a small smile.

'He said I wasn't a proper Jew because I didn't do anything, like go to *shul* and that's why I couldn't commit.'

Eli rolled his eyes. 'I don't know what a proper Jew is and I have no idea what he means. But one thing I don't think it means – and that's going through a load of rituals created thousands of years ago. Did you know Rafi's wife has got the bug?'

'Bug?'

'She's gone religious, ever since October 7. No milk and meat, no seafood, no TV on Saturday until the sun goes down.'

'Yeah, he said.'

'You know, in the middle of all this unbelievable shit that's going on, where people in Gaza are starving to death in the cold of their bombed out houses, hostages are dying in tunnels, people torn apart by grief, sixty thousand people forced out of their homes in the north because they're being attacked by Hezbollah, where there's a shortage of ceramic body armour for our soldiers, where the economy is going down the toilet because the reservists are at the front, the government is giving money to the proper Jews so they can set up training programmes to teach the likes of you and me how to pray. Proper Jew.' Eli almost snarled.

'You sound angry,' Petra said. 'Why don't we go for a walk on deck and look at the pretty lights.'

They made their way past the trestle tables where the operation to repackage the pagers was underway and stepped through sliding doors onto the wraparound deck. The cold was sharp, lights sparkled across the river and the skyline was lit up by the Hungarian Parliament Building. Its golden Gothic turrets reeked of an empire's power. Silhouetted against the building, Petra saw the red-headed boy, a few metres away, gazing avidly at the building.

Eli glanced at him and then leaned over the railing and seemed to be studying the water below. The music loop paused and then started again. Petra saw Eli check his watch.

'The kid's family probably came from here and he grew up with stories of the city. You know, Hungarian Jews consider themselves elite.' Eli sounded as if he had his anger under check, but he was looking at the water. 'But he's still a Jew.'

'A proper Jew?' Petra teased.

'I tell you what I think makes a proper Jew. One thing. One thing alone. It's asking questions. And when we stop asking questions of what is possible or not, what is right and what is wrong, well, then we lose our humanity. Sometimes, I genuinely don't know whether we, proper Jew or not, can ever get over this.'

'I know what you mean,' Petra said. There was silence between them. The water slapped against the side of the boat as they moved through it.

Eli looked up, reached out and took Petra's hand in his own. 'Go on, say it. What are you thinking?'

'If you despise someone and reject them, they get angry and they hate you. Just like Matt hates me. On a macro scale, didn't we despise and reject the people of Gaza? Didn't we underestimate their ability to organise themselves so effectively? Didn't we underestimate their anger?'

'I can't argue with any of that.'

Petra was aware of the warmth from Eli's hand as he held her own. She went on, 'You know, Eli, there's one thing about this work, among the lies and the games that we play where we manipulate people for our benefit; one thing that only we, who actually do the work, understand. It's the privilege of working under cover. Of not being Jews. And moving around without the yellow star of society's prejudices and expectations. Of meeting people like Sahar, who, like her brother, was brave and kind and intelligent and funny.'

'Yes, it is a privilege to see the other side of the argument because they don't know who we really are.' Eli took Petra's hand to his lips and kissed it. 'You know, you need a man who's your equal. That's not going to be easy.'

Petra looked up and away. She didn't know how to respond. But in looking up, she noticed something. The red-headed boy had moved. He was now holding up a bottle, his arm was outstretched towards the shoreline and the Parliament Building, as if in a silent toast. Then he drank.

Just then Petra heard the throttle of a grey dinghy with two Hungarian river police before she saw them in the black water. The boat swished through the water and a searchlight that almost blinded Petra snapped on as the boat kept up with the cruiser. Eli started to talk rapidly into his phone and she heard a judder from the cruise boat's engines as it began to slow down.

Petra leaned over the side and waved at a grim-faced woman standing in the prow of the boat with a conical device held to her mouth. 'Any ideas?' Petra said to Eli.

'Be accommodating.'

'*Figyelem*, attention!' boomed from the device, which was a loudspeaker.

'I'm sorry, do you speak English?' Petra yelled down. 'We're slowing down. Do you want to come aboard?'

'This vessel is not in the correct lane and the bridge is not responding.'

'I am so sorry; I apologise on behalf of Rendal Tours, who I represent. We are a British cultural music tour celebrating the international impact of Liszt and Strauss.'

Even in the darkness, the red-headed boy's face had gone

paler. He opened his mouth to say something, but Eli pre-empted any comment. 'Keep your mouth shut.'

'I—'

'*Sheket*,' Eli hissed and ran down the deck towards the bridge.

'We will rectify that immediately,' Petra said. 'Thank you for bringing it to our attention. Please accept our apologies.'

Petra could see a muttered exchange between the two cops, the woman who was at the prow and a stocky, crop-haired man at the controls. From her vantage point there seemed to be some disagreement. Then a decision.

The woman said, 'Do not repeat offence. We will stay here while you manoeuvre correctly. Understand?'

'Thank you.' Petra leaned over the rail. 'We are deeply appreciative of your tolerance.'

A long two minutes passed before the engine of the cruise ship juddered and slowly, slowly, the angle changed to head closer to the shore. All the while *The Blue Danube Waltz* was blasting out of the deck speakers. Ever after, the sound of the music made Petra's heart rate increase.

The police launch stayed with them for fifteen long minutes more. No doubt waiting to see if they would stray back to the middle of the Danube. When the police finally fired up the engine and disappeared into the darkness, Petra went down to the bar and helped herself to a drink. Long night or not, she needed it.

Chapter 30

Eli briefed the team in the first-class carriage on the 7.06 a.m. from King's Cross to Newark North Gate. They'd arrived at the station separately, in the morning darkness, and had bagged their seats around a table without online reservations. Each of them had paid for their tickets with cash at their different departure stations. Each of them had the unfamiliarity of a wallet of notes and change, plus a pencil and notebook to note down their expenses.

Last to arrive was Rafi, who strode down the almost empty carriage and tossed his rucksack and briefcase into the rack above the seats and settled into the aisle seat, next to Petra. He had that early-morning, freshly showered smell and his hair was wet. There was another big difference – he was clean-shaven; the beard that had made him look so striking was gone. He also looked a lot younger. Petra stroked her own chin. 'New look?'

'Eli,' Rafi said by word of explanation. 'He said it was giving him a rash.'

Across the table Segev smiled with politeness at the weak joke and Eli scowled but he didn't really look angry, he just had the expression Petra had come to expect lately: exhaustion. It was the first time she'd seen him since coming back from

Budapest and the moment of sentimentality on the deck might never have happened.

The shrill sound of the guard's whistle rang across the carriage and the train began to move along the grey platform. It rumbled out of the station, past the flats with lights on in the early morning while within the train the announcements played to welcome them on board.

Eli said, 'Any problems so far?'

'I feel naked,' Petra said. 'No phone, no ID, only cash and a bag of change. How are we supposed to communicate with each other?'

'Phone boxes and pre-arranged meets at set times.'

'You're kidding.'

From the rucksack that was on his lap Eli took out four ordnance-survey maps. 'I've marked the phone boxes closest to our locations. Once we have our transport organised, Segev will dismantle any nearby cameras. We'll use the boxes as back-up drops. Other than that, we will have our pre-arranged meets.'

'Is this really necessary?' Petra said.

'Yes, I'm trying to make sure that we leave no imprint of ever having been here. Understood?'

Just then the guard came through the carriage asking to see their tickets and the orange-striped pieces of card were scanned. They nodded thanks and he passed on.

Eli went on, 'Petra and Segev will be staying at the Travelodge near the station. You pay cash for two nights. Rafi and I are at the Premier Inn, slightly out of town fifty metres away from a second-hand car dealer.'

'So what's the plan?' Rafi said.

'This afternoon you and I are will source transport. Meanwhile, Petra and Segev will talk their way into the location and assess the security weak spots. Then tonight, Rafi and I will do the plumbing and see what we can find.'

'Something I want to say,' Rafi said. 'I want to do the plumbing on my own.'

'Why?' Eli sounded surprised.

'I'm younger, fitter and more experienced at this type of activity. Eli, when was the last time you did a plumbing job?'

'When I was with you and that worked out just fine, didn't it?'

'This is an entirely different situation. Come on, man, this is my area, not yours, I know how to do this and if it goes wrong let's minimise the fall-out.'

'Forget it, if this goes wrong it's my responsibility. You need to be able to say it was my idea. You can only do that if I'm with you. And it won't go wrong.' Eli said.

'Oh yeah.'

'We're not expected and that's the biggest advantage. All we need is some luck and as Napoleon said… give me generals who are lucky.'

Rafi was about to answer when the breakfast trolley rattled down the aisle. They took advantage of what was on offer. For once, Petra's appetite was flagging and she pushed around the reheated flakes of scrambled egg and made a show of nibbling on the toast, while around her the men tucked in.

There was a lot about this operation that was making her feel uncomfortable, not least that she was assisting in breaking and entering, when she didn't have diplomatic immunity. Rafi was also uneasy which wasn't like him. If this went wrong, she could find herself under arrest with a prison sentence hanging over her. No wonder she didn't feel like food.

Four hours later Petra stood on the doorstep of a red brick house in the middle of a village near Newark. It was raining, as it seemed to have done for months, and she was cold in her corporate outfit of suit and raincoat. It was a damp cold, the type that penetrates bones. By her side Segev was holding up an umbrella with a freshly stencilled logo. Petra nodded to him and pressed the doorbell of the target house.

The target house was the third in the operational sequence. The first house was a neat cottage and on that dark, wet afternoon, both the lights and the TV were on. A woman had opened the door and looked as if she was in the middle of cooking.

Petra had apologised profusely and said she and her assistant worked for a marketing company and they were surveying ten random houses in five villages on the perimeter of Newark to establish attitudes about building on green belt land. It was a short qualitative survey to 'hear the truth of local people's voices'. This was a hot issue in rural areas and moments later Petra found herself in the large and lovely kitchen, jotting down the answers to the survey. Segev had stood nearby as if observing.

At the end of the short and successful interview, Petra eschewed the tea and biscuits, which were now cooling on a rack, and asked if there might be anyone else in the village who would agree to an interview. She left with a couple of names; she now had the makings of what they called a *glima*, a cloak for their approach to the target house.

As the door opened Petra put on her most charming smile. 'Good afternoon. I'm sorry to trouble you but your neighbours

Mrs George at 11 Summer Lane and Mrs Bruce at The Pantiles said you might be able to help me.'

'Oh, yes, Edna George is by the letter box, isn't she? I don't know about Mrs Bruce. You see, I'm not from round here,' a woman said in what Petra thought might have been a Cornish accent. 'I don't know a lot of people you see, I'm house-sitting. How can I help you?'

The woman was in her mid-50s. Short, grey hair and an unlined face clean of make-up. She looked tidy, orderly, sensible; the type of woman who made lists and did her chores on the same day every week. From another room Petra could hear the sound of Classic FM and a Mendelssohn symphony and, in the kitchen itself, Petra spotted a well-thumbed book of Wordsearch.

Without delay Petra launched into her spiel and by now she was fluent. She was Philippa Braham, with her colleague, Edmund Perez, who was shadowing her in his first job. Ms Kelly was a retired nurse and, for the last year or so, she'd supplemented her income by house- and pet-sitting. This job was for three months' duration and, since there were no pets, she had little to do except collect the post when it came, pay the utility bills from the account that had been opened and which she was authorised to use and keep the place dust-free. She'd never met the owners; everything had been organised through the agency who hired her and who took a percentage of her fee. Ms Kelly told Petra she reckoned the owners were a wealthy foreign family. Once a week a groundsman came by to check the property and also to see how the barns and outhouses were faring in the wet weather Ms Kelly reckoned that's where the family stored their personal belongings because there was nothing in the house. All of this she'd confided within ten minutes of Petra being there. It was like a dam breaking. It seemed that the woman spent a lot of time on her own and was only too pleased for the interruption.

Five minutes into the survey itself, Segev made his polite request to use the facilities.

'If you go into the hall, it's down the steps by the main staircase,' Ms Kelly said.

Segev disappeared and Petra rolled her eyes at Ms Kelly. 'Thanks. This is his first job and you know how hard it is for young people. Sorry for him to be a nuisance.'

'Don't you worry, seems like a nice young man,' the woman said. 'I detect an accent. Where's he from?'

'Montenegro,' Petra cited the agreed cover story for Segev, in the hope that they wouldn't find the one person in the UK who was fluent in Montenegrin. It seemed as if they were in luck. Ms Kelly smiled and said that she wasn't quite sure where that was. This allowed Petra to say she wasn't sure either. The two women were still laughing at their mutual ignorance when Segev slid into the kitchen and gave Petra the smallest of nods. It meant he had what he needed. But Petra wasn't happy about either the groundsman or what he was supposedly coming to check.

It was still raining and, from the kitchen window, Petra could barely see to the bottom of the garden and the barns attached to the property. She had no reason to go out there. As she shrugged herself into her wet raincoat, she nodded out at the rolling clouds. 'It's set for today. What are you supposed to do if the groundsman's not here to check on the barns if there's a storm? I hope they don't expect you to get a ladder out and fix a tile.'

Ms Kelly shrugged. 'Nothing. They told me that the insurance has specified key holders to the barn and it's the groundsman's responsibility.' As she spoke, she gave Petra an appraising look.

Had she pushed too hard? Back off, smooth over the rough patch.

Petra flashed a wide smile, 'Forgive me, I see loose tiles everywhere. I've just had to replace my own roof and that was a horrible job.'

Ms Kelly smiled and moved towards the door to open it for them; it was a signal, their time was up. If they didn't go, she would remember the people from the marketing company who were overly curious and who also overstayed their welcome.

Chapter 31

The corner of the pub where they sat was dark and too far from the fire to make much difference, but the food was okay and it sat in Petra's gut like a cushion, warming her for what she knew was going to be a long night ahead.

Across the table she sensed anxiety coming off Eli – it was like static and it had spread to the rest of them. Rafi's usual upbeat chat was absent and Segev seemed to retreat further into himself, if that was at all possible. While they ate, Petra studied Eli, his grey eyes, the crease between his brows – if Eli was anxious, maybe he was considering the consequences of failure.

From the laminated menu Petra chose a pudding to follow the steak and jacket potato. This was Petra's pre-operation choice, particularly on a cold night. How many times had she racked up the calorie count in the expectation of a long night of surveillance? Too many to count.

Eli was talking. 'Okay. We have some facts, and we have some questions. Unfortunately, we have more questions than facts and that's what tonight is about. Our target is now not the house, it's the barns. However, as Rafi and I observed this afternoon, to get to the barns we have to either go through the house or climb over the perimeter walls of the property and adjoining houses. It's a well-chosen location, which is a clue in itself.'

'Who do we congratulate?' Rafi said.

'That's what we want to know.' Eli took out a pen and a Moleskine notebook from his inner pocket. With deliberation. he drew a diagram. 'Using the information Segev gathered, the easiest route to the barns is through the ground floor of the house.'

'With that woman sleeping upstairs?' Petra said, aware it was an unnecessary comment.

'It's not ideal but I've done this before,' Rafi said pointedly.

Eli went on, 'Petra is in the car here, Segev disables the motion sensors on the perimeter, then he positions himself on the roof of this garage here. Okay? He has sightlines to Rafi and me, the street in front of the house and Petra. Segev is the comms hub. He has a torch. Two rapid flashes is a warning. Three flashes is Daylight and we abort the mission. Understood?'

'Do you have any idea what you're looking for in the barn?' Petra said.

'Good question. Once Rafi and I are in the first barn, we split up and tackle two quadrants each.' Eli looked over at Rafi to emphasise the point. 'That's why it needs two of us.'

'If you insist,' Rafi said.

'I do. We're looking for evidence. If there is paper, we take it; we don't have time to photograph it. Boxes, then we open, but we won't have time to reseal them. We'll be inside each barn for no more than ten minutes. And I hope it will take Rafi no more than five minutes to disarm any motion sensors on the outside of the barns.'

'It should be enough,' Rafi said.

Eli held her gaze in a concentrated way. It told her not to

argue the point. 'If it's Daylight, Petra, you drive off and leave us. Is that understood?'

'Okay I get it,' she said now feeling as anxious as Eli looked. This could all go very wrong.

'What is your story in the event that you're challenged by a passing policeman? How are you going to explain sitting in a car on your own, in the middle of the night, two hundred miles from your home?'

'I'm going to say that I've been having some mental-health issues, I couldn't sleep and so I just drove. I was too tired to keep driving, so I thought I would sleep in the car.'

Eli frowned. 'That's really not great. Let's just hope you don't have to use it.'

Three hours later, Petra was in the Ford Fiesta, still trying to think of a better reason for her to be there if she was challenged. The yellow light she'd noticed on the dashboard had turned to red when she was parking. No doubt the car needed an urgent oil change but it only had to get them back to Newark so that should be possible. The only other light was from the houses, where an outside light twinkled and made the puddles on the road shine like oil. What was she doing there? If she was given the opportunity to say that she had mental-health issues, it didn't seem that far from the truth.

It was still raining and so much water ran down the windscreen that she had to use the wipers just to see if Segev's torch flicked on. It didn't. This village was dead – there was no shop, no pub, no street lights, and as Petra sat in the cold discomfort, she willed herself not to keep checking her watch. On automatic, she scanned the darkness for any movement and also wondered what people inside the houses were doing. How about the woman who was baking biscuits? Why wasn't Petra indoors, pottering in some domestic way? Yeah, right, she could just imagine it, her baking a cake and Matt in the background putting up shelves for the collection of trinkets they'd bought on holiday.

What was Ms Kelly, the retired nurse, doing? How suspicious was she of her visitors? Had she gone to bed, or was she waiting for the creak of a board in the house that would signal that there was a break-in.

Petra checked her watch again.

'Ready?' Eli said.

'Yeah.'

Eli had his back to the door to try to shield Rafi from the street. Rafi was busy; he held a 5x5-centimetre key pad with a small screen and two plastic-coated wires coming out of the base. He slid the wires in the gap between the wooden door and the door frame, just below the lock, and keyed in the details from the reading, pressed 'enter' and there was a click as the latch slipped back.

'Ready,' Rafi said.

'Yeah.'

Rafi nudged the door open, so that it was wide enough for them both to slip in. He was first, Eli right behind him, and the two men stood in the darkness of the hall, hearing each other's breathing in the silence. Eli closed the door behind them.

For a few moments they stood trying to adjust to the darkness and listening, listening hard. From the first floor there was no sound, no snoring, no radio, no indication that there was anyone else in the house. The house slept. Eli watched

Rafi lead the way in the direction of the kitchen. It was the second door on the left and he walked as if he knew where he was going. Clearly, he did. Rafi had studied the floorplan and was prepared.

Despite his seniority, Eli was content that Rafi lead; in fact, he'd planned it this way. The younger man's experience in this type of illegal-entry operation was unsurpassed and it was necessary that experts did what experts did – Rafi was an expert.

Ahead, Rafi paused on the threshold of the door between hallway and kitchen and beckoned Eli to follow him. Inside the kitchen Eli was aware of the radiant heat from an Aga lodged in an alcove against a brick wall. It was a rectangular room with a solid table in the middle and, a bow window next to a side door that showed a patch of dark night. Just enough to see. The two men padded towards the door and Rafi crouched over the lock. Eli tried to get closer to see what was holding them up and felt rather than saw Rafi's glare. He stood still as Rafi opened his rucksack and took out a spraycan that was about the size of his palm. He sprayed both lock and bolt and the hiss of the canister seemed loud in the silent room. At last, he stopped and Rafi eased back the latch; the back door clicked open. At once there was a rush of cold damp air but, with two steps, they were outside, standing by a wooden chair and some empty plant pots. Eli took a deep breath of rain-soaked air. They'd cleared the first hurdle.

Ahead of them, its shape blocking out the moonlit sky, stood the first barn.

'Ready?' Rafi said.

Eli nodded. He glanced up at the roof of the garage to the side of the house and could just make out Segev's silhouette.

Gaining entry to the barn was far more complex than the house, and noisier. The door bolts around the door had to be removed with miniature detonators that were so small, they had to be applied with what looked like a pen. They stuck to the metal with magnets. Once again, Rafi showed his expertise, and all Eli could do was stand back and admire how deft he was and continue to monitor darkness around Segev's torch.

Despite Rafi's skill, time was passing, and Eli felt the tension in every muscle of his body. He forced himself to check Segev, check his watch and scan the house behind them. It would only take one sleepless neighbour glancing out of the window on this rainy night and not only would his career be over, but Harel's operation would continue on its unstoppable course.

'*Gamanu*,' Rafi said and the small door swung off one hinge and they went into the darkness of the first barn.

Outside in the blue Ford Fiesta, Petra shifted in her seat and once more swept the street for movement. That was when she noticed Segev's torch flash twice in succession, then pause and then flash twice again. She checked the controls on the car, the ignition, the mirrors, the doors and her surroundings. If she was going to have to start driving, she needed to be ready to put her foot down and go. That's when she saw a shape approaching her; it was coming out of the cottage on the opposite side of the street, a bundle of dressing gown, rubber boots and umbrella. It was a woman.

She swayed from side to side, but she was steadfast in her approach towards the car and Petra had no choice but to wind down the window before the woman tapped on it.

'Are you all right, my lovely?' Her face was like currant bun, round with small eyes. 'I don't sleep, what with my back, and I've been watching you sitting here. Is there something wrong with your car?'

'It's very kind of you,' Petra said. 'Nothing to worry about. Honestly. I... I... please go back inside the house, you'll get wet out here.'

'You're not police, are you? You know, I've been watching the farmhouse that's rented out, the one where the house-sitter lives. There used to be a nice old couple there, lived there forever, then he had a fall and she couldn't cope on her own, so now they moved down south to be close to their son. The son, I think it's the son, comes by once a week or so and, of course, there's that pasty-faced woman living there. You're not police, are you?'

'No... no... nothing like that,' Petra said. 'The thing is... you see, I've been having some problems with my husband. I know it sounds crazy, but I didn't want to stay with any of my friends and we had a row and, well, I got in the car and started driving.'

Even to Petra's ear, the story sounded weak but she now put everything she had into it and her voice cracked with emotion. 'Please... please... you're very kind. I'm okay, I promise, I just need a little space and then I'll be on my way home. I'm terribly sorry if I disturbed you.'

That was a mistake. The woman's face crinkled with sympathy. 'What's your name? Mine's Kathy Boughton and I'm a trained counsellor. Why don't you come into the house and have a cup of tea?'

Oh, Christ!

'Honestly, Kathy, I'm okay.' Petra had changed the tone of her voice to make herself sound less crazy and more matter-of-fact. 'Really, I am. It was just a row. Nothing major, and I don't want to trouble you. I've made my point; he'll be worried about where I am, so I'll head home now.' Petra turned on the ignition and slipped the car into gear. 'So kind of you to come out in the rain and talk to me.' She drove off, watching in her rearview mirror the woman standing by the side of the deserted street, still clutching the umbrella over her fluffy dressing gown. Talk about bad luck. Oh, for the streets of central London where no one ever came out if anything looked suspicious and most times, they didn't even bother to call the police.

Petra drove 100 metres down the main road of the village at a gentle pace, all the time looking in her mirror, waiting for the woman to walk back into her house. As soon as she'd disappeared, Petra took a right turn into a small estate of modern houses and found a parking spot. She'd have to leave the car and go back to the meeting point on foot. It was still raining.

The interior of the barn was ordered. Eli positioned the head torch, switched it on and then stepped among the pallets that were lined up with precision. There were wooden crates on the pallets and nearby cardboard boxes and filing cabinets. From the other side of the barn, Eli could barely hear Rafi moving around, just the slash of his Stanley knife on boxes and the rasp of splitting wood on the crates. Eli unzipped his own rucksack and took out the eight-inch prybar and he set to work levering open the lid of the nearest crate. The wood creaked.

'*Ma yesh?*' Eli heard Rafi say from the other side of the barn. 'I don't know yet.'

Eli plunged his hand down through a layer of protective straw and felt before he saw something hard – was it plastic or

221

metal? 'Rafi, come here.' Eli pushed the straw aside and looked down at the grey block. It was about the size of a shoebox, with two vents at the top.

'I think I know what that is,' Rafi said.

'We'd better take one for evidence,' Eli said. 'And we'd better check the other crates. How many crates do you reckon there are?'

'Ten, twenty?'

'Rafi, see what's in those cardboard boxes while I open every second crate.'

The cardboard boxes were less interesting. They were filled with boxes of paper, artwork, drawings, as well as some still photographs. 'I don't know what this shit is,' Rafi said from across the barn.

'Take as much as you can, c'mon, we need to get on to the second barn. Let's finish up here.'

The two men emptied the rucksack and took out the pre-prepared pack; some empty beer cans, a used vape and a hoodie they'd picked up in a charity shop and prepared by treading into it some local mud. They spread the straw from the crates around as if the thieves had been looking for something of value but hadn't found it.

Eli looked around at the mess and packed the mystery machine into his now empty rucksack along with the paper evidence.

'On to the next barn.'

Eli stepped out into the darkness of the garden just as the air around him split from the sound of an alarm.

'Get back in the barn,' Eli said to Rafi. 'What is it?'

'Multi-tone siren. It's a car, about 50 metres due north.'

'That's too close,' Eli said.

'It might stop, and our car is west,' Rafi peered out of the barn door. He was completely calm. 'Segev has just double flashed. Your call, Eli. Wait for it to stop and do the other barn? Or run like hell.'

Chapter 32

Petra had taken up position on the same side of the street as the counsellor, behind a hedge and away from any sightlines the woman might have from her house. Before she crouched down, she signalled to Segev where she was and then dropped out of sight. Now in the darkness, by a hedge, she felt the rain drip, drip, drip down her neck and her nose run.

Just then she heard the high and low pitch of a car siren. It was coming from the direction of the road where she'd parked the car. Segev must have heard it too, his light flashed twice. Shit. There was nothing else for it. The car alarm might bring people onto the street. But without the car they were finished.

Petra heard the crunch of steps on the gravel beyond the hedge. She tensed and turned. It was Rafi and Eli.

'Where's the car?' Eli said.

'I moved it. There was a red light on the dashboard. I thought it was oil.'

'Don't tell me.'

Petra started running and heard them following her.

Eli insisted on getting back to London before they assessed what they'd found and they also had to travel by the same circuitous route. This time it was worse, as they travelled separately. First thing in the morning Eli sold the Ford Fiesta back to the second-hand dealer at a considerable loss but with the understanding that the ownership documents wouldn't be registered at DVLA. They separated at Newark Station and were on different platforms, from where they took trains in different directions.

Some hours later she lugged her overnight case through the London terminals; the case was now stuffed with the paperwork they'd gathered. It was going to be her job to assess it. But she had something else to do because, when Eli had called into the Office to pick up his messages, there was a coded message for Petra. It was Wasim. He had requested a contact. This was unusual and ahead of when they were supposed to be meeting. As soon as she was home, as soon as she'd dumped the case by her dining-room table, while she still had her coat on, she retrieved her work phone and called him.

'Hey, how's everything?' Petra affected the breezy tone of a social call.

'Hi,' Wasim said. 'Thank you for calling back.'

There was something in his tone that was tight; he sounded constrained.

Petra went on, 'What's up? Can it wait until tomorrow or do you want to meet this evening?'

'Thank you. I'm very happy that you're able to send someone to fix the heating. It keeps turning itself off. Yes… yes… at four o'clock? Yes, I'll be there.'

The call ended; Petra looked at the phone. 'Heating' was the danger code. He was with someone, that was obvious. While she thought about it, Petra opened her case and extracted the bag of documents. She took it upstairs, where she used a metal pole to open the door to the attic and spent five minutes uncovering a broken suitcase under a rolled-up carpet. She put the documents in the suitcase and, still with her coat on but now with cobwebs in her hair, sat at the top of the attic stairs and called Rafi on the work phone.

'I think there's a problem with Dove.'

'Just what we need from the golden boy.' Rafi sounded tired. 'Go on.'

'He messaged me, I called back. He wants to meet but he was with someone and he used the expression we agreed for danger. He suggested we meet this afternoon.' Petra gave Rafi the details and she could almost hear his mind whirring as went through the options.

'Call him back, record and send to me, we'll let the experts run it through the system to see if they can pick up anything from his voice. Meantime, change the location of the meet with him to *Meshi*.'

Meshi was one of the code words for meeting locations. It was a cafe next to Ealing Station. It was rarely used because it was at the end of the Central line, so a distance from central London, but it had great vantage points from the station and shops nearby. It was also safer than meeting at Dove's flat or exposing another safe house to an operation that might be compromised.

'Okay,' Petra said as she tried to keep both weariness and disappointment out of her voice. If the operation was going to go down the toilet, the implications were too much to consider.

'I'll set about the protocols necessary to meet Dove,' Rafi said. 'Listen, it might not be a big deal. It usually isn't. The real problem is that we're all doing three jobs at once.'

'I hope you're right.'

Petra made the second call to Wasim, pretending to be the plumbing company, and sent him the co-ordinates of the new location in Ealing. From his voice, she couldn't tell whether he was with someone or not. He was certainly strained but, as Rafi said, it could mean anything. Then Petra stood by the coffee machine and made and drank a double espresso while she sent the voice recording of her conversation with Wasim to Rafi. There was nothing more could she do but place the security pill in its slot in the front door and, once again, go out. This time to meet Rafi and then find out what was going on with Wasim.

Outside her front door, Petra checked herself and the surroundings. Because of Wasim's status, this was more important than ever, no matter how tired she was. Petra had picked her home with care and the cottage looked out onto the village green, where she could scan 180° with a single sweep. There was no bus stop within half a mile, inconvenient for people without cars but, more importantly, inconvenient for a watcher. Side to side, near and across the green she scanned. Were there any unusual cars parked? Maybe someone feeding the ducks who seemed out of place? A figure with that indiscernible aura of not fitting in, a look only recognisable to someone who knew what to check for; a certain stiffness of gait or a tightness around the eye.

There was nothing.

Petra walked to her parked car and thought about how only hours ago she'd been crouched behind a hedge in a village in the Midlands. She was exhausted. With so little sleep, how good was her judgement going to be for this meeting with Wasim?

* * *

Two hours later Petra sat next to Rafi in the back of the Techtruck in a side alley near Ealing Broadway. It was a scuzzy corner that provided parking behind an Indian restaurant and a paint shop – unkempt, with rain-filled potholes, cracked asphalt and discarded rubbish, but it was secure and it would be a simple task for Segev to hack the few cameras on the backs of the shops. Inside the Techtruck Segev sat hunched over the screens, scanning input from two watchers as well as a small drone that looked exactly like a wood pigeon and was perched aloft on a street light across the road from the station itself.

After more coffee, Petra was about as ready as she was ever going to be and she had a clear plan in her head for the meeting as well as exit strategies if necessary. Eyes down to aid concentration, she was mentally running through her key objectives when she became aware of Rafi's intake of breath. She looked up.

'Eyes on *Daledshin*,' Segev said and on the screen Petra saw Wasim's loping gait. He came out of the station, hovered for a few moments as if not sure which way to go, then turned left, crossed by the pedestrian crossing and went into Starbucks.

Behind him one of the watchers emerged from the station, a woman Petra hadn't seen before. She was a mishmash of styles, a red bandana on her head, an Afghan coat and biker boots. She had long spiky nails that had to be fake and was talking animatedly into her phone. Any passer-by might have thought she was sharing thoughts about a date or a dress. Only those who were close enough would have heard the clipped conversation and might have wondered.

'*Lenakot*,' Petra heard the voice in the small space of the Techtruck. Wasim was clean.

'Ready?' Rafi said to Petra.

'Yep.'

Rafi unlocked the door and Petra stepped out of the back of the truck, careful not to step on the accumulation of mouldering leaves that had survived winter. The door slammed behind her and she marched towards the high street and around the corner. Her earpiece crackled into life and she winced as the sound level was adjusted.

'Sorry,' she heard.

The smell of spices from the Indian restaurant reminded her that she'd forgotten to eat but she was also aware that she felt no hunger. She was concentrating on her surroundings and the commentary in her ear.

'All clean, all clear,' Rafi said. 'Proceed.'

Minutes later Petra sat across the table from Wasim and sipped at yet another espresso.

'How's everything?' Petra asked as if there'd been no emergency call, no escalated security, and this was merely a social meeting. Wasim exhaled. There was a crease around his eyebrows that Petra hadn't remembered seeing.

'There's a few things going on. I think I've screwed things up with Sam.'

'How? Wasn't he your best buddy because you got him out of trouble and warned him about the MI5 raid on his flat?'

'I'm seeing Becca, that's who I was with when you rang.'

'Becca? Isn't that the young woman with the green hair? Does this mean Sam is jealous or something?'

'He wants me to go on the marches,' Wasim said. 'I've told him that the people at the marches are all photographed, whether or not they're wearing masks. He said how do I know that, as if I'm working for MI5. I said everyone knows that unless they're completely stupid.'

'Did you actually say that?' Petra said.

'He is stupid. Breathtakingly stupid. Stupid in ways you can't possibly imagine and anyway, this is all about Becca.' Wasim shook his head. 'Realistically, why would a young, talented woman want to sleep with a loser like Sam? He spends half his life talking about the sanctity of using the correct pronoun and how J K Rowling betrayed a generation.'

In her ear Petra heard Rafi chuckle. At least he was getting some entertainment out of this. She was starting to feel irritated; this was hardly an emergency.

'And the other half?' Petra said, trying to lighten up Wasim.

He waved a hand dismissively. 'Oh, that's word spaghetti about Zionism, colonialism, imperialism, fascism. It's like a rap.'

'And you've pissed him off? You might want to think about how you can change that situation.'

'Maybe. What really bugs me is how ignorant he is. I asked him if he had any thoughts about the Abbasid caliphate. It stretched from Africa to Portugal, Spain, as far as China. That was colonialism. And then I asked him about the third caliphate, the Ottoman Empire. He thinks I'm making it up when I tell him that a fifth of the population in the Ottoman Empire were slaves in the seventeenth century. I'm not right-wing and, God knows, slavery was appalling. I'm just tired of listening to crap. And so was Becca.'

'Listen,' Petra leaned forward in her chair. 'He wants you to go on the marches. Do it. What difference does it make?'

Petra was thinking how quickly she could end this waste-of-time meeting and get back home, where she had a pile of documentation in the attic that needed to be analysed.

Wasim's voice broke in on her thoughts. 'There's something else. Sam told Becca something. I think he was trying to impress her and he said it was absolutely secret.'

'Go on.' Petra was unconvinced.

'I don't know whether it's true or not. I don't think she's lying to me. But that's why I messaged.'

Across the table, Wasim pursed his lips. It was a look that Petra remembered his sister made. Petra leaned forward, elbows on the table, and supported her head with her hands. 'What is it, Wasim? What did Becca say?'

'She said Sam told her he has a connection with people he calls "The Brothers" and he stores things for them in a lock-up on an industrial estate near Wembley that he rents but they give him the cash.'

Petra sat up a little straighter. 'What things? Who are they? A crime gang or something?'

'I don't know. And she doesn't know. But I thought it was important enough to tell you.'

'Does she know anything about you? About me?' Petra shot at him, studying hard for his reaction.

Wasim shook his head. 'No, never. I barely know her and while I may have pissed off her old boyfriend, I'm not that stupid.'

'What if Sam is suspicious of you and he set her up to tell you that story, to test you in some way.'

'I don't think he's smart enough,' Wasim said.

'Never, ever underestimate how hatred can make people react,' Petra said. 'I'm not kidding.'

Thirty minutes later Petra was back in the fug of the Techtruck as it made its way along the North Circular towards the A4. Petra felt wrecked. By contrast, Rafi looked annoyingly fresh for someone who'd had so little sleep.

'Your debrief was okay. In parts,' Rafi said.

'Fuck you.'

'Not enough information about the green-haired girlfriend, not enough digging into who these Brothers are. But your *narativ mitchave* was okay.'

'What?'

'It means…' Rafi seemed to be searching for the translation. Then he said, 'Counternarrative – when you warned him about making Sam angry.'

'Thank you.' Despite herself she was mollified.

'But is he lying?' Rafi said. 'Is she lying? Has she been set up to mess with Dove?'

'I've no idea.' Petra rubbed her face with her hands. 'I haven't slept or eaten since I don't know when, and I just don't know. I don't like the sound of these Brothers, whatever they're supposed to be, and whether or not it's true. It could just be drugs – Sam has that look about him. But, I agree, what if Wasim's playing us?'

'He wouldn't be the first,' Rafi said. 'We need to talk to Eli. What are you doing now?'

'I'm going home and I'm going to have a hot bath and something to eat, and then I'm going to start looking at those papers we brought back.'

'Want some help?'

'From you?'

'That was the general idea,' Rafi said.

'Where's Eli? Isn't he expecting us to have gone through everything? When can we talk to him about Dove?'

'Out of town. He had to go back to Budapest to tidy up loose ends, so we've got at least a day to think about all this. A day to think, a day to write your report on Dove and a day to go through the documentation we brought back from Newark.'

'What about your—' Petra said.

Rafi put his hand over Petra's. 'If I have to spend one more evening with my wife trying to convince me that October 7 was a punishment from God and I need to start laying *tefillin* and doing morning prayers, I'll lose my mind.'

'Is she doing that?'

'Yes,' Rafi said. 'Not that I don't want to help you go through those documents.'

Three hours later they were sitting at Petra's dining-room table with the remains of a takeaway from Petra's favourite restaurant at one end and the documents at the other. After a shower, and a thirty-minute nap, Petra was at her laptop while Rafi sat on the other side of the open-plan area, his long legs stretched out on the vermilion sofa and a second laptop on his thighs. The harvested documents were now in piles divided by subject and Petra had the necessary but laborious task of numbering the documents, detailing what was in them and cataloguing it. If there was something significant, something that would prove Eli's theory and that would later be needed to be presented to an inquiry, it was important that they followed a clear process for their conclusions.

It was the type of work that Petra had done when she worked at Corudon and had delved into the activities of companies targeted for potential takeover. Forensic research was another name for it but it was all the same, sifting through evidence, looking for oddities and inconsistencies. So far there was nothing.

She had a snippet of a script in her hand. It seemed to have been written for Grant D Miller, for an interview on Fox News that had found its way to YouTube. Rafi had pulled it up on his computer.

'Here.' Rafi uncurled from the sofa and brought the open laptop towards Petra. 'Take a look at this.'

It was shortly after 9/11 and what looked like a much younger Grant D Miller was spouting fire and brimstone against Osama bin Laden and anyone who had supported him. Even then he was a middle-aged man with the cropped hair of someone who'd been in the military. His eyes were intense and stared, not at the interviewer, but at the camera.

'We need leadership,' he said. 'We need to forget about the rules of war, because these people don't play by the rules. They treat us like patsies, fools; they despise us. They despise America, they burn our flag and they laugh at us. Yes, they laugh at us. While we weep for our murdered citizens, they dance, laugh and burn our flag. We cannot, we must not, we will not, allow that to happen.'

There was some sweat on his upper lip, which went with the rant and it matched the script that Petra had in front of her, if not one hundred per cent, certainly close enough to indicate that he'd prepped the speech for this impassioned delivery.

'What do you think?' Petra looked up at Rafi.

'I'm surprised he didn't get a job in the first Trump admin-istration, when there was a revolving door,' Rafi said.

234

'Probably too dirty.' Petra stood up to reach for the pile furthest from her laptop. 'It's all here. Flight manifests from the planes that went to Jeffrey Epstein's island. He was on the plane a lot and here,' she reached for a photo of an older Miller walking through what looked like Central Park, with Epstein.

'That looks to me like the same route Epstein did with Prince Andrew,' Petra said, holding the print. 'Except now it's spring or early summer, look at the foliage.'

'So what?' Rafi shrugged. 'Most people do the same route with different people. I do it. Not here, of course, and certainly not now, but when I'm home, I go on the same run every day. By the beach from the Sharon to the Dan just as the sun comes up. It's beautiful – I wish you could see it.'

Petra wasn't listening. She stood up and walked to the kitchen, where she filled the coffee reservoir at the sink.

'You know something, I'm actually starting to believe Eli.'

'What?'

'That there's something here, something doesn't feel right, but I can't put my finger on it. Where's Segev?'

'Off grid, taking apart the unit we took away with us some-where safe.'

'It's not some sort of bomb, is it?' Petra said.

'No… but he's checking everything thoroughly. He's like that.'

Petra pressed the buttons on the coffee machine and then turned to face Rafi. 'I think you and I should have a little outing.'

Chapter 33

It was the next day and Rafi had stayed over, which was strange in itself. While he sat up in bed drinking the coffee she'd just brought upstairs, Petra held her own mug, standing by the window, looking out over the green. It had flooded and seagulls were gliding across the patches of water covering the cricket pitch.

'I've been thinking about what you said about counter narratives – that was it, wasn't it?' Petra said.

'Always thinking, that's Petra.'

'Yes, and I think you should apply that skill to your wife and this religious thing.' Petra turned to face him. 'You can't walk away from her now, not when she's in such a dark place. And this…' She gestured back and forth with her finger. 'This isn't the answer. Never was and you know it.'

Rafi was silent for a few minutes. 'You're probably right. Whatever happens in the future, I should try.'

Rafi put the coffee cup on the bedside table and threw back the covers. He stood up and walked towards the bathroom, giving Petra a view of broad shoulders, slim hips and long legs. He was a fine-looking man, but he wasn't for her.

Rafi looked over his shoulder. 'What's the plan?'

'I told you last night, we're going on an outing.'

* * *

Later that day Rafi was in a less compliant mood. They were in a hired Ford Focus, sitting in the car park of the National Archives. The sun had just gone down and dusk was closing in like a grey blanket. 'This wasn't what I had in mind when I accepted your invitation,' Rafi said. 'An afternoon in that miserable coffee shop waiting while you went through files.'

'It's not a miserable coffee shop,' Petra said. 'I don't know what you're complaining about. There's a bookshop and an exhibition. And you couldn't have gone upstairs because you don't have a reader's card.'

'And now I'm stuck in this miserable car park, waiting for some museum dork to go home so we can follow him.'

'Stop complaining, I know you love it,' Petra said through mouthfuls of a sandwich. She swallowed. 'If he cycles, we follow him in the car. If he goes by public transport, then I follow him and I'll call you when I have a location.'

'What if he goes out with friends? Or has a date, or goes to visit his old mother?'

'Then we change the plan. You know, improvise. Rafi, you can go home now if you want to and I'll do this on my own. I'm perfectly capable of doing this without you, but I'm sure he's our guy and he's been instrumental in tampering with the file.'

'Like you thought that Silver Dove was the messiah,' Rafi said, 'instead of just being another agent.'

'Silver Dove is a human being, like all of us. If you don't want to do this— There he is.'

Adrian Farlow, senior librarian at the National Archives, had just come out of the entrance and was heading straight towards them. Slightly above average height, with wayward hair and specs, he looked studious and thoughtful; in fact, he was central-casting librarian, Petra thought. Also, he looked extremely worried. So he should be. Using her Corudon research card, Petra had requested the World War I military records of the original Grant D Miller, the man cited in the YouTube video, the cowboy from Colorado, the man with the Military Cross for his heroic endeavours in World War I, who'd gone to Canada so he could enlist in the RAF and be an ace. The man who'd met his wife, a nurse from Newark, in the American military hospital in Portsmouth after he'd been shot down fighting the Hun. What a story his grandson had told the Fox interviewer. It ticked all the boxes of an American patriot.

But when Petra sat in her allotted space in the reading room at the National Archives she also studied Adrian Farlow, the librarian who had handled her request. With his flushed and sweaty face, he looked like a man who realised that his guilty little secret was about to catch up with him.

Consequently, it was no surprise to Petra that when she opened the file and examined the document that detailed Grant D Miller's military record and his award of the Military Cross, the ink on the handwritten document hadn't aged in the same way that the comparison document she'd also ordered.

'Lazy bastards,' she'd muttered to herself. But, of course, they didn't expect someone to go down to Richmond, order up the file, hold up the document to the light and look at it with Adrian Farlow observing from a distance and no doubt having palpitations.

And now several hours later, Adrian was on his bike, pedalling north, along Kew Road, over the bridge, left at the Thames and then down the back streets towards Ealing. All the while his bike light flashed on and his hi-vis vest lit him up like a beacon telling them which way to go.

Finally, Adrian cycled onto the cracked concrete in front of an Edwardian villa with multiple flats.

Just ahead, Rafi pulled up and Petra jumped out of the car and strolled past the house, where she saw Adrian take off his helmet and hi-vis jacket, pack it away in the panniers of the bike before opening the front door and manoeuvring the bike into the communal hall. The librarian didn't think to look around or check himself, which Petra took to be a good sign. Also this was more than likely to be home or, at the very least, somewhere he visited frequently. Petra sensed, rather than heard, Rafi at her elbow. Ever since they'd started to follow the librarian, Rafi had stopped complaining and she recognised his engagement now that they were doing something.

'What's the plan?' Rafi said.

'Let him get inside. If we're lucky, the lights will go on at the front of the house before he draws the blinds, which means he lives alone.'

For a minute or so they stood in the dark holding hands, acting like a couple having an intense conversation. A jogger came past them panting, then a man tugged along by a brown spaniel. But still the bay window of the villa remained dark.

'Let's go back to the car.' Petra took Rafi's arm, maintaining the couple fiction. 'It was too much to hope that we'd get that lucky. His flat's got to be at the back, which is no help to us, and doesn't answer the question of whether he's alone.'

Together, they walked back to the car and found a spot fifty feet down the road, where they could watch the property through the wing mirrors. If he came out, they'd see him but if he didn't come out, they could be there all night.

'Why don't we call it a day?' Rafi said. 'We've established who he is, what he's done and where he lives, that's a lot for just a few hours. If we were putting in an official report, that would look like real progress.'

'And we'd have a couple of watchers and the Techtruck out here, instead of it just being you and me.' Petra sighed. 'I suppose we could jack it in and come back at 7 a.m. Wait for him to go to work, gain access to the flat after he goes and be there when he comes back in the evening. Or...' Petra had her hand on the door of the car and was opening it.

'What are you doing?' Rafi said.

'Why don't I just ring his doorbell, invite myself in and ask him what he knows about putting a fake document in a file?'

'What happens if he's not on his own?'

'Then I don't ask him.'

It didn't happen quite the way Petra described it to Rafi. In fact, she pressed Adrian's doorbell, which he'd conveniently labelled with his name on the buzzer, and she said she had a package for one of the other flats. He buzzed her in. Once inside, she made her way through the common parts, which needed a refurb and climbed the stairs to the first-floor landing, where there were two doors. This was a potentially dangerous moment.

She tapped on the door and moments later Adrian opened it. Before he could say a word, she'd stepped inside and closed the door behind her.

'Remember me?' Petra walked through the tiny hall into a small sitting room with a two-seater sofa and a bookcase and island separating it from a kitchen. In one corner the TV was on and in the kitchen the microwave pinged its completion.

'What… what…?' Adrian said.

He'd changed out of the navy corduroys and navy jumper he wore for work and was in a tracksuit. He looked younger and more vulnerable and more scared.

'I think you know why I'm here,' Petra said. She sat on the windowsill across from the door. It gave her a perfect position to signal to Rafi who was now in the garden beneath the first-floor window.

'I want you to leave,' Adrian said. 'I don't know who you are or what you want but I want you to leave and, if you leave now, I won't call the police.'

'Don't make me laugh. Adrian, you need to understand, it's been a long day for me. I'm tired and that makes me more bad-tempered than usual.'

'Who are you?'

'I'm someone who is doing you a favour, that's who.' Petra got up from the windowsill where she was sitting and stood close to Adrian. She was less than six inches away from him and she was the same height. She prodded his shoulder with her pointed finger as she spoke. 'I need you to tell me everything you know about the document that even to my untrained eye has been forged.'

She pulled her arm back and slapped him across the face. He stumbled and she pushed him back into the two-seater sofa and stood over him. 'Adrian, why is a fake document in that file?'

His face was red where she'd slapped him and her fingers were clearly marked on his pallid skin. 'If you don't go right now, I will call the police.'

'No, you won't and that's not just because I'll stop you physically. It will be because you'll lose your job if this comes to light and worse, you won't be employable in any meaningful profession. After all, who is going to trust someone who has betrayed the fundamental tenet of what the National Archives is all about, which is preserving the truth.'

At that he seemed to crumple as if he was collapsing internally. Petra went on, 'To repeat, I'm extremely tired and that makes me impatient and bad-tempered. You may think this is irrelevant but it's a problem… for you because although I really don't want to hurt you, and as a rule, I only hurt people when I'm threatened, I have a reputation… for…' Petra held up her hands in a gesture meant to suggest inverted commas. She went on, '"Not being afraid of getting blood on her hands." Do you understand? That's what's been said of me. I don't like it any more than you would, but it's a fact, Adrian. It's other people's perception of me. What I'm trying to say, Adrian, in the nicest and most respectful and least threatening way…, is if you don't tell me right now everything you know about that document, I'm really going to have to hurt you.'

His eyes seemed to be bulging out of his head in fear.

Petra studied the man for a moment or two and then went on in a resigned voice, 'I presume you keep your household tools either in that cupboard by the front door or under the sink.'

He didn't respond. He just gaped at her. Petra was starting to wonder whether she'd misjudged him or worse, overdone it and he would have a heart attack from fear. Maybe he was paralysed like a small bird or a squirrel that gets trapped in the mouth of a dog. Either way it was too late to change tack now, she had no choice but to go on.

Petra stepped away from the man and strode towards the cupboard by the front door. There was an iron and an ironing board, a caddy of cleaning materials and a toolbox. She lifted it out.

'He said... he said... it was for his grandfather...' Adrian's voice quavered.

'Go on.'

'He said that it would mean so much to the family if he had a military record. And that if I just slipped the document in with all the others, that's all I had to do. So it would be there, for posterity. Honestly, I didn't think it would do any harm.'

Petra carried the toolbox into the sitting room with her and sat back on the windowsill with it at her feet.

'Okay,' she said. 'Let's take it from the top. When did this guy turn up? And how much did he pay you?'

Chapter 34

They met in a safe house, a flat on the top floor of an empty Victorian semi in Willesden Green. The other flats had been vacated and there was evidence of recent departure, overflowing black bags of rubbish, the cupboard with the fuse boards hung open on one hinge and there was a pile of mail on the doormat. Yet it had been swept and scanned by Segev and for this particular meeting the recording equipment had been disabled.

On the way there Rafi had told Petra that disabling the recording equipment would mean the end of Segev's career if it became known, but it was a measure of Eli's trust in the progress of this investigation into Grant D Miller that he had taken the risk.

'But I should warn you,' Rafi said, 'Eli's not happy about your session with the librarian. You could have been arrested, and we would have had to shut down and go home if he really had called the police.'

'But he didn't,' Petra said. She felt defensive, and that made her want to fight her corner. After all, who was Eli to complain about how she'd got the information? Wasn't the first rule of intelligence that an operation was deemed a success if it worked? They were climbing the stairs of the safe house and there was a bad smell from the first-floor-landing flat, she diverted the conversation. 'Never mind about disabling the kit, or me being in trouble, why can't you ever get these places cleaned? It's rank.'

Eli was by the front door, beckoning them in. 'That's part of the charm.' He was undoing the topmost button of his shirt and loosening his tie as he spoke. 'Come on in. I understand from Rafi you are to be congratulated. You got some hard data on the Nottingham job.'

'And I understand from Rafi you're pissed off about how I did it.'

'There is that,' Eli said. 'We'll talk about it later. Meanwhile…' They followed him into the flat. On the table there was a spread of food and some fresh bread and beer. 'You have to try this,' Eli said. '*Baracskai* cheese, aged for four months. Very special.'

Petra wasn't fooled. It was Eli's methodology to create a warm environment before the bollocking but that was fine, she was able to prepare. After they'd eaten, Eli took his laptop out of a rucksack and opened it up.

'Let's start with Silver Dove,' Eli said.

'I'm sure Rafi told you everything. I had an urgent request for a meeting. Silver Dove screwed some woman that Sam was interested in. And she told Dove that Sam has a connection with something called The Brothers, who apparently have a storage facility.'

'What else?' Eli said.

'Sam wants Silver Dove to go on the marches and demonstrations and Silver Dove wants to stay out of it. I just said, do whatever it takes. After all, it's part of his cover.'

'How did he look?'

Petra went into a detailed description of what Wasim had been wearing, his apparent energy levels, what he ate and exactly what he'd said during the course of the meeting. Not only had it been recorded but it had all gone into her report. Petra had also been thinking about it. Alon had been obsessive about minuscule details and she remembered him asking whether a target ate a cheesecake with his left or right hand. Something she'd considered to be an unnecessary detail. 'No,' Alon had said. 'It all adds up. Each element joins another and another and another until we join all the dots and get the whole picture.'

By contrast, Eli was more direct. 'What's your gut feeling, Petra? You've had time to think about this. Is Dove lying? He wouldn't be the first agent to pull us into a trap and, let's face it, agents are professional liars.'

'Like us,' Rafi said.

'Yeah, just like us.' Eli held Petra's gaze with his own. 'Well?'

'What worries me is that he guessed who we are and, at the time, he said he was okay with it. But maybe he isn't, maybe he changed his mind? Or maybe he was conning us all along?'

'That just about sums it up.' Eli leaned back in his chair and rubbed his hand across the flesh of his lower face. 'I don't like it.'

Petra went on, 'You think I do? The flat's wired so we know what happens when he's home, but we don't know what's happening outside. Why can't we do what we did with the Ukrainian? Watch him round the clock?'

'Impossible,' Rafi said. 'Not now. If it wasn't for the war, we'd pull in a team of watchers from Europe, another one from home and cover Dove round the clock. But we can't do that now. We don't have the resources. We barely have enough people to secure the London Embassy staff. Nathan is running around the UK visiting communities and advising on security. We've got joint ops running with *Aman*, so that's our Syrian speaker gone, and we've lost Adam to the Germany Station for the duration. It's so bad that one of the watchers we used when you met Dove was our unit analyst.'

There was silence around the table. The three of them sat under the stark overhead light, on a stained sofa and chair that were one step away from the dump. Petra looked for ideas in the corner where the paper was peeling. She thought about Wasim, pictured him, his expression, his eyes. Could he be trusted? How could she find out if he was telling the truth?

Outside the flat, an ambulance siren split the air and it seemed to shatter the moment of group rumination. Eli stirred in his chair and stretched his shoulders. 'The greater problem is that he knows who Petra is, which, if he has been turned, could put her in serious danger.'

Rafi was swirling the remnants of coffee around his cup. 'We could walk away.'

'No,' Petra and Eli said in unison.

Eli shot an intense look at Petra, nodded at their agreement and went on with renewed energy, 'It's too important to walk away without concrete evidence that the operation is blown. Okay? What do we need to know?' He held up his thumb and then fingers as he spoke. 'Three things, first if Dove is lying. Second, if this Brothers story is bullshit. Third, if it's a threat to us. But the point is that there is no urgency to clarify any of these issues. We can afford to wait a few days. Then Petra meets him. Turns up at the flat unexpectedly so he has no time to prepare, and she establishes whether or not he's lying.'

'Okay,' Petra said. 'I can do that.'

'I know you can,' Eli said. 'Everything to date indicates that you have a strong relationship with him. He is doing what we want him to do. And you have the skills and experience. Let's not overthink this.'

Eli turned to Rafi. 'Can you check to see if there's enough coffee in the kitchen? If not, there's a shop at the end of the street. And keep an eye out for Segev. He should be on his way.'

As soon as Rafi left the room, Petra braced herself for the slap on the knuckles about the librarian. Eli was back on his laptop, tapping keys. No doubt he was pulling up her report on the librarian. He scanned it before he turned to her. She felt as if she was at the doctor's surgery and some bad medical results were being looked at on the screen.

'Exactly what happened last night?' Eli didn't look up.

Petra repeated all the pertinent information that she'd gathered from Adrian. How he'd been approached in the car park of the National Archives by a man with a 'foreign accent'.

'Did he describe him?' Eli said.

'Thirty to forty, medium height, dark clothes, clean-shaven, nondescript.'

'Great,' Eli said without colour in his voice. 'He could be anybody. How much did the librarian get for putting that document in the file?'

'Two grand,' Petra said, 'plus the sob story about a dying grandfather, who said that he would go to his grave as being irrelevant and it was a way to make him feel that he was leaving a legacy.'

'Do you think the librarian believed that?'

'He might have. I don't know.'

'Why don't you know?' Eli said.

'Because by the time I got the information out of him, he

was distressed. And he was distressed because I threatened him, so I wasn't able to get any nuance out of him. All I had were the facts. Is that what you want to hear, Eli?'

'Is it the truth?'

Petra felt something burn inside her. She closed her eyes and took a deep breath. Still keeping her eyes shut, she said, 'I am so angry. It was nothing to do with that wretched man, who just happened to be there. It's me, Eli. Ever since October 7, I've been keeping it in, tamping it down, but then... I keep thinking about Alon's wife, an 85-year-old woman, stuck in some fucking tunnel, being starved to death.'

Petra was aware of Eli's hand on her shoulder. 'We are all feeling that pain and anger—'

'It's not just that, it's the cruelty. People relishing the cruelty of what was done. I can't help wanting revenge on them, those cruel people, and I know it's not helpful. But it's eating me up, Eli, and I push it down and I push it down and then when I least expect it, it overcomes me and I lash out. That poor guy just happened to be there.'

He was holding both her hands between his own; it seemed as if he was trying to make her stronger. 'Petra, it's grief. It's not just the entire country, there are 16 million Jews worldwide grieving and when people grieve, they do crazy things. And whatever anybody says in the press, that it's like the Holocaust, it isn't, it's worse. Because, for many Jews in the US and UK, the Holocaust was far away and a creeping realisation. Even when hard evidence started to come through, people didn't think it was possible. Didn't believe that it was true. But October 7 was different; streamed in real time. It was documented minute by minute and we, collectively, will never, ever get over it. What's more, instead of being denied, there's a competing narrative. The attack is being justified and that's a good reason to be angry; the problem is that anger dilutes power, it makes you vulnerable, it shows that you're vulnerable.'

'Maybe,' Petra said. 'I don't want to be vulnerable, like my grandparents, like my father who wouldn't talk about it.'

Petra's eyes were shut and she felt, rather than saw, Eli release one of her hands and stroke the side of her face with his finger. He traced a line from her damp cheek down to the corner of her mouth. She opened her eyes and saw that he was looking at her with an intensity in his own grey eyes.

Just then, Petra heard the front door open and Eli moved back. She turned and caught Rafi's surprised expression as he ushered in Segev, who was carrying a battered bag for life from Aldi.

In one swift movement Eli stood up. '*Manyamin, achi,*' Eli said and clapped the young man on the back. 'What have you got for us?'

Chapter 35

Petra remained at the table and observed the bustle of the three men as if from a distance. She was trying to process what Eli had said, and also that moment when he had looked almost inside her. There was a rapid interchange in Hebrew and Eli and Rafi disappeared into the kitchen area, where they were apparently making coffee. She didn't want to try to understand what they were saying; she had too much to think about. Meanwhile, Segev had taken Eli's empty seat at the table and was unpacking the carrier bag with careful deliberation. He seemed oblivious to everything apart from the object on the table that was wrapped in a towel.

'I presume that thing isn't dangerous,' Petra said.

He was a serious young man, and she realised that she'd never seen him quip with the others. It wasn't his style. 'No, not dangerous in its current state but it can certainly be used for dangerous activities.'

'What is it?'

Segev reached for a corner and unwrapped the grey metal and plastic component. 'It is a dedicated GPU – that means, graphics processing unit.'

Eli held two mugs of instant coffee and put one in front of Petra and the other in front of Segev. There was also a Hungarian cheese roll for Segev on a piece of kitchen towel.

Rafi wasn't sitting down. He just stood in the open door frame of the kitchen, leaning to one side and watched while Eli beavered about.

'Okay,' Eli said. 'This is the unit we brought back from Newark. You said it's a GPU. What does it do that we would find interesting?'

Segev took the cheese roll in both hands and bit deeply into it. He spoke as he chewed and swallowed. 'Thank you, Eli. I worked through the night and I forgot to eat.'

'*Bete avon,*' Eli said. 'Take your time. God forbid we should rush you.'

Segev swallowed, took a gulp of coffee and went on, 'Okay, so there are two types of GPUs, integrated and dedicated. This one is dedicated and it makes it far more powerful.'

'Do you know who made it?' Rafi said from the doorway.

'Irrelevant,' Segev said. 'Could be South Korea, Vietnam or Taiwan, or made under licence somewhere else. Anywhere else. It's just a processing unit but what it does is interesting. We use them when we hack into CCTV and adjust the footage. It both enhances the images and speeds up the process.'

Rafi left his position by the door and came to stand over the table where the grey box with its built-in fans sat like a magnet that was drawing them all in.

'I knew what it was as soon as I saw it,' Segev said. 'But I wanted to tie it in with the data that Petra got from Corudon about localised surges. I managed to hack into the control room at the National Energy System.'

'And?'

'You were right, Eli. That's why I was up all night. There was a series of localised power surges two weeks before this terminating operation was suggested. The surges came from a location 50 metres from where we found the GPUs. I'm sure there was another barn or property in the vicinity; if we'd looked, we might have found the servers.'

'Do we go back and look for it?' Rafi said.

'Not necessary,' Segev said. 'Unless they're actually in use, it's irrelevant. But what proves Eli's theory is a series of uploads from the address onto the internet via a dark-web file hosting service. They took place at exactly the same time. I'm still looking for a signature but I can say with confidence that all the footage you saw on YouTube, Facebook, Ted, X and Ancestry.com of this Grant D Miller is fake.'

'Somebody has gone to a lot of trouble to create a cover story for him,' Petra said.

'Yes, but is it us?' Eli said. 'Well, Segev?'

'I can't say. Not yet. It could be us. We have the capability.'

'And we have the imagination,' Rafi said. 'It feels like it's us, it's the kind of operation we like to do.'

'I agree,' Eli said.

There was silence in the room until Segev said, 'I have some friends in Unit 8600. I did induction training with them and I'm sure I can get in touch and ask a few questions.'

'No... no... don't do that,' Eli held up a finger. 'That would be a mistake. You'd be compromised before we had confirmed the truth. I don't want you involved, Segev. You've done enough. All of you.'

Eli stood up from the table. 'Okay, let's clear up this place, like we were never here. I need to work out what to do next.'

Chapter 36

Eli was the last to leave the safe house. He stood over Segev as he fiddled around with a box in the broken-down hall cupboard. It was next to the meters and Segev was recalibrating the recording equipment. Not that Eli knew exactly what Segev was doing with the exquisitely arranged tools in his rucksack but bearing him company was the right thing to do. This was his show. His responsibility. To use the English expression, every 't' needed to be crossed and every 'i' dotted.

After Segev had gone, Eli waited seven minutes and then left the deserted house and walked south, down Walm Lane towards Willesden Green Station. The afternoon had turned into early evening as Eli trudged past the terraced houses. Along the way he dodged burnt-out mothers, who wheeled prams with one hand and with the other clutched a toddler. Life was hard for many in London.

As Eli crossed the road near Station Parade, something made him turn, pause and look at the mounds of fruit arranged outside a shop. He pretended to be interested in some custard fruit and took the opportunity to check himself. There was nothing. Nothing except a feeling.

Instead of going into the station and travelling the two stops home, Eli walked past the entrance and turned right into St

Paul's Avenue, past the big old Edwardian villas that had long ago been turned into flats. He picked up his pace, trying to identify a vantage point where he could linger unseen, but there was nowhere obvious. After fifty feet, Eli paused and knelt down to tie up the already secure laces on his trainers. When he stood up, he again checked himself and again, there was nothing. Just a feeling.

Eli crossed the road, dodged between some cars and turned left into Dean Road. Now he broke into a jog. There was a low metal side gate to a house and no obvious external security light. Eli glanced up and down the road and for the moment it was quiet. He opened the gate and sheltered by the side door of the house, ready if he was challenged by the home owner to say he was looking for a young woman he was supposed to be taking on a date. For five minutes Eli stood by the door and waited, looking out onto the street, trying to see if anyone passed who might have been following him, someone who had the telltale stride of the hunter stalking a quarry. But there was nobody, only the sounds of the city and the smell of the bins. Had he imagined it?

Eli left the safety of his hide by the side of the house and returned to the quiet street. He turned left, intent on heading back to Willesden Green Station and home and there, leaning against a metal post with a sign indicating parking charges, was Rafi. He was smiling.

'What the hell are you doing here?' Eli said.

'Just checking that you were up to speed with your safety protocols.'

'Fuck off,' Eli said and walked at a clip towards the station. 'You've just wasted half an hour of my time.'

'I also wanted to talk to you,' Rafi said.

'What about?'

'Is there something going on with you and Petra?'

'No, of course there isn't,' Eli said. 'When are you going to stop thinking with your dick and start thinking about some of the bigger problems that are going on?'

'I'll take that as a no,' Rafi said. 'Now explain to me why, having established that Grant D Miller is fake, you don't want to talk about the implications with your handpicked team.'

'Because you might want to have a career after all this hits the fan. You might even still want to live in Israel and not find yourself in the diaspora in some shitty security job, or, if things really go wrong, on the run because *Kidon* are coming after you.'

'Don't you think you might be exaggerating a little?'

By now they were by the station and were being buffeted by people swerving around them to go through the barriers.

Eli sighed heavily. 'First of all, when you came in, I was just about to talk to Petra about *Tohar Haneshek*.'

'And you had to hold her hand to do that?'

Eli ignored the comment. '*Tohar Haneshek* is what this is all about. Purity of Arms. If we become hired mercenaries for other countries' political parties, we may as well join the Mafia and get paid properly.'

'And you still had to hold her hand?'

'*Sheket*, Rafi. What are you doing now? There's a good Chinese in Willesden High Road. I'll buy you dinner if you stop whining like a little bitch about me holding Petra's hand.'

Thirty minutes later Eli and Rafi sat across from each other and ate Peking duck in a Chinese restaurant, where they were the only diners apart from what looked like a couple of pensioners having the early bird special. As they loaded up the pancakes, Eli tried to explain to the least politicised person he knew why the situation was so serious and also why it would be best for all of them if Eli bore the burden of the discovery. And he needed to do it without being patronising. This wasn't Rafi's world, Rafi was a kibbutz boy, a soldier, a plumber, a watcher – he did the job. Broke some rules but he didn't question them. He was fully aligned to the notion that the job of the Office was to carry out the government policy, whatever that happened to be.

'There are two problems,' Eli said. 'The first problem is that we now know this so-called Grant D Miller is a construct. A fake. He looks like he is closely connected to the Republican Party and has the ear of Trump but that could be completely untrue. Or partially true. We don't know. Putting aside the problem that someone, possibly us, is allocating enormous resources to initiate a targeted assassination, the greater issue is where this goes next.'

Rafi had stopped eating and was fully focused on Eli, who went on, 'Back in the day, when I was a rookie case officer and Alon was head of station, whenever we were developing an agent, he always suggested taking them to see *Evita*. I must have seen it eight or ten times. I hated it. But you know why Alon liked it? Because afterwards it gave us a chance to talk to the target about authoritarian regimes and how they screw over the people. Whether it was Assad or Saddam or Gaddafi, the Ayatollah or Hamas or Hezbollah or any of those charmers who took people into their torture chambers and stuck electrodes up their arses.'

257

'Did *Evita* work?' Rafi said.

'Sometimes,' Eli said and took a mouthful of beer. 'But that's not the point. The point is that authoritarian regimes have a way of sneaking up on you. There's a recognisable recipe; they seek to control the judiciary, dilute or control the media and often try to create a dynasty, whether it's as a brother or a son, they like to keep it in the family. They're also seriously corrupt, use their power for personal gain and will do anything, absolutely anything, to hold onto power because they can't get off the tiger. For an authoritarian leader, there is no retirement plan.'

'What are you saying, Eli? Bibi's been in and out of power for our entire careers. It's not our job to get involved in politics. You know that as well as I do.'

'Sure, I know that. But does there come a point where we have to? And while I'm not suggesting a coup, what I am saying is that this operation of Harel's, authorised by the Prime Minister's office, is not something that the Mossad should be doing. And I'm going to find a way to stop it.'

Eli leaned back in his chair. 'Now you know why I figured you should stay out of it.'

Rafi said nothing. His head was on one side and he appeared to be absorbing what Eli was saying. A waiter hovered into range and backed off when Rafi glared at him with a fierce expression.

'I just want to ask you one thing. Are you sure this isn't about Harel?'

'I admit I loathe him and everything about him. But part of that is his ethics. Or lack of. Rafi, man, if we... the premier intelligence service – the elite, if you will – can't at least try to have some honour and maintain purity of arms, then what the hell are we doing? What sort of people are we?'

'I'm the wrong person to ask, *achi*. Ever since October 7, I've been asking myself that question. But I'll tell you one thing, I think you need to talk to Yuval. Tell him everything we know and do it before you do anything else that's crazy.'

Chapter 37

When Eli finally got home, he felt easier than he had for a long while. Yes, there was still a slew of thoughts, questions and ideas that swirled around his mind, but the isolated act of articulating to Rafi his greatest fears diluted them. Rafi was real. There was nothing fake about him. He didn't get tangled up in intellectual arguments to try to justify a political stance, something was either right or it was wrong, legal or illegal, and, as far as Rafi was concerned, you made the choices and took the consequences. As Eli padded into the kitchen, he smiled to himself because in so many ways talking to Rafi was better than talking to Gal.

Eli set his work bag down on the kitchen table and drifted over to the sink to fill the kettle. He glanced at his watch. It was just after 9.30 p.m. in Israel. Maybe now would be a good time to try to find Gal and hope that she wasn't doing yet another one of her sleep clinics for traumatised kids. With one hand he poured boiling water into a mug, onto one of Gal's weird teabags, while with the other he keyed her contact into his phone.

No luck again. It went straight to voicemail, so he hung up.

Like all Office employees, Eli retained a land line in the eventuality of a cyberattack. It was an extra level of security that was mandatory for every member of the Mossad, even though most of the handsets just gathered dust. This was along with the battery-operated short-wave radio that had now become part of every Israeli's emergency pack, along with the tinned goods, water and batteries. The land line might be worth a go, Eli thought, as he carried the mug to the table. Not only would he have tried but he was also aware of just how much he wanted to hear her voice even if he couldn't see her.

Eli took a sip of the hot unrecognisable liquid from the mug and keyed in the land-line number. He heard the long ring in his ears and waited for it to switch to voicemail.

'*Ken*,' Eli heard and started. It was a man's voice.

'Who's that?' Eli said.

'It's me, *Abba*. Who were you expecting?' Doron said.

An unexpected rush of joy flooded through Eli and he felt his eyes tear up. 'What are you doing there? Are you on leave? How long for? Let me speak to your mother, *motek*.' Eli knew his voice sounded odd but, if he spoke to Gal, he could recover.

'She's not here,' Doron said. 'And there's no food either, not even that birdseed she eats for breakfast. I was so desperate I was going to eat that, but there was no birdseed and no milk either.'

'Is there nothing in the freezer, schnitzel or a goulash?' Eli said.

'I'll have a look,' Eli heard rustling in the background and the sound of the freezer door being wrenched open.

'Make sure you close it properly,' Eli said. 'The seal needs attention.'

'Yeah, yeah, yeah.'

Eli smiled at his son's dismissal.

'How's it going?' Eli said. 'How long are you there for?'

'Just the weekend and I'm going to eat, shower and sleep,' Doron said. 'Ah… this looks like steak.' There was more rustling and then he said. 'I've got some frozen vegetables. That will do.'

'Wish I was there,' Eli said. 'That'll be those South American steaks your mother gets. What else do you need. Mustard?'

'I've got everything.' Now Eli heard the clatter of drawers being pulled open and the frying pan going on the hob.

'Shall I call you later?' Eli said, sensing the hunger urgency in his son's voice.

'You can try, but… I might be asleep, *Abba*. I've been awake for 36 hours, on patrol with our guys, clearing houses, room by room.' His voice shifted from the breezy tone he was putting on. It was now brittle. 'It's bad, Dad, really bad.'

'I'm sorry, Doron.'

'It's the smell that's the worst. It's like an abattoir.'

'Doron, my darling boy, you are home now,' Eli said. 'Eat, shower, sleep. It will seem better tomorrow, I promise. It's always better in the morning, remember?'

'Yeah, yeah.' Doron replaced the mental shell. 'Always better in the morning, the bears aren't there. They never were. Always better in the morning.'

When he was a kid, Eli used to sing his son a nonsense song when he couldn't sleep.

'Tell your mom I called,' Eli said. 'Love you. And it will be better in the morning, I promise.'

For a while after finishing the phone call, Eli sat unmoving. He was with his son, in the kitchen he knew so well, visualising him cooking the steak, microwaving the vegetables and then sitting at the table, eating in his usual enormous mouthfuls.

With all his heart, Eli hoped that Gal got back soon, imagined her coming in the front door and putting her arms round his son, as he would do if only he was there.

Eli pushed the mug of tea aside and went to the cupboard, where he had a bottle of Pinot Noir. He'd been saving it to go with a meal that merited its excellence but, since that was likely to be some time coming, he opened it and poured and swirled before sipping. It was a way of delaying the moment. Eli had a difficult call to make and he wasn't sure how he was going to explain to Yuval what he'd found out about Harel's operation.

After Eli had sipped the wine, he made a few handwritten notes on a pad, then he went through the security protocols for the pre-arranged conference call with Yuval. The screen on the laptop was black and then exactly at 10 o'clock UK time, it flickered into life and Yuval's face stared out at him. Behind his old boss, Eli could see drawn curtains and the ubiquity of the international hotel. Yuval was in a room outside Cairo but he could have been in any of a hundred or a thousand hotels across the planet that all looked exactly the same. He looked tired, defeated and Eli had a moment's qualm about burdening his boss and mentor any further but tamped down the idea.

'*Manyanim*,' Yuval said. 'Tell me some good news.'

Eli smiled. This type of comment was unlike Yuval in the extreme. Maybe he was on the Pinot too.

'How's it going your end? How are the negotiations?'

'Couldn't be much worse, since you ask. We make a proposal, they agree to the proposal, then we change our demands and so do they. It's like being a rat in a maze, we go round and we go round but we're trapped and so are they. And we both know why. Neither Sinwar nor Bibi even want a deal to release the hostages. Whatever he may say, Sinwar doesn't want any political competition from the movers and shakers that we've got in our prisons, so he certainly doesn't want them back. And, on the other side, Bibi wants to keep the war going forever, so that he doesn't have to face the inevitable inquiry and corruption trial.'

'What can you do?'

'Nothing. Eli, I really don't know what I'm doing here, apart from carrying the boss's briefcase and having a whisky with him at the end of yet another unproductive day. The Americans are getting sick of us as well. So are the Qataris and the Jordanians. I don't blame them. So I'm relying on you, Eli. Tell me some good news. How is my old friend, Oliver Milne of MI6? Does he miss me because I certainly miss him. Tell him. I'm not cut out for this diplomacy crap.'

Eli had never seen Yuval like this and it was alarming. It reminded him of the day that he'd seen his father cry when he received the posthumous medal given to the uncle that Eli could only barely remember. Yuval had always been there. He was a rock. He was always thinking his way out of a corner. If he was giving up, which is what it sounded like, then what hope was there?

'Yuval, I know it's bad and I don't think it's ever been worse than this, but we are still here. And we *can* do something. We can stop Harel from using *Kidon* to murder for Bibi's political expediency.'

Yuval seemed to have heard this. He straightened up a little in the chair.

'Go on.'

'The situation is like this,' Eli said, consciously using his boss's introductory expression. Eli described what they had found out about Grant D Miller and he had a sense of satisfaction from seeing Yuval shift from despondency into engagement as he unwound the proofs they had. By the time Eli had told him about the librarian and the GPUs, he could see that Yuval was fired up.

'How did you find this out?'

'I went to the house that's connected with this Grant D Miller and… found a barn out the back with GPUs.'

'A barn out the back with GPUs?' Yuval repeated. 'Are you telling me that you… the head of the station, did a break-in? Are you crazy, Eli? How would that have looked on the BBC, who already hate us?'

'I didn't get caught. I had Rafi with me.'

'Was this his idea? I should have known better than to put you two together. Rafi's a liability, always has been. There's something wrong with his brain. He does something and then thinks about it half an hour afterwards.'

'It was my idea,' Eli insisted.

'Then you've been spending too much time with him.'

'It was done properly,' Eli said. 'We were off grid, but I followed all the necessary protocols and, for God's sake, Yuval, it worked. Isn't that the most important thing?'

There was silence for a few moments while Yuval glared at Eli. Then he nodded and almost growled. 'You're right. I'm spending too much time in these damn meetings. Now, at least, we have options,' Yuval said. 'Good work.'

'Harel is back in London tomorrow,' Eli said. 'And the *Kidon* team are arriving at the end of the week for pre-operation training. I'm going to tell Harel what we know and tell him to back off.'

'You are going to have to play this carefully,' Yuval said. 'You can't put a fire under him until you find out if we created the cover story. And if Harel knows that it's bullshit.' Yuval rocked back and forth in his chair, seeming to be thinking hard. He went on, 'Let me tell you, Eli, if I was in the Prime Minister's office and I wanted to do something dirty before the American elections, Harel would be my top pick. He has history. He's ambitious. He cuts corners and he wants to be on the winning side.'

'I've got no proof. I can't find out if it's us who created the cover story or some other nation state's advanced persistent threat group – you know, an APT. Not without leaving a trail in our systems.'

Yuval massaged his jaw and he was frowning. 'Don't patronise me, Eli. I know what an APT group is. I did the same cyber-security course you did.'

'Sorry,' Eli said. 'But it doesn't solve the problem. I can't use our systems to check the authenticity of the cover story without being exposed.'

'No, you can't. If I was back in Washington, I could get someone on it who worked for 8600, who just might do me a favour. But I'm not.' Yuval shifted in his chair. 'I'm attached to the hostage negotiations – I can't be seen to be involved. That means that this is on you, Eli. You have to tell Harel that there are proofs and get him to understand what the implications are of going ahead with this operation.'

'Understood,' Eli said.

'Do you really understand? If it is us, and we have that piece of information and it's leaked, it will bring down the government and it will impact the American election. It will also be illegal and we could find ourselves in one of those prisons alongside the guys that Sinwar doesn't want back.'

'That's why you needed to know,' Eli said.

'Thank you. I need another headache,' Yuval said. 'But it's good news, Eli. We're not dead yet.'

Chapter 38

Two days later, Eli was at his desk waiting in his office on the third floor of the embassy in Palace Gardens. It was 5 o'clock. Eli pushed the laptop away from him, stood up and stretched. His muscles were stiff. He hadn't managed to get down to the gym for weeks and he was feeling it. Eli walked to the window that looked out on Palace Gardens, at the tree that he'd seen through summer and winter since he'd got his posting. The branches were sharp and made stark silhouettes against a sky that changed minute by minute as dusk fell. It was now ochre and warned of high winds that were surely on the way. High winds that just might blow some fresher air into the Office. He could hope. The embassy was quiet. There was an event that evening, a screening in Finchley of a film about the attacks on October 7 and a lot of the embassy staff would be in attendance. Either as security or guests, it was perceived to be a significant event.

But Eli wasn't on the guest list. He was waiting for Harel, who was in London and was coming to see him.

For the past two days, Eli had spent hours preparing for this meeting. Preparing to convince Harel that the course he was on had to be diverted. Rafi was part of it and they talked about likely ways of trying to reach Harel and turn him away from the headlong tumble into a diplomatic abyss.

On one thing Rafi and Eli were in total agreement, there was no point trying to appeal to Harel's sense of history, of honour or ethics, since they were concepts that would be alien to him. But there had to be something that would make him realise that this targeted assassination would end in disaster.

Eli walked back to his desk and sank into the chair, he turned on the desk lamp and there was a pool of light in the darkening room. There he reread his notes for what was likely to be the most consequential meeting of his life. He was going to push back against his boss, the acting head of Washington Station and that meant pushing back against the head of the Mossad, the Prime Minister's office and indeed pushing back against the country. It didn't feel good.

The door buzzed and Eli looked at the image on his desktop. It was Harel; on time. Eli pressed a key on his laptop and it activated the lock. Harel strode into the room.

'I understand you have something significant to pass on to me,' Harel said without preamble.

'Yes, please sit down. Let me get you a drink or something.'

'I'm only here because I got a personal message from *Memune*. No doubt this was engineered by your master, Yuval. What exactly is it you want to say to me, Eli?'

'I appreciate you coming, I really do,' Eli said, 'I'll get to the point. There's no easy way of saying this, but you've been duped about Grant D Miller. He's a fake. His backstory is a construct and I have the proofs to support what I'm saying.'

'What proofs?'

Eli ticked them off on his fingers, ending with the annotated document that showed Grant D Miller's illustrious heritage, as detailed at the National Archives. Harel shook his head. 'That's not possible. I've met the man. He knows who we are. He did a Ted talk, he's all over YouTube.'

'Did you think to ask any of our people if they saw him with Driver at the White House during the presidency? Or after?'

Harel fiddled with the cuff on his shirt and tugged it down to cover his oversized watch. He was rattled.

'He was in Thailand, he spent a lot of time in Thailand because of the Jeffrey Epstein business. We know that.'

'Do we?' Eli said.

'Everything's organised. The team are arriving, I can't stop it. I can't stop it without explaining to the Prime Minister's office that the guy is fake and I'm not doing that.'

'What?' Eli said. Stunned at the direction the conversation was taking. 'You have to stop it.'

'No, I don't,' Harel said. 'As far as I can see, you haven't got any hard-edge proof that anything more serious has happened other than someone slipped a document into a file in a museum. Eli, you found a bunch of graphic processors in an unauthorised illegal-entry operation. So what? Someone could be designing a video porn game. That sounds exactly like the sort of thing Miller would do. We're not stopping the operation without more evidence.'

'But he's fake,' Eli said.

'We're all fake,' Harel said. 'Nobody is who they say they are, that's our business, isn't it?'

Eli stood up from his desk and went to his bookcase. It was something to do, a way of dispersing the anger that had built up inside him. A way of stopping him trying to throttle Harel, who, having made up his mind and overcome what no doubt he now saw as a minor glitch, had now assumed his habitual superior expression.

'It will come out,' Eli said. 'These things always come out in the end. Remember the Palestinian who scammed us in 1967.'

'I wasn't born then,' Harel said.

'It came out. How about Lillehammer, when we shot a waiter instead of a terrorist, or the blood on the pillowcase in Bahrain and everyone was filmed on the hotel CCTV. It came out. The mistakes always come out and this is more than just a mistake, Harel. This is knowingly murdering someone.'

'Eli, unless you have authenticated proof that will stand up in an internal inquiry and not something that you stole during an unauthorised break-in, then you'd better shut up and let the professionals get on with it. Grant Miller says the target is a thorn in Trump's side.'

'Grant Miller is a fake,' Eli said.

'The target still has a podcast that gets millions of downloads and he's pissing off Trump because he's funny.'

'Harel, think for a minute,' Eli said. 'What makes you think that Trump would be okay if a vocal critic is murdered? He's not Putin. Or MBA.'

'The target's not going to be murdered,' Harel said.

'What?'

'He's not going to be lured into an embassy and cut up in the basement. It will look like a heart attack and my guess is that Trump will be delighted. As happy as I would be if someone I loathed dropped down dead.'

'That's puerile,' Eli said.

In an instant Harel's expression changed and softened. His voice mellowed along with it. 'You're right,' Harel raised his hands and showed his palms. 'That was puerile and I apologise. But, Eli, let me ask you something, do you ever go to the casino, play cards or gamble in any way?'

'No.'

'I thought as much. Let me put it in simple terms – we are spreading our bets. We need to prepare for either election outcome in the US. Your *lochesh* operation will fit neatly into a Democratic win. But it's long-term. Short-term we need arms flow and, throughout all of this, we have one duty, and you know what that is?'

'I'm sure you're going to tell me.'

'It's to survive.'

'As what? A Mafia state?'

'You're being dramatic, Eli, but with good reason. We're facing an existential threat. Listen, my wife has one of her uncles in Washington for a visit. Irritating man, he's one of the old-timers. He was in the Unit at the same time as Bibi and Yonni. Said Yonni was always the star and Bibi was nothing much.'

'He probably wasn't.'

'But no one denies that he is a remarkable politician. Anyway, that's not the point,' Harel said. 'The point is that this bitter old fool, who I currently have staying in my apartment, eating my food and driving my wife crazy, says we're finished. Says the State of Israel, everything we've fought for over 75 years, is finished, and he's been saying that ever since Bibi was re-elected in 2022, before any of this happened. He gave us seven years then.'

'So what? Where are you going with this? How does it justify this unethical and entirely illegal operation?'

'Because we are facing an existential threat,' Harel said. 'We have a duty to survive when all bets are off.'

Despite himself, Eli had to admire Harel's argument. His taste for ostentation concealed a feral intellect. But there was a way in; a counter argument to make Harel change course, because citing survival suggested that Harel would be determined that his career survived and even prospered. He wouldn't want to get buried in an ugly internal inquiry once the war ended and the inquiries began.

Eli modified his voice to sound equally reasonable. 'I'm genuinely not sure that you understand all the implications of this situation. Unless we assume that all our institutions are going to break down, this would be murder. As such, it's not legal.'

Harel stood up, straightened his jacket and headed towards the door. 'I'm not sure that *you* understand, Eli. This operation has been authorised by the Prime Minister's office. I've got the red page to prove it and that's what makes it legal. Try to get your thick head round that.'

'Yuval—'

'Forget Yuval and *Memune*. Like my wife's uncle, they're yesterday's men. If I were you, I'd think hard about your future and where that's going to be.'

Chapter 39

After Harel has left his office, Eli sat at his desk and watched the afternoon slip into evening and felt darkness settle on him.

Eli remembered the day he'd signed the document swearing secrecy to the activities of the organisation. It was the day he'd been accepted on to the training programme and it was a moment of solemnity and excitement. How long ago that seemed. A time when he thought there would be a way ahead for Israel, but that was something he was starting to doubt as events spiralled out of control. It wasn't just Harel, it was Doron, his son. What was this doing to him? Eli shook his head and, in the shadowed office, made his way to the small fridge under the bookcase and helped himself to a beer. He needed to get some perspective. He needed to speak to Gal.

Back at his desk with his beer, Eli called his wife and waited for the phone to go to voicemail again. It did. And he leaned back in his chair and imagined what she might be doing back home. Maybe she was driving. She hated to pick up the phone when she was driving and at any given opportunity would describe how dangerous it was because the brain couldn't cope with the complexities of driving and having remote conversations and she had the MRI scans from an academic study that had been done to prove it. In the dark of his office, Eli closed his eyes and imagined what he would say to Gal if she was sitting opposite him. How he would explain to her his fears and frustrations.

Eli's phone rang and it was *Ode to Joy*. Gal. He grabbed the phone and slid open the call.

'*Motek*,' Eli said. 'I can't tell you how pleased I am to hear your voice. Where have you been? How are you? Where are you? Are you home? Have you seen Doron?'

'Eli, Eli, one question at a time,' Gal said. 'Doron is okay. I just took him to the bus station so he could get back to his unit. He's eaten and he has a clean uniform.'

'Did you think he was okay?' Eli said. 'He said it's bad.'

'Of course it's bad. What do you think he's going to say? It would be more worrying if he said it wasn't and he had everything under control.'

'Okay, okay, I get it. It's hard to be so far away from him… and hard to be far away from you.'

Something had made Eli add that last comment. Afterwards, when he thought about it, he realised he must have known what was coming, even if it was on a subliminal level. A level that Gal would have written a paper about.

'Eli,' Gal said. 'Eli… this is going to be a difficult conversation, but I need to tell you something.'

'What?' Eli felt cold.

'I wish I was there. I wish I was in the room with you, and I could tell you in person but I can't. I am here and you are there.'

'You could come here. The planes are still flying,' Eli said.

'There's no point. I think you know. I feel that you already know,' Gal said. 'Eli…' She exhaled heavily. Eli felt sick but he wasn't going to help her. Oh no, that would be asking too much. Let her own it. Eli heard her swallow. Maybe she was having a *shlook* of one of her favoured wines.

'Eli, there is no easy way of saying this, so I'm just going to do it. No preamble. From the hip. After the business with the Ukrainian, we patched it up but, Eli, something broke. There were cracks and the stress of the last few months have opened them up again.'

'You can spare me the metaphor,' Eli said.

'Okay, if that would be easier for you. I met someone. I'm not going to attempt to justify it but he's in my world, another academic. He understands what I do, what I'm trying to do, in a way that you can't possibly understand.'

'What? He told you you're a genius child shrink so he could fuck you. Is that how it went?'

'Don't make this ugly,' Gal said.

'But it is ugly. You can dress it up any way you want to, but it's ugly,' Eli said. 'You're screwing someone else. How did it go, a special moment over the water cooler and then a shag in a conference room after hours, or did you wait for a missile attack and fuck in a safe room?'

'I can't talk to you if you're going to be like this. I'm trying to be civilised and behave in an honourable and respectful way by telling you. And you're behaving like a child.'

'What would you like me to do? Say, "Okay, fine"? Is that what you imagined I would say when you did your Venn chart on the likely outcome of this conversation?'

There was silence at the end of the phone. Eli could hear his wife breathing and he detected a sob but, if that was supposed to soften him, it wasn't going to work.

'I'm busy,' Eli said. 'Goodbye.'

He ended the call. The office was now dark. The lights through the window and the distant sound of traffic were his reality. Whatever Gal was doing 5000 miles away was in another world, a world he couldn't be part of because he had his job to do and that was more important than anything else.

PART FOUR

Truth

A lie gets halfway around the world before the truth has a chance to get its pants on.

Winston Churchill 1874–1965

All truths are easy to understand once they are discovered; the point is to discover them.

Galileo Galilei 1564–1642

Chapter 40

Ever since Petra had met Eli and Rafi to discuss Wasim, she'd also been ruminating about her heavy-handedness, no, her anger, with the librarian. Wasim's truthfulness was a 'yes or no' question – either he was lying or he wasn't, and if he was lying at this stage in the operation, about anything, the operation would be stopped. Despite potential disappointment, Petra was okay with that; the incident with the librarian ran deeper.

She didn't know how to deal with it. It felt like being on a plane in a cloud, bumping through air pockets and yearning to break through to clear blue sky, clear thought. It wasn't only what Eli had said that made herself ask who she was and what she'd done, but the moment when he'd been tender. She was confused. Was there something there? She was sure that he felt it but the question she asked herself was whether it was simply two damaged people recognising each other for what they were. Was it any different from her own parents, whose only point of connection seemed to be that they were both displaced, lonely and trying to start a new life in a country where they were outsiders? Petra remembered winter evenings in the flat in Swiss Cottage, her father deep in an armchair, deeper in a newspaper, and her mother at the table totting up figures in an accounts book, meticulous about what they had and what they could afford. And silence. There might be music in the background, always classical, of course. Or TV, either the news or a documentary. But as Petra recalled it, there was no idle chat, no jokes, no loving words between her parents. Not even any rows; they just jogged along, day by day, week by week, until illness and death released them.

It was cold and dark out on the street near Wasim's flat and Petra looked with longing at the lights inside the flats. Since she wasn't sure how late she was going to be, she'd parked the Ford Puma hire car in a private two-bay space behind Prontaprint. She had made an arrangement with the franchise owner of the business where she paid cash and he turned off the security camera. He probably thought she was meeting a lover in her tweed skirt and county outfit; a buttoned-up wife of a city guy looking for some rough and tumble with an escort. The thought made her chuckle to herself and again, it made her think of Eli. He'd enjoy the joke, he understood her. He also knew what it was to yearn to be on the inside, as she stood at the bus stop across the road from Wasim's flat and saw people bustle off home from their offices. Or on the way out for evenings in the pubs and bars of Westbourne Grove, where the glow and chatter would welcome them in and keep the February dark at bay. That would be a nice life to have, wouldn't it? One where you didn't have to stop and check and double back and check over and over and over again before you got anywhere. Sometimes when she was doing her security checks before she got to a meeting, she imagined she was like a rat in a maze going round and around, trying to find the way out but, in fact, just trying to get to the next meeting. And Eli would understand all of that too.

Petra was well prepared for this meeting with Wasim, she was leaving nothing to chance. Using the kinesic interview method that she'd practised with Rafi, she was going to steer this interrogation without it being apparent to Dove. She had one goal, to catch him in a lie. Everything else would follow from that. If he was lying about anything, anything at all, they would abort.

Three days earlier, Petra had phoned Wasim to say that she would come by if she was in the area but had not specified exactly when. But she'd asked him to use the entry signal on his window. Despite the shortage of watchers during those three days, external spot checks had been carried out and Wasim had been shadowed to and from Imperial on two days. Within the flat he was monitored and they were able to watch him as well as pick up on his phone calls. All data had been run through machine learning programs and nothing so far indicated collusion with any outside actor.

From the other side of the street, Petra looked up at his window and then down at her watch. The blinds were down one third and the sidelight was on the left of the window. That was the agreed entry signal that it was safe for her to cross the road and visit the agent. Now was the time to move.

One more scan up and down the street and Petra left her perch at the bus stop to walk the twenty metres towards the traffic lights. There she pressed the button and gave yet another 180-degree scan of the street. That's when she noticed a car on the corner of the side road, near to where her car was parked. Its lights were on.

A dark saloon, an old Mercedes, someone in the driver's seat, interior light on. Could it be an Uber? It had a dent on the streetside rear, so probably not. Just to be on the safe side, Petra decided to take a turn past the car but maintain distance. Wasim would just have to wait another ten minutes.

That's when she saw her agent.

Petra gaped at the entrance to the flats. It was either Wasim or somebody who looked a hell of a lot like him. He was coming out of the block of flats. On either side there was a man and Wasim was being hustled along, his feet barely grazing the pavement. Was he being carried? The group seemed to be heading towards the parked car and they moved at a pace.

For a second Petra was rooted to the spot trying to decide what to do. If Wasim was simply going out with a couple of student buddies who'd turned up at his flat unexpectedly and she charged in, then he'd be blown. Decision taken, Petra headed towards the parked car. She took out her phone and in the guise of answering it and having a conversation, she took a photograph of the car, the number plate and also Wasim and his escort.

'Yes, yes, I'll pick up some milk and yoghurt,' Petra said to no one. 'See you soon.'

She was now just ten metres away from both Wasim and the car, and able to see more; his expression and also the way that the man on his right grasped his forearm. This wasn't camaraderie. This wasn't a couple of pals dragging Wasim towards a bar for a night out drinking shots. The agent was in trouble.

Petra broke into a trot.

Chapter 41

Less than two kilometres away, Eli and Rafi sat in the third-floor office, drinking beer. Eli had just told Rafi about both Harel and Gal. Twin disasters, and Eli appreciated that Rafi wasn't in a hurry to go home. Eli, of course, had no home to go to, at least, he had no wife.

'Listen, man.' Rafi stretched his legs in front of him as he lounged back in the armchair by the window. 'It might just be a war thing. Give it time, give her some space and see. How many times have you told me that crap about Tolstoy? Be patient.'

'Shut up, Rafi. I'm sorry I told you.'

'No, you're not. I'm here for you, I cover for you, you cover for me, we're our own unit, brothers in arms.'

Eli didn't respond to the comment, but it had sunk in. He nodded a silent acknowledgement as he studied the label on the bottle of Italian beer and tried to shape his thoughts into words. Nothing came. Nothing that made sense anyway.

'What made you say that?' Eli said. 'Now? The Tolstoy quote?'

'Because that's what you'd say.'

Gal had been a constant in his life ever since the first moment he'd seen her. And the Tolstoy quote was part of that first meeting. He remembered the moment – a Purim party in Jaffa, a lofty warehouse, where everyone was drinking shots and admiring each other's outfits. Eli hadn't dressed up. It was only hours after he'd arrived back from an intensive language course in Europe. It was on that course that Eli learnt his one sentence in Russian, and at that party that he'd used it on Gal to try to impress her. '*Dva samykh sil'nykh voina terpeniye i vremy.*' The two most powerful warriors are patience and time.

Eli had arrived at Ben-Gurion Airport and gone straight to the party. Eli couldn't remember why he was there, whose party it was and why he'd been invited but, boy, did he remember Gal. She was by a table loaded with snacks, her dark hair gleamed in the light, her head was thrown back and she was laughing at something one of the people with her had just said. Eli had no recollection of the rest of the group. All he saw was Gal, all he heard was her laugh, and he remembered thinking that he wanted to be near her and hear that laugh every day of his life. He'd approached her with a fresh drink, hovered outside the group and eventually he caught her eye. She had a way of looking at him – it was frank and challenging.

'Why aren't you in a costume for Purim?' she said. 'Or are you?'

'I just came from the airport.' He told her about the course and she asked him to say something in a language that she didn't know, so he rattled out his one sentence of Russian. A week later he admitted that it was his only Russian and she laughed as if it was the funniest thing. It made him feel good. But that was then.

Eli looked up from his examination of the beer bottle. 'I said some pretty bad things to her tonight.'

Rafi shrugged, 'You were angry. She'd have known that, she's a shrink. What were you supposed to say, "Yeah fine, go with my good wishes"?'

Eli shook his head. 'I don't know. I'm not sure I know anything any more. Maybe Gal is still angry with me after that crap with the Ukrainian. She said things hadn't been okay since then.'

'You saved her patient's mother's ass.' Rafi sat up from his supine position. 'No, really, Eli. You take too much on yourself. If Gal can't see that and this is some sort of revenge thing…' he tailed off. 'I don't know her that well, but I don't think that's how she operates.'

'How's Hannah?' Eli said, to change the subject.

'Don't ask. She went to a *mikvah* last week, left the kids with Urit's mother and took herself off to Leeds and some *Chabad* retreat where she had her first *mikvah* since we got married. You know what she said when she came back? She said she felt renewed and then told me that the word *mikvah* has the same root letters as hope. And that's why she'd done it. Because we need hope. What am I supposed to say to that?'

'What did you say?' Eli said.

'That if she wants to go back to Israel and sit in a safe room and talk about hope, then she can leave the girls here and I'll get my mother to come over and look after them. I don't understand what she's thinking.'

'Maybe it's us. Maybe we don't understand how the rest of the world thinks. I don't understand how Harel thinks.'

'That's easy. He thinks with his future career prospects in mind.' Rafi gulped back the rest of his bottle and strode over to the bin, where it clinked down with the others. 'Come on, let's go eat.'

The buzzer on the office door rang and Eli glanced at his phone. 'Segev.' Eli released the lock and the young man came into the office. There were dark shadows under his eyes and his usual air of detachment was frayed. Eli noted stains on the sleeve edges of his hoodie as if he'd rolled them up with grimy hands.

'What's up?' Rafi said. 'Something happened?'

'Maybe, yes… yes… something's happened.' His voice was raspy. 'I've checked and double-checked. I even got Michael to see what I was looking for and, to make sure, I had to tell him what we were doing, but he's okay. You know we're close.'

Eli remembered seeing Segev comfort Michael in the immediate aftermath of October 7. It was more than camaraderie and he was pleased they had each other.

'Come, sit down,' Eli said. 'What do you want – beer, coffee, juice? When did you sleep last?'

'That doesn't matter. I can't remember. I knew it was important that we find out and I know.'

Eli guided the young man to the armchair that Rafi had just vacated and pulled up a chair to sit in front of him. At his elbow, Eli felt, rather than saw, Rafi with a carton of juice with a straw poking through the top. 'Here, drink this. If you haven't slept, you probably haven't drunk or eaten anything either.'

'I tried to.'

'Drink this, take a deep breath and then talk.'

Eli glanced at Rafi who, by the merest nod, indicated his approval about how Eli was handling the wired young man. It crossed Eli's mind that if Segev had been working non-stop, then he may have had some drugs, recreational or otherwise, to keep him going. If so, that would be something he'd need to deal with, but later. For the moment, Segev had some information.

After sucking deeply at the juice, Segev spoke. 'Not just us but a lot of actors have been engaging in active measures using cyber and there are distinct operational styles.'

'So?' Rafi said with a hint of impatience. 'Everybody knows that.'

Eli turned to Rafi and frowned. 'Ignore Rafi. Go on.'

'If you're going for volume in terms of cyberattacks, you have to develop efficient protocols. Distinct patterns of TTPs – that's—'

'Tactics, techniques and procedures,' Rafi said. 'And?'

'GRU has a five-phase playbook, which they always stick to. Always. I've checked the procedures followed on establishing Grant D Miller's backstory. Everything, apart from the hard-copy document at the National Archives, has followed the exact same pattern—'

'GRU… are you saying it's not us, but it's the Russians?' Eli said. 'Are you absolutely sure, Segev?'

'Yes. One hundred per cent.'

'Why would the Russians put all those resources into getting us to kill someone? It doesn't make sense,' Rafi said.

'Oh yes, it does. It makes a whole lot of sense,' Eli said. 'They want to drive a wedge between us and the US, whoever gets elected. The US is our oldest and most trusted ally; if we're duped into killing one of their nationals, it won't matter who's elected – we will lose that support. And we need them more than they need us. It nearly happened when we allowed Jonathan Pollard to spy for us. The fall-out from this would be much worse. And the fact that this takes place in the UK is also part of it. It makes the UK security services look bad and Russia will enjoy that. They've probably never got over the British attempts to mess with the Bolshevik Revolution. It's all part of the big plan: Putin wants to get the US to distrust everyone except Mother Russia. It's his way back to the big table. It pains me to admit it but it's exceptionally clever. Nearly as good as The Protocols of Zion.'

For a few moments there was silence in the room, just the sound of breathing. Then there was a trill from Rafi's work phone. He glanced at the number and strode to the bookcase.

'Yeah,' Eli heard Rafi's voice from across the room. 'How many?' Rafi continued, 'Don't take chances, Petra, not with three. Okay? I'll call you back in ten minutes.'

Rafi closed the call and pocketed the phone. 'It looks like Silver Dove has been kidnapped.'

'And the Russians have fucked us over,' Eli said. 'How much better does it get?'

Chapter 42

'Call back in ten minutes?' Petra repeated to the empty car. 'Thank you very much, Rafi.'

Petra was two cars behind the old black Mercedes, on the A404, around Kensal Rise, heading northwest. Just making that call to Rafi had meant she'd lost concentration on the car ahead of her, so she was far from pleased with the curt dismissal.

'Git,' she said aloud and then went back to focusing her attention on the black Mercedes.

Stay close, but not too close. Do not attract the attention of the target car.

Rafi's voice rang in her ears. It was all very well for him to drop these pearls on a sunny afternoon outside a shooting range, quite another thing to be out here on her own with no back-up. Git. Fortunately, the driver wasn't racing ahead and also, fortunately, despite being old, the black Merc had big fat brake lights that announced its stately presence.

'Steady as we go,' Petra spoke aloud again and the sound of her own voice calmed her.

If she could find out where they were taking Wasim, it would be a simple task of calling Rafi and bringing in the police if necessary. The other voice inside her head broke in with one

291

word: simple? Let's not think about that too much at the moment. Concentrate on not losing the Mercedes.

Just then the white Yaris ahead of Petra indicated and took a left, down a side street. It left Petra exposed behind the black car. Damn. If the Merc driver was observant, he had to see her. All he had to do was glance in his rearview mirror. Without considering her actions, Petra hunched down into her seat and kept her head down, though much good that would do.

Ahead, there was no light coming from the interior of the car. The privacy glass was effective. They could have been doing anything to Wasim and there'd be nothing she could do. Nothing. Once again, Petra glanced at the phone. Surely ten minutes must have passed.

The traffic lights changed and Petra delayed, hoping that the BMW in the right lane would lose patience and push in front of her, giving her some cover, but the boy racer didn't. Bloody Beamers. He just hooted and shook his head at her, an action which had completely the wrong effect. It drew attention to her tail.

Christ.

Petra ignored the scowling BMW driver and continued to follow the Merc, through the traffic lights and further, further, further along the A404.

Where the hell were they taking Wasim? Bloody Scotland? Maybe she should call the police, but what would she say? I think someone I know has been kidnapped? No, not yet. For the moment it would appear that Wasim was in no danger. She chose to believe that.

Through Willesden she followed, right behind the black car, until they did a left at a T-junction and Petra was able to shift back two cars and breathe a sigh of relief. This was good. Steady progress. She could handle this. All she had to do was see where they stopped and then call it in to Rafi and he could deal with it.

To her left she recognised the white arches of Wembley soaring out of the darkness; so they were coming up to the A1 and M1, maybe they really were heading up north. But before she'd worked out how far she'd be able to go before refuelling, the Merc suddenly turned off the main road. Petra sped up and followed. Moments later she found herself in an industrial estate. There was absolutely no traffic ahead, nothing but the Mercedes, its big lights guiding her onwards. As slowly as she could, Petra cruised past small units, a sign advertising vacancies, a sign for plumbing supplies, a sign for MOTs and a sign for marble and quartz at bargain prices. The further she went into the maze of the industrial estate, the more pitted the road and, as she bumped across a pothole, she hoped she hadn't screwed the tyres.

Now that she was deep into the deserted industrial estate, Petra felt more conspicuous than ever. Fifty feet ahead of her there was the Mercedes. It slowed and took a turn to the left. That was way too close for her to follow. Petra pulled into a space outside the MOT unit, where an external light cast a single point of illumination in the darkness, and turned off the engine.

There was no choice. If she was going to find out what they were going to do to Wasim, she would have to walk from here.

Chapter 43

'Thank you, Segev,' Eli said. 'Good work. Now, go home, get some food, go to bed, and I don't want to see you until tomorrow.'

Segev shifted from one foot to the other. It was hard to see whether he was just jittery or whether he was going to argue.

'Go on, get out,' Eli said. 'If we need you, we know where you are.'

Segev turned and left the office, leaving Eli alone with Rafi, who was dialling a number on his phone.

'She's not answering.' He fiddled with his own phone and studied the screen. 'She's somewhere in north-west London, near Wembley. She's stationary, so she's either in traffic or she's at the destination. She must have got out of the car.'

Eli was looking at his laptop. He had a sudden sense of awareness that, in the midst of the moment, he'd forgotten that his marriage was over, that Gal had met someone else, that she was screwing someone else. A moment when he realised how he was so engaged in what was happening, what was important, what would have huge implications, he'd forgotten about himself.

'Doesn't amount to a hill of beans,' Eli muttered as he scanned his laptop and the list of London safe houses and their current occupants.

'What?' Rafi said.

'Doesn't matter. The *Kidon* guys are split between the Chiswick safe house and the one in Acton. Both good for the airport and central London. We need transport, Rafi, but I want a motorbike. It'll be the fastest way to get there. If we can't get Harel to see reason, we're going to have to find some other way of putting a stop to this madness.'

Rafi stood up and was shrugging himself into his leather jacket.

'The car-hire *sayan* has got a brand-new BMW M1000XR in his garage. I'll call him. Let's take that. It's got some guts.'

'Rafi, I'm going to have to tolerate your driving. Don't make this worse than necessary.'

Rafi grinned.

'Here is the plan,' Eli said. 'One – we hit on the ambassador. If she knows and we warned her and this blows up, her career is over. We get the authority from her to abort. Two – we corner Menachem. Your old unit won't use guns in the UK – my guess is that it will be poison and Menachem will have had to sign off the drug, the antidote and the delivery system.'

'Isn't this wasting time?' Rafi said.

They were outside the office now and striding along the third-floor corridor. The floor of the old building creaked a little and they walked with the purpose that implied they were unstoppable.

'No, because we need to be carrying our own supply of the antidote and the delivery mechanism, it's insurance,' Eli said. 'Three – we get to Acton, pull rank on the *Kidon* guys in the safe house and tell them to abort. If they don't agree to abort, we phone it in to Oliver Milne which will bring the whole of

London Station crashing down and result in our swift return home. Are you okay with that, Rafi?'

'The nuclear option.'

'Yes. If you want to put it like that. This cannot be allowed to happen,' Eli said.

'What about Petra?'

'The problem is the ambassador. If she was at home, we could have borrowed her security detail for a few hours and sent them to Wembley. But she's not, she's at an event. That means Petra will have to handle the situation until we get there.'

'Understood,' Rafi said. They were by the lift. The doors opened and both got inside. Eli pushed the buttons to the basement. 'We need to get kitted out for the bike. We need helmets and comms as well as leathers. I'll do that while you try to reach Petra. Make it crystal-clear that she's there to assess the situation and not to engage under any circumstances.'

Chapter 44

'I get it, okay?' Petra said. 'I won't engage. I'll just observe. But how quickly can you get here?'

'There's a problem,' Rafi said. 'Remember my friend's crazy hunch? He was right. So now we have to sort it out, otherwise I'd be with you in fifteen minutes. You know I would.'

'I see.'

Petra heard noise in the background from wherever Rafi was calling from and he went on, 'Babe, I've got to go. Remember what I said. We'll call back soon.'

Petra sat back in the Puma and stared at the screen on her phone until it went dark. She was on her own with no idea how long she'd be waiting for the cavalry to turn up. She was 'in the mud', as Alon would have put it. For the briefest of seconds she wondered how his wife was, alive and an ailing hostage or dead, having died alone and her body rotting in a tunnel. That was certainly 'in the mud'.

For all the warning not to engage, she couldn't just sit there and wait for Rafi to turn up and make a decision about what to do next. Doing a thorough scan of her surroundings could hardly be considered engaging; she was just going to observe. In preparation, Petra switched her phone to vibrate and pocketed it, then she reached into the bag on the front seat of the

297

car to see if there was anything useful. Since she hadn't expected to be doing a surveillance job, for once she was without her usual kit. What was there? A miniature bottle of gin she hadn't felt like drinking on the plane back from Budapest. What was she going to do with that? It might come in handy if she had to stand outside waiting for Rafi to turn up God knows when. She reached further down into the bag. Notepad, pen, the credit-card-sized gizmo with the scissors and the magnifying glass, the Bic lighter she'd used for Sandie's fireworks, a pouch bag for shopping and antibac hand gel. Hardly tooled up.

As quietly as she could, Petra slipped out of the car and shut the door. Keeping to the darkness, Petra crept towards the MOT centre and the turning where she'd last seen the Mercedes's fat lights. There she stopped. She scanned ahead for movement and then eased herself around the corner of the building. Her view was blocked by a commercial waste bin that overflowed with black bags, sodden cardboard and a mangled bike. Petra had to step out and be exposed if she was going to see where the Mercedes was.

Just observe. Don't engage.

As soon as Petra stepped away from the bin, she saw the Merc, you couldn't miss it. It was parked in front of a run-down Portakabin. Even in the darkness she could see loose strands of wiring and dead leaves. There was a light on inside but the window was covered. Petra stopped. Waited. Nothing.

She edged closer, past a corrugated one-storey building. Outside, stacked in neat piles, were squares of granite and quartz, samples, about the size of coasters.

With all the stealth she could muster, Petra edged closer to the Merc. As close as she dared, squinting in the gloom. The car was empty. They must have hustled Wasim inside.

Just observe. Don't engage.

Petra scanned the area, she needed somewhere where she could hide that had a vantage point. The door to the offices of the granite outlet was too exposed and, worse, white. She'd show up like a black crow against a white cloud. Turning, she saw a possible spot; a narrow space between the MOT office and the works themselves. Petra darted into the darkness. It smelt as if someone had dossed down there or taken drugs; they'd certainly pissed. She wedged herself in on top of some broken glass underfoot and wrapped her scarf around her face, just exposing her eyes so she was as concealed as possible. Despite the location's foul smell, it was a decent vantage point; at 90 degrees, she could see any cars coming or going and, if she poked her head out, she had a clear view of the Portakabin.

Just then her phone vibrated, and Petra didn't have to look to guess that it was Rafi checking up on her. Great timing. She ignored the call.

Chapter 45

'This is nice,' Eli said, as he swung a leg over the bike and stepped away from it.

'What?' Rafi was absorbed in the bike and running his fingers over the gleaming handlebars. He looked up at Eli and followed his gaze. They were 50 metres away from the front of the Phoenix Cinema in East Finchley and, even from that distance, the small group of protestors was evident. Green, black, white and red flags were waving and they could hear the chants of 'Fuck Israel', 'Genocide', 'Ceasefire Now'.

The police were there, stopping the protestors from touching people arriving at the cinema, but the shouting was loud and, even from a distance of fifty metres, intimidating.

Eli saw a black Range Rover sweep up to the front of the building. Two security guys got out, followed by the ambassador. She swept through the shouting crowd and looked neither left nor right. Eli remembered the woman he'd seen trembling with anguish in the meeting room at the sight of the live footage being streamed from the massacre. She had got herself together. She was majestic as she swept past the protestors. Less attractive was the sight of Nathan at her heels, but that might prove useful.

Eli and Rafi marched towards the cinema and Eli made eye

contact with Hillel, one of the embassy security jocks, who was scanning the area outside. The square man in the black suit was talking to one of the cops and pointing at a protestor. It looked as if he was making his own protest at the lack of security for the ambassador, but it seemed that at least she was now inside.

'We're with him,' Eli said when they drew abreast of Hillel, who nodded at the cop, and Eli had the oddest sensation of what it would be like to walk on a red carpet into a cinema. For Eli, to be exposed in this way was far from an ideal situation, but then, if the cultural attacheé of the Israeli government, as Eli was described when his credentials were presented to His Majesty's Government, and his deputy, couldn't attend a screening of the documentary about the massacre of 400 people at the trance music event, *They Will Dance Again*, then who the hell could?

Minutes later, Eli was inside and found his hand being shaken by a bespectacled man, who introduced himself as a London literary agent. Eli had no idea who he was and muttered something, trying to keep his eye on the ambassador and her progress through the crowd of people there for the event.

'Excuse me,' Eli said. 'I just want to make sure that everything is ready for the ambassador's speech.'

With Rafi in tow and feeling a little like Darth Vader in his motorbike leathers, Eli marched up to the ambassador. She was bent over a little old lady with coiffed white hair. The ambassador held the woman's hand and presumably was saying something comforting about the hostile crowds outside. Too bad. Eli nudged the ambassador's elbow.

'I need a word. Urgently.'

A minute later Eli was in the empty cinema with the ambassador, her deputy Yossi, Nathan and Rafi. Hillel was at the door to stop anyone from coming in.

'I need your authority to abort a mission that has been greenlit by the Prime Minister's office,' Eli said without preamble.

'I can't do that, it's not my—'

'It's a termination operation and we've been duped into thinking it's real by the Russians.'

'You have no idea how much I hate you people,' Yossi said. 'Haven't we got enough to worry about without you lot playing cowboys and Indians? Every problem we ever have always comes back to you and your so-called intelligence.'

'Shut up, Yossi. Let me deal with this,' the ambassador said. She held his gaze for a moment. 'Eli, I trust you. You have my authority to abort the operation. I will make that a matter of public record.' She knew what was at stake and Eli reckoned that she was planning to come out of this smelling sweet. And why the hell not?

'Thank you.' Eli turned towards Nathan and pointed a finger at him. 'You're with me.'

Nathan looked like a rabbit frozen in the headlights of a car but, before he had the chance to dissemble, Rafi's hand was on his elbow, guiding him along. As Eli swept through the lobby of the cinema and out onto the street, without looking back, he knew that the two men were bringing up the rear.

They frogmarched Nathan through the crowd of protestors, who were banging drums and chanting an enthusiastic 'From the River to the Sea' refrain. Once past them, they turned down the street towards the bike. There they stopped and, by a garage

different brands and logos. In the winter night, they were tawdry ghosts of summer, scuffed, faded and filled with battered boxes of stale cones.

After five minutes of exploration it seemed to Petra that her first choice of hide might be about as good as it was going to get. It was at least close to the Portakabin. Just then Petra heard a noise. A car. She saw the headlights of a car coming around the corner. Petra squeezed next to the overflowing industrial waste container and crouched, head down.

The car drew closer and slowed. It went right past where Petra squatted. She heard it stop. Still keeping low, Petra stepped around the waste container and peered around the corner. Parked outside the Portakabin was a Volkswagen Golf. Silver. A few years old but in decent condition. The car door opened, the internal light came on and Petra got a clear view of Sam as he stood up, leaned back into the car and took a bag from the passenger front seat. The door to the Portakabin door opened and she heard a few indecipherable words. Sam disappeared inside. The door shut and she was alone, behind the skip, in the dark.

After a few moments Petra straightened up. The arrival of Sam demanded a better view of the Portakabin door. Further away, across the rutted path in front of the MOT centre, rows of dumped cars were either being rebuilt or stripped for parts. The shell of a Toyota truck was propped up on two old wooden sawhorses. Behind it a black Fiat 600, its upholstery ripped out and piled on the roof.

Petra looked around – if she slipped into the Fiat wreck, she would be concealed and she would also have a direct view of the Portakabin.

Taking out her phone, she dialled Rafi.

Chapter 47

They were making steady progress down Hoop Lane, towards the Finchley Road, and, while Eli was far from relaxed riding pillion behind Rafi, he had stopped clenching both his hands and jaw. He was surprised. Rafi might be casual to the point of dangerous behind the wheel of a car, he might slide from lane to lane with zero traffic awareness, but on the BMW he showed both concentration and riding skill. Maybe it was because it was a fancy new motorbike, but it was still impressive. While Rafi would never approach Segev's skill as an operational driver, Eli was confident that they would reach Menachem, the embassy doctor's flat in one piece.

The Bluetooth link between the two helmets was live, so that when Petra's call came through, it became a conference call.

'I don't know how long it will take us to get to you,' Rafi said. They were at traffic lights. 'But it makes no difference. The situation is still the same. You observe. You do not engage. Do you understand?'

Rafi sounded tetchy. He should know better. That was never going to work with Petra, that was like encouraging her to do something. With his gloved hand, Eli dug Rafi in the ribs; it was a signal to shut up while Eli prepared to modulate his voice, to be both reassuring and authoritative. If Petra recognised it, it's what she would have called his spy-runner shit. He only hoped that in the moment she didn't recognise it for what it was.

'It's extremely significant that Treesmith is there,' Eli said, using Sam's code name. 'I'd be lying if I said this looks like a great situation. It's not. Something must have happened that's put Silver Dove under suspicion. So much so that Treesmith felt empowered to effectively kidnap him and presumably try to interrogate him.'

'My point entirely,' Petra said. 'What am I supposed to do, leave him there and let him get beaten to a bloody pulp? He's my agent.'

'You know this as well as I do. Sometimes we lose agents—'

'Oh, no. Don't you say another word. That's not happening. I promise you that's not going to happen. I'm not losing him.'

The motorbike had stopped at traffic lights and, while the lights were on red, Rafi's helmeted head turned to look at Eli. Even behind the visor his face looked grim and he shook his head. Eli ignored it.

'Listen to me,' Eli said. 'If he's at risk, really at risk, you take action. That's an order. You get in your car and drive to a call box at least half a mile away from your current location. Okay? Then you put in a call to the emergency services. You cannot compromise yourself, Petra. Remember that interview you had with our British friends? You have to understand this. Promise me.'

'Half a mile away? That's crazy. That's not going to help him.'

They were now outside the block of flats where Menachem lived and Rafi had pulled into one of the bays reserved for bikes.

'I'm sorry but I have to go. We will call you soon and we will be there as soon as possible, but please, I'm begging you, Petra. Please do not engage.'

Chapter 48

It was all very well for them to tell her not to engage and slope off to a phone box and call it in, even if she could find one that worked, but could she really do that? Could she do that and live with herself? As Petra sat in the wreck of the car, watching the Portakabin, she could only imagine what was going on beyond it. At the very least they would be trying to frighten Wasim. At worst they would be torturing or killing him.

She thought about his sister, Sahar. Petra could see her big eyes behind specs, the same wiry hair that Wasim had. And in her case, the trust that she had in Petra, her friend, her imagined friend, that she hoped she'd see in *Jennah* after she became *Shahida*.

How that young woman had been betrayed. Sahar, with her belief that she was going to make a difference by blowing herself up. Sahar, who never found out that she was just a tool, something to be used to further other people's political agendas and even careers. Sahar, who had been rejected by her husband's family because she was unable to have children. Sent back to her own family as a disgrace and becoming *Shahida* to win respect.

Petra had failed her. She'd tried to save the young woman, but she'd failed.

Even more unforgivable was Tom. Petra had used him. She'd manipulated him and lied to him; she used his young ambition to be an investigative journalist who was going to change the world to recruit him.

Oh yes, Eli might mouth the refrain that we lose agents, it's part of the job. But she knew him better than that, she knew the pain he'd felt when he'd lost an agent who'd been more than an agent, who'd been a friend.

Over and again, as Petra hunched inside the shell of the gutted car, watching her breath cloud despite the scarf wrapped round her face, her mind returned to Alon. Alon, whose wife was dead or dying in a Gaza tunnel. She remembered how he spoke of his childhood with her father, the grim story of loneliness, danger and privation her father kept from her. Alon talked about it, but he always spoke with a casual shrug, as if dismissing the pain. 'Everybody in Israel has got a story of survival,' he'd often say. 'Everybody. Everybody has a story about decisions that were right or wrong. Of getting on the train to occupied Germany, where work was promised, or waiting for the Russians to come. Of running away from Turkey after the Thrace pogroms and finding it more dangerous in the British Mandate of Palestine.'

'Right decisions and wrong decisions,' Alon had said the last time they'd met.

Her wrong decision had been not to keep in touch with the man who'd looked after her father when he was a child. Not to see him before he died. That must have hurt him. Her right decision would be to keep faith with him and his wretched wife and do the right thing by Wasim.

There was no way she was going to lose him, nor would she

drive off to try to find a functioning phone box half a mile away and make an anonymous call the police would probably think was a crank call. Either she called the police right now and dealt with the fall-out of being on an MI5 watch list. Or she got Wasim out of there herself.

Either way, she was not going to lose her agent.

Chapter 49

Menachem, the embassy doctor, looked worried as he led Eli and Rafi through the sitting room, where Yiscah, his wife, nestled on the sofa under a throw and an episode of *Bridgerton* was frozen on pause. She was an exceptionally beautiful young woman dressed for an evening in on a cold night in a cashmere hoodie and tracksuit trousers. At their entrance she started to get up, possibly to offer them coffee but, at a glance from Menachem, she sank down again into the sofa's plump cushions.

The fact that Menachem looked worried was normal. It was his perpetual expression but, as the young medic shut the door of the small room next to the sitting room and the three men crowded in next to desk, computer and a bookshelf, he was sweating with anxiety. Eli perched himself on the corner of the desk and Rafi followed his lead and settled himself into the ergonomic office chair. The Mossad men had history with the embassy doctor, and it hadn't been that long ago when Eli had been compelled to write a report describing Menachem's work and attitude as obstructive to the activities of the unit. It seemed that for Menachem, the posting to the London Embassy was a sinecure. Vaccinations, health checks, sick notes and first aid.

The disconnect between Menachem's job expectations and its reality collided when there'd been a first-aid requirement to set the broken arm of an intelligence source, a source who'd jumped out of a first-floor window, trying to run away. Menachem's performance in setting the man's arm so that the unit could avoid a visit to A&E and embarrassing questions had been woeful. Mutual animosity had only grown. Eli could see from the deep cleft between the doctor's brows that the notion of being involved in any way with the Office and a termination operation was making him wish he was back in the medical centre in Herzliya, dealing with ingrown toenails.

This was all to the good.

'I've got it ready for you,' Menachem said without preamble. 'It doesn't have to be kept refrigerated. Only the Scoline does. But you do have to sign for it before I can give it to you. Protocol.'

Eli ignored the tablet with the authorisation document that Menachem was thrusting at him. 'How much has the *Kidon* team got?'

'Two multivials of the Scoline, in case one isn't enough.'

'Enough to kill a horse,' Rafi chipped in and earned a glare from Eli.

'How about the antidote?' Eli said.

'Again, two. Dantrolene. But it needs to be administered within minutes of the Scoline to work. If the target goes into cardiac arrest or has pre-existing conditions, it's not going to work.'

'Great.' Eli reached for the tablet and touched the box on the screen.

Instantly, Menachem looked relieved. His face said it all. *Off his desk. Onto someone else's. Not his problem.*

From the bottom drawer Menachem pulled out a small padded bag. It was turquoise and looked like a child's sandwich bag. Menachem wrenched the Velcro seal open and showed Eli the contents.

'Two vials of Dantrolene, already loaded into the delivery mechanism. If he's coming round, don't use the second dose; it will make him vomit.'

Eli reached in and took out a white plastic device only a little smaller than a pen. It had a rectangular head at one end.

'It's a transducer that works a little like ultrasound. It doesn't pierce the skin but, for best results, you need to locate a main artery or the thoracic cavity.'

'He means heart,' Rafi said. He was flicking through the pages of a theatre programme that was on the desk.

Eli glared at his deputy for the self-evident explanation, though, of course, this was Rafi's area and it would be foolhardy to deny it.

In the lift on the way out, Eli asked, 'Have you actually used one of these devices before?'

'Of course I have,' Rafi said. 'No matter what that *shmock* thinks, this isn't new technology, not for *Kidon* anyway. Incidentally, Scoline is the same drug used in intubation or thoracic examinations. It's just the quantity that kills people.'

'Well, I'm pleased that's settled.' The two men came out into the lobby and approached the exit and the bikes. 'If we get through this, I promise you one thing, we get our own medic who is attached to the unit. That guy proves time and time again how totally unfit he is for our requirements.'

Rafi paused in the process of strapping on his helmet. His tone was conversational and he might have been asking for Eli's view on the results of a soccer match. 'Do you actually think we will get through this?'

'I don't know. Ask me in half an hour; meantime, we need to check in with Petra, make sure *that* situation is contained.'

Eli mounted the bike, Rafi engaged the ignition and it roared like the machine beast it was. As Rafi nosed out of the private parking area and onto the Finchley Road, Eli called Petra. There was no reply.

Chapter 50

Now that she'd made up her mind that she was going to act, Petra stopped feeling cold and tired and guilty about her failures. She had a plan. Keeping the Portakabin in her direct view, she eased herself out of the Fiat and crept towards the bin and the mutilated bike. It had one wheel that was flat and almost hanging off the outer rim. That would do. With cold hands she picked up the bike and carried it back to her post and knelt by the shell of the Fiat. There she used the letter opener to lever off the outer tube and unwind the soft rubber off the inner tube.

Petra retired inside what was left of the car and pulled the tiny scissors out of the credit-card gizmo. There she unwound the grey scarf around her neck.

The viscose scarf was going to make the ultimate sacrifice, along with the rubber tubing from the bike. Petra cut both into multiple pieces and blessed the size of it. Next she slid out of the Fiat and straightened up. With resolution she approached the Portakabin but stopped ten metres away, outside the offices of the granite works, where the samples had been stacked on the ground for potential buyers. Petra picked up four squares of granite and slipped them into her unfolded pouch bag. If the polyester fabric could hold her shopping of a litre of milk and a bottle of wine, it could certainly hold the granite samples.

Petra checked her watch. Sam had been in the Portakabin for ten minutes. If it was going to get ugly, and even if it wasn't, she couldn't delay. At pace Petra moved towards the ice-cream vans around the corner. She picked the one that had the most cardboard cartons piled on the front seat and, after positioning herself to swivel for maximum shoulder power, she raised the shopper-weapon and swung it into the side window. Crash.

Then she waited. Her breath from the exertion sent clouds of moisture in front of her. She waited but was poised to run. All quiet.

Next Petra took off one of her gloves and reached through the broken window to feel the cardboard box that was closest to her. It was cold but it was dry. Result. Petra spread a handful of the scarf remnants over the boxes and sprinkled some of the precious gin and some drops of hand gel. Then she went round the corner to the overflowing bin. Petra did the same thing but this time, before she distributed the remaining pieces of scarf, she doused them in the rest of the flammable liquid. Standing back for a moment, she looked at her work. There was more chance of the ice-cream van burning up but there might be something combustible in the commercial bin – oil or petrol-soaked material from the MOT site. She thought about what Eli had said on the train to Newark. 'Give me generals who are lucky…' She was no general but she was owed some bloody luck.

Chapter 51

Eli and Rafi climbed the safe-house steps two at a time and together. For once they skipped the protocol of arriving separately and doing a security sweep of the area. If the operation was underway, corners had to be cut and Eli was cutting them. The jumping-off safe house wouldn't be re-used for another operation and, if London Station was going to go down in flames because of Harel's ambition and stupidity, then the exposure of a Mossad safe house wasn't going to make any difference anyway.

They stood on the doorstep and Rafi pressed the entry bell. The house was run-down, scratched. There was faded paint on the front door and weeds sprouting through the cracked tarmac, but the entry bell was an anomaly. It was bright and shiny with an overhead camera.

'Smile,' Eli said to Rafi. 'These are your guys. If Harel isn't here, I'm relying on you to convince them it's Daylight.'

Daylight was the code to abort. It meant chaos, which was the usual result of an operation that had gone wrong, when the only option was to pull out.

'Surprised to see me, darling,' Rafi said.

That guy just couldn't help himself, Eli thought.

The door clicked open, and the two men came in, slammed

it behind them and thundered up the narrow stairs to the first-floor apartment. The door was open and a slight young man with curly brown hair was standing on the doorstep.

'Dov,' Rafi said and hugged him. 'How's your Dad? Is he well?'

'Rafi, this isn't a social call,' Eli said.

'No, it isn't. But this young man's father is as good as my own,' Rafi said as he strode into the shabby sitting room.

'Shit,' Eli said. There was nobody in the room apart from Dov. The space was empty, apart from four different carry-on bags, a rail with clothes on a rack and open plastic bin bags, ready for the post-operation clean-up, when the unit would swap clothes and identities for fresh ones before they left the country by plane, Eurostar or ferry.

'Shit,' Eli said again. 'We're too late.'

It took them less than five minutes to not only convince Dov that it was Daylight but also to establish that since the operation was now underway, comms were down. They couldn't be reached by outside information. It was protocol and was a way of putting the team in a bubble of responsibility if it went wrong. They would only be able to communicate with each other.

The three-man team were in two rooms at the Strathearn Hotel in Back Hill, Clerkenwell. Harel was with them. The plan was that he would be with Ze'ev in one room on the second floor, where they would monitor and adjust the hotel's CCTV feed. Gidi and Oren were going to waylay the target when he came out of the lift, hustle him into his hotel room and there they would complete the termination operation. Apply the drug, hold the target down until he was paralysed and had stopped breathing. Once death was confirmed, by checking his pulse in two locations, they would undress him, hang up his clothes in the wardrobe and put him to bed. All in complete silence. Until the target was dead, he was paralysed but conscious. He would be able to see his assailants and hear what they were saying, so silence was protocol.

'When did they go?' Eli said.

'Three hours ago,' Dov said. 'Gidi had to get into camouflage on site. And they wanted to be set up for when the target came back from dinner. Or if he came back early for some reason.'

It was now 10 o'clock. If they were lucky, it would take them thirty minutes to get to Clerkenwell from Acton.

Chapter 52

It was 10 o'clock and Petra was ready. Or as ready as she ever would be. She got out of the Fiat and approached the Portakabin. She needed to see what was happening and the only way was to peer through the almost-covered window. It was far from ideal and she grimaced at the thought of what Eli and Rafi would say, but they weren't there. She was. This was her show.

Step by step Petra approached the Portakabin, ready to run if the door opened. Now closer, she heard voices. They were aggressive. Four more steps and she was by the covered window. Petra crouched and pressed her head to the window. The glass was icy against her cheek but she held it there while she peered through the inch of light.

Inside she saw one of the two guys who'd brought Wasim. He had his arms folded. He was behind what must be Wasim, who was on a chair. In front of him Sam paced up and down. He leaned into her agent and he shouted, 'WHO ARE YOU?' Then he hit Wasim across the face.

Petra flinched at the sight. It was a reflex, as strong as if she'd been the one tied to a chair and beaten. She'd seen enough and crept away.

A minute later she was in front of the ice-cream van and was watching the rubber and the scarf kindle the dry cardboard.

It stank and billows of black smoke rose out of the broken window. Rafi had been right – whether it was the gin or the viscose or the hand gel or last year's ice-cream wafers, the ice-cream van was going up like a rocket. Petra ran to her second operational site and watched the grey yarn from her scarf twist and ignite the boxes and old newspapers. This time it was slower, but then there was a flash of blue and the flame had found something to play with – Petra stood back as the fire took hold.

She couldn't have asked for more. Despite wanting to watch the flames now crackling and the sparks of some combustible material, Petra ran back to her original hide, the fetid alley near the Portakabin. She was there, crouched in the darkness, when the shrill beep of the smoke alarm by the MOT centre went off.

Chapter 53

The door to the hotel room opened and Harel stood glaring at Eli and Rafi. For once he wasn't wearing some overpriced suit but was kitted out in what he no doubt considered to be appropriate. A black polo neck, black jacket and black jeans. Behind his aviator specs his eyes blazed.

'Aren't you going to invite us in?' Eli said as he walked past Harel into the suite. At the coffee table Ze'ev was poised with a laptop on his thighs, connected to a monitor. Eli glanced around. The ops site was tidy to the point of obsession. They were ready to exit and clear the room in less than a minute if they had to evacuate.

The images on the monitor were split into boxes. It was the feed from the hotel's CCTV that Ze'ev had hacked into. In a corner of each image was the actual image and the bigger image was the doctored image. Despite having seen a demonstration of the system, this was the first time that Eli had seen it in an operational setting and it was impressive. But this wasn't the time to admire the tech.

'Where are Gidi and Oren?' Eli said. 'It's Daylight. You have to abort and I have authorisation from the ambassador.'

'I don't know what you're doing here, Eli,' Harel said. 'Or what you're trying to achieve but you're too late. Look. Ze'ev, close up.'

On the monitor Eli saw one of the boxes expand until it filled the screen. It was a view of the hallway. The real image showed a man and a woman by the lift. The woman, who was about the same height as the man, was wearing a bulky coat, she had shoulder-length dark hair and knee boots. The man was in a suit. They looked like the type of couple you'd expect to see in a central London hotel, business types, passing through.

'Oren looks kind of cute, doesn't he?' Harel said.

'What floor?' Eli said. 'What floor are they on?'

'I'm not stopping it for whatever weak reason you've cooked up,' Harel said.

'How about that I've got the proof that this is a Russian disinformation operation and I don't know who Grant D Miller actually is but he sure as hell isn't who you think he is.'

'Proof,' Harel sneered. 'What proof?'

'Evidence that his cover was faked using the specific protocols that Russian cyberattacks use. Do you understand?'

The expression on Harel's face changed. It was as noticeable and as sudden as a light turning on. His eyes narrowed and he looked as if he was calculating a chess move.

Had he suspected that Grant Miller was fake?

Eli pushed on, 'There is a very narrow window for you to stop this and at the inevitable inquiry it will be justifiable error. If you proceed and you don't abort, then it will be over for you. It will be over for you and the government. The Russians will do what they always do when they have an active-measures win, it will be all over *Telegram*. And if Driver does win the election, you'll still be fucked, because he doesn't like losers and he doesn't like people who get caught.'

'It's too late.' Harel gestured at the screen. The lift doors had opened and a man in his forties got out. The lift closed behind him and he was alone in the hotel corridor with the man and the woman, with Oren and Gidi. In one move they grabbed him on either side and marched him down the corridor, away from the camera.

'WHAT FLOOR, WHAT ROOM?' Eli said.

'828,' Harel said.

Rafi was by the door, ready to haul it open and start running.

Chapter 54

Crouched down in the hide, Petra took a few deep breaths. She'd seen Rafi do this before going into action. After they'd both been injured and spent some time together, he'd tried to teach her this pre-action meditation.

It wasn't working.

Her breath came in ragged gasps as if it was being ripped out of her. Even at a distance she could hear the smoke alarm and see some billowing smoke over one of the low industrial units. It was hard to be specific about where it was coming from. Was it dumpster or ice-cream truck? Either way, it smelt acrid.

The door to the Portakabin burst open and Petra heard voices. She shrank back into the hide and crunched on the broken glass underfoot. *Shit.* Petra stopped, one foot in the air, fearful of the noise if she put the other foot down.

She heard the sound of running.

'It's a fucking fire, man. I don't know where it's coming from.'

The voice was young, scared.

'I'm not waiting to see where the fire is, no fucking way. I'm on bail and there's no way I'm going to stick around to find out. Fire engines, cops. Fuck off! Come on man, let's go.'

'I demand that you stay here.'

That sounded like Sam.

'No fucking way. We got the guy here. We've done what you asked. You said nothing about beating up on him.'

Petra heard the heavy thunk as the Mercedes door shut. The engine started. Then she saw the Merc pass by. For several long seconds, Petra waited, then she stepped out to where she could get a look at the Portakabin.

The door was wide open. Hard light from an overhead tube sliced down and in the middle of the space, Wasim sat tied to the chair. His head was slumped down on his chest.

Petra straightened up and stepped out of her hide. In one hand she held her weighted shopping pouch. She strode towards the Portakabin aping the bravery that she didn't feel.

'Hello,' Petra said as she reached the open door and walked in and scanned the room. On one side of the space there was a row of dumpy bags filled with wooden logs.

'What on earth is going on here?' Petra said. 'Wasim? Are you all right?'

He lifted his head and croaked. 'I've been better.'

Sam emerged from the shadows and he looked rattled by Petra's frontal attack. She pressed on. 'What are you doing?'

'I don't know who the fuck you are or what you've got to do with Wasim but my advice to you is mind your own business and fuck off.'

'How dare you talk to me like that,' Petra said channelling a Home Counties matron. 'I object to that language, it's vulgar and inappropriate. And I will tell you exactly who I am and perhaps, if you so wish, you may explain yourself.'

Sam seemed to consciously shake off the shock of her appearance and he unwound the keffiyeh that was draped around his neck, twisted it into a spiral so that the fabric was tight and rearranged it around Wasim's neck. He held the two edges in one hand.

'Who are you? What are you doing here?'

However much Wasim despised him, Sam didn't look like a fool to Petra. She could feel his eyes scan her, checking her over, trying to work out who she was. Her entrance had been too theatrical; she needed to dial it down while she worked out what he was capable of doing.

Petra smiled, 'Since you ask, I'm a friend of Wasim's family. My father and my grandfather served in the British Army in the British Mandate in Palestine. In fact, my grandfather was an army chaplain and he received an OBE.'

'You and people like you are why we're fighting.'

'Forgive me, but I'm not quite sure what you mean. Why have you got Wasim tied up in this unpleasant place? What's he done?'

'Why are you here?'

'I was supposed to be having supper with Wasim. It's something I do from time to time. You may not realise this but his grandfather was Sheikh Al-Arikhi, from a very prominent family who were terribly kind to my grandfather when he was a young man.' Petra shrugged in her most dismissive way. 'When I arrived at Wasim's flat, I saw him being taken off. I wasn't sure if he'd forgotten our date and, since I had nothing else to do, I followed them.'

Sam nodded. 'I get it. Your family, his family. Colonialists, imperialists, Zionists, you're all the same. You think you control the world. What are you doing? You're killing the world with your fossil fuels and arms and drone industries. You're all fascists and should be struck down.'

'Is that why Wasim is here? Because of disagreements about political doctrine?'

'Oh, no. Wasim is here because I don't trust him. You see, he has no real interest in his people's struggle for independence. That's clear. And then I kept asking myself how he knew that MI5 were going to raid my flat. I think he's a spy, a Zionist spy.'

Petra frowned, as if she was confused. 'MI5? They raided your flat? Why on earth would they do that?'

Sam nodded. He was watching Petra as if she was the most fascinating creature he'd ever seen. Holding her gaze, he reached around his waist, took out a gun and pointed it at her.

Chapter 55

Eli and Rafi stood in front of the hotel door and Eli rapped on the wood. No reply. Then he heard a voice, 'No service, thank you. We have everything we need.'

'It's Daylight,' Rafi hissed. 'Open the door, Oren.'

There was a second's delay when every second counted. Eli tried to sound calm, as they were no doubt panicked behind the door. He said, 'You are authorised to open the door right now. This mission is aborted.'

The door opened and they stepped in. Oren's face was one big question mark while Gidi, in a dress and knee boots, was leaning over the target, Jimbob Loxlee. The American was slumped in the armchair with his shirt pulled up over a rotund belly. Oren held his wrist and was checking his pulse.

Eli put a finger to his lips. They needed to maintain silence in front of the target. He nodded to Rafi, who already had the transducer out of its pouch and was approaching Loxlee.

'*Dva samykh sil'nykh voina*,' Eli said. '*Terpeniye i vremy*.'

Both Oren and Gidi frowned, but Rafi understood immediately.

'*Da*,' he said and leaned over Loxlee to apply the antidote. Nothing happened.

Gidi started to rub one of Loxlee's hands while Eli grabbed the man's coat and covered him with it.

'*Dvah samykh.*' Eli leaned right into Loxlee's face. Then, Eli gently slapped his face and tried to imbue the Russian he was using out of context with meaning.

'*Dvah samykh*, Mr Loxlee?' Eli said.

An eyelid flickered. Yes. Then the other one. He was focusing his gaze on Eli, who put his fingers to the man's neck to check his pulse. It was slow, it was faint, but it was there. Oren, who was checking the pulse on Loxlee's wrist, nodded.

'*Pravda,*' he said.

Eli smiled. Oren was quick. He got it. And his one word of Russian was perfect for the occasion. *Pravda* meant 'truth'.

Within thirty seconds, the four men were out of the hotel room, walking in pairs down the corridor towards the ops hub, six rooms along. They maintained a distance from each other and walked in a manner that suggested they were relaxed, an exercise that they'd all done on the training course as rookies when they'd learnt about the golden hour after an operation, the most dangerous time, when the risk quotient was at its highest. Sure, the CCTV in the hotel would be manipulated and they would vanish from the footage, but if someone was to open a bedroom door or come out of the lift during those few seconds, then no amount of electronic solutions would help. All Eli could do was try to look forgettable and quell the desire to run like hell and bang on the door of the ops hub and, once inside, punch Harel's lights out for putting him, the unit, the Mossad and the bloody country in this situation.

No, not anger, that was no good. It solved nothing. Control it, control it, control it. Eli took a deep breath and quashed down the flood of fury before he tapped on the door of the room.

Harel opened it and Eli stepped inside. At the table Ze'ev's fingers were flying across the keys of the laptop at such a pace his hands were almost a blur.

Before Eli could say anything to Harel, there was another tap on the door and Oren and Gidi slipped in. They were too well trained to ask why the mission had been aborted, or maybe they sensed the atmosphere between Eli and Harel. With the barest of nods, the two men went to their designated spots and packed up their kit, only spending a moment to look over Ze'ev's shoulders at what he was doing on the computer.

Eli looked at Harel, who was already packed and ready to leave the ops hub. He was shrugging himself into a black cashmere coat.

'I am clearing up your shit.' Eli pointed his finger at Harel. 'You will contact this Grant D Miller, who we will no doubt shortly discover was born Vasily Volkov and is an SVR Major. You will maintain the fiction and tell him that for operational reasons the job was aborted but it will resume within the next week. Understood? You will get this Russian to come to the UK to meet you.'

'How do I do that?' Harel said.

'I don't care. Think of something. You're supposed to be an intelligence professional, God help us. Tell him he's going to meet the ambassador, who's going to give him a medal.'

'That would probably work,' Harel said.

Faced with Harel's lack of remorse, Eli felt the anger coming up again like bile, but he fought it.

'As no doubt you saw, Oren and Gidi responded well to the situation. Oren even managed to contribute a word of Russian.'

'I saw that,' Harel said. 'Bravo, and I also saw the target come round, so your night's work is now done and you can plod back to your office and write your report for Yuval, who will no doubt be delighted. I'll deal with Grant D Miller.'

'And while you're at it, you can go to your, no doubt, over-priced hotel and start planning how you're going to respond to the inquiry and consider what your future job prospects might be.'

'Oh, Eli, you do overreact, don't you?' Harel tied a scarf around his neck. 'I think you'll find that I continue to have powerful allies but don't worry, I will assist in clearing up this misunder-standing. In the meantime, the only way I'm going to disappear is if you kill me.' He glanced down at the transducers that Oren was putting into the empty slots of a medical roll. 'I'm surprised you haven't tried.'

'Because I'm better than that,' Eli said. 'We're better than that. That's what you and your allies need to understand. The Mossad is better than that and so is Israel.'

Eli took a step towards Harel and slapped him hard across the face.

Chapter 56

Twelve miles away, Petra was rigid. She'd recognised the gun instantly. It was a Makarov pistol, popular in south London shootings, and no doubt easily available in a pub or on the dark web. Petra cast her mind back to the session with Rafi at the firing range. She remembered; the Makarov had a heavy trigger mechanism, and it was designed in that way to enhance safety. It also meant that the first shot was less likely to be accurate. Helpful though that knowledge was, it didn't answer the question as to whether Sam knew how to use the gun that he was pointing at her.

'I'm not a Muslim, I'm not anything,' he said. 'But Gaza is a catalyst. It's our generation's call to action, and what happens there will change how we all live.'

'I'm not arguing with any of that, believe me, but I can't see how that's going to work for you. If you're going to shoot me in a place where a fire alarm has just gone off. If not the police, certainly a fire engine will be here at any moment, how's that going to work for you?'

'The Brothers will know what to do,' Sam said. 'I help them. Wasim will be a good hostage and so will you.'

'Who are The Brothers? Are they Muslim?'

'You'll find out.' His voice was clipped. It meant he was concentrating.

'Is that why MI5 raided your flat? Because of these Brothers?'

Petra didn't dare to look at her watch to see how much time had elapsed since the smoke alarms had gone off. It was certainly less than fifteen minutes, which would be the optimum amount of time for a fire engine to arrive. And Sam did seem confident. Maybe he had already heard from his reinforcements. Maybe they were close by. Or maybe he was confident because he was standing with a gun in his hand in front of a man who was trussed up and a woman in a skirt. If she was going to disarm him, she needed to rattle his cage first.

'You know, Sam.'

'Samir,' he corrected. 'It's out of respect for my friends.'

'Samir.' Petra took a step to the side of Wasim to get closer to Sam's gun. 'I think you're in a lot of trouble. I don't exactly know who these Brothers of yours are, but...' Petra was making calculations about the distance between the gun and the shopping pouch. 'They may be your friends, but I don't think they're coming and I think they're going to leave you to carry the can with whatever they're storing here. What is it? Drugs, arms, stolen goods?'

'I don't need to know. I just need to do what's right. You and people like you are history. You're imperialists, colonialists, occupiers. You don't understand or care how people are exploited and oppressed simply because of their race and identity. I have a duty to right the wrongs of the oppressed.'

'I can see that, and I genuinely think a lot of what you're saying is important and needs to be said.' Petra edged closer and kept her voice calm, despite the dryness in her throat. 'I can also see you're pissed off with Wasim because he stole your girl, didn't he?'

Sam flinched. Petra had touched a nerve but she wasn't sure if it would work in her favour. Too late to turn back, she ploughed on, creasing her brow with concern. 'I know that's painful and I don't blame you for being angry, because Wasim can be an arrogant twat. But these Brothers of yours are not going to turn up with the alarms going off. They'd be crazy. Which leaves you with a massive problem, how are you going to get out of this? Maybe I can help.'

Sam opened his mouth to respond but Petra didn't hear what he had to say. In one movement she both stepped forward and raised the bag with the granite samples. Down it went, with all the power from her shoulder, across her body and aimed at Sam's outstretched arm with the gun.

But it missed. His head was in the way. His right side, above the ear, took the full force of the blow. Petra raised her arm again and paused. Despite her poor aim, the granite samples had done their job, the gun clattered to the concrete floor and Sam was staggering back, clutching the side of his head. Without delay Petra followed up. She took one step forward, tilted back and kick-punched him in the groin, the blow delivered with a grunt of exertion from her. Sam's head dipped and a second, harder kick followed; this one slammed into his chest and knocked him right off balance. Slowly, slowly, as if in slow motion, he toppled back and fell. Petra heard his skull hit the concrete.

The exertion had left her breathless but she needed to focus. He was unconscious, but there was no telling how long it would be before he came round.

'I'll take that.' Petra snatched the handgun and slid it into the shopper. Then she knelt at Wasim's feet and kept her eyes on Sam's immobile body in case he stirred. The scissors on Petra's gizmo came out and in deft moves she sliced through the plastic ties that bound Wasim.

'What are we going to do with him?' Wasim stood up and rubbed his wrists.

'Take him with us, hand him over to the cops. Someone else can patch him up. Five are going to love hearing about the Muslim Brotherhood in Wembley.'

Petra moved over to Sam and, still kneeling, looked at him. 'Maybe he can walk if we get him on his feet. I really don't feel like carrying him. Come on, arsehole.'

Wasim was by her side and he slipped his hands under Sam's shoulders. 'Up you get, man…' Sam's head lolled forward. 'Petra… Petra, I think he's dead.'

'Oh, shit.'

Wasim laid him down again and placed his fingers on Sam's neck, then he held his wrist. He shook his head. 'He's dead. Probably a brain aneurysm. It can be quick.'

'Then we'd better get him out of here. No body, no crime,' Petra said, scrambling to the dumpy bags and tipping the logs of wood out onto the cement floor. 'Oh shit,' Petra said again. Underneath the wood at the bottom of the bag there was a black case. It might have been mistaken for a laptop carrier with its handles and reinforced fabric cover but Petra knew what it was; she'd seen the exact same brand at the range in Hampshire. It had been in one of the display cases with all the other gun accessories.

'We'd better take that with us too,' Petra said. 'Come on, let's get Sam in the bag. You take his shoulders.'

Together they lifted Sam into the dumpy bag and then, taking one handle each, dragged the bag out of the Portakabin and across the bumpy asphalt.

At Petra's hire car they had another problem. At first glance, the boot of the Ford Puma looked too small to get the dumpy bag in.

'That's never going to fit,' Wasim said. 'We're going to have to leave it and just get out of here.'

'Oh no, we're not.' Petra opened the side door and felt around in the dark. There had to be a way of doing this. She felt the top of the rear seat and then felt down the sides and the base.

'What are you doing, Petra? We've got to go, we're gonna have to leave the body.'

Then she felt it. A lever. Petra hoicked it up and the seat tipped forward.

'How about that?' Petra said as she straightened up. 'Come on.'

Together they lifted the dumpy bag and lowered it into the boot of the Puma. They had just got into the front seats when lights striated the road into the industrial estate. A pale VW van swung in and pulled up in front of the Portakabin. Petra heard, rather than saw, Wasim's fear in his breathing.

'It's Sam's Brotherhood friends. Now what?' he whispered.

'Can you drive?' Even to her own ears she sounded preternaturally calm.

'Yes.'

'Move over, I'm going to slow them down. Keep my door open.'

'Petra...'

But she was already out of the car and moving in a crouched position towards the VW van. It was side-on to the door of the Portakabin. In her hand she held the Makarov. Now would be the time to find out how accurate it was on a first shot. And a second. From the Portakabin she heard voices, then she heard the back door of the van open. They were loading up.

Two shots. Petra positioned herself and aimed the gun at the front wheel. The damn thing was heavy; she used her left hand to steady her outstretched forearm, took a deep breath and squeezed the trigger. The bastard *was* stiff. The recoil jolted her arm and shoulder, the shoulder that had once been dislocated, but adrenalin soothed the pain. Immediately, Petra shifted her aim to the back wheel of the truck. She shot off two bullets and, without waiting, ran for the Puma.

Moments later, they were through the gates and onto the road but ahead, blue lights strafed the darkness, sirens wailed, all racing in their direction.

'Full house,' Petra said as the fire engine sped past.

Wasim slowed down to the twenty-mile-an-hour speed limit as an unmarked police car joined the cavalcade of fire brigade and police. Just then Petra's phone rang.

'I can't talk. I'll call you back but we need to meet,' Petra ended the call. 'Left here,' she said to Wasim.

He took a hard left into Corringham Road and then Petra directed him to drive left and right, right and left, until there were no cars either behind or in front of them.

'Pull up,' Petra said outside a suburban semi with a neat Honda Civic in the front drive. 'Wasim, this is where you get out. Your nearest tube station is Wembley Park. Okay? I want you to go home, put everything you were wearing into a bin bag and take it to a clothing bank. Tonight. Then go home, have a shower and I'll call you tomorrow.'

As she spoke, Wasim was nodding. Not arguing. Not coming back with a better idea for the sake of it. Just nodding. Petra thought of what Eli had said about establishing authority. She'd certainly done that.

'I want to… I want to… thank—'

Petra cut him off. 'Go on. Wembley Park is about half a mile from here. Jubilee Line. Go.'

Without argument, Wasim got out of the car and began to walk. Petra shifted into the driver's seat and started the car up, overtook him and reached for her phone to call Eli back.

Chapter 57

The drive from Wembley into central London gave Petra plenty of time to think about the last few hours. Despite it being late, there was still heavy traffic down the A40 towards central London. In the four-second call with Eli, he'd said *Adom* as the place to meet. It was one of the designated locations he'd set up before they went to Newark and was at the back of the Adelphi building, off the Strand. The street was an oddly quiet spot in the middle of central London. No doubt there were CCTV cameras, as there were in all of Westminster, but it was none-theless dark and, for their purposes, dark was always attractive.

As she drove, Petra checked in with herself, aware that there was a dead man in the boot of the Ford Puma. A corpse, the weapon that had killed him – by her hand – and a gun bag that she had yet to open. It started to rain and the wipers squeaked back and forth, a hypnotic rasp across the windscreen as Petra adhered with almost religious dedication to the speed limit.

Why wasn't she scared? If she got pulled up by the cops for any reason at all, she'd find herself at Paddington Green police station, in the cells they reserved for terror suspects. That's where, hopefully, they'd shortly be busy with the guys in the VW van but it would take some hours before they started to ask why two tyres had been shot. And more time to find the fragments of her scarf in the fires. And even more time to start analysing any scraps of CCTV footage they might have found on the cameras on the industrial estate.

But Petra wasn't scared. By the time the cops contacted MI5 and they got round to investigating, Segev would have hacked into and manipulated the feeds. He would make the truth of what had just happened disappear.

Was that why she wasn't scared? How about the presence of death only feet away from her? Maybe she should be feeling remorse, but she wasn't. She wasn't angry either. There was just a feeling of satisfaction. She'd done what she'd set out to do. She'd saved Wasim and protected him in a way that she hadn't been able to protect either his sister or Tom. Both people who should have been saved, who deserved to be saved, because they would have made a difference.

The traffic stacked up as she ascended the slope over Edgware Road before descending on to Marylebone Road. Petra indicated right in preparation for the turn down Baker Street, careful and courteous, not to push, but to wait. To be invisible when she was visible. After nodding her thanks at a woman in a Clio who let her in, Petra sighed.

Maybe Sam would have found his way out of the fetid citadel of his belief system, where violence was justified, where the massacre on October 7 was an act against imperialism, colonialism, the capitalists, the Zionists, the establishment, the racists, the fascists. Justified resistance against evil.

In every successful lie there needs to be a seed of truth – that's what makes it convincing. That was one of the fascinating and satisfying aspects of the work, the juxtaposition of truth and lies and the need to find a path through the maze to try to identify what was real.

Only Eli would understand where she was in all of this. Only Eli might be able to explain to her what she was feeling, because he felt it too. He'd be able to contextualise it, to frame it, like a picture, what should be in the foreground, what should fade into the horizon. What colours to use.

Twenty minutes later, Petra turned into John Adam Street, took a right onto Adelphi Terrace and parked across the road from a BMW bike, by the side of which stood two helmeted riders, Rafi and Eli.

Eli crossed the road to Petra's side of the car and leaned down as he opened the door for her.

'How was it? I'm sorry we couldn't get to you sooner but we've had quite an evening.'

Petra got out of the car. A wave of exhaustion came over her as she faced Eli and, as she stood up, she felt heady. Eli took her arm and guided her towards where Rafi was standing by the bike.

'I'm okay,' Petra said trying to shake off Eli and not look weak. 'Probably just hungry. It was bloody cold out there.'

'Where's Silver Dove?' Rafi said.

'Home, I hope. Safe. I dropped him off near a tube station and said I would find him tomorrow.'

'What about Treesmith?' Rafi said.

Eli said, 'Give her a minute, man.'

Petra held out the car keys. 'Rafi, please, do me a favour and take the car back to the hire garage. There's something in the boot that needs to be taken care of first. If you do that, I'll explain to Eli what happened.'

Rafi took the keys and gave Petra his helmet. Eli walked with him to the car and she saw them open the boot and exchange a few words.

Then Eli was back by her side, rootling through the pannier on the bike. He handed Petra a black balaclava. 'This will help with the fit of big head's helmet. Now put the helmet on. I'm driving.'

Hoicking up her skirt, Petra slipped one leg over the seat and put her arms around Eli's waist. Through the leather she felt his back against her chest and closed her eyes as the engine thrummed into life.

Chapter 58

It was a week later, early March, and wind blustered through London blowing debris across the streets. It was the end of a storm and there were the usual stories of travel disruption on Eli's newsfeed. It was refreshing after the news from Israel and Gaza, where food shortages in the Strip and an ongoing assault on the Al-Shifa Hospital made him ache for a time when the weather was the top story.

But at least he had the day ahead to distract him, and the need to focus. As Eli walked up the stairs to the Travellers Club and his meeting with Oliver Milne, he felt a little lighter. There was something comforting about working with the Brits that Yuval had never appreciated. Behind the politesse they were devious bastards and they'd somehow managed to manoeuvre their way through choppy waves without societal collapse. A scene that took place at the Capitol on 6 January 2020 would never happen in the UK. How much of that was because people in Milne's sister agency at Five had sophisticated tech was hard to say. More likely it was cultural. Despite the artificial heat generated by online activity, some of it enhanced by interested parties, there was less anger. Was that to do with the weather, the constant rain and grey skies that damped down fire? Maybe, Eli thought. More likely it was to do with history and the way

Britain had absorbed the cultures of their colonies; it wasn't just a land and resource grab, it was a cultural osmosis over many years. They loved the countries where they sent their young doctors and administrators in a way that other European countries didn't. Eli thought about Kipling and Kim, the first literary spy. And about the other Kim who would have stood on these same stairs and betrayed everyone around him. He didn't appreciate what he had.

Eli pressed the white bell and a uniformed doorman greeted him.

'Good morning, Mr Amiram. Mr Milne is expecting you.'

The door closed behind him and shut out the world; Eli was led into the reception area and was guided to a seat, where he was probably being observed by security before meeting Milne. Five minutes later, he was in the high-ceilinged coffee room, by one of the windows with reinforced glass. Opposite him sat Milne, immaculate as ever, in one of his charcoal suits.

'Are we set your end?' Milne said after a preamble that mentioned the weather.

'Yes,' Eli said. 'Everything is in place.'

'Good. We won't be officially telling Charlene until after today's activities. That's how she wants it. The attempted murder of this American national is too combustible at the moment. She wants it buried.'

'Understood.' Eli sipped at the coffee.

'I'm not entirely sure why you feel the requirement to meet our Russian friend.' Milne buttered a triangle of toast and smeared marmalade on it.

'Call it sentiment.'

'More like *Schadenfreude*, from where I'm sitting.' Milne

looked up. 'But I can't say I blame you. The raid on the Newark location will happen simultaneously with the rest of our activities today. I've been charged with expressing our thanks.'

'We're happy to help.' Eli drained the rest of his coffee and pushed the chair back, but Milne raised a finger to halt him. 'If you have time this morning, there are a couple of other issues I'd like to cover.'

'Certainly,' Eli said.

'Do you recall that tip you gave us about a student regional organiser, one Sam Scedding? I passed it on to Five and they did a dawn raid. They found nothing.'

'I remember.'

'Five are currently investigating his connection with a Muslim Brotherhood cell, who had a cache of arms in a lock-up on an industrial estate in northwest London.'

'So it was a good tip after all,' Eli said. 'Scedding just didn't keep whatever it was at home.'

Milne gave Eli a look of weariness. 'Scedding has disappeared. Under interrogation members of the cell said they were expecting to meet him at the lock-up.'

'So?' Eli shrugged.

'Our people think the CCTV has been tampered with in a way which looks like one of your procedures.'

'Is this official?' Eli said. 'Because if it is—'

'Not yet. But let me repeat, Eli. Despite this Russian sleeper that you've just dropped into our laps, for which we are grateful, you're on thin ice. Do you understand? I don't have to tell you that we're war-gaming the impact of radicalisation all over the West as a consequence of the war in Gaza. The government is also looking at terrorism legislation. That means we require everything you've got that's pertinent to us. If Scedding has left the country to join a terrorist group—'

'He hasn't,' Eli broke in. 'I can assure you, Oliver, he's not going to do anybody any harm, ever.'

Milne gave Eli a long look. 'Very well. I accept your assurance on that issue. Now, let's keep the channel flowing for all our interests.'

'Agreed.'

Chapter 59

Eli was early. He'd overestimated the time it would take to get from Pall Mall to Richmond, despite the two changes on the District line and doubling back from Earl's Court. Since this was a meeting of such significance, Segev was heading the watchers team. Eli felt that he should be there at the kill, he deserved to be. The Techtruck was now parked near a health centre off Twickenham Road. It was a perfect location; it had both visibility and flexibility, if for any reason the meeting had to be abruptly ended.

The restaurant itself, where Eli currently sat in the deserted upstairs area, was a gem in terms of operational hygiene, *hygiena tif'ulit*, as they called it. It was tucked down one of the passages between King Street and the adjoining green and was the perfect place for the team to see if there was surveillance. There were no vantage points to watch entries and exits beyond the shop on the other side of the passage, which was shut. Again, Segev had sourced the location and Eli reckoned that if he ever got poached by another unit, he'd be impossible to replace.

Eli felt in his ear for the concealed earpiece and adjusted it. Then he glanced at the laminated menu of Sardinian specialities and made his choice. As ever, the downside of restaurants was interruptions from staff, but this place was discreet and the £100 cash advance on the bill helped. Eli had no doubt the restaurant had its share of clandestine meetings of a domestic nature but not, Eli thought, on this grey March day.

Eli had seen the lunch crowd as he came into the restaurant. It was less of a crowd, more a speckle of pensioners who shared health news over their food. At one table a couple were talking with animation over half-eaten bowls of pasta. The man looked like a journalist or an academic, the woman had been harder to place but, for sure, they didn't know each other well. There was too much conversation for that.

In the week since Harel's exposure as the ambitious snake that he was, Eli had been busy mopping up the mess. Today's meeting with Nicolai would be the last of the cleaning operation and then Eli would be able to consider the other aspects of his life. Despite the pressure of work, Eli had managed to speak to Gal twice and both times he'd controlled his feelings.

After the first video call, he'd felt some remorse at the amount of relief in her face when she realised that he wasn't going to rant and howl or even beg. That he was just going to accept that this is where they were, this is what she wanted to do. And discuss like adults how they were going to do it. She agreed to keep the decision to separate under wraps until he finished his term so as not to arm the enemies in the Office.

'You're okay with this, aren't you, Eli?' Gal had said at the end of the call.

'Yes, I am. I think you're right. It's time.'

She nodded. She almost looked tearful.

When the call was concluded, Eli had spent a few moments, but only a few, asking himself if his acceptance of the end of his marriage had anything to do with Petra. It was possible. Eli was thinking about that when Nicolai strode into the space and the Russian made the low-ceilinged room seem smaller.

Nicolai held out his hand for Eli to shake, then shucked off a greatcoat that wouldn't have looked out of place on Red Square and hauled out the chair. Even without the coat, he was a striking man, with wide cheekbones and hair just greying at the temples. As Eli already had done, Nicolai took out his phone buffer and placed it on the table between them.

They ordered and engaged in the usual chit-chat about the political landscape, what Eli considered to be the *amuse-bouche* of the meeting. Nicolai was ebullient and speculated about the British election, when there was hardly anything to speculate about, and the American election, in which there was plenty.

'At least your elections leave little room for doubt,' Eli said. 'That must make working with the government easier if you're certain that policy is unlikely to change.'

'It does,' Nicolai said. 'There's clarity. Continuity if you like.' Nicolai had been pushing around his tortellini, but had made inroads into the bottle of red wine in front of them. Now he held up a finger-smeared wine glass and studied the blood-red liquid. 'Continuity is good, Eli. No government can achieve anything with only a four- or five-year mandate. You people know that. That's why Bibi keeps coming back. You know, we really do have a lot in common. Ashkenazi, aren't you?'

Nicolai pronounced it, Ashke-nazi. The bastard was goading Eli. Milne had been right when he talked about *Schadenfreude*.

'That's right,' Eli said. 'My great-grandfather was born in Gorki. He walked two thousand miles to get out of Mother Russia. How about you, where do you come from? Heroes of the Party or Aristocracy?'

'Heroes of the Party, of course. My grandfather was in the Politburo and my old man was Minister of Education until… it all collapsed.'

'How was that?' Eli poured more wine into Nicolai's glass.

'Not good. I was just a kid… it killed my father. Not literally. That was one of the previous administration's specialities. No, this was worse. It killed my father's soul. The West did that to us and for that, we will never forgive you. At least, I won't.'

'What was the West supposed to do?' Eli said, genuinely interested and not just trying to prolong the lunch.

Nicolai shrugged. 'Something like the Marshall Plan? Then maybe we wouldn't have been ripped to pieces by criminal gangs. But there was nothing. Ultimately, we always have to rely on ourselves. And we've always been betrayed by the West. We lost more people in the great patriotic war than everybody put together. Twenty-seven million.'

'We also lost a few people,' Eli said.

Nicolai ignored him. 'That's why we should have been allies. Our service and yours are the two premier services on the planet. We have different styles; you favour these flashy headlines that your government can deny.'

Eli thought about the pagers, now nestling in pockets in south Lebanon. When that button was pressed, it would certainly meet Nicolai's criteria of flashy operations.

Nicolai was waving the glass around to make his point. 'Our expertise is in *dezinformatsiya*. No other country, no other service, has had as much success as us. Tell me if I'm wrong.'

He leaned back in his chair and looked at Eli as if he was a morsel on a plate that he was going to gobble up.

'Why would I argue with that?' Eli said.

351

'What we do is beautiful, creative, original. How about the Protocols of Zion? That document is as fresh today as the day it was written in 1903. We did that.'

'Masterly,' Eli said.

'We took an existing idea, in this case anti-Semitism, and we wrote and distributed a document that is cited as truth after more than a century. What other intelligence service in the world has had such success with one document? Tell me, Eli. Or CND – again, we took an idea that was in the ether, a fear, it always must be a fear, and we used it for our benefit. Or immigration. We're doing a lot of work in that area at the moment, and the disruption it causes, the wasted resources – it all benefits us. We are world experts, Eli.'

'Nicolai, I won't deny it. But I think there's a fundamental weakness in a tactic where the goal is to get your enemy to kill each other over a rumour. Maybe something to do with morality?'

Nicolai laughed. He showed fine dental work as he threw back his head.

'You people. You think you're so clever.'

'Sometimes we are. Sometimes we're not, I won't deny that. But we ask questions and try to find answers. That's the way of it. May I take this opportunity to ask you a question?'

'What would that be?' Nicolai smiled with benevolence.

'Is anything you've been involved in recently payback for embarrassment you may have experienced because of the Ukrainian?'

'Ukrainian?'

'The one who fell out of the window, which was why you were expelled.'

'Oh, that Ukrainian,' Nicolai said, still smiling. 'That was… embarrassing.'

Eli's earpiece buzzed into life. One word. '*Gamanu*'. Done.

He stood up from the table, 'For that I apologise, Nicolai, but for this… I don't.'

Nicolai frowned.

Eli went on. 'You might want to check your newsfeed in the next fifteen minutes. While we've been having lunch, which I shall pay for, it being the least I can do, your sleeper, Grant D Miller, has been arrested at Heathrow and the operations hub in the Midlands has been raided.'

At the mention of Grant D Miller, the Russian's face was a picture; it caved in. He reached inside his pocket for his phone.

Eli went on, 'You people.' He emphasised the expression. He repeated it, 'You people may be skilled at *dezinformatsiya*, at poison gossip and at finding ways to make angry people more angry, but when it comes to operations, Nicolai, you're not quite as clever as you think you are. In fact, I'd say you were clumsy.'

Eli turned and strode towards the stairs. At the bottom, where the service station was, he passed two fifty-pound notes to the server by the till.

'Please ask my guest if he'd like anything else. He may want another drink.'

The End

Author's Notes & Thanks

I've been writing for some thirty years and this is the hardest narrative I've ever written. It wasn't the plot or the characters, it was the world after October 7 2023 and the horror that continues. At the moment it's uncomfortable to be a Jew of any type, observant, non-observant, left, right or centre, Israeli or Diaspora. If I hadn't established my characters, their arcs and set up storylines in the previous two books that I wanted to pay off in the third I'd never have attempted to write this book. It's too current, too painful and I didn't want to exploit the ongoing anger and anguish for entertainment. However, given all those circumstances I felt compelled to give it a go and do my best. Let the reader be the judge.

Thematically, this third Amiram book was always going to be about disinformation and truth, which fascinates and worries me. Before I wrote fiction, I worked in news and PR and I believe there is something fundamentally problematic about how we use emotions to sell products and disperse information. I don't think emotions solve problems, they amplify them. But emotions also help us to connect with each other. If we don't have empathy and try to sense someone else's emotions, then we don't have humanity.

Storytelling is about choreographing emotions, which is

exactly what spies do. I don't know what the answer is to all this but it's something I think about.

The upside of writing this book has been the research and those moments when I think 'well I never'. I'd like to thank Nigel Bagster for the weapons information and the introduction to Mick Cook. I'm still thinking about that fascinating interview. David Brummer wrote a neat little piece about GPUs, which I plundered, and he was kind enough to answer my follow-up questions. I'm immensely grateful to Felicity Main of Mandiant, who helped me with the issue of bad actors' signatures. It's a real thing.

My brainy cousin Adam Nygate set me off on the fake legend trail and my literary cousin Joseph Millis checked my sometimes-invented Hebrew expressions and also the sensibility of the piece. Thank you to both.

Early in the research period, I came upon a paper by Professor Dror Ze'evi on Palestinian clans. He was kind enough to talk to me. There were so many interesting ideas about society in his paper and the subsequent brief conversation we had. I'm sorry I was unable to use more.

I'd like to thank Jamie Hodder-Williams and Ion Mills for their patience and for asking me to write the book. Also, Bill Massey for asking the questions that helped me refocus. And Polly Halsey and everyone at No Exit Press for their kindness.

The best thing about writing is other writers and friends, who are endlessly supportive about my need for isolation and bad temper, when the writing is going badly. I'd like to thank Suzanne Mustacich for telling me I can do it, when I don't think I can. Isabelle Grey for saying the book will write itself, when it never does. Tika Cope for being first reader, babe. Helen

Soffa for thinking I'm brilliant whatever I do. Gary Sutton for good champagne and the company to enjoy it. Kasia Crane for coffee, cinnamon buns and flammable materials. Mike 20 Minutes Emery for culinary advice. Gavin Collinson for describing me as a skilled technician – I liked that. Marcella Forster for long-time support and memorable lunches. Shane Whaley, Alex Gerlis, Charles Beaumont, Ilana Berry, Antonia Senior, Paul Burke and all the Spybrary spooksters, who make the spy writing biz fun. Peter Strange, without whose diligent work on my behalf I would be unable to spend time writing.

While I'm at it, I'd like to thank the journalists on *The Economist*, *FT*, *Foreign Affairs*, *Ha'aretz* and all the other journos who take their work seriously and try to make sense of what's going on. Hats off.

And James. I would not have written this book if it hadn't been for you. Thank you for ideas, support, love, patience, dinner, love, cups of tea and chocolate. And love. Always.

About the Author

Author photo courtesy of Merle Nygate

Merle Nygate is a screenwriter, screenwriting lecturer and novelist. Her career has taken her from working on BAFTA winning TV to New York Festival audio drama to writing original sitcoms. She previously worked for BBC Comedy Commissioning. She has been a writer and script editor across multiple genres; from factual drama to high end fantasy. Her first espionage novel, *The Righteous Spy* won the Little Brown/UEA Crime Fiction award. Her second, *Honour Among Spies* was a 2024 SpyMasters Book of the Year, a 2024 Five Best Books pick and a *Sunday Times* Thriller of 2024.

merlenygate.com
@MerleNygate

NO EXIT PRESS
More than just the usual suspects

'A very smart, independent publisher delivering the finest literary crime fiction' **Big Issue**

MEET NO EXIT PRESS, an award-winning crime imprint bringing you the best in crime and suspense fiction. From classic detective novels, to page-turning spy thrillers and literary writing that grabs the attention. Our books are carefully crafted by some of the world's finest writers and delivered to you by a small, but passionate, team.

In over 30 years of business, we have published award-winning fiction and non-fiction including the work of a Pulitzer Prize winner, the British Crime Book of the Year, numerous CWA Dagger Awards, a British million-copy bestselling author, the winner of the Canadian Governor General's Award for Fiction and the Scotiabank Giller Prize, to name but a few. We are the home of many crime and noir legends from the USA whose work includes iconic film adaptations and TV sensations. We pride ourselves in uncovering the most exciting new or undiscovered talents. New and not so new – you know who you are!

We are a proactive team committed to delivering the very best, both for our authors and our readers.

Want to join the conversation and find out more about what we do?

Catch us on social media or sign up to our newsletter for all the latest news from No Exit Press.

f fb.me/noexitpress   **X** @noexitpress

noexit.co.uk